Academy of Secrets

From the Outcast Angels®
Christian Fantasy & Science Fiction Series

Michael Carney

Sign up at http://outcastangels.com/subscribe for our newsletter and receive a free copy of the *Outcast Angels* story "Time Loop" along with sneak peeks at future Outcast Angels stories and other exclusives.

http://OutcastAngels.com

Follow us:
http://facebook.com/outcastangels
http://twitter.com/outcastangels
http://pinterest.com/outcastangels
https://plus.google.com/+Outcastangels
https://www.youtube.com/user/Outcastangelsbooks

Enquiries about the OUTCAST ANGELS series should be directed to contact@outcastangels.com

ISBN-13: 978-0-473-35572-2

Other Outcast Angels Stories by Michael Carney

Time Loop

A contribution to the "Realms Of Our Own" multiverse
http://bit.ly/timeloopbook
Available free exclusively to those who sign up for our newsletter at
http://outcastangels.com/subscribe

PROLOGUE I
The Ice Pits of Hades, April 27 1605

i

"Tāw ʾālep kāphē mēmhē tāwhēt hērēšhē"

As it slammed its pickaxe into a thick vein of frost-crystal deep within the Ice Pits of Hades, the Outcast Angel known only as Prisoner Eleven silently chanted the phrase that could mean either freedom or eternal torment.

Eleven had overheard a demon recite the spell five hundred years earlier. Fearful of forgetting, it repeated the words to itself many times each and every day. The same agonized thought followed every repetition. *What if these words are wrong?*

There was only one way to find out. *Get to the portal and try to use the spell to escape.*

But that prospect seemed as impossible as ever.

# # #

Eleven—no Outcast Angel captives were permitted names, by personal order of the leader of the Darke Warriors, Lord Hurakan—was the only living prisoner on Hades. Every other prisoner had died at least once and been resurrected to suffer the eternal damnation of the netherworld.

Eleven's appearance was indistinguishable from that of the humans around it. All heads were hairless—condemned Ice Pit workers had their heads shaved once a week as a simple identification measure. And each worker wore a tunic fashioned from the hides of helldragons. The toughened skins were a practical solution to the harsh conditions of the Ice Pits, but did little to protect the wearers from the bitterly cold environment that was Hades.

The excavation of the Ice Pits continued for hour after hour, as it did every single day. There was a brief pause during Hour 15, when one of the workers was crushed in a rockslide. "Get that body out of the pit," snarled one of the demon guards, "and add another thousand years to its sentence for clumsiness." Those whose bodies died on Hades were simply resurrected there—but then their new bodies had to be retrained, reducing their productivity for many weeks, which the demons hated.

After twenty hours, Eleven's shift was over for another day. *Four hours of rest before tomorrow's shift begins.* Eleven joined the thousands of human workers swarming from the pits and making their way up the roughly-cut paths to the higher levels. Eleven was halfway to the top when most of the demons began shouting and cheering.

ii

The Darke Warrior Nekhbet, sitting alone in her palace office on the top level of Hades, allowed herself a brief smile of satisfaction. *The pope has been killed.* She had already sensed the resulting probability changes, minutes before the confirming mind-message had arrived from Rome. *<It's done. Congratulations, Nekhbet, we're now one major step closer to the Lost War.>*

It was the 27th of April 1605 on Earth and the new Roman Catholic Pope Leo XI, formerly Alessandro Ottaviano de' Medici, had just died. He had served as pontiff for less than a month before unexpectedly passing away, ostensibly as the result of a cold. Nekhbet knew better. *As a cousin of the Queen of France, Alessandro would have kept the peace between France and the Papal States in the coming war. That future possibility has now been wiped from existence.*

Nekhbet was beginning to examine the new probability implications when she heard loud noises outside. Frowning, she strode across to the main window with its panoramic view of the city of Tartaros, home to the millions of demons that inhabited Hades. *What's happening out there?* Despite all her prophetic powers, Nekhbet was usually oblivious to the going-on of the ordinary demons around her.

Row after row of two-thousand-foot-high buildings stretched out as far as the eye could see. They were usually so grim and silent, but now dozens of helldragons circled over the city, their riders crying out to each other. Furious at the disruption, Nekhbet tuned into some of the thousands of mind-messages flooding across the city—and then relaxed. *They're celebrating the killing of the pope,* she realized. *I suppose it's about time. There hasn't been much to party about lately, especially since our failure with the Spanish Armada.*

Nekhbet returned to the battered stone table that served as her desk. *If you think this little success is worth celebrating,* she thought before turning her attention back to her calculations, *wait until we win the Lost War.*

iii

Eleven reached the surface of the Ice Pits and looked around in amazement. Everywhere, demons were running amok. *They haven't been this crazy since they caught that other Outcast Angel and dragged its newly-resurrected body through Hades.*

That cruel event was the catalyst that had triggered Eleven's determination to escape, thirteen hundred years earlier. The memory of that same event prompted Eleven now. *There are nearly four hours until the next shift, that's how long until they notice that someone is missing. With the demons all distracted, there'll never be a better chance to try to escape.*

Still, Eleven hesitated. If the escape failed and its body was killed by the demons in the process, Eleven would be doomed to eternity in Hades—its body would be resurrected in that hellhole and it would forevermore be under the mind-control of Lucifer and his demons.

Will the spell work? That was the single question that mattered—and Eleven could only find out by somehow getting to the palace chamber which housed the portal, the one physical gateway between Hades and Earth. *That means passing through the city—and several heavily-guarded checkpoints.*

Eleven agonized over its decision for another minute—but in the end, it had no choice. Eleven had already been imprisoned in Hades for more than ten thousand Earth years, effectively condemned to eternal torment. This was its best and probably only chance to escape.

Eleven bent its shoulders and lowered its head. That pose was typical of the weary, desolate stance of the Barren—those resurrected humans that the demons considered useless for all but the most menial of tasks.

In that uncomfortable position, Eleven shuffled its way out of the main gate that separated the Ice Pits from the city of Tartaros and headed for the first checkpoint.

iv

Nekhbet, in the midst of complex planning for the Lost War, sat back with a start. There had just been a change to one of the hundreds of individuals whose futures she monitored in the back of her mind.

Unsure of exactly who that individual might be, and what the change might entail, Nekhbet spent several minutes sorting through the many possibilities. Eventually, she identified the source.

Ah, Eleven, decided to try to escape after all these years, did we? That will cost you your soul, if not your secret.

Nekhbet reached out with her mind, preparing to issue orders for one of the Ice Pit guards to stop the runaway—and then had a better idea. *Let's see how far you get, young Eleven.*

Nekhbet began to actively track Eleven's progress, enjoying the brief distraction from the arduous task of planning the war.

V

Eleven shuffled slowly towards the first checkpoint. *Here goes.*

"What do you want?" snapped the demon at the checkpoint. "Where are you going?"

Eleven bent even lower, adopting the typical droning, listless voice of a Barren. "Lord Kasdaye requires a message to be taken to Lord Dalkiel." Eleven deliberately named two of Hades' most senior Darke Warriors.

"What is the message?" demanded the demon.

Eleven cowered. "Th-th-th-the Lord instructs that the message is only for Lord Dalkiel."

"That's not good enough," said the demon. "I need to know the message before I can let you pass."

"Th-th-then, you can m-m-m-mind-call Lord Kasdaye," Eleven stuttered.

The demon paused, and for a frightening moment, Eleven feared that the demon would call its bluff and mind-call the Darke Warrior. *Surely, it won't be willing to disturb such a senior Darke Warrior on such a minor matter?*

It was and it did.

vi

Eleven couldn't hear the mind-conversation that ensued, but the demon's facial expressions suggested that the chat wasn't going well. After a minute or two, it was apparent that Lord Kasdaye had abruptly terminated the discussion.

The demon turned back to the nervous Eleven. "Lord Kasdaye says—that he is otherwise engaged and doesn't wish to be disturbed. I don't have time for this either, it's Leo-day and I'm off-shift in a few minutes. Get out of here." The demon waved Eleven through. "Go now, before I change my mind."

Eleven shuffled slowly past the checkpoint, wanting desperately to run but being careful to continue to act like a Barren.

# # #

That went better for you than I had expected, Eleven, thought Nekhbet, who had observed the proceedings through the eyes of the checkpoint guard. *Let's see how you cope if I make your journey a little more difficult.* Nekhbet placed a quick mind-call, issued several instructions, and then leaned back in her chair to observe.

vii

Eleven shuffled through the Tartaros city streets, belatedly wishing it had adopted a speedier disguise. *Still, there's no doubting that this is highly effective—none of the demons are paying any attention to a Barren.*

The passing demons had other things on their mind—they were going to party, hard. Many of the demons scurrying past Eleven carried supplies of the usual brew, fermented manblood, harvested from mostly-accidental human deaths. A fortunate few had scored very rare basiliskblood from the palace reserves. *Those demons definitely won't be doing any work tomorrow,* thought Eleven as it turned onto one of the main Tartaros thoroughfares.

Eleven reduced its already slow pace. Something odd was happening at the checkpoint ahead. Three helldragons hovered nearby, their massive scaly wings flapping languidly as they maintained their stationary position above the checkpoint.

Their riders, clearly annoyed at having to miss out on the festivities, were closely inspecting everyone who approached. *There's no way to get past there without being spotted as a fake,* thought Eleven.

Eleven lingered, pretending to consult instructions from its master, while it considered its options. *Can't go back and can't go around.*

#

Nekhbet, watching Eleven through the multifaceted eyes of one of the helldragons, was getting bored. *Come on Eleven. Make your move,* she demanded, making her helldragon-host uneasy but achieving little else. *Your four hours are slipping away and I have a war to plan. If you don't move along soon, I'll have to send for Nemesis.*

viii

Eleven was still one block away from the checkpoint. With few options ahead, it slipped into the last remaining side street. The street itself was effectively indistinguishable from all the other streets in the neighborhood, with tightly packed rows of two-thousand-foot-high apartment buildings. It was also, for the moment, empty of demons.

A wild idea seized Eleven. It looked around in all directions. *Nobody in sight.*

Without stopping to decide whether this was just a stupid idea or actually a really stupid idea, Eleven summoned its wings from the aether. The glorious, white feathered appendages, sixteen feet from wingtip to wingtip, shimmered into ectoplasmic existence on Eleven's back.

Eleven had not used them for more than ten thousand years— Outcast Angels were forbidden to use their wings in Hades, on pain of instant and prolonged punishment—but they felt as comfortable and familiar as ever.

Driving the wings with its mind, Eleven launched into the air and quickly flew to the top of the nearest apartment building, two thousand feet up. It was a maneuver that should have been impossible in Hades— and would have been, on any other day but this. The demonic eyes that normally would have spotted and reported such a heresy were otherwise occupied.

# # #

Even Nekhbet didn't know what Eleven had done. She knew that some factor had changed—the probabilities told her so—but the helldragon hadn't seen anything, and Nekhbet didn't think to redirect its gaze upwards.

Before Nekhbet could determine what was happening, she sensed that Eleven had slipped past the checkpoint and was moving towards the palace chamber that contained the portal.

Very well, thought Nekhbet, releasing her mental grip on the helldragon, *I'll do this myself.*

She headed towards the steps that led down to the portal chamber.

ix

Eleven scrambled across the rooftops, making short flying hops from one roof to another, bypassing the remaining checkpoints that stood between it and the palace. Once past all the guards, Eleven flew back down to ground level, rapidly dismissing its wings before they could be noticed. It then resumed its slow shuffle towards the cheerless grounds of the Hades palace that housed Lucifer's most trusted Darke Warriors.

Eventually, Eleven arrived at the palace and made its way down to the chamber containing the portal. The room was empty and unguarded.

Eleven straightened up, discarding its Barren disguise. It walked over to the portal that occupied the center of the room. *Hope this works.*

Eleven took a deep breath. Its entire future was on the line. *"Tāw ʾālep kāphē mēmhē tāwhēt hērēšhē"*

Nothing happened.

# # #

Nekhbet, who had been watching from a hidden control room, almost laughed aloud. *Fool. We change the portal spell every day. What else would you expect?*

Then she noticed a critical change that had just emerged in Eleven's probability patterns. *How very interesting. Your potentialities have now changed dramatically. If you escape from Hades now, you might well become the one who actually triggers the Lost War.*

She cast a quick spell.

# # #

Eleven was thrown into darkest despair. *It didn't work.* The most likely outcome now was to be arrested and handed over to the Darke Warrior executioner, Nemesis.

Then, belatedly, wonderfully, the portal flared into life—

accompanied by a deafening series of alarm bells that filled the chamber and that every demon for miles around would have heard.

Even Leo-day won't be enough for them to miss those alarms. Time to go. Eleven plunged into the portal and was instantly translated to Alepotrypa.

PROLOGUE II
Alepotrypa, Morea [Greece],
Midnight Wednesday April 27 1605

Fireballs exploded into the midnight sky high above the Peloponnesian peninsula. The sole onlookers, a few shepherds tending their flocks on the rugged mountainside nearby, looked up in terror.

What followed left the shepherds utterly convinced that the cave at Alepotrypa was indeed, as ancient tales suggested, the gateway to Hades.

Hundreds of demonic creatures poured out from the cave like swarming bats and soared into the night sky, their terrifying armored bodies illuminated by the half-moon.

Demon after demon flexed black, leathery wings and flew into the sky, branching out in all directions, searching for some mysterious prey. Their collective wingbeats created an intense angry buzz as they circled round and round.

One of the demons flew down to the mountains and hovered near one poor shepherd. The nightmarish apparition raised a flaming sword— and shrieked with delight as the shepherd ran for his life.

Two of the shepherds, afraid that they could not escape without being spotted, hid behind some large boulders high on the side of the mountain. From that vantage point, they could see large numbers of demons flying around far above, blanketing the sky, whilst small groups combed the mountainous landscape.

Then the shepherds heard a new sound cutting through the buzz.

The sound came from what the shepherds decided must be an angel, white wings beating furiously as it fought through the layer of demons and plunged down through the sky, down towards the water below, at an incredible, impossible velocity.

Many of the demons broke off from their formation and chased after their angelic quarry as it continued to increase its speed, heading towards what must surely be a fatal collision with the Mediterranean Sea.

Before the angel could come anywhere near its intended destination however, two fireballs struck its feathered wings. The wings burst into flames.

Like a modern-day Icarus, the figure plummeted from the sky.

PART ONE

ONE
Naples, Kingdom of Naples [Italy],
9 p.m. Monday January 18 1610

"Don't let her escape!" shouted Henricus, as he watched the young woman scrambling across the badly-damaged top floor of a derelict building in the residential quarter of Naples. Several of the Alchemae, Academy graduates with enhanced powers, closely pursued her. A handful of hired thugs, whose not-so-unique talent was primarily brute force, joined in the chase.

The two groups were effectively herding the young woman towards the most unstable corner of the building, where large sections of the floor had collapsed into the darkness below. Even Girardus, whose acrobatic abilities were unmatched, proceeded carefully across this hazardous surface.

The woman suddenly checked her headlong flight—not because of any concerns about the void into which she might have plunged, but rather because a ten-foot-tall, double-headed monster had just blocked her path. This terrifying creature—conjured up by the Alchemae's master of illusion, Apollinaris—breathed out great torrents of flame. Its two heads—on the left a hissing serpent, on the right a snarling lion—were poised, apparently ready to strike the woman at any moment.

"Excellent," Henricus remarked to his Academy colleague, Zulian, "Apollinaris has outdone himself tonight. His latest creation looks like a cross between a hydra and a chimera, if I remember my Greek mythology correctly."

Henricus and Zulian stood on the far side of the building, close to a bonfire which the Academy's men had lit earlier in the evening with the goal of attracting the *lazzaroni*, Naples' teeming masses of beggars, poor and homeless. It was a cold, wet night and the bonfire had proven an effective lure. Unfortunately, as Zulian's nose told him only too clearly, the lazzaroni might be better described as the *non lavato*, the unwashed. He could smell their choking stench everywhere, especially as the bonfire liberated the odors from their wet clothing. Zulian, for one, hoped that this recruitment mission would swiftly conclude so that he could escape the horrific smell.

When the Academy's trap was sprung, several of the lazzaroni had drawn their swords—only priests or the most wretched of paupers would go around unarmed in seventeenth century Europe—but the supernatural powers of the Academy's enhanced had quickly discouraged any significant opposition. Some had sought to run but only the young woman had successfully eluded the Academy's grasp. It seemed, however, that her freedom would be short-lived.

"She's trapped," smirked Zulian, "nowhere to run. Even if she has the nerve to get past Apollinaris's monster, she'd be crazy to try to jump the gap—it's a very long way down. We've caught her now."

And so it seemed, until their quarry appeared to notice that the creature in front of her had done little more than look threatening. Then she thrust her hand directly into the path of one of the bursts of flame that the monster spat out.

"Amazing," said Henricus. "She's much braver than I would be. Most of the lazzaroni would be shaking in absolute terror if they came face to face with one of Apollinaris's monsters. Not this one, though. Now she knows for certain that the monster is an illusion." Before he could instruct his men to close in, the young woman made her own move.

She plunged straight through the creature's false image and rushed over to the collapsed section of the floor. Before anyone could reach her, she leapt across the vast gap, somehow made it almost to safety, and then could be heard scrabbling desperately for a handhold as her grasp slipped on the rain-splattered bricks at the edge of the abyss.

Henricus and Zulian could no longer see the young woman, because of the darkness enshrouding that section of the building. The crescent moon now hid behind rain clouds and the corner itself was too far away to be illuminated by the bonfire.

Henricus squinted into the darkness, fearing the worst. He could hear the occasional impacts of a few dislodged fragments of rock, but no sound of a body crashing down to the lower floors.

Then one of the searchers shouted out. "She's made it to the stairwell! She's going to get away!"

There was a brief, torrential rain-burst directly over the stairwell down which the woman was fleeing—conjured up by Tranquilo, who despite his name was one of the Alchemae's more powerful members and could manipulate the weather—but the tightly-focused downpour merely served to delay the young woman, not to stop her.

Zulian swiftly turned to Henricus. "Do we follow her? Or shall we let her go and focus on the other street people that we've already caught?"

"Send everyone after her. Don't bother about the rest of the lazzaroni. She's the one we want."

Zulian stopped and stared at his colleague. "A woman student? In the Academy? Are you crazy? The Master will be furious. And can you imagine what Father Carracci will say?"

"Doesn't matter. Just do it." Henricus had no interest in debating the topic. "Once this woman receives her powers, the Master will finally achieve his greatest success in the forthcoming Lost War."

Zulian reluctantly gave the necessary orders and then turned back to Henricus. "Mannaggia!" It was most unusual for Zulian to swear, even so mildly—he came from a prominent local Napoletano family, which had already provided the Church with several nuns and three Jesuit priests. "What is it with you tonight? Where did that prophecy come from? Since when did you turn into an oracle?"

Henricus possessed the potion-enhanced ability to identify people with powers, or those who had the potential to develop powers, but this latest pronouncement was far beyond his usual capabilities.

"I haven't," admitted Henricus, "I'm simply repeating what the Contessa told me this morning."

Zulian didn't know what to reply—one didn't argue with the wife of the Master of the Academy.

Meanwhile the Academy's recruiting team, powered and unpowered alike, swarmed out of the derelict building to resume the hunt. Most of the lazzaroni—including three young children—slipped away as soon as their captors were out of sight, though a foolhardy few remained by the fire. Roving gangs, forcibly recruiting for various navies, were a commonplace hazard in a major port city like Naples, but a roaring bonfire freely available to the homeless on a cold, wet winter's night?

That was a unique and welcome event well worth the risk.

# # #

No-one noticed a shadowy figure observing from the rooftop of an adjoining building. As the Academy's men poured into the street in search of their prey, the unseen watcher summoned her wings with a thought and launched herself into the air, following the chase from high above.

TWO
At the same time
**High above Wallachia [Romania],
10 p.m. local time Monday January 18 1610**

The Outcast Angel Jesse, flying vigorously in pursuit of the fleeing Vlad Ţepeş in the skies above Wallachia, gasped aloud. Wave upon psychic wave buffeted his mind as massive numbers of probabilities suddenly became fluid.

Everywhere, future timelines were in turmoil.

Some disruptive event was occurring at this very moment—some crucial trigger that would have profound implications for the future of a great many, people and nations alike.

Jesse's prophetic powers—his ability to determine the possible futures of specific individuals—could show him what would be the most likely outcomes if events continued along their current paths.

Most of the probabilities that Jesse monitored had been fixed and largely favorable until a moment ago. Now they were almost universally grim.

Some critical element was changing. Jesse could clearly enough predict the probable results if the changed circumstances actually became the new reality—but his powers did not allow him to identify the cause.

Jesse paused in his chase long enough to send a prayer skyward. *<Father God, not for me, but for Your children on Earth, I ask You to intervene and prevent this change, whatever it is. Otherwise, the powers that You gave me reveal that great evil will again be unleashed on this world.>*

As had been the case ever since Jesse and his fellow Outcasts had been exiled from Heaven, there was no reply.

THREE
A few minutes later
Naples, Kingdom of Naples,
9.05 p.m. Monday January 18 1610

Chrymos—the young woman being sought so energetically by the Academy—raced through the narrow streets of Naples' residential district, heading towards the port area. She wasn't running as fast as she might, she had a different goal than merely to escape. She paused for a moment and listened to the clatter of footsteps on the streets behind her. *Sounds like they're all chasing after me. Hopefully that means the children will be able to get away.*

Chrymos ran on, slowing her pace even further to match that of her pursuers. It was a wise move. She could barely see a few steps in front of her in these narrow, unlit streets and the lava slabs with which the streets were paved—harvested from Mount Vesuvius's occasional volcanic tantrums—were still slippery from the evening's frequent showers. One wrong step and the chase would be over too soon.

Her heart was still pounding after her encounter with the monster. *Who are these people,* Chrymos wondered, *and how can they have such powers?* When the monster breathed fire at her she was terrified at first, and mere seconds from surrender. She would have stopped running immediately, had it not been for her desire to protect the three children in her care. Now, she hoped to lure her pursuers away from the bonfire so that the young ones might be able to escape.

Chrymos turned a street corner and ran downhill, towards the port. Her current position, surrounded by towering city buildings mostly constructed from dark stone, was in an area that she always considered grim and unfriendly, even in daylight hours. At this hour, the neighborhood seemed even more pitiless. Building after building showed no outward sign of life. Any doors or shutters that might face onto the street were tightly closed and barred, to keep out unwelcome guests and to keep in the heat—which also meant that no light escaped to guide passersby down the treacherous rain-glazed streets.

As usual, the streets reeked of discarded human waste, though the evening's wind and rain helped to disperse the worst of the odors.

As she ran, Chrymos clutched Adric's schiavona. She had picked up the broadsword when Adric had been knocked unconscious, intending to keep it safe for him until he awoke. Instead, she had found herself wielding the weapon, poorly but successfully, to defend herself and protect the children when the thugs ventured too close.

Now Chrymos needed to secure the schiavona so that her hands would be free. She eased the sword into her belt, wincing slightly as she was obliged to use her left hand—badly cut and bruised from desperately grabbing the jagged bricks a few minutes earlier—to push the intricate basket-hilted sword into place.

Her headlong journey soon took Chrymos to an intersection. The cross street was slightly wider, which enabled the crescent moon to illuminate her limited choices. She stopped. *Left, right or straight ahead?*

Chrymos looked to the left, spotted the elaborate façade of one of Naples' most respected convents and smiled bitterly. *If I had been seeking sanctuary right now, that convent would never let me in. Those nuns come from some of Naples' wealthiest families. They don't want any lazzaroni befouling their bedsheets.*

Imagine how they would react if they opened their shutters and saw me. They would shudder in well-bred disgust. This ragged coif, a simple cap that barely covers my head. A cloak that might have looked presentable once but which is now both dirty and shredded beyond repair. No fine jewelry, only a plain neck chain—and this bronze ring from little Olivia.

She smiled ruefully, inspecting her injured hand, crowned by chipped nails edged in black. *They definitely won't think much of these filthy hands. And as for my cord sandals, I can hear the nuns now—'My dear, those will never do!' Well, my tunic dress is modest enough, even by convent standards, and at least it's clean—mostly.*

She could hear her pursuers growing nearer, which prompted Chrymos into action. She opted to ignore the left and right options and plunged straight ahead, into yet another tight street—but this new passageway began narrowing almost as soon as she had entered it. In less than a dozen feet, the passage became too constricted for her to force her way through. *It's not a thoroughfare,* she belatedly realized, *it's a small and shrinking gap between buildings.*

Chrymos turned, intending to retrace her steps, but came to a sudden halt. Her pursuers could be seen coming down the street that she had just left. They would soon be at the intersection—it was too late for her to change direction without being seen. *I can't go back to the crossroads or they'll catch me for sure. I'm trapped.*

FOUR
Moments later
Naples, Kingdom of Naples,
9.10 p.m., Monday January 18 1610

Chrymos quickly dismissed the notion of simply trying to hide in the narrow passageway. *Most of those searchers are carrying flaming torches so the darkness won't protect me for long.*

She turned back to examine her current surroundings more closely, not an easy task in the cloud-shrouded moonlight. *I can't get any further forward down this alleyway and I can't see any doors or windows at ground level. How about further up?*

She looked up, squinting, searching for possibilities up above. *That could be a shutter up there, on the third or fourth floor. But can I even get all the way up there? And dare I hope that the shutter will be unlocked?*

Increasing noise levels from behind Chrymos, as the searchers arrived at the intersection, suggested that whatever she decided to do, she needed to get moving, fast.

She pushed herself forward into the passageway until both of her elbows were touching—constricted by—opposite walls. The walls on both sides were constructed of large stone blocks, with just enough mortar between blocks to provide regular footholds for climbing. *I must be pazzo to do this,* thought Chrymos as, using her forearms and her sandal-clad feet, she began to leverage her way up towards the shutter she hoped she'd seen far above her. The blocks were slightly wet, but the direction of the prevailing wind and the narrowness of the passageway had limited the amount of rain that could reach the lower walls. *That's some good news.*

Up one block, two blocks, three blocks, four. The presumed shutter still seemed almost as far away as ever, but Chrymos could hear footsteps coming closer so she redoubled her climbing efforts, cruelly scraping her elbows and forearms as she did so. Five, six, seven, eight, nine blocks. *Keep going, just keep going, almost there.*

Finally, she reached her intended destination. It was indeed a shuttered window. Bracing herself, Chrymos tried to yank the shutter open from the outside but it was firmly bolted shut, with no light or even noise evident within. *Now what?*

Before Chrymos could even start to construct a new plan, there was a shout from below.

"There she is!"

Chrymos looked down. Several of her pursuers had ventured into the alleyway, armed with torches, and at least one of them had thought to look up when it became obvious that the street led nowhere. One of the thugs ran back to the cross-street and called out. "Get Girardus, we need him. She's here."

Chrymos had already seen the man they called Girardus in action, back at the bonfire. He was like a human frog, jumping easily from one spot to another, bouncing off walls or any available surface. *If anyone can easily reach me up here, he can.*

Chrymos looked upwards. She was now closer to the roof of the building than the ground, so she made the inevitable choice and resumed shimmying up the walls. Her elbows and forearms were now bleeding steadily from the climb, and her toes were badly stubbed as well, but there was no time to worry about the pain. *Girardus will bounce up here far faster than I can.*

Up, up, up—and then Chrymos ran into a major problem. The wall on the left abruptly ended—it was about ten feet shorter than the wall on the right. *Should I go left here?*

A quick glance changed her mind. That building stood on its own at the end of the row, a long way from any other building except the one on her right. *If I climb onto that roof, I'll be trapped.*

She glanced down. Although there was still no sign of Girardus, the other searchers had begun to scale the walls using the same method as she was, urged on by their colleagues. *I'm running out of options.*

Some choice curses floated up from below as the climbers started to realize that the ascent was not as easy as Chrymos had made it seem. *Even so, they're still coming,* she thought. *Either they're very well paid or they truly fear their masters.*

Whatever the answer, Chrymos still had little choice. Twisting her body around until she could stand on the edge of the lower building, Chrymos steadied herself and then reached out with both hands to the wall opposite. She stretched to the top of the next block of stone and began pulling herself up with both hands until she could get a proper foothold. Her efforts were rewarded with a shot of pain. *Ouch! I'd forgotten about those bruises.* It was an unpleasant reminder that her left hand was already damaged.

Two more blocks of stone to go. The building's roof was tantalizingly close, almost within reach. Then Chrymos heard another shout from below, from near the passageway entrance.

"Girardus, over here!"

Chrymos risked another glance down, saw the new arrival leaping into the alleyway, jumping high into the air and bouncing easily from one wall to another. Before she could even realize she was holding her breath, Girardus had reached the shuttered window halfway up the wall and was comfortably perched beside it, deciding his next options.

No more time to lose. Chrymos stretched up to the next block, pulled herself up in almost a single movement, despite the agonizing pain in her left hand. The surfaces of the highest blocks of stone were wet and slippery—unlike the lower blocks, these had no protection from the intermittent rain—and she almost lost her grip. Fortunately, she was able to retain enough traction to hold on with her fingers until her flailing feet found the gap between blocks. *He's nearly on me,* she thought as she hurriedly stretched up to the top of the last block and began the final pain-punctuated ascent.

As Chrymos pulled her body up, over the ledge that encompassed the roof and then dropped untidily about three feet onto the flat surface below, the rapidly-arriving Girardus overtook her. He leapt above her head, twirling in mid-air, landed on the rooftop, rolled and then jumped to his feet, in a virtually single movement. He turned to face Chrymos, crossing his arms and adopting a self-satisfied expression as he did so.

"We're done here," Girardus said. "You put up a good race, but it's over. Come quietly. The Academy needs you."

FIVE
An instant later
**Naples, Kingdom of Naples,
9.15 p.m., Monday January 18 1610**

"I don't think so," said Chrymos, pulling herself to her feet and drawing the schiavona from her belt. She waved it, menacingly she hoped, in the direction of her assailant.

"Really? A sword?" scoffed Girardus. "You think that will save you? After you've seen what I can do?" To illustrate his point, he jumped vertically into the air, somersaulted twice in mid-jump and then landed lightly, legs bent, arms held straight out towards Chrymos. The effect was spoiled slightly when one of Girardus's feet slipped on the rain-soaked stones and gravel, airborne gifts from nearby Mount Vesuvius, which littered the roof.

The schiavona did have one useful effect—it discouraged Girardus from coming too close, which gave Chrymos valuable time to examine her new surroundings. The crescent moon also began to emerge from concealing clouds and partly illuminate the roof, another precious gift.

Even so, there wasn't much to see, at least not on the rooftop upon which Chrymos and Girardus were perched. The roof itself was flat, except for a three-foot-high ledge that acted as a safety barrier between the roof and the perilous depths below. Over to the left, Chrymos could see the outline of a trapdoor, flush with the roof's surface, which presumably led down inside the building. In the right-hand corner, a castellated chimney-pot coughed out smoke and soot—clearly the building was indeed occupied, even though there had been no external signs of life when Chrymos made her agonizing climb.

What particularly caught her eye, however, was a reflected glow from about four buildings away.

She looked again, glanced towards the port where the lighthouse, *La Lanterna*, dutifully warned away ships, did some quick distance calculations in her head. *That nearby glow,* she realized, *must be the*

Strada di Toledo. If I can make it over to that street, hopefully I can get lost in the crowds.

First, though, she needed to get past Girardus.

"You want me for your 'Academy', don't you?"

"So I've been told," said Girardus, "I have no idea why—you'd be the first and only female student there."

"Then—" Chrymos hopped up onto the nearest ledge, wavering for a moment but then quickly regaining her balance "—you'd better stand back. You won't want to have to report to your bosses that you made me fall down because you CAME TOO CLOSE!"

Chrymos shouted these last words because Girardus was edging nearer and nearer. He looked suitably guilty as he took a step backwards.

"Good," said Chrymos. "So tell me about your Academy. What's so bad about it that you have to drag recruits off the streets?"

As Chrymos talked, she slowly, carefully, slid her sandals along the ledge, aiming to work around the building. She hoped to distract Girardus from noticing her movements—and to distract herself from noticing that she was five floors above the ground, inching along a slippery, narrow ledge from which she might topple at any moment.

Neither distraction worked. Chrymos felt more and more unsafe as she edged along. And Girardus simply kept pace with her as she made her way from the left ledge to the center. She nearly tumbled as she navigated the ninety degree turn at the corner without looking down, but managed—just—to retain her balance.

Girardus made no effort to seize her. He was keen to talk, to evangelize on behalf of the Academy, perhaps hoping that he could convince her to abandon her resistance. He launched into an explanation.

"We're recruiting on behalf of the *Accademia dei Segreti*."

"The Academy of Secrets? That sounds ominous," said Chrymos, although her attention was mostly on where she placed her feet as she continued her perilous journey around the edge of the building.

"As it happens, the Academy gained its name because of the many secrets we learn. Fascinating subjects. Diplomacy, battle strategies, hands-on training in various fighting styles, we even study—" Girardus looked around to ensure that no-one else was listening. "—weapons, deadly poisons and my personal favorite, spy craft."

He looked around once more, lowered his voice conspiratorially. "The most important topic we learn about is alchemy. As you may be aware, the Church has banned the use of alchemy, so that's the main reason why we can't promote the Academy openly. Even so, we still attract many new students every year, from some of Naples' finest families. In addition, we're always seeking candidates with the right kind of potential—" Girardus looked around yet again to ensure that no-one else was listening, a rather pointless exercise on this deserted rooftop in the middle of the night. "—because once we graduate, we're given a very special *Exousía* potion—that's Greek, it means "power"—which provides us with our own unique abilities. Henricus—he's the one leading our team tonight—he's told us that you yourself have immense potential."

Chrymos was both intrigued and horrified. "Sounds like someone's planning a war."

"Oh, the Lost War's coming, alright," Girardus said nonchalantly. "The Academy's helping to ensure that we're ready for it."

Exactly who is 'we'? Chrymos wondered. But she didn't pose that question to Girardus, because she had now reached the right-hand ledge that was her intended destination and needed to focus on her next move. She turned and then, before wiser thoughts could prevail, threw herself towards the building that was her next destination.

SIX
One second later
Naples, Kingdom of Naples,
9.20 p.m., Monday January 18 1610

Chrymos leapt unsteadily across the deadly gap, grasping desperately at the ledge of her target. After a nervous moment, her left hand and the hilt of her sword combined to gain her a safe perch on the other side.

She lay on the newly-achieved rooftop briefly, steadying her nerves, until Girardus inevitably joined her. For him, the leap from rooftop to rooftop had been a trivial feat.

Once Girardus could see that Chrymos was unhurt, he began to deliver a stern lecture.

"That was so foolish. You could have been killed—"

"I wasn't, so spare me the lecture," Chrymos snapped back. She stood up, sword still threatening Girardus, and confirmed her earlier impression. This building was under repair and the rooftop was crowded with construction equipment and materials, including a treadwheel-powered crane. *This I can use.*

She adopted a more conciliatory tone. "Thanks for your concern, though. Your jumping skills," she asked, "are they natural or as a result of Academy training?"

"Both," came the quick response. "I was always nimble, but the Academy training very definitely helped—and then the Exousía potion multiplied my skills immensely."

"So what exactly can you do?" Chrymos asked. "Could you, for example—" She singled out a number of places on the rooftop. "—leap from where you are up to the ledge, down to that pile of bricks and from there to the top of the chimney, then onto that scaffold and down onto the roof beside that crane?"

"Watch me," said Girardus. He launched himself into a spectacular display of hopping, sliding, tumbling, rolling and jumping, as he ricocheted along the route that Chrymos had indicated.

She wasn't really watching him, though. Rather she was poised expectantly. As soon as Girardus completed his final somersault and spiraled in to land at precisely the designated rooftop position beside the crane, Chrymos sent the schiavona hurtling towards his landing spot.

"Missed me," he laughed, landing safely while the sword flashed past him.

"Not really," she said. The sword embedded itself into the stack of wooden beams near the chimney, having sliced neatly through a rope on its short journey.

That rope, in its turn, had been threaded through a pulley attached to the crane, and had been securing a load of building materials which had been painstakingly hauled up from street level using the crane and treadwheel. Without the rope's support, the wooden beams were no longer suspended, but cascaded downwards onto the unsuspecting Girardus, simultaneously pinning him to the ground and knocking him unconscious.

Chrymos casually walked over, retrieved her sword, and secured it to her belt. "Thanks for the offer," she said to the unheeding Girardus, "but I think I'll pass."

Shouts from behind extinguished her own cockiness. Chrymos glanced back to see that several of the Academy's men had successfully repeated her original climb and were even now starting to clamber onto the rooftop of the building that she had so recently left. It would be the work of but a few moments for them to rush across that building's roof and then leap to her current location. *I need to move.*

Chrymos rushed to the side of the building furthest away from her pursuers and peered down to the street below. *No good—there are even more of them down there, they'll see me if I try to climb down. I'll simply have to keep going over the rooftops.*

The distance from her current position across to the next building was significantly greater. *I'm going to need a decent run-up for this.*

Chrymos selected a plank of timber and dragged it into place against the top of the far ledge, forming a makeshift ramp. Ignoring the growing shouts from behind her, as her pursuers saw what she was doing, she repeated the action with a second plank, allowing herself a margin of error—at least in the run-up.

Once I start that jump—Chrymos feared that if she finished that sentence, she wouldn't have the nerve to make the attempt.

Instead, she ran back to the opposite side of the building, startling her pursuers who were deciding whether or not they could successfully cross a much narrower gap. Chrymos took a deep breath and then ran at full acceleration across the roof and up the ramp, launching herself over the wide chasm that stood between her and freedom.

Too late, Chrymos realized that she had misjudged the distance, or the angle, or both. Her trajectory was not enough to take her to the top of the building. Instead, she slammed into the side of the wall, about two feet short of the top, and began to slide down.

SEVEN
Long seconds later
Naples, Kingdom of Naples,
9.25 p.m., Monday January 18 1610

Scratching, scraping, Chrymos desperately sought to find some handhold, something to stop her fall. Unfortunately this wall was plastered—there were no blocks or bricks that she could grasp.

Chrymos slid down another two feet. She was moments away from losing contact with the wall entirely, when her left hand finally gained some purchase—a small area of plaster had chipped away, providing a scant edge that she could grasp. She clung fearfully to this small lifeline, but at the same time, she despaired. Her entire bodyweight dangled from that single, damaged hand. *I can't hold on for very long, I can already feel my hand starting to lose its strength.*

Frantically, Chrymos reached around with her right hand, hoping she could find another handhold. She found none—the section where the plaster had broken away was a fortunate but all too rare exception—and its usefulness would soon come to an end, when the bruised hand finally failed.

Hope was fading—and, even though her mind labored at fever pitch, cycling through possible alternatives, Chrymos couldn't think of any. The muscles in her left hand were beginning to spasm. The end was near.

And then—a rope came spiraling down from above and a voice shouted. "Hold on, don't let go. I'll be right there."

A few seconds later, sure enough, someone began climbing down the wall towards Chrymos, holding on to the rope with two hands—while using two more hands to reach out and grab Chrymos by the arms and another two hands to hold her around the waist.

Her six-armed savior held her firmly in his grasp and began climbing back up the rope.

EIGHT

A few minutes later
Naples, Kingdom of Naples,
9.27 p.m., Monday January 18 1610

Chrymos was released as soon as her rescuer reached the rooftop.

She was not alone. In fact, it seemed that most of the Academy's men were now clustered around her. Listening to their chatter, she gathered that their ascent to the rooftop was rather easier than hers—their leaders had encouraged the building's residents to allow them access through the building's internal stairs.

A well-dressed young man introduced himself as "Henricus, at your service," and politely asked for her name.

"You chase me halfway across Naples and you don't know who I am?" Chrymos was indignant.

"True, I don't know who you are," said Henricus, "but I do know what you are—the most ideal candidate for the Academy that we've ever come across." Henricus bowed low, no irony intended.

Chrymos appreciated the gesture, though she was convinced that Henricus must be either lying or mistaken, at least about her suitability for the Academy. *I'm merely a street orphan. But perhaps I can use that belief to get him to tell me what I desperately want to know.*

"My name," she informed him as she sat up, "is Chrymos."

"Pleased to meet you," said Henricus, extending his hand. Chrymos simultaneously shook the offered hand and used it to pull herself to her feet. Henricus continued: "I look forward to getting to know you better at the Academy. It is my very real pleasure to invite you to join our little community."

"Really?" Chrymos was non-committal. "But before I can even start to consider your 'offer', I need to know what has happened to the others that your men had detained near the bonfire."

"Which others?" Henricus looked genuinely puzzled.

"I guess you would call them all lazzaroni, though only a few deserve to be labeled beggars," said Chrymos.

"Oh, those. We let them all go when we chased after you," said Henricus. Chrymos let out a deep sigh of relief, but Henricus wasn't quite finished. "Well, most of them."

Chrymos almost panicked, until Henricus added, "We held onto one fellow, called—what was his name, Zulian?"

"Adric."

"That's right, Adric. He's another talent bound for the Academy, along with one other fellow we picked up earlier this evening."

Chrymos was finally free to relax. Adric was taken—that was a major concern. But at least the children were safe—safe from these particular marauders, anyway. *Now all I have to do is escape so that I can rendezvous with the three of them.*

Chrymos scrutinized her current surroundings. Another plain rooftop, except that its roof sloped sharply down on one side. She gazed back at the building from which she had launched her nearly-fatal leap. Several more of her former pursuers were busily lifting up a stack of wooden beams, presumably those that had collapsed onto Girardus. *They don't seem to be in any hurry, so hopefully Girardus isn't badly hurt.*

Henricus interrupted her train of thought. "Chrymos, let me introduce you to your rescuer, Uicenzo."

He beckoned to the young man, who came forward and bowed, his six hands performing intricate supplication gestures in perfect unison. "It was my pleasure to be of service to you, signorina."

"Thank you for your rescue, Uicenzo," said Chrymos, "I am very grateful."

"Chrymos here," Henricus informed Uicenzo, "has been trying very hard not to be noticed while she inspects her surroundings. I very much fear that she will soon try to run away from us again. Uicenzo, would you be so kind as to secure her so that such temptations are—out of reach."

Before Chrymos could even blink, Uicenzo sprang into action. With one hand, he seized the rope that he had previously employed to rescue her. He used several other hands to wind the rope around and around her arms and torso until Chrymos was completely wrapped in loops of strong cord. Uicenzo tucked one end under the coils of rope behind her back—the other end was still secured to the chimney to which it had been attached during the rescue effort.

"There—that should hold you safely, signorina," said Uicenzo politely.

Chrymos stood stunned. *He was so fast. He moves like a spider! How did he do that?*

Henricus looked indecently pleased with himself as he smiled at Chrymos. "We will continue this conversation down below." Then he turned away from Chrymos and began issuing instructions. "Let's get off this rooftop and take her to the cart."

Chrymos glanced at Henricus, and saw that his attention was momentarily diverted. She looked carefully at the knot securing the rope to the chimney and then examined the manner in which most of the rope had been wound around her body. She had a split second to act. Her mind rebelled. *I can't believe I'm going to do this!*

She ran to the edge, the rope tightening behind her, and threw herself off the roof.

NINE
Seconds later
Naples, Kingdom of Naples,
9.30 p.m., Monday January 18 1610

Henricus stood frozen for a moment—he could not believe what had just happened. Then he rushed to the edge of the roof and looked down, expecting to see the young woman's body splattered on the ground.

Instead he saw an incredible sight. Chrymos was unraveling the rope around her body, whirling round and round like an adult-sized spinning top while the rope unwound around her, slowing her descent. Henricus glanced back at the chimney—the other end of the rope was still firmly attached, a factor that Chrymos had clearly taken into account before throwing herself off the roof.

He turned his attention back to Chrymos, grinning in admiration. *Well played, signorina, well played indeed.*

He waited a moment, watched as the rope completed its unwinding. Chrymos had now freed her hands and was well able to control her final descent to the street below. She stooped to retrieve her cap—the solitary casualty of the rooftop plunge, it had tumbled off her head as she spun. Then Chrymos curtsied daintily towards the rooftop where Henricus stood, before accelerating down the street towards the bustle and noise of the Strada di Toledo. *Was that curtsey for me, Chrymos? This isn't goodbye. We're not done with you yet.*

Shouting out instructions as he rushed towards the trapdoor which led to the interior stairwell, Henricus couldn't help but grin. He was still smiling as he led the chase down the stairs and back out onto the streets.

TEN
Earlier That Night
In the woods, Naples, Kingdom of Naples,
7 p.m. Monday January 18 1610

The rain had settled in for the evening, intermittent showers adding to the misery of an already cold night in the city of Naples. To make matters worse, Chrymos and the three children in her care were living rough. A week earlier, they had been forced to leave the rooftop attic that had been their home for the past year—Naples was now the fastest growing city in Europe and every available building was needed to house the population explosion. Even properties of dubious merit such as the dilapidated attic—*which,* thought Chrymos, *should actually have been demolished*—were being pressed back into service to meet the desperate demand.

Chrymos and the children—Olivia, Madalena and Sirus—had not yet found a new place to live and so for the past several nights they had found rudimentary shelter in the woods on the edge of Naples' central residential district. Most of the trees in that area had shed their leaves for the winter so, with rain imminent, the foursome had set up for the night under a stand of evergreen cypress trees. Unfortunately the rain had now arrived and was proving heavier than expected. As a result, the trees and their leaves were becoming more and more soaked, and so were Chrymos and her charges.

"It's going to be another dreadful night, I'm afraid," said Chrymos as the four of them huddled together under a cloak at the base of one of the largest cypress trees they could find, "but at least this rain will discourage the lazzaroni." The previous night, they'd been forced to move when a group of beggars had turned up in the middle of the night and decided that they wanted the spot that Chrymos and the children were occupying. It hadn't been worth getting into a fight about, so the four of them had moved further into the woods. This latest location was a compromise— far enough into the woods that they probably wouldn't be disturbed, yet not so far that the children might get lost.

"Is there any bread left?" asked Olivia. At around eleven years old—Chrymos' best guess at her age—Olivia was the youngest of the three children. She was a bright and bubbly girl, usually the most optimistic of them all. Two years earlier, Chrymos had found Olivia, starving and nearly dead, outside Naples' vice-regal palace. The palace guards had shown absolutely no interest in the young waif, ignoring her feeble cries for help. Chrymos had rescued the girl and taken her to the *Pio Monte Della Misericordia,* the charity brotherhood, where they nursed her back to some semblance of health. Once she had recovered sufficiently, unfortunately, Olivia was no longer permitted to remain amongst the sick and incurable so Chrymos once again stepped in and took the young girl under her wing.

Chrymos reached for her treasured *swete bagge,* the large embroidered bag that she had recovered from discarded trash outside one of Florence's aristocratic homes. She fossicked around inside the oh-so-carefully repaired bag, careful to shield its contents from the rain, and fished out a solitary chunk of stale millet bread.

Chrymos broke the loaf into three smaller segments and handed a piece to each child. "We'll get some more tomorrow." *I hope.* She tried not to think of eating, despite the urgings of her stomach, as she watched the children nibbling at what remained of their food.

"At least we're going to have fresh water tonight," said thirteen-year-old Madalena, nodding towards the makeshift bowl they had placed in the nearby clearing to catch rainwater. Occasionally Chrymos was able to draw clean drinking water from one of the hundreds of public wells fed by the Bolla aqueduct, though more often than not the locals chased her away—there were now too many people in Naples and the aqueducts simply couldn't supply enough fresh water for them all. On those occasions, Chrymos and the children had to settle for foul-smelling—and worse-tasting—water from a horse trough.

Madalena, quiet by nature, stayed with Chrymos and the others out of choice rather than necessity. The alternative was to live with her mother, Caterina, a woman who survived on the streets by entertaining male guests. Madalena hadn't said much about her mother to Chrymos—but had clearly opted to run away and hide rather than observe her mother's slow disintegration. As for Madalena's father, if the girl did know who he was she hadn't shared that fact with Chrymos.

Sirus—newly fourteen and increasingly impetuous—unexpectedly leapt to his feet and began climbing the tree they had all been sheltering under, dislodging showers of droplets that cascaded down onto the others. He responded to their loud protests semi-apologetically. "Sorry about that, but I need to check out one of those buildings."

Without stopping to explain further, Sirus clambered up the tree, grabbing rain-drenched branches. Sirus had been living with Chrymos and the others for three months, and had said little about his past life except a gruff "I ran away". From his occasional comments since, Chrymos had concluded that Sirus must have taken exception to his father's future plans for his life and had opted to strike out on his own. She had refrained from suggesting to Sirus that life back with his family surely must be an improvement on this current existence—*it would be best if Sirus reached that conclusion on his own.*

Sirus kept climbing until he arrived at a suitable vantage point on a branch high above. He raised a hand to cover his eyes from the rain and stared down at the residential area bordering the woods. The buildings in that part of the city were mostly tall, multi-story affairs of brick or stone construction, dark and gloomy in midwinter. It didn't take long for Sirus to discover the exception.

He shouted down to the others. "Someone's lit a bonfire on the roof of the old Tirabosco building!" The building in question, once owned by a leading local family, had been abandoned for many years, and not even the current property boom could make it habitable again—scavengers regularly looted the building, carrying off bricks, timbers and whatever else they could cut or chip away, effectively rendering the whole building unsafe.

"What else can you see?"

Sirus squinted through the rain. "It's not easy to see from here, but—no, wait!" Forgetting where he was, Sirus jumped a little in excitement—not enough to make him fall, but enough to send a fresh wave of raindrops hurtling downward. "I can see people standing beside the bonfire, and at least some of them are local street people that we know. There's Gasparo, I'd know that limp of his anywhere. And that must be, I'm sure it is, Signore Spizega, he used to chase me away when I was younger." Sirus smiled at the memory.

Olivia hopped up and down, tugging at Chrymos' tunic. "Can we go? Can we go? I'm so cold here."

Chrymos looked over at Madalena, who nodded. For such a quiet girl, that tiny movement constituted a ringing endorsement.

"Get yourself down here, Sirus, we're going to a bonfire," called Chrymos. The two girls showed their excitement in their own way, Olivia by clapping her hands and burbling with glee, Madalena with a slight smile.

While she waited for Sirus to make his descent, Chrymos gathered her precious swete bagge and stashed it inside a gap in a nearby tree-trunk, out of sight and away from the rain. Then she reached down to the ground, scooped up some mud and smeared it on the faces of Madalena and Olivia. It wasn't much protection, but it might help render them both a little less desirable to some of the street predators who preyed on the weak and helpless.

Once Sirus had reached the ground, Chrymos called them all together. "We're going over to the bonfire, but we need to be alert. This could be a good Samaritan being generous—or it could be a trap, perhaps some sailors recruiting for their navy. So let's go through our standard precautions again. What do we do if strangers get too close?"

"We run," Olivia said.

"To where?" Chrymos knew that the three of them would be annoyed having to go through all this again and again, but she considered it vital that they were all quite certain of what they had to do in the event of danger.

"Where we always go," said Madalena quietly. "La Lanterna—the lighthouse at the port."

Chrymos persisted. "And what should you do if anything goes wrong at La Lanterna?"

"Really? Again?" asked Sirus, rolling his eyes.

Chrymos nodded.

Sirus sighed. "Run to the soldiers guarding the customs building."

"Correct," said Chrymos. "Remember, they won't actually help you, but anyone who might want to harm you should run away once they see

42

the soldiers and their muskets."

"Yeah, I think we know that now," said Sirus. "After all, you've only told us fifty times this month."

I suppose I deserved that, Chrymos thought as they began to thread through the trees towards the welcoming bonfire. *They're not helpless, merely young—and getting older and more street-savvy every day.*

Madalena and Sirus strode along quietly by themselves, but Olivia clung to Chrymos' hand. She looked up at Chrymos, smiling as she spoke. "You're so wise. I guess you had to learn all this when you were a similar age to us."

Chrymos had been dreading this moment.

"I don't know. I can't remember anything before five years ago."

ELEVEN
Several minutes after Chrymos escaped from the rooftop
**Strada di Toledo, Naples, Kingdom of Naples,
9.40 p.m., Monday January 18 1610**

As soon as Chrymos was out of sight of Henricus and the others on the rooftop, she turned down towards the port, hoping to find a shortcut through which she could head directly to La Lanterna where the children should be waiting. But every street she inspected had groups of what must surely be Academy thugs loitering at the other end. *I'd better try to lose them all on the Strada di Toledo,* she finally decided, *especially now that it's stopped raining.*

The Strada di Toledo was the boisterous heart of Naples in 1610—the noisiest place in the world, some called it—bursting with life, art, and commerce, even at this hour of the night. The street was crowded, with artisans plying their trade, with street vendors hawking their wares in a flurry of gesticulating arms and frenetic voices, with beggars pouring out their sad stories to any sympathetic mark—and with pickpockets and other ne'er-do-wells slithering through the crowds in search of easy pickings. Sometimes it seemed that the entire population of Naples was crammed into this single street, endlessly searching for cheap goods, quick meals, transitory entertainment or the promise of exotic treasures from around the world. In short, the Strada di Toledo was a never-ending marketplace that was the envy of Europe, vice and virtue on display day and night—and usually for sale for the right price.

Chrymos emerged from a side street, paused until she spotted a momentary break in the streaming parade of passersby and then plunged into the mêlée. Obliged to move at the same pace as those around her, she waited as the crowd paused to watch a shoemaker cut out an intricate pattern, advanced a little as the crowd surged in response to entreaties from butchers offering sausages, entrails, and other supposed delicacies, then stopped again as trinket traders displayed a wide range of colorful ornaments made from lava. Locals were dismissive of this cheap junk but out-of-town visitors tended to stop and admire such unusual offerings.

Chrymos typically avoided the Strada di Toledo—it was a place to buy, sell, steal or beg, none of which Chrymos had any interest in doing—but on this chaotic evening it was an ideal place to hide. The street also slanted down towards the port, her ultimate destination, so Chrymos was content to move with the crowd, despite its stop-start progress. *There's another benefit to being here,* observed Chrymos as she waited for the crowd to move along. *The Academy people won't be able to use their powers openly in the midst of this crowd. Witchcraft like that is quickly punished by the most gruesome tortures, even in these more enlightened times.*

The lava baubles were left behind as the crowd inched forward again, and for a moment Chrymos thought that the parade might move along at a faster pace. But no. A popular vendor of macaroni, Naples' favorite dish—at least among the poorer classes—had his stall set up a short distance ahead, and he was swamped by eager buyers, once again bringing the procession to a standstill.

Chrymos, hoping to bypass this latest obstruction, squeezed through the crowd to its outer edge. It was a risky move—not only might Chrymos be seen by the Academy's men, she could also fall or be accidentally pushed into the hectic carriageway that bordered this pedestrian area. A steady stream of carts and carriages, containing the wealthy and the wannabes of Naples aristocracy, constantly clattered through the Strada di Toledo. The noise from carriage wheels on lava slabs was bad enough, but the continual clanging of bells exaggerated the commotion. The bells, fastened to the necks of the donkeys ferrying their passengers through the city streets, were intended to warn away the unwary. Unfortunately, the combined cacophony had the opposite effect, overwhelming the senses of all those within range.

The crowd ahead was still not moving—this vendor's macaroni dishes were the most popular on the whole Strada di Toledo—so Chrymos spent some minutes considering her best course of action. *Should I continue to move along gradually with the crowd, and wait to cross the road when they do—or should I dash across the street right here, through the carriage traffic? Of course, if I do that I'll be in plain sight if any of the Academy's men happen to be watching.*

A shout from one of the carts made the decision for her. "There she is!" Several men on that cart were searching the crowd as their vehicle clattered down the street and she had been spotted.

Chrymos plunged back into the crowd, pushing through despite protests from those waiting their turn for the delicious macaroni. Politeness was no longer a luxury she could afford. Behind her, she heard even more strident complaints—two of the Academy's men had jumped from the cart and were in hot pursuit. They were in no mood to be gentle as they elbowed through the crowd.

The crowd thinned again once she was past the macaroni vendor, which was both good and bad news. *I can move faster now, but so can they. How can I slow them down?*

As she ran, Chrymos constantly scanned her surroundings, turning left and right in a desperate search for some distraction that would slow down her pursuers. In another fifty feet, she saw that she would be faced with another dense crowd of onlookers, watching enthralled as an itinerant gleeman told bawdy tales whilst showing off his juggling skills. *If I can't think of how to stop those chasing me, they'll definitely catch up when I hit that next crowd.*

Another ten feet and she was panting now, she still hadn't fully recovered from her earlier rooftop exertions. She started to lose hope—and then she saw a possible solution.

A stand not far ahead belonged to a seafood seller, deeply engaged in haggling with a customer who was trying not to appear too eager. Chrymos wasn't interested in the seller or the transaction—several large barrels caught her eye. The barrels, lying on their side near the stand, were clearly empty, having served their primary purpose of transporting their contents to market. A few boxes had been tossed in front of the barrels to stop them from rolling away.

The deal successfully completed, the seafood seller turned aside to wrap a large fish that his customer had just agreed to purchase. Chrymos seized her moment.

The men chasing her were a few feet away when Chrymos kicked the boxes out from in front of the barrels and then began rolling barrels towards her pursuers. They might have avoided a single barrel—in fact, one did so rather easily—but Chrymos rolled three barrels straight at them. The combination of multiple barrels plus the greasy seawater pouring out of each barrel proved too much and the two men slipped, slid, and went down.

With the aggrieved shouts of the seafood seller ringing in her ear, Chrymos rushed past the fallen duo and dashed across the carriageway, heading for the left-hand side of the street. She heard a mix of screams, shouts, and frantic bells as she did so, and half-turned to discover that a rearing donkey was mere seconds away from trampling her beneath its hooves.

TWELVE
Moments later
Strada di Toledo, Naples, Kingdom of Naples,
10 p.m., Monday January 18 1610

Henricus, twenty feet back in the midst of the group that Chrymos had recently abandoned, watched open-mouthed as his chosen candidate faced imminent disaster.

Chrymos would probably have been killed, if not for the quick thinking of the carriage driver. He pulled hard on the right hand reins, redirecting the donkey's path away from Chrymos. Even so, she was still in real danger of being side-swiped by one of the back wheels as the carriage's momentum took it inexorably towards her despite the donkey's change in direction.

There was no time for anything but an enormous leap, which took Chrymos out of immediate peril—but saw her cannon into several people on the other side of the carriageway, knocking them to the ground.

"I'm so sorry, I'm so sorry. Are you hurt, are you okay?" Chrymos managed several heartfelt but extremely brief apologies as she hastily picked herself up from amongst the innocent bystanders that she had just knocked down. Then, plunging into the midst of this new crowd, Chrymos was quickly lost from sight.

Behind her, chaos reigned. The carriage Chrymos that had so narrowly avoided had managed to pull up short before anyone in the crowd was hurt, but the other carts and carriages hurtling down the carriageway had not been so attentive and had little chance to stop. Several carriages plowed into each other, resulting in much shouting and gesturing—but thankfully no broken bones or seriously injured donkeys. The carriages had not escaped so lightly and the remnants of these broken down wagons effectively blocked the carriageway.

Zulian, emerging from the crowd some distance away from Henricus, took one look at the tumultuous scene and posed a rhetorical question. "That was her, wasn't it?"

"Indeed it was."

"Are you absolutely certain we want her for the Academy? She is quite the chaos-maker, don't you think?"

Henricus turned away from the escalating turmoil on the carriageway—the drivers of the broken carriages were growing increasingly heated as they argued with each other about who was at fault and who would pay, whilst their aristocratic passengers expressed their unhappiness in more refined but no less dogmatic statements. He smiled at Zulian.

"As I told you earlier," said Henricus, "Chrymos was the Contessa's choice, not mine. Still—" Henricus looked across the carriageway, gazing in the direction in which Chrymos had vanished. "—I do like her. I think she'll bring a certain—excitement—to the Academy."

"Yeah—like the Black Death," muttered Zulian.

But Henricus had moved on and was now wrinkling his nose at the fish-laden stench coming from the two men who had been unlucky enough to come into relatively close contact with Chrymos. "Go and clean yourselves up. If I can still smell you coming, you'll need to find your own way back to the Academy."

That hygiene matter addressed, Henricus issued a simple order to the rest of his team. "She went thataway. Let's go."

With the carriageway currently closed until the debris of the broken carriages had been cleared away, it was a simple matter for the Academy's men to cross over and resume the search.

THIRTEEN
Twenty minutes later
**Strada di Toledo, Naples, Kingdom of Naples,
10.30 p.m., Monday January 18 1610**

Chrymos stood on the street corner and watched, smothering a smile, as once again Henricus and his men walked right past her. It was the third time that they had ventured along this street from one end to the other, searching fruitlessly, and they were clearly growing increasingly frustrated as they failed to find any trace of the object of their quest.

Finally, Henricus had clearly decided to change tactics. He gathered his team together and, as Chrymos continued to observe, tasked the men with checking out many of the side streets that branched off the Strada di Toledo. Chrymos wasn't close enough to hear what he said, but she did take careful note of the streets to which he pointed. *If I stay away from those streets, I should be able to sneak off to La Lanterna before he can catch me.*

A few more minutes and then Henricus waved his men into action. He took one last look around and then headed back across the carriageway, which was finally starting to return to normal as the last of the broken-down carriages was hauled away.

Chrymos watched Henricus disappear into the crowd on the other side. Only then did she deem it safe to move.

She stepped down from the box on which she had been standing, startling a couple of children who had been admiring her 'living statue' pose. "Time to eat," she whispered to the children, making her voice as gruff and masculine as she could. *No point shattering their illusions. Pulcinella is supposed to be male.*

Chrymos scooped up the handful of coins that had been tossed into the hat beneath her while she was pretending to be the much-loved *commedia dell'arte* character. She grabbed hat and box and carried them all back to the stall where she had found the Pulcinella costume and the other props. Slipping behind the curtained-off area at the back of the stall, Chrymos removed the borrowed costume, smoothing out her tunic dress, which had been stuffed out of sight beneath the classic fat-bellied top and baggy trousers that every Pulcinella actor wore. The traditional floppy hat was next to go, allowing Chrymos to shake out her pigtails and let them flow freely down her back. She retrieved her own cap from the pocket of her tunic and pulled it onto her head.

Finally, Chrymos removed the black mask, which had hidden most of her face from the Academy's searchers. "Goodbye, Pulcinella, thanks for your help," she whispered as she placed the costume back where she had found it.

Chrymos left the donated coins beside the Pulcinella costume, a token payment to the street theater performers who had unknowingly provided her disguise. Then she put on her cloak and slipped away before the performing troupe might find her when they returned from their supper break.

Glancing around to ensure that she was still unobserved, Chrymos finally left the Strada di Toledo behind, heading down one of the streets that, as far as she knew, wasn't being watched by the Academy's men.

Next stop, the port and La Lanterna!

FOURTEEN
Earlier That Evening
**In the woods, Naples, Kingdom of Naples,
7.30 p.m. Monday January 18 1610**

All three children stopped in their tracks upon hearing Chrymos' surprise revelation. The bonfire was forgotten for the moment as they stared at her in disbelief. Sirus, inevitably, was first to speak. "What do you mean, you don't remember anything before five years ago?"

"Simply what I said," replied Chrymos, simultaneously urging the children to keep moving towards their destination, the bonfire. "I woke up one day on the streets of Florence, not far from the *Ponte Vecchio*. I had nothing—only the clothes that I'm wearing now. I had no memory, I struggled with the language, and I didn't even know my own name."

"Then how do you know," asked Olivia reasonably, avoiding a large puddle as she walked along, "that your name is Chrymos?"

"It probably isn't," admitted Chrymos, "but I needed to call myself something. On the streets of Florence I heard plenty of possible names bandied around—I even tried out a few of them." She smiled. "Would you be friends with me if I was still called *Agnesina*?"

Olivia giggled. "Certainly not."

"How about *Euphrosina*?" Chrymos directed that question at Madalena, who solemnly shook her head.

The group emerged from the woods and turned to walk down the street as Chrymos aimed the next option at Sirus. "*Polixena*?"

"I don't think so," said Sirus, joining in the game.

"What about *Sicambria*?" Chrymos put on a sour face as she offered that alternative.

The combination of odd name and comical facial expression brought fresh peals of laughter from Olivia, who struggled to choke out a question: "So how did you pick *Chrymos* as a name?"

"It came to me in a dream," Chrymos said, "and it just seemed right. So I took it, and I've used it ever since. I'm not sure if it's actually my name, or perhaps it's simply the name of a donkey I used to ride—" Olivia spluttered at the thought. "—but it's mine now and here I am."

"And here we are," she added, because the four of them had arrived outside the Tirabosco building. The bonfire still blazed merrily on the top floor so, with one final warning to remember the escape plan, Chrymos led them up the stairs towards the welcoming warmth.

FIFTEEN
After Chrymos left the Strada di Toledo
The Port of Naples, Kingdom of Naples,
11.00 p.m. Monday January 18 1610

The chosen escape route took Chrymos past *San Giacomo degli Spagnoli*, another church that ministered to the city's poor and infirm. The church had been a lifesaver for Chrymos during her first weeks in Naples, providing food and occasional shelter until she had been in a position to make her own living arrangements. She still occasionally accepted gifts of food from the church when she was unable to find any odd jobs. Chrymos could subsist on very little but the children needed to eat regularly, even if it was only stale bread—the good people of San Giacomo degli Spagnoli visited local shops and bakeries at the end of each day and gathered up unsold leftovers to distribute to the needy.

Tonight, even that former haven was cold and quiet. Chrymos hurried past, her attention focused on the lighthouse still some distance away at the edge of the harbor. She pulled her cloak around her as she passed through the large open area that lay beyond the church. *The rain, thankfully, seems to have stopped but that wind is definitely unpleasant.*

Chrymos turned one final corner, past the wall bordering *L'Argo del Castello*—the imposing castle that towered over the port of Naples—and there it was, straight ahead, down the street and along the pier, La Lanterna. The basket of flames flickering at the top of the lighthouse had never seemed so welcoming.

Chrymos walked briskly down the street towards the pier, her cord sandals making little noise on the lava slabs beneath her feet. Coming up on her left, she spied the *Dogana Grande*, the customs house, patrolled as always by several armed soldiers. They watched her warily as she came down the street towards them. *Nearly there*, she told herself.

Chrymos heard a sudden clattering of footsteps behind her, running at first and then slowing down to a more measured walking pace. She risked a glance backwards and recognized several of the Academy's men.

They must have slowed down because they saw the soldiers, she realized. Another Academy thug was fast disappearing up the hill, obviously scurrying back to summon the others. *It's about to get crowded here,* she thought as she kept walking towards the pier.

It was an odd procession, and in any other circumstances Chrymos might have laughed. She led the way, walking as briskly as she dared under the suspicious gaze of the customs house guardians. Twenty feet behind her, a half-dozen of the Academy's men strained to walk quickly yet innocently—though if any of the watching soldiers were fooled, it was not evident in the manner in which they straightened at their posts, muskets at the ready.

Chrymos kept walking, drew level with the soldiers, and then moved beyond the customs house and onto the pier itself. The lighthouse was tantalizingly close, a few hundred feet away, and although she could see no sign of the children, she expected that they would be nearby, hiding at the side or rear of La Lanterna.

Chrymos glanced back. The Academy thugs were now abreast of the customs house and the soldiers were on heightened alert, watching closely as the intruders marched past. *Their movements look so ludicrously false,* Chrymos thought. *It wouldn't take much for the soldiers to open fire.*

No such incident occurred, however, and the Academy's men reached the pier. They split up and spread out, moving purposefully towards Chrymos.

She had already abandoned any idea of joining up with the children—*no sense bringing them back into this, they've already escaped once tonight*—but now she was trapped on the narrow pier, with her pursuers moving relentlessly towards her.

SIXTEEN
A few seconds later
The Pier, Port of Naples, Kingdom of Naples,
11.15 p.m. Monday January 18 1610

Once again, Chrymos found herself scanning her surroundings searching for viable alternatives to simple surrender. The pier itself offered little in terms of either protection or offensive maneuvering—it was a weathered wooden platform that stretched between dry land and the lighthouse, with occasional bollards along each side to which visiting ships might be moored.

On this particular night, there was merely a single visitor tied up at the Naples pier—a Spanish war galleon, on the pier's left hand side. Chrymos cast an eye over the imposing vessel, noted two watchmen in the stern who were likewise observing both her and the men behind her. *No escape there*, she thought.

Almost, Chrymos failed to notice the decaying hulk moored on the right hand side of the pier. To her, as to most city residents, the *Napolitana* was just part of the scenery, an eyesore that should have long ago been towed out to deep waters and sunk. And yet, in its own way, this galleass was a hero—it was the lone survivor of the four warships provided by the Kingdom of Naples as its contribution to the ill-fated Spanish Armada of 1588.

More than two decades later, the Napolitana was rotting away on the Naples waterfront—unwanted until, as Chrymos realized with a jolt, this very moment. She walked over to the once-proud ship, noting as she did so that Academy reinforcements had arrived—a large group, several carrying flaming torches, ran rapidly down the street, causing further consternation amongst the soldiers guarding the customs house. A second group, accompanied by cart and donkey, followed close behind. *At least,* Chrymos thought as she looked desperately for some way to climb onto the Napolitana, *the men already on the pier are waiting for the new arrivals before they come any closer.*

She smiled briefly. *You'd think they were afraid of me.*

The momentary pause gave Chrymos time to scramble onboard. The tide was low, so the old ship was more accessible than it might otherwise have been. Chrymos was able to climb up the side of the ship easily enough, thanks to conveniently-placed oar holes. Despite her injured hand, Chrymos quickly pulled herself over the side and onto the deck of the Napolitana.

What she saw gave her pause. In fact, there wasn't much to see, even with the combined light of the crescent moon and the lighthouse. The deck itself was barren, long since stripped of any usable materials, except for a handful of tattered ropes dangling down from the masts. The galleass was a crossbreed ship, which could be powered by either sail or oar—but there was little remaining evidence of its rowing capabilities, except for a couple of long rowing benches which, by the look of them, had been too badly mangled by English cannon-fire to be worth looting.

At this point, Chrymos might have despaired. She heard voices growing nearer—*sounds like Henricus, giving orders as usual*—and decided that her best chance was to hide below deck.

Chrymos took off her sandals and then, as quietly as she could, tiptoed over to the stern of the ship, where a dark passage appeared to promise entry to the lower decks.

SEVENTEEN
Naples, Kingdom of Naples,
11.30 p.m. Monday January 18 1610

Zulian was tired of this seemingly never-ending hunt, even if Henricus appeared to remain exhilarated by it all. He didn't even try to hide his annoyance. Zulian's own potion-bestowed skill, the ability to command flocks of birds to do his bidding, was of little use in this extended chase. "More hide and seek? In a ship, this time? Why don't we just blow it up and go home? I'm cold, I'm wet, I'm tired, and I've had more than enough of all this."

Henricus could still muster a smile, even if, truth be told, he was becoming exhausted as well. "Think of it as practice for the grim days that lie ahead, Zulian. When the Lost War begins, whose side would you rather this woman be on, theirs or ours?"

"What makes you think you can win Chrymos over, Henricus?" Zulian was far from convinced. "She's made it quite clear that she wants us to stay well away."

"Yes, at the moment she probably does, but then I haven't yet had a chance to impress her with my sparkling personality," Henricus replied with a grin. "Once she's properly exposed to the full Henricus charm, her resistance will simply melt away."

Zulian couldn't help but smile, even though his opinion hadn't really changed. Henricus turned his attention back to the search for the elusive Chrymos, instructing his men to search the crumbling warship from stem to stern.

Several of the hired thugs, who clearly shared Zulian's views on the undesirable nature of this long drawn-out chase, rushed to the side of the ship and scrambled aboard.

Then they stopped short. With the deck scraped so bare, there was little to search. Only the entrance to the lower decks appeared to hold any promise—but it also screamed danger to these wary toughs.

None seemed in any rush to put themselves in the line of fire until

Zulian, who had climbed up the side of the vessel and was clinging to the top, called out. "Are you too afraid of this vicious young woman to go below? Or is it that you don't like the dark?"

He called down to the pier. "Bring me a couple of those torches."

Two torchbearers hastened to obey, climbing up the side of the derelict ship and passing their torches to Zulian. Two of the thugs already on the deck, either braver than their companions or more likely stung by Zulian's words, stepped forward to claim the flaming lights.

In a show of bravado, one of the torch-carrying thugs strode determinedly to the darkened passageway and plunged below, followed a minute later by his slightly less enthusiastic colleague.

Not much could be heard at first but the clomping of the men's boots on the wooden steps. Then the protesting screeches of wood on wood, as the men below pushed open long-unused hatches in search of their prey. Next came a few low murmurs as the men exchanged information and then—a sudden commotion, shouting, crashes, banging.

The men on deck exchanged glances and smiles. This long night would soon be over—and successfully, too, based on the noises emanating from below. All eyes went to the doorway, now not quite so dark as flickering torches began to emerge.

The first surprise was that the two torchbearers were backing rapidly out of the doorway, propelled backwards by whatever was in front of them.

The second surprise was that when their prey came into sight behind the two searchers, the young woman was clutching a small gunpowder barrel under one arm.

The third and most unwelcome surprise of all was that the gunpowder barrel had a fuse cord attached, and the fuse was fizzing and sparking and burning steadily, perhaps a third of its way towards what promised to be a highly explosive encounter with the gunpowder within the barrel.

EIGHTEEN
Naples, Kingdom of Naples,
11.45 p.m. Monday January 18 1610

Chrymos stood on the deck, heart pounding, fuse cord fizzing a few inches from her face. Pretending a calmness she almost certainly did not feel, Chrymos called out to the men around her, who were all backing away from the explosive threat she carried. "Run. Get out of here. Otherwise—" She glanced down at the burning fuse, the fire now halfway through its journey to the barrel. "—I think you know what will happen."

One of the thugs found his voice. "You wouldn't dare. You'll be blown up as well."

"Are you willing to risk your life to find out who has the biggest *fede*?" Chrymos threw the challenge back at him.

That did it. The men on the deck of the Napolitana rushed to the side of the ship and threw themselves over, some managing to climb down carefully, others slipping and falling with muffled thumps on the pier below. At least one of the thugs must have injured himself—his panicked screams contrasted with the peace that now reigned on the ship's deck.

Chrymos could see only a single man remaining—not standing on the deck but rather clinging to its side. She recognized him from her earlier encounter. "Zulian, isn't it?" He nodded. "Do you have a death wish, Zulian, or are you too afraid to move?"

Zulian smiled. "Neither." He turned to another Academy man who was just climbing into view. "Tranquilo, it's all yours."

The newcomer braced himself with one arm against the side of the ship and then stretched the other arm skywards. A moment later, torrential rain poured down from above, drenching the Napolitana deck in general and Chrymos in particular.

The fuse, overwhelmed by this intense downpour, hissed, sizzled and then died with a whimper, still two inches short of its goal.

Chrymos, still getting soaked as the rain bucketed down upon her, acted almost instinctively. She grabbed the barrel with both hands and threw it towards Zulian, while at the same time rushing to the seaward side of the *Napolitana*, away from the pier. *Perhaps I can swim to safety,* she thought as she climbed over the rail and scrambled downwards towards the water.

Alas, her hastily-constructed escape wasn't to be. The moment that her trailing foot touched the freezing waters of the Gulf of Naples, Chrymos realized that there would be no exit that way, only a miserable death. She looked up. Zulian was gazing down at her from the deck above. "A little bit cold even for you, I think," he said. He turned, called to someone that Chrymos couldn't see from her position. "Help her up."

A few moments later, two of the Academy's men had climbed down, one on each side of Chrymos, and roughly hauled her back up to the deck. She was still soaking wet, courtesy of Tranquilo's torrential rain, so at a nod from Zulian one of her rescuers went to fetch a blanket from the cart. The other rescuer held her arm firmly—he was obviously taking no chances that she might escape again.

Chrymos reached up to seize the chain around her neck but her captor was on the alert for such moves. He reached around and tugged on the neck chain, breaking it in the process. "Oh no you don't, signorina!"

The chain fell to the deck, along with its attached bodice dagger which had been hidden under Chrymos' tunic dress. A nearby thug quickly scooped up the dagger and tucked it into his belt, well out of her reach.

Chrymos was finally defenseless. Zulian walked over to her, frowning. He held the gunpowder barrel with which Chrymos had threatened her pursuers. "Empty, I see," he said, peering under the lid of the barrel.

"The ship's been tied up here for twenty years," said Chrymos. "Did you truly think there'd be any weapons left onboard? I found what little was left of the armory—a few empty barrels and a couple of fuse cords— and that gave me an idea. I fastened a fuse cord to one of the barrels. Then when your men came below, I was able to light the fuse from one of their flaming torches. They lost interest in capturing me as soon as I threatened to blow us all up."

"Nice bluff," said Zulian, "and it might have worked, too, if it wasn't for Tranquilo and his storm powers."

He beckoned to Chrymos. "Now let's get off this wreck. I'm sure Henricus will be very glad to see you."

NINETEEN
Naples, Kingdom of Naples,
11.55 p.m. Monday January 18 1610

A few minutes later, Chrymos, a blanket now wrapped around her, was escorted to the Academy's cart. Henricus, standing nearby, smiled as she approached.

Henricus was surprisingly friendly, despite the fact that he and his men had been led on such a merry chase. He took her aside and spoke quietly. "What happens now is up to you, Chrymos. If you hadn't thrown yourself off that roof—which was amazingly brave, by the way—we would already have had this conversation, and you would either be happily accompanying me to the Academy or heading back for yet another freezing night on the streets."

Henricus shivered and pulled his cloak around himself before continuing. "Here's what you need to know. The Academy represents an incredible opportunity for you. I've already told you that you show more potential than anybody else at the Academy. What I didn't have the chance to tell you—" Chrymos blushed, conscious that her own actions had prevented that part of the conversation. "—is that this prediction comes from Contessa Della Porta. She's the wife of the Master of the Academy, and she's definitely the power behind his throne."

"But how," asked Chrymos, "can she possibly know of my potential? She's never met me, I can't believe she's even heard of me. I'm just an orphan from the streets. I don't even know who my parents were."

"I don't know the answer to your question," replied Henricus, "but what I can tell you is that the Contessa is one of the most gifted of the Alchemae. That's what we call members of the Academy who have been provided with the Exousía potion," he added. "After years of intensive study, those who graduate are given that very special treatment. We all gain powers, but those gifts vary from person to person. Clearly, the Contessa believes that you have great potential. Once you graduate successfully from the Academy, she expects you to manifest mighty powers, to use for the greater good of the Kingdom of Naples, the Spanish Empire, and the Holy Catholic Church."

Chrymos was shocked—and more than a little flattered. For as long as she could remember—admittedly, only five years—she had been nobody. Rejected by her parents—whomever they were—then ignored, chased or spat upon by the good citizens of first Florence and then Naples.

"So you're saying—" she began.

"—that if you don't want to take advantage of this once-in-a-lifetime offer," continued Henricus, "then off you go, sorry to bother you, have a nice life. Otherwise, come with us tonight. Regular meals, clean clothing, a little money and the opportunity to really make a difference."

Probably without realizing it—at least, not consciously—Henricus had said the words that Chrymos most wanted to hear. Not food, not money, but being able to do something meaningful in the world. But there was one problem. *The children. How can I leave them? Could I still help them if I was at the Academy?*

There was one way to find out. She had to ask Henricus. "Could I bring any children with me?"

Henricus was startled. "You have children?"

"No, certainly not—but I've been caring for three street kids. Can I bring them along as well?"

Henricus gave an unwelcome answer. "No, sorry, I don't see how. The Academy is—not a safe place for children. Too many things that could poison them, blow them up or turn them into pillars of stone—and too many reckless students experimenting, sometimes with powers beyond their control."

"What about free time?" asked Chrymos. "If I can't bring the children with me, could I at least go and visit them regularly?"

Henricus replied honestly. "You'll be kept extremely busy, you won't have many hours to yourself."

"I was afraid that would be your answer," said Chrymos sadly.

Henricus wasn't finished. "Every Sunday, after Mass, we do have the afternoon off. You could visit the children then—the Academy isn't far from the city. We're on the Capodimonte hill, close to the Catacombs of San Gennaro."

Chrymos was about to decline the offer when Henricus spoke again. And his next words suggested that he could finally understand what mattered to his potential recruit. "Let me say this, Chrymos. If you simply care about what happens to those particular children, then leave us and go home now. If you believe that you are absolutely the only person who can look after them and ensure that they survive right now, don't let me stop you."

Chrymos started to respond, but Henricus held up his hand. "Let me finish. On the other hand, if you want to be in a position to save not just those three children but in fact a great many people, young and old alike, then the very best thing you could do is join the Academy. This is your big chance to escape the streets, to become somebody—not merely for yourself but for them as well. Then, when the critical moment comes, when you graduate and attain your full powers, you will finally be in a position to reach out and help those in need."

Henricus' comments touched Chrymos. "Thank you for saying that," she said quietly.

She wasn't decided yet. "I have another question. From what Girardus said, most of the classes at the Academy are geared towards war, fighting, or spying. They don't sound like topics that I'd enjoy, or even be good at learning."

Henricus stood very still and stared into her eyes. When he spoke, it was so softly that no-one but Chrymos could hear him. "There's a war coming, Chrymos, a titanic war in which we will be fighting powers beyond imagining. For reasons that we don't yet understand, it will be called the Lost War. This war will dwarf the petty battles we've seen between countries such as Spain, the Netherlands, France, or England. The only way—the *only* way," he stressed, "that any of us can make a difference in this war is if we also have powers. Special powers that, yes, will require us to fight, on behalf of humanity—but powers that will also enable us to protect those we care about."

Henricus sighed. "My own skill, such as it is, is very minor. It allows me to identify people who have powers—or who have the potential to respond favorably to the transforming Exousía potion that the Academy uses. But you, my dear—" He stood back for a moment, staring so intently at Chrymos that she blushed. "The Contessa prophesied this very morning that you will gain such mighty powers that, in her words, 'the Master will achieve his greatest success in the forthcoming Lost War.'"

Henricus took another step back, and then bowed. "In other words, Chrymos, you are the secret weapon that can turn the tide in this war. You're that important to us."

Chrymos was definitely attracted to the offer. *But I can't leave the children on their own—I just can't.*

"I'm sorry, Henricus, I'd like to come with you but I simply can't do it," she told him. "The children depend on me."

Henricus was taken aback, but he wasn't about to give in so easily. "Okay, I think I understand. This isn't just about you. It's about those children as well. So what would it take to make them comfortable? Money? I can give you that—the Academy pays a signing bonus. Five piastres. The Master is very generous. In fact, let's say six piastres. Then the children can easily split the money three ways." He reached into an inside pocket and pulled out six coins. "There you go."

Chrymos thought quickly. Two piastres were a typical week's wages in Naples—and represented a small fortune for the homeless. Two piastres each would enable the children to survive for several months.

She took the money. "This isn't a decision I can make by myself—I need to speak to the children. They're waiting down by the lighthouse. Can you give me a few minutes?"

"Yes, of course," said Henricus. "But please don't take too long. We need to get back to the Academy as soon as we can. This evening's escapades have already gone on for far longer than we planned. Our allies—" He looked over at the thugs milling around near the cart. "—will be expecting a much larger purse than usual for their efforts tonight."

Chrymos blushed again—*sorry, my fault*—as she bustled down the pier towards La Lanterna. She still clutched the borrowed blanket around her but it failed to ease the chill that she felt in her heart.

TWENTY
A few minutes later
La Lanterna, Port of Naples, Kingdom of Naples,
12.05 a.m. Tuesday January 19 1610

Chrymos was immensely relieved to see that the children were unharmed, and waiting for her at the base of the lighthouse as arranged.

"You got away! I was so worried that you wouldn't, especially when I saw so many of them running after you," said Olivia, rushing to hug Chrymos. Madalena as usual said nothing but reached for her hand and clasped it fiercely. It was the injured hand, the left hand—Chrymos winced silently but squeezed Madalena's hand tightly in response.

"Of course she would, I told you so, didn't I?" said Sirus. He played with a stick of driftwood, pretending unconcern, but Chrymos could see that underneath the bravado he too was greatly relieved to see Chrymos alive, well, and evidently free. He hung back, but allowed himself to be pulled into an embrace as well.

Chrymos hugged the three children close to her for a minute or two. Then, conscious of Henricus' request for a speedy return, she knelt down, bringing herself to the same height as the children. *It's now or never.*

"I need the three of you to listen carefully," Chrymos began, "because I have something very important to ask you." She looked into the eyes of each of the children in turn. Madalena looked expectant, Olivia worried and Sirus—*He looks belligerent,* she decided. *He thinks he knows what's coming. And, sadly, he's right.*

Chrymos took a deep breath. "I realized tonight that I've been treating you all as if you can't take care of yourselves. That's no longer true. Perhaps it never was. You survived on the streets by yourselves long before you met me. I've showed you a few things but you already knew most of them."

She turned to Madalena. "You know, your mother Caterina always told me that she would look after you—all three of you—if anything ever happened to me."

Olivia's eyes began to tear up. "But nothing's happened to you, Chrymos, has it? Has it?"

Chrymos struggled to find the right words. "No, I'm okay. But I've been offered a—a job, I suppose, a very important job. But if I take this job, it would mean that I have to leave you for a while."

Sirus was instantly on the attack. "When?"

Here it comes. "Now."

"For how long?" That was Madalena.

Chrymos hated to answer that question. "It may be several years. But," she hastened to add, "I will be able to visit you every Sunday afternoon."

What happened next was exactly what Chrymos had feared. Olivia burst into tears, Madalena's face went completely blank and Sirus—Sirus pulled himself away from Chrymos' grasp and glared at her, as angry and sullen as he had been on the day they had first met.

His response was scathing. "You want us to make your decision for you, don't you? You want us to absolve you of your guilt at dumping us. Sorry. Not going to happen. This is all on you."

Sirus stepped back from Chrymos and then turned to the others. "Come on girls, let's go."

"What? No!" snapped Olivia, shocked. "She won't leave us, will you Chrymos?" Her beseeching eyes combed Chrymos' face, searching for reassurance.

Chrymos could give none. "I desperately wish I could stay with you," she admitted, "but I can achieve so much more for all of us by seizing this opportunity."

"More for you, you mean," scoffed Sirus. "You get the job and the home and we get the street. Thank you so much for the 'opportunity'." He spat in disgust and turned his back.

Chrymos spoke quickly. "Wait—I have some money for you all. A signing bonus. Two piastres each." She held out the coins as a peace offering.

Sirus didn't even turn around. "Thirty pieces of silver? We don't need your blood money, Chrymos. Like you said, we can manage perfectly well without you."

Reluctantly, first Olivia and then Madalena slowly backed away from Chrymos and joined Sirus. He spoke again to Chrymos. "We're going back to the tree. That's where we'll be tonight, if you decide to turn down this 'job.' After that, we move on. Don't bother coming to 'look after us' on Sunday afternoons. We're not interested."

The three children began to walk up the pier, away from Chrymos. Only Olivia looked back, once, her eyes pleading.

The children walked past the wreck of the Napolitana, past the Academy's men. Then they were gone.

TWENTY-ONE
A few long minutes later
Port of Naples, Kingdom of Naples,
12.15 a.m. Tuesday January 19 1610

Even though she knew that Henricus was standing by, waiting for her decision, Chrymos lingered underneath the lighthouse, pacing nervously.

The only sensible thing to do, she told herself, *is to agree to the Academy's offer. I have no future on the streets—and no other means of escaping my fate. No dowry, so no-one will marry me. No illustrious family lineage, so even the nuns won't take me. I'll end up like Madalena's mother, forced to become a woman of the night just to survive.*

But what about the children? The question kept echoing in her mind. *Perhaps they don't really need me anymore—but do I still need them?*

She could think of no satisfactory answer.

In the end, she pulled the blanket tightly around her and simply trudged back up the pier.

TWENTY-TWO
A minute later
Port of Naples, Kingdom of Naples,
12.17 a.m. Tuesday January 19 1610

"Have you decided?" asked Henricus as soon as Chrymos returned.

"Yes," she said. "Take me to the Academy. I'll study hard. I'll take your potion. I'll be the special one. I'll fight in the Lost War. And, God willing, I'll save the world. Okay? Just don't ask me any more questions tonight."

Chrymos went over to the Academy cart, where Adric sat talking to a fellow recruit. Adric wasn't exactly dressed for the wintry conditions—his cloak had been ripped off during the scuffle back at the Tirabosco building, leaving him dressed in a light shirt and linen breeches. As usual, his legs were bare and his shoes were torn and ragged. He must have been freezing.

Even so, he greeted Chrymos cheerfully as he helped her onto the cart. "Hiya C! Are your ears burning? They've been talking about you tonight—a lot!"

"I guess they have," agreed Chrymos. "It's been a long night." She looked him over—no sign of chains or any other restraints. "So you've agreed to join the Academy as well?"

"Sure, why not? I didn't have anything else to do." Adric had previously signed up for an expedition team scheduled to sail to Monterey in the Americas, accompanying the explorer Sebastián Vizcaíno, but the trip had been cancelled before it could even begin.

Adric also answered her unspoken question. "They made me a promise I couldn't refuse."

Adric appeared about to ask Chrymos a question of his own, but she shook her head. *Not now, Adric. Maybe not ever. I simply don't want to talk about it.*

Adric, appearing to understand, changed the subject. "By the way, here's another Academy recruit who's also been scraped off the streets tonight. Chrymos, Ruben. Ruben, Chrymos."

The pair exchanged nods. Ruben looked to be about the same age as Adric—mid-twenties or so. His hair was light brown, long and scruffy, though his beard was more neatly trimmed. Ruben was dressed more appropriately for a mid-winter evening—thick cloak over the top of a matching dark green doublet and jerkin combination. Below, he wore padded brown trunk hose squared-off at the bottom in the Spanish style, with knitted stockings stretching from his knees presumably to his toes, underneath the elegant boots that completed his attire. *They may have snatched this fellow off the streets but I doubt that he lives there*, thought Chrymos. *He's too smartly dressed.*

They had no more time for private conversations, because at that moment Henricus took his place at the front of the cart. Zulian soon joined him.

As the donkey began to pull the cart and its passengers towards a hopeful but still uncertain future, Chrymos heard what sounded like a flutter of wings above her. She looked up, expecting perhaps to find a bird of ill omen—probably a vulture—but the crescent moon had hidden itself again behind yet another cloud, and nothing could be seen in the darkness.

TWENTY-THREE
At exactly the same time
In the skies above Transylvania, [Romania]
1.17 a.m. local time, Tuesday January 19 1610

Jesse's wings were beating steadily as he hovered over the Ialomiţa River, on the outskirts of Târgovişte. His quarry Vlad Ţepeş had vanished, finding shelter somewhere in the city below. *<He's escaped, for now anyway,>* Jesse began, mind-calling fellow Outcast Angel Ravid, who had remained back in Sibiu to free Ţepeş's prisoners. *<We'll have to—>*

Jesse broke off his conversation as his mind was again assaulted. Now the psychic attack was far worse, as a thousand times a thousand futures solidified into a new and horrific reality.

Jesse fainted from the mental barrage. Without his mind to sustain them, Jesse's ectoplasmic wings vanished and his unconscious body plummeted towards the river below.

It was a close call. The falling angel narrowly missed a bridge that spanned the river, instead plunging into the bitterly cold water in the center of the river with an almighty splash.

The cold water revived Jesse and he struggled to the surface, spluttering and coughing, before dragging himself to the nearest riverbank. He considered the aches and pains of his aging body, which had been due for replacement at the time of the Rebellion. The events of those days had postponed replacement forever. *I'm getting too old for this.*

Once Jesse had recovered sufficiently, he sent another mind-call to Ravid. *<We face deadly danger. Not immediately, but soon enough. Unless we can stop it, there will be war—a war that will consume the entire world, bringing death and destruction on a scale never seen before. Nations will fall, millions will die or be enslaved, and perhaps not even we can stop it now. Continue freeing the prisoners, there's nothing else you can do as yet. I will fly back to England and examine the new futures. Unless we can find*

the right answers, this world faces a new and treacherous Dark Age.>

Despite his prophetic powers, Jesse had no idea where to start searching for an answer.

TWENTY-FOUR
The Tower, Academy of Secrets, Naples, Kingdom of Naples, 12.30 a.m. Tuesday January 19 1610

Contessa Stefani Della Porta seldom had reason to be on the wall-walk at the very top of the Academy's Tower—but tonight she had received an urgent summons, delivered by a terrified Janus twin, that compelled her attendance.

The Tower itself was dark and unwelcoming, a frightening place even for those who had been fortified with the necessary elixirs and enchantments—but for the Contessa, mistress of the Academy, the Tower was a powerful symbol of her strength and that of her family. She strode confidently along the wall-walk, pausing occasionally to look down at the Academy's lands below.

The crescent moon slipped in and out of the clouds high above the Tower, which seemed to absorb rather than reflect the moonlight. Lesser mortals would have shuddered. The Contessa merely smiled, a bitter, icy grimace, while she waited.

A short while later, the Contessa's vigil was rewarded. The occasional moonbeams revealed a shape rising from above the city, wings rhythmically rising and falling, heading towards the Tower. The Contessa watched, seemingly indifferent but in fact intensely fascinated, as the being drew closer and closer.

Thanks to the flickering moonlight, the Contessa could begin to make out a female figure clad in form-fitting dark armor from head to toe.

The creature's wings were bat-like, black and leathery. Even the Contessa felt a moment's dread as she awaited her visitor.

A few minutes later, the Darke Warrior Nekhbet landed. She was unusually tall, with long black hair that cascaded down her back. Her complexion was dusky, offset by glowing green eyes that usually entranced her victims. Those unfortunates who found themselves under her spell discovered only too late that she was needlessly cruel and completely merciless.

Unlike her fellow Darke Warriors, Nekhbet did not bother to carry a sword, relying instead on several chakrams attached to her belt. When Nekhbet threw a chakram with a single flick of her wrist, the circular blade would spin through the air and strike its target with deadly force, usually slicing completely through whatever it struck. Only Nekhbet herself could catch her impossibly sharp chakram without being cut to ribbons.

One unfortunate characteristic that Nekhbet did share with her fellows was the inescapable stench of brimstone.

The Contessa, trying not to recoil in distaste at the smell, greeted the new arrival with a question. "You asked to see me. Is this about the woman?"

Nekhbet nodded. "It is done. Your people have convinced her to join your Academy."

"Does she suspect?" asked the Contessa.

"Not from what I could see."

"Good," said the Contessa, "I shall advise the *Consiglio dei Quattro*."

"You know what you have to do. But remember, time is limited. You have less than six months," warned Nekhbet as she stretched her wings, preparing to depart.

"That's not long enough," protested the Contessa.

But the Darke Warrior had already flown away.

PART TWO

TWENTY-FIVE
Academy of Secrets, Naples, Kingdom of Naples, Early Morning, Wednesday April 7 1610

Chrymos awoke drowning. Again. A colossal storm still raged in her mind. Huge waves pounded the battered shoreline incessantly, first demolishing, and then scraping the land bare of, any infestation of civilization.

Through the cascading spray from endless waves, despite the sheeting torrential rain, despite the malevolent storm clouds propelled at breakneck speed across the sky, Chrymos caught a fragmentary glimpse of a fearsome demon flying high above. This apparition was clad from head to toe in black armor, vast leathery wings keeping it airborne whilst with one arm, it cast mighty lightning bolts and with the other, it seemed to control the impossibly violent winds. The surely-hell-spawned creature seemed to be the cause of all this horrendous destruction—and it laughed and reveled in the chaos.

Chrymos herself was stranded far out to sea, an angry black sea whose surface was swollen with broken bricks and dislodged boulders, wooden beams, tree roots, branches—all slamming together in a gigantic whirlpool of debris. She clung to the remains of a thatched roof that was being steadily reduced to its component pieces by the relentless elements. Chrymos knew that unless she could escape from the tumult she would never survive. Then a faint cry caught her attention.

Just beyond Chrymos' reach, the sea threatened to engulf a terrified young boy. He screamed for help, his cries barely audible against the unfettered fury of the elements, as he tried and failed to make any headway against the outgoing monster tide. Despite the fact that any attempt to save the boy would take her even further away from land, Chrymos desperately swam towards him. Kicking frantically against the walls of water, Chrymos threw herself towards the distressed youngster, forcing her way through the crashing waves. Before she could make much progress, she found herself hammered against a jagged chunk of broken wall that carved a deep, bloody furrow in her left leg. Her lungs were bursting as she swallowed large mouthfuls of seawater.

At the very moment that she thought she was finally making headway towards the child, Chrymos felt a hand grip her shoulder. *No, not a hand, a claw.* She felt herself being pulled around to face whatever it was—and then the nightmare finally released her, the moldy smell of straw and mildewed earth broke through her nostrils to her brain and reminded her where she actually was. On solid if uneven ground, in her basement chamber underneath the stately mansion of Giambattista Della Porta, home of the forbidden Academy of Secrets.

This is crazy! I have these drowning dreams constantly, but I've never even left dry land! At least this time dead bodies didn't surround me. On the too-frequent occasions when Chrymos suffered such nightmares, they invariably left her physically and mentally exhausted. *That's the last thing I need, today of all days.*

Thankfully, Chrymos was alone. No other students had witnessed her desperate panic because Chrymos had this tiny subterranean shelter all to herself. She was the only female student in the Academy and the Academy's Master, Giambattista Della Porta—or, more likely, his wife, Contessa Stefani—had decreed that Chrymos should get her own room.

Not that the room was anything much. The space allocated to Chrymos was in fact little more than a converted food storage bin below the scullery. If Chrymos looked too closely—which she usually tried not to do—there was still plenty of evidence of the room's previous purpose: partly-germinated seeds, coarsely ground grains, the rotting remains of a few hardy vegetables. Entry and exit into the chamber was by way of a rickety ladder, which Chrymos had to climb up every morning and down every night.

There was no natural light—the room had been dug deep within the bowels of the Della Porta estate, it was really just a pit—and the only available illumination trickled down from any candle that might be lit in the scullery above. When Chrymos first arrived at the Academy, Luca—a venom-tongued student from the class a year ahead of her—had initially made a nightly ritual of sneaking in and closing the scullery hatch so that Chrymos found herself in total darkness. Luca eventually tired of the game though, because Chrymos never screamed or complained. Not because she wasn't affected—in fact, Chrymos felt nauseous and had trouble breathing every single night that she climbed down into her bedroom pit. She hated being enclosed in such a small room and her panic dramatically intensified when there was no light at all. But Chrymos would never give Luca the satisfaction of knowing that he could affect her, so instead she suffered in agonized, lip-biting silence.

Luca didn't give up on mischief-making, though. Every so often, Chrymos would be in her basement dungeon and hear muffled thumping, accompanied by unpleasant moaning sounds. At such times, she would simply shake her head. *Luca, when will you get it through your thick skull that you can't scare me away from the Academy with your cheap tricks?*

There were no such distractions this morning, fortunately, and candles from above partly illuminated the room, which helped soothe Chrymos as she lay quietly in her bed of straw.

It must be time to get up. Chrymos fancied she could hear quiet voices above, probably in the main kitchen, as the staff began to prepare breakfast for the Master and the Contessa. *If I hurry, I should be able to eat before the others get up.*

Chrymos preferred not to eat with the other students. Far too often, she was the target of mindless bullying by several of the older students, sons of the rich gentry of the Kingdom of Naples, who thought that their fathers' exalted status somehow made them special as well. Chrymos' scathing responses usually showed them otherwise. However, the inevitable backlash—tutors tended to favor the students whose families had paid handsomely to attend the Academy ahead of those like her who had been abducted from the city's streets—was best avoided wherever possible.

Chrymos had also shown herself to be a natural with the sword—or, at least, its wooden equivalent in the practice rooms of the Academy. More than one tormentor had expected to engage in school-sanctioned violence against this presumptuous lazzarone, only to be sent sprawling to the stone floor, blood streaming from nose or limb painfully broken. Those raised amidst the pampering comforts of the Vice-Regal Court of Naples tended to be less than capable swordsmen. Unfortunately, Chrymos' successes tended to create enemies rather than admirers.

Time I was going. Chrymos stood up, smoothing out the straw that served as mattress and blanket, and straightened her hemp under-tunic. Stretching her arm out to gather the woolen tunic dress that was her usual outerwear, Chrymos pulled the blue tunic over her head and arranged it so that it fell modestly to her ankles. She then reached around behind her head, clasped her long strands of braided hair and tugged them out from beneath the tunic. Shaking her head briskly so that the braids of hair would rearrange themselves obligingly down her back, Chrymos pulled her cap out of her tunic pocket and adjusted it on her head.

As she lowered her hand, Chrymos caught an unwelcome glimpse of the bronze ring that was a constant reminder of Olivia, Madalena, and Sirus. She shuddered, closed her eyes, and offered up her usual prayer. *Lord, please protect the children, wherever they are.* Chrymos had not seen the children since they left the pier and walked away from her three months earlier, despite many Sunday afternoons spent searching the city streets.

As ever, her guilty conscience condemned her. *You, Chrymos, you were the one who was supposed to protect the children. Instead, you sacrificed them—for this pathetic existence. Save the world? You can't even save yourself!*

Why don't you just leave the Academy? No-one would stop you. In fact, they'd probably applaud as they watched you crawl away!

Such sentiments had become a regular refrain. In her stronger moments, Chrymos had a ready reply. *Because I'm not doing this for the Academy and their mysterious "Lost War". I'm here to gain special powers so that I can protect all the Olivias, all the Madalenas, all the Siruses.*

At her weakest moments, Chrymos could not bring herself to believe that argument. But the alternative—walking away and abandoning any chance to redeem herself and remedy at least some of the injustice in the world—was intolerable. So, she persisted—but the self-doubt took its toll.

Eventually, Chrymos composed herself. She slipped her feet into the well-worn cord sandals that were her only footwear and climbed up the ladder. She was first to the table and was able to have breakfast by herself.

TWENTY-SIX
Academy of Secrets, Naples, Kingdom of Naples,
Early Morning, Wednesday April 7 1610

Her morning meal completed, Chrymos made her way upstairs through the servants' narrow stairwell, which emerged into a small passageway near the main staircase. The servants were already hard at work, polishing the many marble statues of Roman emperors that dominated the grand entranceway into the Della Porta mansion.

These were not mere busts of the Caesars, carefully bland and anonymous in the usual style of official portraits. These were life-sized, full-bodied statues, rendered by an amazingly talented if unknown craftsman. Each depicted a Roman emperor in dynamic action, memorializing an epic moment from the subject's life.

On the far right, first among equals was Gaius Julius Caesar, represented here in his glory days as the mighty military leader who conquered Gaul. The sculptor had captured the moment when Caesar had brought his sword flashing down, perhaps to sever the head of an enemy. The sweat could be seen glistening off Caesar's muscled forearm as he clasped the sword tightly, delivering a mortal blow to his unknown foe.

Far left, at the other end of this glorious parade of the mightiest Roman emperors, stood Gaius Aurelius Valerius Diocletianus Augustus, commonly known as Diocletian. This emperor's sculpture showed him standing triumphant, winner of the Civil War that had nearly torn Rome apart. Diocletian wielded a pike that pierced the mangled corpse lying at his feet, Diocletian's unlamented imperial rival Carinus.

Even after three months at the Academy, Chrymos still hated the opulence on display here. It was calculated to impress even the wealthiest visitors so that they might be persuaded to send their sons to the Academy, inevitably accompanied by a healthy endowment. *Meanwhile, so many of those in the city around us starve.*

Apart from the statues, other compelling sights that a visitor would see on entering the Academy building included the frescoes that adorned the glorious dome that topped the entrance hall. The dome was rumored to have been created by Michelangelo himself, a refinement of his design for the St. Peter's Basilica dome in Rome. The frescoes, though reportedly painted by lesser artists, were still utterly breathtaking, though nowhere near as magnificent as Michelangelo's own creations in the Sistine Chapel.

Beneath the dome, a grand circular staircase wound its way up to the drawing rooms and the Great Hall on the first floor. Beyond lay yet another staircase, this one providing access to the second, third and fourth floors and to the mysterious Tower, rumored to contain the Academy's most precious secrets.

The Tower was off-limits to students, as indeed were the two upper floors, which were reserved for the Alchemae. This elite group was comprised of graduates of the Academy who at the end of their studies had gained supernatural powers. The opportunity to gain such powers and then make a difference—that was the only reason that Chrymos had stayed at the Academy and endured three tough months of study so far, fending off bullies, dealing with intransigent teachers and defying more than a few of her peers who believed that she had no place at the Academy. The Contessa's prophecy, which had allowed Chrymos to enter the Academy, seemed to have been forgotten. In any event, that prophecy gave Chrymos no privileges nor did it save her from being treated badly by those around her.

As she paused for a moment, yet again disgusted by the wastefulness, Chrymos spotted fellow recruit Adric, who had been striding purposefully towards the main staircase. She waved and he took that as an invitation to come over and join her.

Adric, a twinkle in his dazzling blue eyes as always, greeted Chrymos with a quick hug and a warm smile. "Hey, C, what's happening?"

Chrymos started to reply but Adric held up his hand. He whispered urgently: "You can tell me your news later, sorry. Right now, you need to come with me. Something seriously important is happening and I'm determined to find out exactly what it is. This could be it—the start of the Lost War."

Chrymos looked around. There was a definite increase in intensity this morning. The servants, who normally polished the statuary with calm, unhurried motions, positively rushed through their chores, barely completing one Caesar before moving onto the next. *The Master would not be pleased with how they're treating his precious emperors.*

Chrymos glanced over at the main entrance. *More than double the usual amount of comings and goings, and at such a pace!*

Was this indecent haste in preparation for this afternoon's ceremony—or did it signal an even more significant event?

Adric waited for her, barely restraining himself. "We need to go—we have just a couple of minutes to get in place."

TWENTY-SEVEN
A Few Minutes Later
Academy of Secrets, Naples, Kingdom of Naples, Wednesday April 7 1610

Chrymos followed Adric as he rushed up the sweeping circular staircase, past several servants industriously polishing the balustrades, past the gleaming marble pillars that flanked the first floor entrance and into the small chapel where Father Carracci celebrated Mass every Sunday.

Adric looked around furtively, reassuring himself that the chapel was indeed empty, and then walked briskly up to the front, near the altar. "Hurry," he called to Chrymos, "we don't have long."

Chrymos reluctantly moved to the front of the chapel, only to see Adric squeezing behind the towering statue of San Gennaro, one of the patron saints of Naples. Legend had it that San Gennaro had proven his claim for sainthood more than a thousand years earlier, at Pozzuoli, when his Roman persecutors had attempted to feed him to wild bears. Instead, the holy man had emerged from the arena untouched.

Chrymos had knelt in front of the statue on many occasions, praying for the saint to protect her children, but she had never thought to go behind the massive sculpture.

Puzzled, she followed Adric, just in time to see him pulling aside a curtain that hung off the back wall. Adric then opened a mostly-hidden wall panel and eased through. *Oh well, in for a grana, in for a piastre,* thought Chrymos, and she followed Adric on what was likely to turn into yet another of his many ill-considered quests.

Slipping through the wall panel, Chrymos found herself in a small room. Adric, a few feet away, indicated that she should close the panel behind her.

"I think this was a priesthole," said Adric. Chrymos looked at him blankly.

"You've never heard of priestholes, C? They're secret rooms where priests can hide if they're wanted by the authorities," Adric explained. Chrymos shook her head.

"Okay, that probably doesn't make much sense in Naples, priests certainly don't need to hide around here," conceded Adric, "but I first came across priestholes when I was over in England a few years ago, hoping to find work. As you probably do know, the English Queen, Elizabeth I, didn't take too kindly to Catholic priests trying to preach in her Protestant country. Believers had to construct secret places where priests could hide, in case the queen's soldiers came looking for someone to string up."

"Okay, now I understand," said Chrymos. "Still, I suppose many of Europe's great mansions would also have secret rooms like this—you never know when you're going to fall out of favor with the ruler of the week." Her comment reflected the reality that so many countries in Europe regularly changed allegiance, through invasion, arranged marriage, or very occasionally citizen revolt.

She inspected her surroundings. *Not much to entertain anyone who's hiding in here*, she thought. *A desk and chairs, bookshelf, a small bed, a wooden chest.* She peered inside the chest, was vaguely disappointed to find it empty.

Clearly, the servants don't know about this place, she thought— everything was absolutely covered in dust, a situation that the Contessa would simply not tolerate if she knew.

"C, over here!"

Adric stood by the far wall, about six feet away, grinning contagiously but with his finger pressed to his lips. She didn't actually need to be told to stay silent—she knew that the two of them had no business being in this room and she had no wish to be discovered.

Again, Adric beckoned her forward. Again Chrymos followed, this time to a small peephole through which they could look down on one of the mansion's large drawing rooms.

Adric whispered directly into Chrymos' ear. "Isn't this amazing? This peephole has obviously been built especially for eavesdropping. I discovered the room by accident about a month ago, when I had to clean up after that unfortunate calcio incident."

Chrymos couldn't help but smile at the memory. On that particular

Sunday, Adric had brought a football with him to Mass, aiming to play a game of calcio soon after the service. Naturally, the ball had chosen the most inopportune moment to escape from his grasp, bounce heavily on the wooden floor, and roll down towards the altar, interrupting one of Father Carracci's more passionate sermons. Adric was fortunate indeed to survive the Dominican friar's wrath with merely a day's servitude scrubbing the chapel floor.

"You know, you can't even see this peephole from down there," whispered Adric, interrupting her reminiscences, "not unless you're as tall as one of those biblical giants that the good Father keeps talking about."

"This is all very interesting Adric," interrupted Chrymos, "but why are we here now, this morning? What's this all about?"

"A few minutes ago, there was an urgent visitor for Master Della Porta," began Adric. "I overheard one of the servants being instructed to take the visitor to the room below. I—shhhh, there's someone coming."

There was a scraping noise coming from behind them—the wall panel was being removed to gain access to the room.

Adric and Chrymos hurried over and hid behind the desk. *Hopefully whoever this is he wants to use the peephole*, thought Chrymos desperately. *If he comes over to the desk, he'll see us for sure.*

The pair held their breath as they heard the panel moved and then replaced. Then quiet footsteps moved towards them—and then, thankfully, passing by, towards the far wall where the peephole lay.

Then silence.

Adric, who had a better view than Chrymos, mouthed one word: "Luca".

Chrymos was caught by surprise. *He's been released early. I wasn't expecting him to show up until the ceremony this afternoon.* She wasn't particularly surprised, though, to find him eavesdropping. From her experience, Luca was always up to no good.

There was one problem, though, and it was a big one. *Our classes are due to start in*—Chrymos guessed the time—*about an hour.*

She and Adric couldn't leave until Luca did—if they tried to get from the desk to the secret panel while he was still here, they would easily be seen.

Luca will happily turn us in to the teachers if he finds us in here and I'm sure he'll concoct a marvelous excuse to explain his own presence.

There was little else they could do but wait.

TWENTY-EIGHT
LOA Headquarters, the Royal Exchange Building, London, England, midday, Wednesday April 7 1610

Jesse began the urgently-arranged meeting of the LOA Directorate with a shock announcement. "Directors, I have grave news. Our messenger was intercepted two days ago. I regret to advise that this is the catalyst that will trigger the forthcoming global disaster. I have established that the pathgem will soon be rediscovered."

The announcement was greeted with puzzlement by most of those present, so Jesse added a further explanation. "The pathgem is one of three powerkeys that were taken from Heaven during the Great Rebellion. It has always been regarded as the least of the keys—but in the wrong hands its use could still destroy this world."

Ravid, a tall, clean-shaven Outcast Angel with short brown hair and sparkling blue eyes, had the grace to look guilty—it was he who had brought the pathgem from Heaven, only to have it stolen by the Darke Warriors when Sanctuary was destroyed. Jesse glossed over Ravid's role and continued to address the LOA Directorate.

"Thirteen hundred years ago, when our enemies last used the pathgem, disaster was averted thanks to the courageous actions of a single individual, our fellow Outcast, Machkiel. You have the details in the briefing paper in front of you. If we cannot again defeat those who wield the pathgem, then evil will triumph, the nations of this world will fall to oppressors and freedom will be a distant memory. We need every available team to take action, fast."

Jesse waited to see how the LOA's ruling Directorate would react. The LOA—named after, and originally created in conjunction with, the legendary Library of Alexandria—sought, like its namesake, to collect information. Unlike the original library, however, this LOA sometimes found it necessary to take direct action, and the organization maintained several small response teams around the known world for precisely that purpose. Jesse now proposed to divert all of those teams to tackle the pathgem threat, an unprecedented step—which was why Jesse was seeking Directorate approval.

The room in which the LOA Directorate met, on the top floor of Sir Thomas Gresham's Royal Exchange building in London, was sparsely furnished, barren except for the substantial oak table that dominated the room and around which the directors now sat in uncomfortable leather chairs. A grasshopper, the Gresham family crest, was carved into the center of the table; otherwise, the table was unadorned except for the briefing papers in front of each director.

The LOA leader, Jesse, was a tall, solidly-built but usually unthreatening figure, typically with a ready smile and gentle words of encouragement. He wore a simple dark green robe and sandals and currently walked with something of a limp, the result of a misadventure in Wallachia a few months earlier. Jesse managed his limp with the aid of a stout quarterstaff, a handy walking aid whose very existence also discouraged undesirable attention.

Jesse's shoulder-length silver hair and foot-long salt-and-pepper beard, both dramatically out of control and desperately in need of trimming, would ordinarily make him appear like a friendly elderly grandfather, perhaps a little on the forgetful side. Not on this occasion—Jesse's whole stance proclaimed stress and tension.

Jesse was one of those who called themselves Outcast Angels. Along with Lucifer and many hundreds of thousands of other angels, they had been banished from Heaven for their actions during the Great Rebellion—but several thousand Outcast Angels had chosen not to continue defying God. Instead, they had been battling against Lucifer and his angels-turned-demons for many millennia.

The Outcast Angels still retained the supernatural powers that they had been given in Heaven. Jesse himself had been blessed with the power of prophecy. He could consider any individuals, perceive their possible futures and determine the most probable outcomes in their lives.

Jesse gazed around at the directors. All but Ravid and Shamar—the other two Outcast Angels who were members of the LOA's governing body, the Directorate—were human. Jesse had individually chosen all of the directors, both for their wisdom and for their commitment to the LOA's long-term mission.

The human members of the LOA Directorate were not personally familiar with situations such as this current crisis—though the Outcast Angels seemed to encounter them all too often over the centuries—and asked to hear more. Jesse leaned on his quarterstaff as he continued his report.

"I have examined a great many possible futures for the world's leaders. These are the most likely outcomes if the pathgem is found.

"King Henri IV of France will be the first to die, in less than six weeks from now. He will be travelling through the streets of Paris in his royal carriage. An assassin lurks, a blade will flash out and the king will die. All this will happen whether the pathgem is recovered or not. Still, the king senses something unusual and unexpected, but does not see it before he dies, and so neither can I."

The French representative, Bishop de Richelieu, at twenty-five the youngest member of the LOA Directorate, was naturally greatly disturbed by this news. He stood up, started pacing, and then spoke quickly. "We must stop this heinous crime *tout de suite*. We must warn His Majesty, keep him off the streets, and double his guard—"

Jesse was sympathetic but cautious. "Your grace, I do understand how you feel. We will do what we can to avoid this tragedy. By all means, you should also set in motion what precautions you can—but quietly, delicately. His majesty's future can still be changed. What I've shared with you is a prophecy, not a certainty. But without proof, without some tangible evidence, I fear that you will put yourself at risk should you tell the king or his courtiers what lies ahead. If your warnings go unheeded, and then the king is still assassinated, I must advise you that you will be considered part of the conspiracy. Your most likely future in that case is that you will be put on trial, found guilty and swiftly put to death. Your holy position will not be enough to protect you."

"My fate is unimportant," said the Bishop, "what matters is the king."

Jesse's next words gave de Richelieu reason to reconsider. "I try to avoid telling anyone their own most likely future, but in this case I believe it is necessary for me to do so. Your Grace, your possible futures are changing before my eyes, as you consider what actions you should take in response to my prophecy. I can tell you this: if you can avoid being caught up in events surrounding the death of King Henri, then you have a very meaningful role to play in the future of France. I will not give details, lest I sway your future choices—suffice to say that you will find yourself in a position of substantial influence, which you will of course use for the betterment of your country. Your Grace, I entreat you, mourn the imminent death of your king in silence, for the greater good."

The bishop resumed his seat, pondering Jesse's comments. The Outcast Angel, his prophetic vision confirming that the worst outcomes for de Richelieu had been averted, continued.

"As I was saying, this first tragedy is not because of the pathgem. But once the jewel is rediscovered—and I fear that this will happen very soon, the probabilities are so strong—the crisis will then escalate rapidly. In mid-summer, in the Dutch Republic, Maurice of Orange will be meeting with the deputies who collectively form the republic's Council of State. Maurice will be arguing with the Council over military budget cuts."

Fellow Outcast Angel Shamar gave a bleak smile. "That sounds familiar."

"Different generation, same old story," agreed Jesse. "Just when the discussion is getting particularly heated, Maurice and the deputies will hear a clap of thunder—and a group of about half-a-dozen brigands, swords at the ready, will appear out of nowhere, right in the middle of the council meeting room. That phenomenon alone is clear evidence that in less than five months from now the pathgem will have been found and put to use."

Ravid and Shamar nodded grimly. The others were on the edge of their seats as Jesse continued.

"Maurice's guards, posted outside the meeting room, will come running but they will be driven back by a relentless blizzard of wind, snow, and ice."

Jesse held up his hand, to forestall any objections.

"Yes, I said that this attack will happen in mid-summer. And yes, there will be a treacherous blizzard—biting, pounding snow, sleet, and ice—and yes, it will happen indoors, while the day outside remains sunny and cloudless. One of the attackers can conjure vast quantities of snow and ice from the very air in the room and then create powerful wind blasts."

The council meeting erupted in chaos, as the LOA directors began to realize the implications. Jesse struggled to regain control of the assembly, eventually raising his quarterstaff and hammering it against the solid oak table. He had to do so several times before the clamor subsided.

"Thank you, gentlemen. We can discuss and debate this situation later. For now, please listen."

The buzz was reduced to low whispers. Jesse continued.

"Yes, all my prophecies indicate that we are facing people with supernatural powers. How and where they get their powers, I do not yet know. But from all that I can foresee, these are humans, not demons. The Darke Warriors are not directly involved, at least not in any of the attacks that I have so far pre-witnessed."

"Small mercies," murmured Shamar.

"Indeed," agreed Jesse. "Returning to Maurice of Orange—his guards will attempt to push through the blizzard towards their attackers. But the blizzard-maker is not the only demonic power in the room.

"A second talent amongst the attackers will choose that moment to manifest his abilities. This individual—Maurice will not be able to see clearly through the blizzard, so I am unable to describe him to you—has the ability to conjure up and hurtle mighty blasts of energy that are as unstoppable as enormous boulders. Each blast is enough to flatten several guards—the Dutch Republic's defenders will be killed in a matter of minutes."

One of the LOA Directorate's senior members, Paolo Sarpi of the Venetian Republic, stammered out a horrified question. "Quello che è successo—your pardon—can you tell us what happened to Maurice of Orange?"

"Precisely what you fear will happen. All will be rounded up and swiftly executed. Maurice of Orange will be the last to be killed. As you would expect from a military captain-general, Maurice will stand tall and face his executioners defiantly. His final thoughts will be of his mistress, Margaretha, the mother of his three young sons. He will worry what will become of her and their sons, and will regret that he never married her."

"You say 'will'?" said Sarpi. "Of course—these events will not happen until summer. Then we can still warn them—"

"Patience, Director Sarpi," said Jesse. "Yes, there is still time—

although how we can warn anyone without being accused of witchcraft or worse, I'm not sure. You know the age in which we live—innocents have been drowned or burned at the stake on the merest gossip about such practices. And you all heard the warning that I gave to Bishop de Richelieu—preventing these murders must be undertaken carefully, or we may face far worse outcomes.

"But what you've heard thus far is merely the beginning of the story. In every land throughout the known world, these pathgem-enabled supernatural attacks will soon take place. In every land, that is, except for Spain and its territories."

"Then Spain must be behind these attacks!" gasped the Venetian director.

"Those who support Spain, yes, so it would seem," agreed Jesse. "But Philip III of Spain or his men? Unlikely. The powers behind these attacks are far beyond those of any earthly government. We do not yet know who is responsible—they will act in stealth, and conceal their motives. Know this, though—as soon as we have any of their operatives in our hands—" Jesse's face turned to stone. "—we will find out the truth."

Many of the directors murmured their agreement.

Ravid was keen to hear more about other threats. "You said you examined the futures of many leaders. What else can you tell us?"

"Look to the east, where Ahmed I, the young Sultan of the Ottoman Empire, will die in similarly unusual circumstances. He is a keen and very experienced horseback rider and that will prove his downfall. He will be racing along a pathway that takes him near the top of a cliff overlooking the Black Sea when his horse will dramatically change direction in mid-stride, almost as if blown off-course by a violent storm. The horse's altered direction will take both horse and rider over the cliff to their doom. The accident is so unnatural that I must conclude that supernatural powers are again at work."

"What about Jamestown, Virginia?" The newest member of the LOA Directorate, Captain John Smith, would naturally ask about the fate of the American colony which he had helped found. Captain Smith had been forced to return to England after being injured in an accidental gunpowder explosion, but he had never lost his passion for the new colony.

"I doubt, Captain," said Jesse, "that the Jamestown colony is large enough to warrant direct action by our enemies—" Jesse paused for a moment, using his powers to evaluate the probable futures of the distant colony's leaders. "—but it appears that I am wrong. Perhaps it's not the colony's present circumstances but its potential that they fear. At this very moment, as we meet in this room, many of the colonists are dying of starvation—but matters will soon become much worse. Later this year, a new governor, Lord de la Warr, will arrive from England. One of the interpreters will convince the new governor that the best approach to deal with Chief Powhatan is through military might."

"What?" said Captain Smith, leaping to his feet, "That's madness. Powhatan will simply respond exactly the same way as he did to the lost colonists of Roanoke. He will attack in force—and he has far more men and resources than we do."

"Exactly," said Jesse. "There will be war. Royal Powhatan women and children will be slaughtered by English soldiers and in retribution many colonists will be ambushed and killed by the Powhatan tribesmen. Finally, the interpreter—who I am now certain is one of those enemies we are seeking—will lure Lord de la Warr away from the Jamestown fort, supposedly to meet a Powhatan turncoat with vital intelligence. Instead, one of the Powhatan tribal leaders, Wowinchopunk, will capture the governor and he will die a prolonged and painful death. In his last moments, Lord de la Warr will see the interpreter he trusted arriving at Wowinchopunk's camp, greeted as an honored guest."

Captain Smith slumped back into his chair, horrified. Jesse couldn't blame him—the captain had spent so many years attempting to build up Jamestown. If the colony failed, England might well lose its foothold on the American continent, leaving the new world for others to exploit. *Giving free reign to the likes of Spain, France, and, unfortunately, evil influences such as the Order of the Dragon,* thought Jesse, though he kept his musings to himself.

There were too many uncertainties for Jesse to predict the colony's most likely future, but for now, none of that mattered. The impending deployment of the pathgem was his all-consuming focus.

The directors sat stunned as they tried to come to grips with what they had just been told. Venetian statesman Paolo Sarpi was the first to recover. "This is intolerable! What exactly can we do and when do we start?"

"Let's talk about that in a moment. First, you should know what happens as a result. As the leaders fall, one by one, chaos will reign—until a powerful new force begins to emerge. There will be a widespread belief that a leader has arisen from the East, who will shortly take command of the known world."

The reaction to this prophecy was such that Jesse was once again forced to pound his quarterstaff on the table to restore order.

"I know—it's inconceivable. But this is definitely one of the most dangerous circumstances we have ever encountered." *<Well,>* amended Jesse, exchanging thoughts with Ravid and Shamar, *<it's certainly the most dangerous situation that this group needs to know about. Some horrors, we simply must keep to ourselves.>*

No-one spoke. No-one could speak—the implications were simply too terrible. Then Captain Smith asked hesitantly, "Jesse, can any of these fates be changed? You announce them as if they were predestined."

"Yes, of course, Director," said Jesse, conscious of the fact that this was the captain's first meeting since being selected to join the LOA Directorate. He was clearly unaware of the nature of Jesse's prophecies. "These are probabilities, not certainties. It's up to us to do everything we possibly can to try to ensure that they don't come true."

"Then I'm sure I speak for all of us," said Captain Smith, "when I propose that we authorize you to do whatever it takes to stop these events—all of these events—from actually happening. Whatever it takes," he emphasized, as his fellow directors endorsed his proposal strenuously, unanimously, and loudly.

"Very well, directors. Thank you," responded Jesse. "We have established that we are dealing with people with supernatural powers, so we will need to assemble as many of our own enhanced warriors as possible. I will check with our training facility at Stonehenge. Archimedes tells me he has several promising recruits so I will see if there are any currently available soldiers that we can add to our ranks.

"We will also begin our own search for the pathgem—we'll start by reviewing the records in the LOA archive. And, since we believe that the same group who are responsible for many of the other atrocities will carry out the assassination of King Henri of France, we will arrange for at least one of our teams to be in Paris by mid-May, when the king's assassination is likely to take place."

Director Sarpi spoke up. "I believe I know of a new invention that might be of some assistance. You should visit the Venetian Republic and meet with one of my University of Padua colleagues, Galileo Galilei—I will write a letter of introduction for you. Galileo has recently developed an improved version of a Dutch invention that will allow you to see from a considerable distance. If you are able to use Galileo's device, perhaps you could identify King Henri's would-be assassins in advance and stop them from carrying through with their plans."

"I'm not sure there's enough time for anybody to travel to Padua and back before the assassination attempt, Councilor," said Jesse. "Ravid or Shamar could fly over, of course, but I'm not sure if their duties allow—I'll discuss it with them after this meeting. What exactly is the device?"

"The Dutch have been calling it a 'perspective glass' or a 'spyglass'," said Director Sarpi.

"Thank you, Director. We'll see what we can do. Now—" Jesse turned to address all the directors. "Gentlemen, you may fear that the situation we face is hopeless. But let me tell you that we have faced many similarly desperate situations over the centuries, yet we are still here."

Jesse smiled defiantly. "Even if this is a battle that we have only a slight chance of winning, we will take that chance or die trying."

The room—and in fact the whole top floor of the Royal Exchange building—echoed mightily as the directors leapt to their feet as one and roared their agreement.

TWENTY-NINE
Some thirteen hundred years earlier
The Margus River, Moesia, [Serbia]
Late night, ante diem tertium Idus Iulias (July 13) 285 AD

The Darke Warrior Ezequeel laughed as he gutted two more Roman soldiers with a single thrust of his viciously barbed broadsword, avoiding their shields and effortlessly penetrating their body armor. *If you want to try to overwhelm me by crowding in close, bring it on,* thought Ezequeel. *The more humans you throw at me, the better. That will simply make the next battle easier, when I bring the true emperor here to reclaim his throne.*

"It's a demon sent by Orcus, god of the underworld!" The deadly whisper, powered by fear, flashed through the Roman legion surrounding Ezequeel.

Ezequeel smiled cruelly as he raised the double-bladed axe in his left hand. *Demon, sure, call me that. But that slimy toad Orcus didn't send me. The true Lord of Darkness entrusted me with this task.* The axe thundered downward and dispatched yet another Roman soldier to his fate.

More and more and still more of the would-be Roman emperor Diocletian's soldiers crowded around Ezequeel, maintaining their discipline despite the fearsome nature of their enemy. The soldiers clustered together, adopting the classic testudo formation. Their shields formed a largely impenetrable barrier, protecting the soldiers from attacks from above and from any side.

Eventually neither the demon's sword nor its axe could find a way through the interlocking shields. *Impressive loyalty to an imperial pretender,* thought Ezequeel. *No matter. I'll simply choose another spot. On the other side of the river looks as good as anywhere.*

Another evil grimace and then Ezequeel clasped the glowing gem on his wrist, muttered a few words, and vanished. The demon reappeared almost instantly about a hundred feet away. He immediately began lashing out at the unprepared soldiers at his new location.

THIRTY
A few hours later
The Margus River, Moesia,
Early morning, pridie Idus Iulias (July 14) 285 AD

Heads bowed low, the military leaders of Diocletian's army were ushered into the imperial presence in the praetorian command tent. In accordance with the custom Diocletian had introduced since the army proclaimed him leader of the Roman Empire, his commanders lowered themselves to the ground, to lie there without speaking, heads down, until the emperor decreed otherwise.

One by one, Diocletian questioned his commanders, tribunes, and centurions alike. Under pain of death, each swore that the story was true. One centurion, bloodied and battered, freshly returned from the front line, told his story while others nodded in fearful agreement. "Yes, Lord, I saw the creature with my own eyes. It was so tall—more than four cubits, I swear. It towered above us all. And this demon is clearly not of this world—from its back sprouted a massive pair of fearsome, dark, leathery wings—like those of a bat but perhaps a hundred times bigger. Those around me damned it for the spawn of Orcus, master of the underworld, and that I can well believe. With every step it reeked of the smell of the underworld, deadly brimstone, and dying flesh.

"This monster was clad head to foot in blackest armor that turned away every blade, javelin, or spear. There was one touch of color—a glowing blue stone on a silver band around the creature's wrist. The armor itself swarmed with maggots, cockroaches, and vermin of every kind, though the demon paid them no heed. And the eyes of the beast, what little I could see of them within its armored helmet, glowed yellow and red like the fires of Hell. But that was not the worst of it.

"In its right hand the demon wielded a mighty barbed sword, at least two cubits in length and sharp enough to cut through our own armor as if it was papyrus. In its left, the creature brandished a gigantic double-bladed axe with which it could fell several of our soldiers in a single swing. But that was still not the worst of it.

"In desperation, we sought to overwhelm the creature through force of numbers. We pressed in close, maintaining our shields in close formation so that it could not get through to us by swinging its sword or raising its axe. And then—" The centurion paused to give the *mano fico*, the sign to ward off evil. "—then the demon just disappeared. It vanished from our sight. We thought at first it must have dropped to the ground to escape us, but a moment later we heard shouts and screams from across the river and there it was again, its sword and axe once again swinging freely to deliver death to our soldiers."

Marcus Augustus, legion deputy commander and easily the most experienced of all Diocletian's officers, took up the tale. "Again and again, we tried to surround the beast. Again and again, it escaped us, vanishing through some type of demonic magic. The only good news is that the creature departed when the sun rose. But many are convinced that it will return tonight." He took a deep breath before continuing.

"My Lord and Master, you know how loyal and brave your soldiers are. They chose you to lead the empire and will fight to the death to defend you against the pretender Carinus. Even though his forces greatly outnumber us, we still expect to triumph against mere mortal men. But this demon—" The battle-hardened officer shuddered. "It strikes bone-numbing fear into the hearts of our soldiers by its very appearance. How can they fight against the minions of the lord of the underworld, they ask themselves? They remember only too well the stories of Orcus that they were told in their youth, spine-chilling tales that left them terrified and sleepless for many long nights."

Diocletian gazed thoughtfully at his commanders. At first, he had been inclined to dismiss the whispers, superstitious gossip spread perhaps by those amongst his army who had been reluctant to take part in this blood-drenched civil war. *But if even Marcus Augustus thinks there is truth in this tale—*

Abruptly, Diocletian made a decision. "I will consider what you say. Leave me now—but send for my advisor, Machkiel."

As the commanders rose and backed out of the imperial tent, they exchanged puzzled glances. They'd never understood why Diocletian had brought along this mysterious "advisor" in the first place.

Now, after completely ignoring the advisor for the first half of the battle, why would Diocletian suddenly decide to summon him? And how could the usually so practical emperor take this news of demonic interference so calmly?

# # #

If the legion commanders were surprised by the sudden summoning of Machkiel, they would have been horrified by the advisor's behavior in front of the emperor.

Thankfully, neither soldiers nor slaves were close at hand to witness his arrival—Diocletian had sent them all away from the imperial tent and chose to wait alone for Machkiel.

Machkiel breezed into the emperor's tent—no bowing, no prostrating—walked directly to a bench at the side of the tent and calmly helped himself to the emperor's finest wine.

"Hail Caesar and all that." He sniffed at the wine. "Not a bad drop. Should I pour one for you, too, sire?" he asked the somewhat scandalized Diocletian.

After a moment, the emperor rallied and nodded, accepting a goblet of his own wine. He needed it to cope with Machkiel's next move. The impertinent advisor strode over to the emperor's own couch and plonked himself down on the imperial purple.

Diocletian's eyes blazed. He gulped down a mouthful of wine and prepared to mete out imperial justice for this brazen impertinence. But Machkiel smiled up at him.

"Relax, mighty emperor, don't expect me to play by your rules. I'm afraid mere emperors don't rate in comparison to The Ruler I've served. Now come and sit down beside me and tell me exactly what troubles you so much that you finally chose to summon me."

Diocletian finally unbent. "Your leader Jesse warned me that this day would come if I agreed to take over the empire. I'm afraid I didn't believe him."

"Yes," said Machkiel, making room on the couch for the emperor. "Jesse's prophecies are often neither welcome nor believed. Nevertheless, they have a distressing tendency to come true—which is, of course, why you called for me."

Diocletian spent a few minutes explaining the events that his military commanders had witnessed. Machkiel thought aloud as he stood up, returned to the bench and helped himself to another wine. "Disappeared, you say. And almost instantly reappeared somewhere else. That doesn't sound like invisibility—plenty of them can do that, of course. I wonder—"

Diocletian looked up expectantly, but Machkiel stopped speaking and slowly paced around the tent as he pondered the implications. The emperor sat back and observed Machkiel. Tall, slight yet powerfully muscled, from what Diocletian could see of his physique. Short black hair. Still wearing the same grey robe that he had worn when advisor and emperor had first met. And yet, around his middle, where most would wear a sturdy belt and carry a sword, Machkiel affected a few strands of rope.

Machkiel finally stopped pacing and turned to face the emperor.

"What you are facing here is a Darke Warrior, one of Lucifer's inner circle of demons. They don't usually interfere directly with human affairs, preferring instead to work through their local minions such as the Brotherhood of Judas or New Phoenicia. Why this demon would personally attack your men, I don't yet know. But he must be stopped—and you will definitely need my help to do that."

Diocletian's heart skipped a beat. *Did that mean—?* He had to ask.

"And you can help because—?"

"Didn't Jesse tell you? Because I am an angel—an Outcast Angel, yes, but still I possess my angelic powers."

Concentrating, Machkiel summoned his wings. They shimmered into existence on his back as if they had always been there, glorious white richly-feathered wings, perhaps twenty feet across when fully extended.

Machkiel shrugged his shoulders and flapped those magnificent wings, almost tentatively at first, then so vigorously that he rose and hovered in the air, nearly touching the roof of the tent. He landed lightly and then dismissed the ectoplasmic wings with a thought. They faded into the oblivion from whence they came.

Diocletian, who had been brought up to believe in or, rather, pay lip service to the traditional Roman collection of gods, was shocked by this casual demonstration of supernatural powers.

Machkiel retrieved his wine and sipped thoughtfully, then spoke to the emperor—not with the fawning respect that Diocletian usually received, but rather with purpose and determination. "Okay, let's start making some plans. That demon is certain to return tonight. Here's what I need your soldiers to do—"

THIRTY-ONE
Academy of Secrets, Naples, Kingdom of Naples, Morning, Wednesday April 7 1610

Adric and Chrymos dashed into the classroom together, panting and nearly out of breath, mere moments before their class was due to begin. It had been a narrow escape—Luca had finally left the priesthole a few minutes before, appearing surprised at what he had heard—but for Adric and Chrymos the whole misadventure had been a complete waste. They had learned nothing about Della Porta's mystery visitor nor his message—the desk behind which they were crouched was simply too far away from the peephole.

The pair's nearly-late arrival for their lessons earned them a severe frown from their class tutor, Dominican priest Thomas Carracci. Because of their tardiness, the two friends were obliged to sit apart—the only empty places were single seats on opposite sides of the room.

Chrymos went to sit near the two students that she always thought of as the class's "poor little rich kids", Bartholomeo and Salvator. They saw her coming, however, and moved their chairs together so that there was no room for her. *Are they really still jealous because I'm in the same class as them after three months' study while they've had to complete three years,* she wondered. *Do they dislike me because I'm poor? Or is it because I'm a woman in this Academy that's supposed to be exclusively male?* She shook her head in amused disbelief.

Instead, Chrymos found a seat near the only other real friend she had in the class, Ruben. She still didn't know very much about him, except that—even though, judging by his extensive wardrobe, he clearly came from a wealthy family—he treated her like a friend and showed no interest in mingling with either Bartholomeo or Salvator.

As Chrymos sat down, Ruben nodded his welcome, adding, "Carracci's on the warpath today. Better not say anything—" He struggled for the right words.

"—like I usually do?" prompted Chrymos, smiling. "Don't worry,

I've already had my fill of trouble today, I'm not planning to create any more just to maintain my reputation."

"That's not like you, Chrymos. Are you not feeling well?" Ruben put just the right amount of caring concern into his voice, but Chrymos knew he was only joking. Before she could respond in kind, Father Carracci called the class to order.

"Quiet, all of you. Now, you're all well aware of what's happening this afternoon," Father Carracci began. "I do hope that you will still be able to concentrate on your lessons this morning, because today we're going to be continuing with our study on the History of Warfare."

A nearly-audible groan ran through the room.

Carracci managed one of his more unpleasant smiles. "I'm so glad you're looking forward to it. But you might want to pay special attention today, because you're going to be learning about our most dangerous adversaries."

That sparked everyone's attention. Carracci continued: "As ever, before we begin, bow your heads in tribute to our Lord Almighty, Jesus Christ. We ask His blessings on us today, and on His servant on Earth, our king, His Majesty, Philip III. Long may King Philip reign over the Kingdom of Naples and the many other territories of the great and powerful Spanish Empire in the name of the Lord."

Carracci moved on to the topic of the day. "This morning, we will be talking about those who dare to call themselves the Outcast Angels."

Chrymos was suddenly thankful that she wasn't in fact sitting beside Adric for this lesson. Adric could be an unfortunate companion—because he often "interpreted" the lessons for the benefit of those around him. Chrymos had successfully endured many of Doctor Odaldi's alchemy classes only because Adric had made them almost interesting, despite the boring monotone that Odaldi inflicted on his students.

Father Carracci was different—usually more stimulating, but also much more alert to any mischief, and his punishments could be draconian. Chrymos still remembered the minor prank, writing a bawdy verse on the class hornbook, which had resulted in Father Carracci demanding—and securing—Mauricio's expulsion from the Academy two months earlier.

Carracci started his lecture—and, as Chrymos watched out of the corner of one eye, she saw that Adric was shaking his head, wishing he had Chrymos as an audience for his own version of the day's teachings. He settled for making faces at her from across the room when Carracci wasn't looking.

"Previously we've talked about Lucifer and his demons, particularly the ones that call themselves Darke Warriors," Carracci began. "The Outcast Angels also rebelled against mighty God, but—they claim—chose not to go along with Lucifer. Instead they serve a different master, the former archangel Eyphah, a creature as monstrous as Lucifer but even more evil because he hides behind the appearance of innocence."

Carracci looked suitably solemn, which made it all the more difficult for Chrymos to keep a straight face with Adric making facial contortions. She tried to focus her attention on the tutor rather than Adric.

"Most of these Outcast Angels have divine powers that were bestowed by God," said Carracci, "and yet those powers were not stripped from them when they were banished, despite their crimes. A small number of Outcast Angels do not appear to have any powers—we believe it is because they are offspring of the Outcasts, *carogna* begotten in the millennia since the angels were banished. Still, the distinction between powered and unpowered does not matter—all of these 'Outcasts' are abominations in the sight of the Church and of God."

Carracci was in full swing now. *At times like this,* thought Chrymos, *I can easily see why Father Carracci went into the priesthood. He truly believes in what he's saying.*

"The reason that the Academy exists," thundered the priest, "and why we practice alchemy here even though the Church officially forbids it, is simple: we may be the Church's sole protection against these Outcast Angels, who have on many occasions shown themselves willing to use their powers directly against us."

# # #

The remainder of the lesson consisted of an extended retelling of the grim misadventures of the Spanish Armada in 1588, with Father Carracci blaming many of the Armada's failures on Outcast Angel interference. Even Niccolo, usually the most gullible student in the class, struggled to believe that argument. Across the room, Adric was almost sniggering—

silently, of course.

Finally, Carracci summed up. "Now you know what you're going to be facing. It's a sobering revelation. That's why you need to be ready. These creatures have rejected their God-given heritage and are misusing their powers for evil beyond belief. That is why, after extensive training, we will give you powers through alchemy, powers which you will use to carry the battle to these Outcast Angels during the forthcoming Lost War—once you have proven yourself worthy.

"This afternoon, of course, we will be celebrating the graduation of your predecessors. As you know, three weeks ago last year's graduates were given potions designed to release their unique powers. In doing so, they became members of the elite group we call the Alchemae. Since then, they've been cloistered, learning about their powers and refining their abilities.

"This afternoon, we will see those powers in action for the first time. We cannot predict in advance what those powers will be, because each person is different, each manifestation of power is different. Although we give all graduates the same Exousía potion, each responds differently. From what we understand of the process, the potion simply releases the supernatural capabilities that dwell uniquely within the individual."

Carracci paused, staring around the room to ensure that every eye was turned towards him.

"So my final question to you all, as we wait for this afternoon's unveiling, is simply this: how will you cope when you receive your powers, capabilities that may be beyond your wildest imaginings? How can you best devote those powers to the service of the Academy, the Kingdom of Naples, the Spanish Empire, the Catholic Church, and for Almighty God?

"Class dismissed."

THIRTY-TWO
Academy of Secrets, Naples, Kingdom of Naples, Afternoon, Wednesday April 7 1610

That afternoon, Chrymos waited alongside the other students in the grand ballroom of the Academy of Secrets for the graduation ceremony to begin. She looked around, as usual mentally condemning the wastefulness of her surroundings. The ballroom was the most richly-decorated of all, in a mansion dripping with conspicuous wealth. The room itself was easily two hundred feet long, the walls stretching thirty feet high to rendezvous with lavishly-illustrated ceiling panels, each a masterpiece of the painter's art, capturing scenes of past glories of the legendary Roman Empire. The walls themselves, though plainer than their elevated ceiling companions, were a mix of elegant marble facings enclosed by embedded gold leaf, which captured and reflected light.

And the light? The ballroom was simply ablaze with candlelight, much of it pouring from the three dozen candles carried by each of the twelve priceless crystal chandeliers that dominated the room. The chandeliers, treasures in their own right, were a gift from the Tsardom of Muscovy with grateful thanks for the Academy's assistance during the recent Time of Troubles.

Chrymos, in her poor and (in her eyes) pitiful blue tunic dress, felt woefully out of place amidst the finery of this glamorous environment—although, in truth, all of her classmates were similarly under-prepared for the splendor of the ballroom within which they now waited. Only the Contessa Stefani was garbed appropriately for the surroundings. The mistress of the Academy wore a richly-embroidered, huge-skirted costume of magnificent black satin, trimmed with the finest lace and carelessly adorned with precious gems. *So that's the royal wedding outfit,* thought Chrymos, *I must admit, it looks spectacular.* The Contessa had, according to kitchen gossip, last worn that particular dress in 1600, to the wedding of King Henri IV of France and Marie de' Medici of Florence. The new queen had, so wagging tongues had reported, personally congratulated the Contessa on her stunning appearance.

The Contessa's white blonde hair was uncovered but carefully curled to her crown and held in place by unseen fastenings. She had opted for a high-backed collar which freed her neck to display a stunning large white diamond affixed to a black silk ribbon. *The effect is outstanding,* thought Chrymos, impressed despite herself, *although imagine what the Contessa might achieve if she could actually bring herself to smile.*

Chrymos turned to watch as each of the five freshly-graduated members of the Alchemae filed in and prepared to demonstrate their newly-acquired powers in front of the students, staff and other graduates of the Academy. Uncharacteristically, the Master of the Academy, Giambattista Della Porta, was not present. The Contessa stood on the podium in his place, her icy expression dampening any expectations that this would be an occasion for celebration.

At a nod from the Contessa, the alchemy tutor Doctor Odaldi opened proceedings, his usually dull monotone showing a hint of life.

"Contessa, honored staff, graduates, students, it is my pleasure to introduce to you the newest members of the Alchemae, five students who have worked diligently these past weeks to achieve mastery over their powers. Gentlemen, please step forward and bow when your names are called out."

Each of the graduates did precisely that. "Luca, Flaminio, Pascol, Simon, Bitino." There was polite applause—the graduates were yet to display any powers.

Odaldi continued. "Now, let us see what our newest Alchemae can do. Luca?"

Luca, the humorless student who had worked so hard to make Chrymos' life in the Academy unpleasant, was more than happy to go first. He was of average height, with blond hair and blue eyes, but a distinctive curved scar, stretching from just below his right ear down to his chin, marred his otherwise handsome face. *Jealous lover or bitter rival,* Chrymos often wondered, but if anyone in the Academy knew how Luca had come by the scar, no-one was talking.

He reached out, plucked a purple-tinged orchid from a nearby vase and, with little more than a thought, transmuted the fragile flower into delicate but solid gold. His next move was to present the golden orchid to

Contessa Stefani, bowing low as he did so.

"Oh yeah, that's so Luca", whispered Adric to Chrymos. "Never misses a chance to suck up."

Chrymos smiled briefly, then returned her attention to the ceremony. The icy Contessa was commenting. "A fine talent, Master Luca. Not, perhaps, suited for the front line, but surely it will help to fund our forthcoming endeavors."

Front line? Chrymos was so busy trying to decipher the meaning of the Contessa's comment that she almost missed the start of the next demonstration, as Odaldi spoke again. "Flaminio, if you please—but remember, proceed more cautiously today."

That last comment piqued everyone's interest. Flaminio, a short but powerfully built student from the island of Sicily, strode forward onto the podium, and then turned to face the audience. He braced himself as if for combat, clasped his large hands together, one clinging to the top of the other, and stood motionless.

Chrymos looked up at his face. Flaminio, never an intellectual, was frowning, brow deeply furrowed, eyes closed, as he concentrated intently.

There was a gasp from one of Chrymos' classmates, Niccolo. Chrymos looked over, saw him point at Flaminio's hands. She turned back to Flaminio, saw that even though his hands were tightly clenched together, something was struggling to push those hands apart.

As Chrymos watched, indeed as the whole auditorium watched, Flaminio's hands were being pushed further and further apart with each passing second.

Odaldi spoke up. "That's large enough, Flaminio. Now toss it to your left."

Flaminio opened his eyes, seized the invisible something that he had just conjured up and prepared to hurtle the burden away. He was aiming to his right, where many of the staff were standing, until Odaldi urgently hissed and pointed. "Left, Flaminio, left. In that direction."

Finally taking the hint, Flaminio tossed his virtual load to the left, where it collided with, and partially destroyed, a small desk—after which the invisible force then ricocheted into two of the servants, knocking them to the floor. As the servants were helped to their feet by other serving staff, Odaldi explained Flaminio's power.

"Flaminio can create virtual boulders with his mind—a very useful tool for any army, to be able to throw invisible objects at your enemy."

Most of the onlookers applauded enthusiastically. Luca clapped politely but looked unimpressed.

Pascol was the next to demonstrate his new skill. A tall, thin individual who originally hailed from Milan, Pascol was incredibly pompous—he typically acted as though he was far better than those around him. He was always impeccably dressed and groomed, usually in the latest fashions from the city of his birth, and today was no different. He cut a dashing figure, ruffled white collar contrasting with a stylish crimson false-sleeved silk doublet and matching hose of patterned damask. *With his fussy moustache and long thin face,* thought Chrymos, *Pascol always reminds me of a ferret.*

Odaldi indicated that the audience should move back, which—after Flaminio's recent demonstration of the perils of being too close—they hastily did. Two servants maneuvered an empty barrel into place on the podium before quickly evacuating the area.

Like Luca, Pascol reached out and took an orchid from a nearby vase. He held the orchid above the empty barrel and then, after checking that his audience was paying attention, blinked his eyes, just once. The flower he was holding simply dissolved into liquid, flowing through Pascol's fingers into the barrel.

Pascol's hand was wet, so he gestured to a nearby servant who was holding a towel. That unfortunate underling, afraid of being turned into water, very tentatively held out the towel at arm's length.

Pascol took the towel, dried his hand and then held the towel itself, pinched between thumb and forefinger, over the barrel. Another blink and the towel also liquefied, flowing into the barrel to join the fluid remains of the former orchid.

Pascol lifted his hand away and shook off a few drops of liquefied towel, then turned that movement into an ornate bow towards Academy staff. As Pascol left the podium to slightly nervous applause, Chrymos shook her head slightly. *None of us will be shaking hands with Pascol any time soon.*

Simon was next. Where Pascol was merely tall, Simon was a veritable giant, at least six foot three inches in height. He was a former grain farmer, press-ganged from the streets of Naples after a wayward night out drinking in the big city to celebrate a record harvest. Simon had no desire to go back to his farming life—he preferred the challenges on offer in the Academy to the back-breaking work in the fields.

Chrymos had always liked Simon. He had a gentle heart and a simplistic view on life, which could be summed up in a single philosophy: do unto others as you would have them do unto you. That attitude made it even more surprising that Simon had such a passion for, and could do wondrous tricks with, knives. He could throw a knife and hit his target dead center or make the knife twist and turn in the air and even somehow find its way around a corner. Simon was forever juggling, sharpening, or whittling with his collection of knives, demonstrating uncanny skills. *Even if Simon turns out to have no useful powers,* thought Chrymos, *he will still be valuable to the Academy.*

As it happened, Simon had indeed acquired a new and noteworthy talent. He stood on the podium, towering over everybody—and then his body began to shrink.

Down, down, down, he went—down to "normal" size, then to child size, then down again still further. He stopped shrinking when he was about the size of a large cat. The watching students went crazy, clapping and whistling, until the Contessa picked up a tiny bell and rang it—once, but that was enough.

She bent down to Simon, speaking quietly. "Can you hear me?"

A tiny, squeaky voice replied. "Yes, there's no need to shout."

Odaldi took over the proceedings at this point, as the Contessa moved out of the way.

"You'll notice," said Odaldi, "that Simon's clothes shrank along with him, as did his knives and anything else that was touching his bare skin."

Father Carracci stepped forward. "Doctor Odaldi, you've had the opportunity to work with Simon on his powers over the last two months. How useful will those skills be in battle, when he is competing against full-sized opponents?"

In response, Odaldi pushed a wooden bench close to the diminutive Simon. With a tiny knife in each hand, Simon was able to climb up the side of the bench, creating his own handholds with each thrust of the two knives. He quickly stood on top of the bench, knives ready to go slashing into action.

Odaldi explained further. "His strength is proportionate to his new size, but he keeps those knives very sharp and they could easily do some significant damage—especially if he dips the blades in poison first."

Carracci nodded, recognizing the possibilities inherent in such skills, but Odaldi wasn't finished.

"Simon's real advantage lies in stealth. He can shrink down to get through any defenses and then enlarge himself and strike from behind."

Chrymos scrutinized Simon as he began to return to his full size. The Simon she thought she knew would have been appalled at such talk but now he seemed unfazed by the prospect of behaving in such a treacherous fashion. *Has he changed or have I simply been getting the wrong impression?*

"Thanks Simon," said Odaldi, indicating that the new graduate should retire to the sidelines. "Finally now, let's see what Bitino has to offer us."

Bitino was the last of the graduating class to be introduced, and he came forward triumphantly, raising his arms as if to acknowledge the adulation that would soon be his. Bitino was one of the group that Adric liked to describe as "the rich and powerless"—Napoletano families who were still wealthy in their own right but who had little influence with the Spanish Empire and its vice-regal representatives governing the Kingdom of Naples. Bitino—and Luca, who came from a similar background—resented the Spanish Empire for a simple reason: they were not part of its power structure.

Today, however, Bitino thinks he's onto a winner, thought Chrymos. *I wonder what power he's received?*

Odaldi nodded to Bitino—and the grand ballroom started to become very, very cold. Then it began to snow—inside. Light flurries of mixed hail and ice pellets and powdered snow at first, then the wind arrived, stirring up the mixture, turning it into deadly missiles that pelted the audience. They endured the discomfort at first, but then as the bad weather intensified the audience broke and ran for the doors.

All except one. Father Carracci stood his ground, clapping slowly and loudly. He shouted out, above the noise and clamor of the blizzard, "We get the idea, Bitino. Stop—now."

Bitino stopped what he was doing. He looked around, surprised and more than a little pleased at the chaos he had caused, then once again turned to the audience, smiled proudly and lifted his arms high above his head. If he expected a standing ovation, he was sadly mistaken—from their vantage points around the exits and at the furthest corners of the room, everyone just stared at him. In particular, the Contessa glared—furious.

Bitino took another, closer look at his surroundings and his eyes opened wide in horror as he finally realized what he had done. The glamorous ballroom was now in ruins. Most of the priceless crystal chandeliers had been torn apart by the deadly wind he had conjured up. A few remnants dangled in tatters from ceiling hooks, but most chandeliers lay in pieces on the ballroom floor. Their candles had been scattered—but thankfully extinguished—by the combination of wind, snow, and rain. And what little light remained in the ballroom was no longer reflected off the gold leaf, which itself had been battered and torn by wind and by shards of ice as the storm pounded the walls.

Odaldi came back to the podium, picking his way carefully through the crystal fragments. "Bitino, wait over there—we will deal with you shortly." Several of the servants rushed out of the room, returning with candle stands so that there would at least be enough light to see by. Odaldi then motioned for everyone to resume their places in the ballroom. He waited until the onlookers found relatively clear spaces near the podium.

Whatever Odaldi planned to say was lost when the Master, Giambattista Della Porta, rushed into the ballroom. He was tall and thin and the little hair that remained on his mostly bald head was short and grey. The Master's beard was closely cropped, which did little to hide his perpetually grim expression. Della Porta usually dressed more formally for graduation ceremonies but on this occasion he was in his everyday attire, a ruffled white shirt and plain black breeches.

Della Porta spoke briefly to the Contessa. From where she stood, Chrymos could hear snatches of the conversation, but understood none of it. "—yōd ʾayin šīntāw wāw ʾaleprēš hētālepšīn nūnhēālep rēšyōdlāmed—" The senior staff often used this secret language, which they called

Mystikó, to talk with each other, to the frustration of many of the students.

Della Porta completed his conversation and then walked over to the podium. Surprisingly, he ignored the chaos in the room but simply addressed the assembly.

"Congratulations to our newest graduates." Della Porta led a brief round of applause. "Regrettably, we will need all of the new graduates to begin working at once. As you may be aware, our Alchemae teams are already involved in special missions. We have now received an urgent assignment that requires us to send today's newcomers on missions of their own."

Della Porta turned to the remaining students, his voice cutting through the hurried whispers that had resulted from his previous announcement. "We also need to advance our next graduation program. Father Carracci, your current group of students will be given their potions tomorrow rather than a year from now. We need them on the front line as soon as possible."

Chrymos' heart leapt. *Tomorrow? Finally! I doubt that I will get much sleep tonight.*

THIRTY-THREE
Academy of Secrets, Naples, Kingdom of Naples, Near Midnight, Wednesday April 7 1610

Chrymos tossed and turned, trying to quieten her overactive mind so that she could get at least some sleep.

When she finally started to doze, she immediately wished she hadn't. Somehow, she was sure that she was in a dream—but that knowledge gave Chrymos no comfort at all.

Olivia stood in front of her. The girl was once again the starving waif she had been when Chrymos had first found her outside the vice-regal palace. Once again, the little girl was clad in a tunic so flimsy that she must have been frozen to the bone.

Olivia's eyes were lifeless and her face, usually so animated, bore no expression at all. The question asked by this apparition sent a bolt of lightning through Chrymos' heart. "Was your power worth the price that we had to pay?"

In her dream, as perhaps in real life, Chrymos had no satisfactory answer to that question. She still could not find the words to explain why she had chosen the Academy over the children. "Wanting to make a difference" seemed so abstract and selfish, even to her.

Chrymos had questions of her own for Olivia. Even though Chrymos had traveled to the city every Sunday afternoon for most of the last three months, she had found no trace of any of the children. Even Madalena's estranged mother Catarina had claimed to have no idea where the three had gone. Chrymos had to ask, even if this was just a dream. "Olivia, where are you? Where are Sirus and Madalena?"

Dream-Olivia's answer reflected Chrymos' worst fears. "They're both dead, Chrymos. They died when you abandoned us, but their bodies took some time to rot."

That transformation began to happen to Olivia's own body as well—it started to disintegrate before Chrymos' very eyes. The child's arms and legs were the first to go, withering away and then turning to dust, sending what remained of Olivia's body crashing to the ground. Chrymos watched in horror, unable to move, as Olivia's torso collapsed in on itself, her ribcage giving way and breaking apart.

In a matter of moments, only the young girl's head remained—and even that was beginning to dissolve. Before it disappeared entirely, this phantom Olivia asked one final question. "Are you happy now, Chrymos?"

Chrymos woke with a start. After that nightmare, she dared not allow herself to go back to sleep.

Gaining those long-awaited powers no longer seemed a joyful prospect.

THIRTY-FOUR
Academy of Secrets, Naples, Kingdom of Naples, Morning, Thursday April 8 1610

The morning finally arrived. Chrymos' nightmare had extinguished any excitement she might have felt, but her determination was as strong as ever. If the world was indeed on the brink of the Lost War, whatever powers Chrymos gained she intended to use to protect the innocent—*which*, she desperately hoped, *includes Olivia, Sirus and Madalena.*

She didn't have to wait long. Directly after the morning meal, Chrymos and the five other members of her class were ushered into Giambattista Della Porta's office, where both Della Porta and Father Carracci were ready for them. The Master of the Academy was first to speak.

"As I have said on many occasions, we owe a great debt of thanks to the late Pope Gregory XIII. If he hadn't forced me to 'close down' the *Accademia dei Segreti* thirty years ago, it would have been but a pale shadow of what it has now become. Instead, operating in secrecy, without having to constantly seek approval from the Church, we have achieved so much more."

Father Carracci looks very unhappy about those comments, thought Chrymos, *but no-one else seems to have noticed.*

Della Porta continued. "You will all naturally be wondering why your class must graduate early." *Of course,* thought Chrymos—that had been virtually the sole topic of conversation amongst the students since the previous day's announcement.

Finally, Della Porta revealed all. "I have received word via the Janus twins of a new agreement, the Treaty of Bruzolo, which is due to be signed later this week by Charles Emmanuel I, Duke of Savoy, and King Henri IV of France. Under the terms of the treaty, Savoy and France have agreed to combine their forces to drive the Spanish Empire from the Kingdom of Naples and all the other Italian territory that Spain controls."

The six students gasped in shock. Naples had been directly under the control of the Spanish Empire for more than a century and its links to Spain through the Kingdom of Aragon stretched much further back, across many hundreds of years. This treaty would rewrite the map of Europe.

Della Porta wasn't finished. "This is an unprecedented situation. We need to take urgent action. I am sending Alchemae teams to France and Savoy immediately—but they may face stern opposition so I am appointing your class to provide additional reinforcements. As a result, those of you deemed ready will be given your dose of Exousía potion today."

The Master of the Academy, never one to display much emotion, was suitably matter-of-fact as he continued. "It is unfortunate that you were unable to complete your final year of training. Instead you will have to learn as you go along. The most important fact that you need to know is that your powers will fade if you do not receive a fresh dose of potion every few months."

A thought flashed through Chrymos' head. *No doubt you will only provide the Exousía potion to those who follow your orders. That explains why the older members of the Alchemae continue to do the Academy's bidding despite their impressive superpowers.*

That thought led her to another, more important concern. *How can I get enough potion to maintain my powers without having to rely on the Academy to provide it?*

Meanwhile, Della Porta continued his speech. "The second essential fact that you should know concerns the purpose of the Academy, especially now that France and Savoy have revealed their true intentions. You have already been reassured that we in the Academy are loyal citizens of the Spanish Empire. That is true—at least, insofar as our loyalty to Spain does not conflict with our far greater purpose, which is to bring about the restoration of the mighty Roman Empire. For more than five hundred years, the Roman Empire was the greatest power in the world. It shall reclaim that throne again."

The Master turned and bowed to the statue of the Emperor Nero, which was displayed proudly in his office. The sculptor had captured Nero on his knees, tears rolling down his cheeks, as he searched desperately through the rubble for survivors of the Great Fire that devastated more than half of Rome.

It's a magnificent work of art, conceded Chrymos. *It obviously reflects the Master's views about Nero, even if not everyone here shares that thinking.* She looked in particular at Father Carracci, who was trying to avoid reacting to Della Porta's speech. *I doubt he believes in the same cause.*

Della Porta stood and stretched out his arm in a traditional Roman salute, palm downward. "I honor you all. *Romae gloria aeterna est.* On behalf of the once and future Roman Empire, welcome to the Alchemae!"

Niccolo, Bartholomeo, and Salvator clapped politely, Ruben bowed in acknowledgement of the welcome. Adric and Chrymos looked at each other and both politely inclined their heads towards the Master.

As Father Carracci began to usher all the students out of the Master's office, Della Porta called out. "Your pardon, Father, I need to speak with you privately."

Carracci nodded, then beckoned to Ruben and passed over a handful of papers. "Take these to Doctor Odaldi—you'll find him in the Tower. As for the rest of you," Carracci continued, "wait for me at the Tower entrance."

THIRTY-FIVE
The Tower, Academy of Secrets, Naples, Kingdom of Naples, Morning, Thursday April 8 1610

It was known simply as "the Tower" and it was at least a thousand years older than the rest of the buildings that formed the Della Porta estate. It was, some said, the reason why Giambattista Della Porta's father had originally chosen the Capodimonte hill on which to build the family mansion. Other gossip disagreed, claiming that the elder Della Porta had striven mightily to remove the Tower from his land, but had died through his failure to do so. "A heart attack," murmured some. "A curse," whispered others.

Whatever the truth, the Tower persists today as it has for a thousand years, dark and foreboding, thought Chrymos as she and the others drew near the Tower's spell-protected entrance, accessible only from the top floor of the Della Porta mansion.

This was as close as she or her classmates had ever come to the Tower—not for lack of desire, but because the Tower's protective enchantments turned away unwelcome attention. Anyone who merely gazed upon the Tower would be stricken with dread and with an urgent wish to be somewhere else, anywhere else. To enter the Tower without permission was, they were taught, simply impossible—even lingering near the entrance was all but intolerable.

Chrymos could feel a powerful urging in her mind. *"Leave this place, leave this instant!"* She managed to keep her feelings in check, both because she knew she was authorized to be there and because she was so desperate to enter the Tower and take the next step towards her ultimate goal.

Chrymos looked around, judging how her classmates were reacting to the intense mental pressure.

Ruben, closest to the Tower entrance, looked distinctly uncomfortable. He clutched the papers entrusted to him by Father Carracci, which explained his proximity to the entranceway, but he shifted his balance from one foot to another, clearly disturbed by the Tower's enchantments. He looked up, saw Chrymos watching him and managed a brief wince of a greeting. Chrymos gave a pale smile in return.

Next, she sought out Adric, found him striding energetically around the antechamber whilst trying not to venture too close to the Tower entrance. He was transparently too bold for the circumstances and was likely trying to distract himself from the unpleasantness through action. *Is it working? I can't tell—but he's certainly going out of his way to avoid eye contact, so I suspect he really wants to run and hide as well,* she thought.

Out of the corner of her eye, Chrymos spotted Niccolo, Bartholomeo and Salvator. The three were as far from the Tower entrance as it was possible to stand and still be described as "waiting nearby." *A quiet "Boo" will send them running helter-skelter out of here,* she thought, almost but not quite inclined to trigger such a reaction. *If I'm going to be locked up with them for the next three weeks, it's probably best not to antagonize them any more than my presence here already does.*

There was a sudden clattering by the Tower entrance. The iron portcullis that physically barred entrance to the Tower was slowly raised and Doctor Odaldi emerged, having unlocked the oversized padlock that had secured the gate beyond.

He beckoned to the class. "Come, come, let's get started. Line up over here."

Odaldi waited impatiently while the six students reluctantly assembled close to the entranceway. The teacher then turned and began to head into the Tower itself. The students might have followed but the enchantment was too strong—they could not move any closer.

After a few moments, Odaldi re-emerged. He frowned at the six students but then realized his mistake. "How foolish of me. You haven't been given the *porta venenum*, have you?"

The students looked uncomprehending. Odaldi explained. "The entrance serum—it allows you into the Tower. Have you received it?"

The students shook their heads. Odaldi scurried away inside the Tower while the students tried desperately, but ultimately without success, to pretend that they were happy to stand so close to the Tower despite its strenuous efforts to chase them away.

Odaldi came back a few minutes later, clutching a vial of slightly-steaming liquid and a couple of goblets. He carefully poured a half-dozen drops into each goblet and handed the goblets to Adric and Ruben, the two students who were standing closest to him.

"This serum will admit you to the Tower. Its effect should last for the next two months, more than enough time for you to be cloistered—no, wait, we won't be able to do that with your class, will we?"

Adric and Chrymos exchanged glances. *Another disruption caused by the Treaty? We really will be on our own.*

Adric and Ruben emptied their goblets, held them out for Odaldi to refill. Adric then handed his refilled goblet to Chrymos, who took a deep breath and swallowed her share of the serum. It tasted as foul as anything she had forced herself to drink when she lived on the streets.

A few moments' pause—and then the mental oppression from the Tower vanished completely. Chrymos could think clearly for the first time since entering the antechamber.

She held out the goblet for Odaldi to pour a few more drops then passed the goblet to Salvator. Niccolo, who had received his goblet from Ruben, ministered likewise to Bartholomeo.

Suitably fortified, the six students were finally able to enter the lobby of the Tower, hot on the heels of Doctor Odaldi, who was clearly in a great hurry.

He waited impatiently until all were inside the lobby and then tugged firmly on the portcullis, dragging it down into place and then securing it with a chain and a giant padlock. *I hardly think that's necessary, given the enchantments,* thought Chrymos.

She took the opportunity to examine her new surroundings, which the protective spells had previously made impossible. Several flaming torches that did the best they could to illuminate the gloomy lobby.

Everywhere she looked, Chrymos saw darkness, an unrelieved blackness that was soul-absorbing even without the aid of mystical enchantments. The stone blocks that formed the Tower walls were of pure black obsidian rock, carved out whole, and then polished so smoothly that each block might have been a precious royal jewel.

As her eyes adjusted to the gloom, Chrymos could see a stone staircase three feet wide, that spiraled both upwards and downwards around a central core perhaps thirty feet in diameter.

At the lobby level the central core was empty but, as Chrymos and the others were soon to discover, other levels bristled with dangerous and forbidden treasures.

THIRTY-SIX
A Few Minutes Later
The Tower, Academy of Secrets, Naples, Kingdom of Naples, Morning, Thursday April 8 1610

Doctor Odaldi led the way up the stone steps, round and round the center core. Finally they reached their immediate destination, two levels up from the Tower lobby. "Come in, come in," said Odaldi, beaming with pleasure. "Now you can finally visit my laboratory." He ushered them into the room and waited for their reactions. He was not disappointed.

"Split my windpipe!" exclaimed Adric, in his surprise slipping into street slang. The object of his amazement was a room in which examples of the alchemists' trade covered every surface, claimed every wall, and even adorned the roof.

Unlike the gleaming black stone in the lobby, this room displayed the cumulative decay of a great many years of regular use. *The walls are encrusted with the after-effects of endless experiments—fragments of who knows what—perhaps the remains of victims who had reacted badly to past potions*, thought Chrymos. There were also scatterings of skin, bones, shells and other residue from creatures sacrificed in the Academy's name.

Chrymos' nose confirmed that this laboratory was also home to a great many unpleasant smells—pungent chemicals battled for supremacy against animal odors, stale sweat and the occasional fragrances from exotic plants, flowers and spices. Thankfully, fresh air came inside from somewhere and Chrymos found a spot where she could breathe more easily.

What was particularly curious was that the room was well-lit—yet there were no torches burning nor were there any windows. Chrymos turned to Odaldi. "Doctor, where is the light coming from?"

Odaldi smiled sheepishly. "Ah, yes, we had a little accident last month. One of the mixtures we were experimenting with proved a little too explosive and blew a large hole in the Tower wall over there." He pointed to a spot that looked exactly the same as all the other parts of the wall.

"The light you are seeing is simply sunshine from outside," Odaldi continued. "I should get the hole fixed, but I have to say I am enjoying the natural lighting. With all the alchemic elements in here, it can be very dangerous to light any candles or torches."

"So that part of the wall over there—" began Chrymos.

"—is an illusion that Apollinaris was kind enough to cast for me," Odaldi put his hand through the 'wall' to show that there was nothing there. "We could have just left the hole as it was—the Tower's enchantments keep everyone away, even the crows that might otherwise blunder inside—but the Contessa does love to see everything neat and tidy."

"I suppose we'll need to get the hole fixed before next winter," Odaldi said as he turned away, "a cold wind coming through the gap isn't much fun—but for now I'm really enjoying the sunshine." *Not to mention the fresh air*, added Chrymos to herself.

He clapped his hands together. "Now come along, take a look around before we get down to business."

Chrymos joined the others and surveyed her surroundings. Ancient wooden shelves stretched around the circular room that was Odaldi's laboratory. And as for those shelves—they housed mysteries such as Chrymos had never encountered before.

Human and animal skulls were a commonplace, dotted here and there. A few skulls appeared recently deceased, still bright and gleaming, but most were dull with age and wear. Most of the shelves were dominated by row upon row of glass jars, occupied by—*anything and everything. That jar contains a reddish powder that glows by itself,* she noted, *while its neighbor contains scorpion bodies—*

She jumped back in surprise when the creatures in the jar she was examining began moving of their own accord, scuttling around inside the jar and attempting to attack each other. One of the scorpions displayed cannibalistic tendencies as it killed and began to eat its companion. Chrymos shivered and moved on.

"Hey, C, did you see this snake?" That was Adric, mischievously drawing her attention to yet another large container, this one containing a silver-scaled coiled creature, hissing softly to itself. As Chrymos watched, the snake raised its head up high, nearly to the lid of the jar, and spread its neck-flap, exposing a deadly black mouth whilst its forked tongue flicked ominously. The swaying snake mesmerized Chrymos. She found herself unable to take her eyes away, which surely was the creature's intention because it suddenly spat at her. The venom sprayed harmlessly against the glass wall of the jar, but still Chrymos jumped.

"Ah, you like my little pet? I call it Cleopatra, in honor of the queen who made such good use of her own snakes," said Doctor Odaldi, who had silently made his approach. He smiled down at the snake. "This Cleopatra is a creation of my own, a cross-breed between a spitting cobra, whose venom is harmful but not usually deadly, and a speedy African serpent whose bite will kill in less than 48 hours. This little darling need not touch you to kill you—its poison will do its deadly worst from as much as a vara away." He stroked the jar. "We keep Cleopatra safely in the jar during the day but allow it free reign to protect my laboratory at nights."

Chrymos backed away from the snake, but Odaldi didn't seem to notice. He had turned his attention elsewhere, responding to a question from Ruben who, along with the other students, was now crowding around Odaldi. "Why would you need snakes to protect the laboratory, Doctor?" asked Ruben. "Surely there are enough safeguards, with the enchantments and the locks?"

"We take precautions that may seem excessive, Ruben, because we face enemies with supernatural powers of their own. And there are a great many dangerous secrets in this laboratory that must not fall into the wrong hands. This metal strip, for example—" Odaldi indicated a piece of metal in a tightly-sealed container. "—would burst into flames if we were to take it out of this jar."

"And these two liquids," said Odaldi, indicating two glass vials, one red and one black, "must always be kept far apart. Their combined effect is most corrosive—they can melt through solid iron in a heartbeat." Adric's interest was piqued by this announcement, Chrymos could see, and he was probably hoping for a demonstration.

Odaldi moved on and was now pointing out an oversized pair of metal gauntlets displayed on a pedestal. "According to Norse legend, these are called the *Járngreipr*, 'iron grippers'. Supposedly, the Norse god Thor needed the gauntlets to hold his mighty hammer *Mjolnir*. Our friends at New Phoenicia acquired them—I'm sure there's quite a story there, but I'm afraid I don't know it—and, for now anyway, they've loaned the iron gauntlets to our little collection." The assembled students made appropriate noises of appreciation.

Chrymos had never seen Doctor Odaldi so animated. Clearly, he delighted in showing off the wonders of the Tower. *This is his true passion*, she realized in that moment. *The Academy lectures are merely a distraction. No, worse—they're a real annoyance, because they take him away from his experiments and treasures in this room.*

Doctor Odaldi moved on to another section of the laboratory. "This," he said, lifting the veil from a pedestal on which an ornate green stone tablet was displayed, "is the most prized resource in my collection. It was thought destroyed in the third century by the plundering forces of the Roman emperor Diocletian, and yet here it is—the *Tabula Smaragdina*, the fabled Emerald Tablet of the great Egyptian adept king Hermes Trismegistus, who knew far more about alchemy three and a half thousand years ago than we have yet to rediscover in this modern age."

The doctor looked longingly at the intricate carvings on the tablet. "So far, we have only been able to translate about a quarter of these instructions."

The tablet was carved with intricate, mysterious shapes, reminiscent of Egyptian hieroglyphics and yet distinctive in their own manner.

"What language is this, Doctor?" asked Ruben.

"The sections that we can read are Phoenician," replied Odaldi. "As for the rest, we're not sure. We cannot read it all yet—and perhaps never will." He looked understandably upset as he replaced the veil over the tablet.

Chrymos, worried that the doctor would launch into even more endless demonstrations of his collected treasures, seized the moment. "Doctor, the Exousía potion—our powers—"

"Oh, right, right." Odaldi was instantly all business. "Now who has the paperwork?"

Ruben, still clutching the papers from Father Carracci, came forward and handed them over to the doctor.

"Thank you, Ruben. I must make sure that everything is in order. Master Della Porta is such a stickler for detail." Odaldi placed the papers on a nearby desk as he moved over to a small cabinet on the left hand side of his laboratory. The cabinet was locked, a problem that Odaldi remedied with the assistance of a key that hung on a chain around his neck. Chrymos took careful note of what he was doing. *If I'm going to steal enough potion to keep my powers indefinitely, I need to figure out how to break into that cabinet.*

Odaldi reached into the cabinet, removed a goblet and two glass vials and carefully measured out a dose from each vial, pouring each into the goblet.

"Two parts blue, one part yellow," Odaldi muttered to himself. "Mustn't mix that up." Chrymos carefully committed the formula to memory as well.

When the two liquids combined in the goblet, they snarled and hissed at each other, stirring up a froth that fought its way to the very rim of the goblet. "Quickly," Odaldi said to the students, "the Exousía potion does not contain itself for long. Now who's first?"

He looked down at the papers. "Adric, your authorization is right here. Drink this first dose, hurry now."

Adric, to his credit, merely gulped once before stepping up and drinking down the potion. "That," he said, coughing a little, "was truly horrible. As bad as choking down a cawdle when I'm sick."

Doctor Odaldi was the first to offer congratulations. "Well done, Adric, welcome. You're now officially a member of the Alchemae. Do you feel any different yet? Any powers bursting to come out?"

"How would I know?" said Adric.

Odaldi shrugged. "It's hard to describe, because the process is different for each person. Some say it's like an itch that they need to scratch. Others, well, there are changes inside their heads. When your tutor, Father Carracci, first received his powers, he didn't even realize that he had changed. It was only when others saw him—or, rather, didn't see him—that he finally understood that he had acquired the power of invisibility."

Chrymos' jaw dropped. "You mean it? Father Carracci can walk around and not be seen?"

"Oh yes." Odaldi managed a wry smile. "You can't imagine how useful the power of invisibility can be for a school teacher—or perhaps you can, if you've ever been on the receiving end of a punishment for a misdemeanor that you thought Father Carracci couldn't possibly know about.

"There are two important points that you should all note. Firstly, there are always physical limits to your powers. The more energy that your power requires, the shorter the duration for which that power can be used. Even your tutor cannot remain invisible for more than an hour at a time, or he will collapse from exhaustion."

Odaldi turned back to Adric. "Anything?"

"No, I don't feel any different yet. How long should I expect to wait?"

Another shrug from Odaldi. "That depends. The longest I've seen anybody wait was six months—but during that period the poor fellow had grown an entire new brain inside his body, which was supposed to double his intellectual capacity but in reality meant that conflicting impulses constantly kept him paralyzed. We had to put him out of his misery, once we realized what was happening. Pity—it could have been a most interesting experiment."

Odaldi managed a vaguely sympathetic smile and then reviewed the papers on his desk. "Bartholomeo, it's your turn."

Niccolo and Salvator watched nervously as Odaldi mixed another batch of Exousía potion and handed it over to Bartholomeo. Chrymos also watched carefully. *Bartholomeo is so bold when he has the backing of his Napoletano classmates,* she thought. *Will he be able to manage this on his own?*

Remarkably, Bartholomeo proved equal to the task, barely hesitating before imbibing the spitting, violent potion. He tipped the goblet high, drained it with a single, fierce draught and then thrust the goblet back into Odaldi's hands.

All eyes were on Bartholomeo. At first, he simply stood, unmoving. After a minute or so, his torso writhed, his face briefly contorted in pain. And then, then—he stretched out one long arm, palm open, towards a wooden shelf. The shelf—shuddered, wavered, then from several knotholes came swiftly-growing tendrils, reaching out to Bartholomeo, expanding into branches and even blossoming with leaves and buds as they grew towards him. The branches touched Bartholomeo, thickened, grew more and yet more branches until it seemed as if there was a forest around the young student.

Odaldi clapped with delight. "A wood wizard, we have a wood wizard among us, one who can manipulate the timbers of buildings and forests to do his bidding! Respect, Bartholomeo, you are welcome indeed into the Alchemae. Now rest, wood wizard, and let others learn their own fate."

Bartholomeo relaxed, stood down and went to chat quietly with Niccolo and Salvator while Odaldi went back to his paperwork. Chrymos walked over and examined the new branches that had somehow grown from centuries-old wood. They looked indistinguishable from normal tree branches, except that they protruded from ancient knotholes.

"Ruben," called Odaldi, "you're next." Again, the two warring ingredients were combined. Again, the designated student consumed the tempestuous brew. Again, all eyes turned to the subject of the experiment. Again, the object of their attention stood motionless.

And then, almost without warning, Ruben—flickered. His shape—changed, reduced, flowed. His blond hair darkened, lengthened, straightened. His face, normally almost cherubic, narrowed, became old and wrinkled. In short, Ruben had become a mirror image of Doctor Odaldi—facial features, hair color and length the same, identical in every physical aspect. Only his clothing remained unchanged. Ruben had even become the same height as the doctor—slightly shorter than Ruben's normal height. Ruben opened his eyes, which were now identical to Doctor Odaldi, and smiled—but his smile was no longer Ruben's but rather Odaldi's. *Ruben even has exactly the same mannerisms as the Doctor. He's like an identical twin,* thought Chrymos.

Odaldi—the real Odaldi—froze. He was clearly both delighted and appalled. Finally, the delight overcame any concerns and Odaldi clapped, even more heartily than before. "Bravo, Ruben, bravo, you have become a chameleon. Oh what a talent that is! Welcome, cousin, welcome to the Alchemae." He paused. "But do," he added hastily, "do change back to yourself, before we become completely befuddled and forget our respective places."

Ruben looked, as surely Odaldi might in similar circumstances, momentarily confused. And then he did indeed change back, his appearance flickering briefly as he reverted back to himself. Chrymos and Adric hustled over. "Well done, Ruben," offered Chrymos, while Adric pounded Ruben's back. "How much control do you have over your mimicry?" asked Chrymos.

"Enough to choose my target, so long as I have a clear image of that person fixed in my mind," advised Ruben. "But," he admitted, "I doubt that I can maintain the impersonation for very long, it does require a large amount of energy to copy someone so exactly."

Whilst the trio talked, Salvator was chosen as the next candidate. He proceeded to down his potion enthusiastically, having seen the results in evidence thus far.

Alas, like Adric, Salvator was destined to be disappointed—his new power stubbornly refused to manifest itself. Odaldi muttered reassuring words. "It will come, in due course, no need to worry, Salvator. I bid you welcome to the Alchemae, we will uncover your new skills in due course."

Niccolo was next. He too swallowed the turbulent potion, awaited the arrival of his new power. At first, nothing seemed to be happening. And then Salvator spoke up, irritated. "Niccolo, get out of my head!"

It soon became apparent that Niccolo had acquired the ability to bombard others with his thoughts—though it seemed he could send his thoughts to just one person at a time. And transmission was one-way. Niccolo could send, but if the recipient had no telepathic powers, Niccolo could not hear their thoughts.

Odaldi was pensive as he issued the traditional welcome. "Your power is an interesting one, Niccolo, we need to consider how best to harness it. Still, be welcomed, the Alchemae take pleasure in your company."

And then, finally, it was Chrymos' turn to receive the potion. But Odaldi hesitated.

"I have no papers for you, Chrymos. I'm sorry, I cannot administer the Exousía potion to you without proper authorization."

THIRTY-SEVEN
Moments Later
**The Tower, Academy of Secrets, Naples, Kingdom of Naples,
Morning, Thursday April 8 1610**

Chrymos was shocked. "What? You can't deny me! I have worked so hard for this."

Odaldi was sympathetic but unyielding. "I'm sure it's merely an oversight, Chrymos. Father Carracci probably has your papers but in all the haste of the last few days has neglected to pass them to Ruben. Salvator, would you be so kind as to slip downstairs and explain the problem to Father Carracci?"

Salvator looked unimpressed at being delegated this menial task but could think of no valid reason to refuse. He reluctantly headed downstairs to talk to the class tutor.

Chrymos had no choice but to wait. She sat in the laboratory, desperately unhappy, while Doctor Odaldi showed the other students more of his treasures.

She did pay careful attention, however, when Adric asked the doctor a question. "Doctor Odaldi, you mentioned earlier that there were two important points we should note, but you only talked about one of them."

"Did I?" said Odaldi. "Which one did I mention?"

"The physical limits to our powers," replied Ruben.

"Oh yes," said Odaldi, "and that's a very important limitation. That's why we allow three weeks for you to learn all about your powers. Well—usually," he added.

"And the second point, Doctor?" prompted Adric.

"Right, right," said Odaldi. "Simply that most of the powers bestowed by the Exousía potion tend to have unwanted side effects of some sort. And it's become apparent that the more potent the powers you receive, the worse the side effects are likely to be. Again, we usually explore those possibilities during the three-week study period."

Chrymos looked over at Niccolo and Bartholomeo who were whispering animatedly to each other. *I bet I know what they're saying,* she thought. *They're probably saying something like "they might have told us much earlier. Some of us might have thought twice about drinking the potion."*

To Chrymos the wait seemed like an eternity, but it was perhaps just twenty minutes until Salvator returned, accompanied by Father Carracci. The tutor did not look pleased.

He spoke harshly to the assembled students. "You were instructed to wait for me at the entrance to the Tower. Which part of 'wait' did you not understand?"

Odaldi came to the students' rescue. "I fear the mistake was mine, Father. I invited them into the Tower, so that we might proceed quickly with the initiation ceremonies."

Carracci looked at Odaldi, bit back what he had intended to say. Instead, he said "That is—unfortunate. I had planned to send up only five of the six students today. He turned to Chrymos. "In my opinion, you're not ready. You will not be receiving any potion today."

Chrymos had been shocked earlier. Now she was furious. "How can you say I'm not ready? I've worked every waking hour to prepare for this. You've seen my performance—and my work!"

Carracci was unrepentant. "You've had just three months' training. These others—" He pointed to Salvator, Niccolo, and Bartholomeo. "—have had three years."

Chrymos virtually shouted at him. "Adric and Ruben have also only had three months. They were brought here at the same time as me. Why am I the solitary one held back? The Contessa herself predicted that I would play a vital role in the Lost War, once I have my powers. "

"So I understand," agreed Carracci, "but her prediction didn't say exactly when. And you certainly won't be given any potion until I decide that you're ready. It's my decision. Yes, your marks are adequate—but emotionally you simply don't make the grade. You don't have the killer instinct necessary to fight this war. In fact, I'm not sure that you ever will."

Chrymos responded calmly, quietly. "Alright then, give me a test. Whatever you like. If I pass, I get the potion immediately. If not—" She shrugged, pretending a composure she did not feel.

"Very well." Carracci smiled in anticipation. "Be ready—we leave tomorrow."

"Leave? To go where?"

"You'll see," smirked Carracci. "You did say you would do anything."

THIRTY-EIGHT
The Road from Naples to Pisa,
Early Evening, Friday April 9 1610

Nekhbet smiled to herself as she caught up with the carriage carrying Chrymos and the Dominican priest Carracci to its mysterious destination. The carriage, emblazoned with the seal of the Kingdom of Naples, had been a gift to the Academy from a well-placed senior official at the vice-regal court—*which will make him a good blackmail prospect in the future*, thought Nekhbet.

Nekhbet knew exactly where the carriage was heading, although it was a mystery to Chrymos. *Strange how much the Lost War depends on Chrymos and her choices*, Nekhbet mused. *If she has the courage to stand up for what she believes, we win—and she will lose everything.*

Nekhbet smiled again as she looked down through the scattered clouds at the horse and carriage trotting along the road. Carracci sat in front, ignoring Chrymos, who was in the back seat, seeing but not really noticing the countryside. *It will take ten days for them to get from Naples to Pisa by road. If the priest won't speak to her, Chrymos is going to have a slow, unpleasant journey.*

For the next few minutes, Nekhbet flew above the carriage, watching Chrymos as a lion stalks an antelope. Then Nekhbet stretched out her mighty black wings and flew off towards her next destination, a place she had wanted to visit for centuries, the underwater city of New Phoenicia

THIRTY-NINE
The Margus River, Moesia,
Early afternoon, pridie Idus Iulias (July 14) 285 AD

It was the calm before the storm. Machkiel sat quietly in the imperial tent, lost in thought. Diocletian dealt with the occasional messages that arrived from the front, where Carinus's forces continued to hold out, but the emperor was much more concerned with what would happen when night fell.

The quiet of the afternoon was interrupted by a disturbance outside—a challenge from the guards, strenuous arguments from whoever was approaching. The flap of the tent opened and a guard entered and prostrated himself before the emperor.

"Yes, yes," grumbled Diocletian, "what is it?"

"It's the Christian leader, Bishop Januarius," ventured the guard nervously, "requesting an urgent audience with you, mighty Caesar."

Diocletian snapped back. "Tell him to go away, we're not interested in him or his pestilent Christian religion."

Machkiel, who a few moments earlier had received a mind-call from Jesse, intervened. "Wait. Jesse says—uh, said—that we should listen to Januarius."

Two pairs of eyes stared at Machkiel in disbelief—Diocletian, surprised that the Outcast Angel would interfere, and the guard shocked that a mere commoner would dare to interrupt the emperor.

Then Diocletian relented. "Oh very well, let him in." The emperor glared at Machkiel, as if to say "this had better be good".

The guard withdrew and then, a few moments later, returned with Januarius. The Christian leader, dressed in a simple white robe, was carrying a white shield marked with a ragged red cross. With a little encouragement from the guard, Januarius knelt down and bowed low to Diocletian, muttering softly to himself "render unto Caesar what is Caesar's."

Still irritated, Diocletian questioned the new arrival. "What do you want?"

"Mighty Caesar," began the bishop, "forgive me for disturbing you. My mission here is not with you but with your companion. I bring him the shield of Evalach for his protection tonight."

Machkiel's mouth dropped open. He didn't know what to say. Diocletian, however, wanted to know more. "What's so special about this shield of—Evalark, you called it?"

"Evalach. He was a Saracen king who lived two and a half centuries ago. He was given the shield by Josephus of Arimathea, the man who provided his own tomb to bury the body of our Savior, Jesus Christ."

An intense stare from Diocletian warned Januarius not to dwell on the subject of religious beliefs. The bishop quickly continued his explanation.

"It was Josephus who painted this red cross upon the shield with his own blood. It is said that this shield grants the owner heavenly protection."

Machkiel finally found his voice. "No, your grace, I cannot accept this shield. I'm not worthy."

"Are any of us on this Earth worthy? And yet the Lord gave this shield and the protection of Heaven to Evalach, a mere mortal who had also sinned and fallen short of the Kingdom of Heaven. Surely you must be at least as unworthy as a fallen human?"

Machkiel might have disputed the point, but a sudden mind-whisper from Jesse told him he should just accept the gift. Reluctantly, he did so, thanking the bishop for his thoughtfulness.

After Januarius had left, Diocletian couldn't help but ask. "An angel needs a shield?"

"Apparently."

Quiet returned to the imperial tent as both Diocletian and Machkiel lost themselves in thought. Each minute that passed brought the impending battle that much closer.

FORTY
Spinalonga, Crete,
2 a.m. Saturday April 10 1610

Nekhbet landed lightly near the blockhouse that guarded the northernmost point of the island of Spinalonga. She was on high alert, chakram poised and ready to throw, because the Venetian guards manning the blockhouse should have seen her clearly in the light from the full moon.

Nekhbet need not have worried. A minute passed and then a figure emerged from the blockhouse and crossed casually to stand in front of her, relaxed, deliberately unthreatening.

Nekhbet inspected the man who stood so unconcernedly facing her, where many would have quaked with fear. He seemed still relatively young in human years, perhaps four decades at most. His face, clean-shaven but for a pencil-thin moustache, was largely unlined.

The man's dark curly hair, little constrained by his plumed hat, cascaded untidily to his shoulders where it met a billowing cloak and ill-fitting white shirt. Two pistols were jammed into a sash around his waist, accompanied by a loosely-suspended sword belt. Dark breeches and sturdy boots completed his wardrobe.

"Captain Easton?" Nekhbet asked the question, although she had little doubt about the answer.

"At your service, Darke Warrior." The new arrival bowed low, removing his hat in an elaborate gesture probably acquired when the now-pirate was still in the service of Queen Elizabeth of England. "Welcome to Spinalonga, gateway to New Phoenicia. I regret that we cannot linger here. We need to begin our journey as soon as possible, we still have many hours ahead of us."

"Lead the way," replied Nekhbet, dissolving her wings and relaxing her hold on the chakram.

Together they walked down past the ruins of an old acropolis, arriving in due course at what appeared to be a sheer rock wall.

"*'ayinpē hēnūn dālet 'ayin 'ayinrēš*" Easton addressed the incantation to the wall, which responded by cracking open to reveal a towering stone door. The pirate captain pushed against the door, which swung open quietly and surprisingly easily given its size and weight.

Nekhbet followed Easton inside, into a stone chamber lit by flickering torches. The room was empty except for a stairwell on the left that led downward.

The captain beckoned to Nekhbet to follow and headed over to the stairway. As Easton's foot touched the first step, the entrance door began to move smoothly back into place, closing off access to the outside world.

FORTY-ONE
Spinalonga, Crete,
Shortly after 2 a.m. Saturday April 10 1610

Nekhbet followed Easton down the winding stairway, which descended further and further into the depths of the earth. Finally, several hundred feet down, the stairway opened into a large chamber.

Easton walked briskly towards a horse-drawn coach that stood waiting at the entrance to what appeared to be a tunnel—evidently one large enough to allow the coach to pass through.

Nekhbet strode over to the coach and then stopped abruptly—the 'horse' at the front of the coach was not a real animal. Yes, it was roughly horse-shaped, but instead of limbs it had metal bars, cogs, gears, and wheels. Instead of a torso, it had a barrel. And its head was a glass jar with a brightly-glowing candle inside.

Nekhbet looked over at the pirate captain in confusion.

He was grinning from ear to ear. "Isn't it great? It's one of our mechanical horses. They're much more practical for pulling these carriages through the tunnels. They don't get tired or hungry or spooked by the darkness, and they can gallop at about three times the speed of real horses."

Easton pulled open the coach door. "In you get. I'll sit on the left, that's where the levers are to control the horse. Not that it needs much controlling," he added as the pair made themselves comfortable in the coach. "These carriages are designed to slot exactly into the tunnels, so there's no need to steer. The 'horse' goes only one way, forward. Its body is fastened to the carriage, which in turn is guided by the slots in the tunnel walls."

Nekhbet watched closely as the mechanical creature began to move forward, mimicking the movements of a real horse but steadily gaining speed until it was galloping along at a considerable pace. "Where did it come from," she asked. "What powers it?"

Easton smiled. "I use it but I don't know all that much about it," he admitted. "I gather that we stole the initial designs from the celebrated inventor Leonardo da Vinci, and then our people refined them into this. As for the power—I think the Academy of Secrets helped us with that."

Nekhbet soon tired of asking questions when it became obvious that the pirate had very little idea exactly how the mechanical marvel operated. There wasn't much to see on the journey either, just mile after mile of tunnel, barely illuminated by the horse's candle-powered head.

In the end, Nekhbet sat back, closed her eyes, and exchanged mind-messages with her fellow Darke Warriors.

Several hours later, the pair arrived at New Phoenicia.

FORTY-TWO
Underwater City of New Phoenicia,
8 a.m. Saturday April 10 1610

Even the supposedly blasé inhabitants of New Phoenicia, the impossible underwater city, were startled by the arrival of a real-life demon. They scuttled out of the way as the Darke Warrior Nekhbet emerged from the coach that had conveyed her to the city. She was so tall and so threatening in her all-encompassing armor that her mere presence—along with the pungent brimstone stench—served to clear her path, no small accomplishment in a city populated by the world's lowlifes.

Captain Easton ushered his guest into the main corridor that connected the coach terminal to the city center. "The coach-tunnel network is not much more than a hundred years old, but the city itself is far older. It dates back nearly two thousand years—" Easton paused for the usual expressions of disbelief that first-time visitors always muttered at this point. Nekhbet was not so easily impressed—she merely raised an eyebrow.

The pirate captain, caught by surprise by his guest's minimalist reaction, attempted to rework his usual tour guide pitch. "Yes, I know, it's, umm, interesting. But the first part of the city was originally built as a refuge around 300 B.C. by the race that the ancient Greeks called the Phoenicians but who were better known to our Oldest Enemy as the Canaanites."

This latest announcement elicited polite murmurings from Nekhbet. She had heard all about those battles from other Darke Warriors.

Easton continued. "New Phoenicia was originally founded by the descendants of the people driven out of the so-called Promised Land in the thirteenth century B.C. by the Jews. The Canaanites resettled on the coast and over the next thousand years became brilliant seafarers and traders. Unfortunately, they were cruelly attacked by Alexander of Macedon—Alexander the 'Great', so-called—in 332 BC, and driven from

Phoenicia as well. That's when they built the first part of this city."

Nekhbet was mildly interested. "How could the Phoenicians build an underwater city, with the few tools that they had two thousand years ago?"

Easton parried this common objection. "You only have to look at the pyramids to see that the ancients weren't as helpless as we modern-day citizens believe them to be. From what our records show, the Phoenicians started with hollow, bell-shaped devices that they lowered into the water from their ships. The diving bells, open at the bottom, contained plenty of air, so that divers could use them as a basecamp, to dive deeper, and stay down longer while they looked for a suitable trench. They wanted a new home that their enemies could never discover."

"Obviously they found their trench," said Nekhbet. "Then what?"

"Then, according to our records, they hauled enormous rocky slabs from the shore and lowered them into place to create a roof over the first trench. From what we can gather, it took as many as ten Phoenician ships harnessed together to haul some of the slabs in place. Quite a few of the Phoenicians' ships were lost to Mediterranean storms, but after about ten years, they finally had the trench covered over. They then sent down divers to plug the gaps between the slabs, to make the trench as watertight as possible."

"Very inventive," said Nekhbet. "But then all they'd have is a covered-over trench full of water."

"True," agreed Easton. "But while the main group was covering over the trench, another group was digging connecting tunnels from the mainland. Now that was an engineering feat to compare with the pyramids! I know they lost thousands of men during the digging, and many tunnels simply collapsed from the water pressure. But eventually, I have no idea how, they managed to dig down deep enough, or maybe found the right sort of soil to dig through, to avoid the tunnels flooding with water. They would have had to dig through solid rock in many places, using primitive tools. Finally, after about thirty years of continuous tunneling, they broke through to the trench. Unfortunately, when the breakthrough came, the water from the trench poured out into the tunnel, drowning more than fifty of the Phoenicians working on the excavation—including the man who had dreamed up the whole idea."

Easton shrugged. "Still—they succeeded. Once the survivors had drained the tunnel and the rest of the trench, they were able to use that as a base for the city. They dug out a number of shafts around the trench, most of which we still use today. In fact, here—" Easton had timed his speech to perfection, reaching a fork in the corridor at precisely the right point. "—here we find ourselves in the oldest part of New Phoenicia."

The left-hand corridor led to a section carved out of solid rock. Easton paused a few moments to point out where the city's original excavators had excelled themselves. "You'll notice these gaps in the walls, where the Phoenicians placed oil lamps to light the way. They carved out the gaps using chisels made of Damascus steel—if we get the chance, I'll show you some of the chisels, we have a couple in our archive on Level Six."

"Steel?" asked Nekhbet, "In 300 BC?"

"It came from India," replied Easton. "The Phoenicians were amazing traders. Supposedly they had regular dealings with India and had acquired some very useful resources as a result."

The tour continued through the older part of the city, arriving next at the original trench. Nekhbet looked up at the roof with some trepidation. Easton reassured her. "We've replaced the rock slabs with more durable materials over the centuries. No need to worry, we're no longer one seaquake away from catastrophe."

Because of the manner in which this part of the city had been built around the trench, Nekhbet could look both up and down from her current vantage point, three layers deep.

Easton explained what they were seeing. "The coach terminal connects with New Phoenicia at the third level. The city itself now goes down six levels and we have room to descend beyond that if that should become necessary. Level One is the Command Level, Levels Two and Four are for living quarters, Level Three, which we're currently on, is for offices and work areas, as well as transportation. Level Five is for—" Easton paused, unsure if he should mention the prison facilities which dominated that level. He quickly decided against doing so.

"Level Five, as I was saying, is for administration, and Level Six, that's storage and archives, along with our alchemic facilities. That's where we take water and turn it into two types of air. One we use for breathing, the other for—well, let's just say that we use it to make our enemies burn."

"Burning air? Isn't that dangerous down here?" asked Nekhbet.

"I don't pretend to understand what's involved," admitted Easton. "If you really want to know the details, I'm sure I could get one of our alchemists—"

"No need," said Nekhbet hastily. "It's not important. One question I'm sure you'll be able to answer for me, though," she added. "Is New Phoenicia still connected to Naples, Spain, France, and England through various tunnels?"

"Of course," said Easton, "that's how we can send our people where they need to go so rapidly."

"Good," said Nekhbet. "Those tunnels will become vitally important in the Lost War."

Satisfied that she had seen enough, Nekhbet turned to her companion. "Now take me to your leader."

FORTY-THREE
Ten days later
Leaning Tower of Pisa, Duchy of Tuscany [Italy], Midday Tuesday April 20 1610

The summit of the famous Leaning Tower of Pisa bustled with people, all seemed to be chattering loudly at the same time—but even so, Chrymos heard Father Carracci clearly enough. She simply couldn't believe what she was hearing. She looked back at the priest, stunned. "You're asking me to push Galileo off the top of this tower?"

"I'm not asking you, Chrymos, I'm ordering you," said Carracci. "What's the matter? Squeamish? I thought you said you were prepared to do 'anything' to become one of the Alchemae?"

Chrymos nodded, still in shock. Yes, she had indeed indicated that she would take on any task, no matter how onerous, to become one of the chosen. But she had never expected this.

Her tutor persisted. "Then follow orders. Carry out the task that I have given you. This is the one chance you have to remain in the Academy and receive the Exousía potion."

Chrymos felt compelled to ask again. "You really want me to push that man off the top of this tower?"

"Silence, Chrymos! Whisper as if you were sharing sweet nothings with your lover. The people over there may not be able to see us but they are not deaf."

One push is surely all it will take to push Galileo off the Leaning Tower to his death eight floors below. But am I actually prepared to kill anyone, especially this poor man? From what she had heard from the noisy students around her, Galileo Galilei was nobody special—just a mathematics professor from the University of Padua.

Chrymos and her tutor stood amongst the bells near the summit of the Leaning Tower, about a dozen paces behind Galileo and his students.

Father Carracci had abandoned his usual friar's outfit for this journey and wore a loose-fitting, plain linen shirt and tan breeches over tall, narrow boots. His shoulder-length blond hair and his beard remained neatly trimmed. When they first began the trip from Naples, Chrymos had been extremely surprised to note that the priest was wearing a sword in his belt, a most unusual choice for a man of the cloth. Upon further reflection, however, she realized that the sword was an integral part of his disguise.

For the moment though, no protective camouflage was needed. Here on the top of the Leaning Tower, despite the midday summer sun, Chrymos and Carracci could not be seen, thanks to the tutor's alchemy-gifted ability to make himself—and whatever he touched—invisible.

Chrymos continued to wrestle with the instruction given by Father Carracci a moment ago. He could see that she was struggling to obey the order, so he spoke firmly to her again. "Chrymos, you know that if you want to join the Alchemae, you must carry out your designated task. I can finally reveal that task: in a few minutes, when Galileo attempts to drop a cannonball and musket ball from the tower, you must ensure that he is the one who falls. It should only take you a single shove."

Chrymos glanced over at the group of students clustered around Galileo. From what she had been able to gather from the students' conversations during the disorienting climb to the top of the Leaning Tower, they were all from his university mathematics classes. When word spread that Galileo might be leaving the University of Padua to take up a post with the Grand Duke of Tuscany, the students had begged their professor for one final favor. Would he replicate his fabled experiment of twenty years prior: dropping a musket ball and a cannonball together from the top of the tower?

Obviously, Galileo had agreed. Unfortunately, that led to the here and now, where she was expected to kill him.

"Why?" Chrymos whispered to her tutor. "Why do you want this man dead? From what those students were saying, he's simply a mathematics professor."

"Isn't that reason enough? Have you never been so angry with a teacher that you wished him dead? From what I can recall from some of my classes, I think you have."

Carracci had an unexpected twinkle in his eye as he spoke, and Chrymos thought for a hopeful moment that the whole "kill Galileo" order was only a sick joke. Then Carracci continued talking.

"It's not who Galileo is, it's what he's about to do that matters. Last year, he developed a spyglass that enables people to see clearly at long distances. The Contessa has predicted that he will shortly provide such devices to the Outcast Angels, which will aid them greatly in the Lost War. We need to stop him before—wait, the students are heading downstairs to watch the experiment. Get ready to make your move."

The students were gingerly beginning to make their return journey down the Leaning Tower's well-worn stairs, so that they could witness the cannonball and musket ball landing together in the courtyard below. *Or at least that's what they're expecting to see*, thought Chrymos. *Instead*—she could not bring herself to finish the thought.

The students gathered near the top of the stairs, laughing and gesturing as they waited their turn to descend the narrow stairwell. Shortly, Galileo would be alone. Chrymos looked over at the professor. *Him or me*, she told herself, *I have to choose between his future and mine.*

She tried to steady herself for the hideous task ahead—even though her every instinct cried out in protest.

FORTY-FOUR
The Margus River, Moesia,
Dusk, pridie Idus Iulias (July 14) 285 AD

Diocletian's soldiers were dreading nightfall. As the last rays of the setting sun threatened to abandon the valley walls, they looked around fearfully. They were some of the Roman Empire's finest soldiers, but they were facing a horror far beyond any of their experiences. It had already been a long day for most—Carinus' soldiers had attacked in wave after wave, no doubt heartened by the demonic support that they had enjoyed the previous night.

The first sign that the demon had returned came quickly. At the furthest reaches of the valley, where Diocletian's army had fought mostly fiercely to claim their ground, fresh sounds of fighting rang out. Shouts and cries of pain intermingled with the clash of swords and the unmistakable thud of the demon's axe as it sliced through the bodies of too many Roman soldiers.

Marcus Augustus was as ready as any military man could expect to be in such circumstances. He had kept several hundred soldiers in reserve, in accordance with Machkiel's instructions, and he dispatched two hundred of them, led by one of his most trusted centurions, to the scene of the latest outbreak.

While that was happening, Machkiel waited for more complete darkness. He and Diocletian had agreed that, if Diocletian's soldiers had seen the Outcast Angel fly from the emperor's tent, they might become even more unsettled and perhaps abandon the fight.

Machkiel was dressed in a light mail shirt that one of the emperor's guardsmen had provided, which he had slipped on over the top of his usual calf-length grey robe. His two concessions to the battle ahead were a gladius—a simple sword sheathed in a belt that dangled over one shoulder—and Evalach's shield, strapped to the Outcast Angel's back.

By the time the reservists had reached the battle scene, Ezequeel had slaughtered most of the soldiers holding that position and was preparing to move further up the valley. Instead, the arrival of fresh victims gave him pause. The Darke Warrior wiped his blood-soaked blades on a nearby corpse and prepared to welcome the new arrivals.

Machkiel quietly slipped past the sentries guarding the imperial tent and found a spot from which he could depart unobserved. He summoned his wings, launched himself into the night air, and flew swiftly around the edge of the valley, aiming to attack Ezequeel from the demon's flank. From the screams and shouts below, Machkiel could hear that the battle was going about as badly as could be expected, given its one-sided nature. Machkiel hovered in place, ready for the next phase.

The centurion gave the prearranged signal and the surviving soldiers swarmed towards the demon, each carrying flaming torches that would illuminate the area. As a result Machkiel could see the demon clearly.

Machkiel timed his descent carefully, aiming to arrive just before the demon concluded that there were too many soldiers and decided to disappear.

Machkiel very nearly missed his chance. The Darke Warrior began to fade as Machkiel reached him. Fortunately, the Outcast Angel was close enough to seize Ezequeel's arm, and Machkiel too began to fade.

A moment or an eternity later, both arrived together in Nowhen.

FORTY-FIVE
Nowhen

Nowhen—a place outside of time, outside of space. An infinite environment inhabited by Kingdom Angels, from whence they could observe the whole of Creation and then travel instantly to any day, any place, to fulfil the Word.

A human description of Nowhen would necessarily fail—but think of it, perhaps, as an endless Garden of Eden. Trees and plants of every shade and hue, watched over not by a few meagre stars but by boundless light pouring in from the entire universe.

After the failed Rebellion, all the rebels had been barred from Nowhen, and if they lingered for very long, both Ezequeel and Machkiel would soon be evicted.

Ezequeel was stunned. He found himself facing a full-blown angel. "How did you—?" he began, then instantly realized. "Of course, you're one of the Outcasts. I should have realized that someone like you would be hanging around a loser like Diocletian. You've chosen the wrong side, Outcast, Diocletian will be history when I bring back the true emperor."

All the while that he was speaking, Ezequeel was preparing to jump again. He had simply been waiting to allow the healing environment of Nowhen to minister to his various bruises and cuts, including one particularly deep slash that a lucky soldier had inflicted after slipping past Ezequeel's defenses.

Machkiel had been watching Ezequeel closely. *If he makes the jump without me, I'll never be able to return to exactly the same when and where we left.* To distract the demon, Machkiel attempted to engage him in conversation.

"Where did you get the pathgem? I thought that it was lost when Sanctuary fell."

Ezequeel was in no mood to provide any information. He simply ignored the question and began to fade back into time.

Machkiel lunged desperately and managed to grasp a small corner of

Ezequeel's axe before the Darke Warrior disappeared completely.

An instant later, both Ezequeel and Machkiel reappeared at the river's edge and then their battle began in earnest.

FORTY-SIX
Leaning Tower of Pisa, Duchy of Tuscany,
1 p.m. Tuesday April 20 1610

The final group of students left the top of the Leaning Tower and began making their way down the spiraling stairs. Carracci turned to Chrymos. "It's time."

Chrymos froze. Finally, when it came to the moment of truth, she knew. She would not, could not, commit murder. Not even to fulfil her destiny. She confessed to Carracci. "I can't do it."

Carracci had expected that Chrymos would fail and he had planned accordingly. He turned towards her and whispered several unintelligible sounds into her ear.

"Pēhēt rēshēhē zayinhē. Dālet 'ayin 'ālepçādē tāw 'ayin lāmeddālet."

Chrymos instantly lost control of her own body. She tried to speak, to shout, but she could not. She could not move a single muscle. Instead, she was a helpless passenger as Carracci's spell triggered some primal impulse and she found herself helplessly following his directions, like a marionette at the mercy of a puppet-master.

For Chrymos, the next few seconds seemed to crawl. Her mind continued to scream 'No' but her body disobeyed. It shuddered forward, step by unwanted step towards Galileo, driven not by her will but by the movements of her tutor.

Every step caused her great discomfort, her muscles driven against her will, as she fought against Carracci. The priest paced alongside her, his iron grip on her shoulder ensuring that she remained both compliant and invisible.

As Carracci's right arm reached out, Chrymos felt her right arm do likewise—*no! no! stop! stop!*—towards an unsuspecting Galileo, just as he turned to peer over the very edge of the tower.

With every fiber of her being, Chrymos fought to reclaim her body, to prevent it being used for this heinous purpose. Catching Carracci by surprise, Chrymos did manage to wrench back control of her arm for a moment. She screamed silently to Galileo to get out of the way.

But the spell was too powerful. Chrymos could utter no sounds, her warning went unheard and then, with another viciously snarled incantation, Carracci regained control. He quickly forced Chrymos' arm to lash out at Galileo and propel him off the edge.

Galileo's hands flailed desperately at the edge of the tower, trying to stop his fall—and then he was gone.

FORTY-SEVEN
Leaning Tower of Pisa, Duchy of Tuscany,
1.05 p.m. Tuesday April 20 1610

Carracci turned towards Chrymos, his eyes flashing triumphantly, and spat out the words that gave her back control of her body. *"ālepwāw ālepkāp hēnūnbēt hēwāw rēšhēhē"*

Chrymos rushed to the edge of the tower, expecting to see Galileo's body lying on the cobblestones far below—and then had to brace herself to stop tumbling off the tower in shock, as Galileo somehow flew up towards her.

No, not 'somehow'—with someone. At second glance, Chrymos could see that Galileo was being carried upwards. Galileo's rescuer looked surprisingly normal—blue eyes, short brown hair, and long dark robe. Oh, normal except for the impressive wings that made it possible for this angel to rescue the professor from certain death.

But this wasn't the dark and evil Outcast Angel of her nightmares. This rescuer's wings were white and richly feathered, not black and leathery.

As Chrymos stared in amazement, the angel looked straight at her— and, surprisingly, gave her a warm smile and cheerfully winked one eye. Belatedly, Chrymos realized that she was no longer invisible. She had moved beyond Carracci's cloaking powers when she rushed to the edge. Chrymos backed out of view before Galileo himself could see her, and hid behind one of the large bells at the top of the tower. She simply could not take her eyes off the angel, who continued flying upward until Galileo could be safely returned to the summit of the tower.

The angel lowered the professor softly to the tower surface, spoke briefly to him and then swiftly flew away, climbing higher and higher into the sky, until he was lost from view in the afternoon sun.

If Chrymos was stunned by the turn of events, Galileo was shocked speechless. He was a devout Catholic and truly believed in angels—but to have one actually intervene to save his life in such a direct manner? That was so foreign to the usually practical academic that he immediately knelt down, crossed himself and gave profound thanks to God for his salvation.

A minute passed. Two. Then Chrymos could hear some of the students calling from the base of the tower. "Okay, Professor, we're ready. Fire away!"

She looked over at Galileo. He was obviously still shaken. As far as she could tell, no-one else had observed what had just happened. Chrymos could almost guess what he must be thinking: *Did I dream all that? What can I say? Who would believe me?*

None of the students would have seen either the fall or the rescue—at the crucial moment, they had all been inside the tower, slowly walking down the uneven stairs.

Galileo shook his head ruefully, stood up and crossed to the edge of the tower—far more carefully now—and called down to his waiting audience. He had to cough and clear his throat before he could speak steadily. "Stand—*cough*—stand by, here they come."

As Galileo reached for the cannonball and musket ball and prepared to drop them simultaneously from the tower, Chrymos quietly walked over to the stairwell. Carracci was nowhere in sight—and then he suddenly reappeared, standing right beside her.

"Well, that was interesting," Carracci said, indicating that Chrymos should precede him down the stairs.

"What was interesting?" asked Chrymos, happy to make conversation that wasn't about her.

"That angel, interfering openly like that. I don't know how many of the students saw him—"

"I don't think any did," said Chrymos. "They were all still inside the tower."

"In that case, the angel was extremely clever," said Carracci as they reached the bottom of the stairwell and prepared to slip away, unseen by the students gathering around the now-fallen objects and excitedly discussing the experiment. "But not quite clever enough. He chose to oppose us directly and openly. The *Consiglio dei Quattro* will be very interested to learn about this development—that's even more important than waiting around for another chance to kill Galileo."

"Why would the Council of Four be interested?" asked Chrymos.

"Never you mind, girl, never you mind," said Carracci, and those were the last words he would say as the pair of them walked back to the clearing where they had hidden their carriage.

That left Chrymos with plenty of time to ponder the mystery of the angelic rescue—and to wonder what lay ahead. *I have no idea what's going to happen when I get back to the Academy, now that I have refused to carry out the task they gave me. I guess I'll find out the consequences soon enough.*

# # #

Back in her office in Hades, Nekhbet gave a shout of pure delight. "Yes!" She sent an instant mind-message to Lord Hurakan. *<The Lost War is as good as won. The girl did exactly what I predicted!>*

<Excellent,> replied Hurakan, *<give the signal. As soon as we have the pathgem, we will begin the war.>*

FORTY-EIGHT
The Margus River, Moesia,
Dusk, pridie Idus Iulias (July 14) 285 AD

The Roman soldiers who had been losing the battle against Ezequeel had cheered when Machkiel had dived down and begun engaging with the demon. The cheers dwindled when the two had faded from sight—and then turned into shouts of horror when the demon popped back into existence a short distance from their position, with apparently no time at all having passed between the two events.

The shouts in turn were replaced by a wary silence when the soldiers could see that the angel had returned as well.

The two combatants stood facing each other for a few seconds, deciding what to do next. Ezequeel was heavily armored as before and once again carried his vicious barbed sword and double-bladed axe. To the Roman observers Machkiel, with a small sword and only his mail shirt to protect him, looked virtually helpless against the hulking demon.

Ezequeel was first to speak, as he began to circle his opponent, planning his opening attack. "You look familiar. Where do I know you from?" He jabbed tentatively at Machkiel with his sword.

Machkiel nimbly dodged out of reach. "From the Kingdom, where else? In those days, you might have known me as Machkiel the star-shaper. It was my role to reach into the hearts of stars and mold them in accordance with the Father's wishes. To aid me in those tasks, He gave me a few special talents." Machkiel bent down, seized a handful of pebbles from the riverbank, held them in cupped hands and began to concentrate.

The pebbles began to glow brightly, as if being heated in a fiery furnace. Machkiel smiled and began to toss white-hot pebbles towards Ezequeel, one by one. He threw the pebbles lightly but with deadly aim.

Ezequeel easily dodged the first few, but a couple inevitably impacted on the Darke Warrior's armor. They sizzled angrily and might even have burned through the armor if the demon had not swiftly brushed them away with his sword. Ezequeel, a little rattled, raised his axe threateningly, intending to strike down this impudent Outcast.

Machkiel simply laughed, snatched another handful of pebbles from the riverbank and then launched himself into the air. He hovered a half-dozen feet above Ezequeel, tantalizingly out of reach, and tossed some more over-heated pebbles at the Darke Warrior. One struck a lucky unprotected spot on Ezequeel's left hand, burning the startled demon and causing him to drop his sword.

That did it. Snarling, Ezequeel squatted down, reclaimed the sword and then, wings flapping furiously, launched himself at his tormentor.

Machkiel had been expecting the reaction and quickly flew higher, further out of reach—but remained close enough to lure his opponent. *I need to keep Ezequeel engaged*—that thought drove Machkiel—*I don't want him to use the pathgem to escape from me or I'll never find him again.*

Higher and higher the pair flew, leaving the battlefield far below. At first, the advantage was all Machkiel's—Ezequeel was still wary of the white-hot pebbles and devoted as much effort to dodging them as to chasing after Machkiel—but, all too soon, the Outcast Angel's small collection of pebbles was exhausted.

Ezequeel, emboldened, mustered extra speed, drew closer to the fleeing Outcast and lashed out with sword and axe simultaneously. Machkiel had now drawn his own sword, much lighter than either of the demon's weapons—but the sword, like the pebbles, now glowed with ferocious heat. As a result it was able to cut through the wooden haft of the thrusting axe, severing the blade and sending it tumbling to earth.

The demon's sword, facing no opposition, sliced towards Machkiel and would have delivered a killing stroke. At the last moment, however, Machkiel was able to twist his body slightly, so that most of the sword's impact fell on—and was dispersed by—the shield fastened to the Outcast Angel's back. Unfortunately, Machkiel didn't escape unscathed—the sword cut through the chainmail shirt and carved a nasty slice out of Machkiel's left shoulder.

Blood gushed out of the open wound.

FORTY-NINE
The Margus River, Moesia,
Night, pridie Idus Iulias (July 14) 285 AD

Machkiel reacted instantly. First he accelerated out of reach of the pursuing demon, so that there was no immediate danger that Ezequeel would land a second blow. Then Machkiel touched the flat surface of his blade to the gaping wound. The flesh was seared and blackened from the intense heat, stopping the blood-flow, but not without consequence.

"Ahhhhh!" The involuntary cry escaped from Machkiel's lips as the pain stabbed through his body. Ezequeel echoed the sound with his own cry of triumph.

"Yeeee-hahhhhh! Not so cocky now, Outcast? Better fly away—or stay and die!" Ezequeel dropped the now useless axe haft and focused his mind on getting more thrust out of his wings. The virtual appendages responded immediately to the increased mental musculature, propelling the Darke Warrior forward at a much faster pace and bringing him almost within hacking distance of the injured angel.

Machkiel rallied, banishing the throbbing pain to the furthest edges of his mind and concentrating on his own wingspeed. Pain-hampered, Machkiel could not fly as far or as fast as his best—but Ezequeel's heavy armor reduced his maximum speed as well. They were closely matched— the angel could not outpace his pursuer but neither could the demon gain on the Outcast.

Higher and higher the pair flew, until eventually the atmosphere began to grow thin. Neither combatant needed air to support their wings—the non-corporeal appendages interacted not with the physical surroundings but with the underlying currents of what the ancient Greeks had named *aether*. These were unseen energy streams that flow everywhere through the universe, providing both carriage and communications for spiritual beings.

Air was, however, useful for breathing. Not essential, at least not for every single angel or demon—some could adapt themselves to airless environments. If needed, their metabolisms could switch autonomously to extracting the necessary life energy from the aether instead—but flying and mind-messaging capabilities would be restricted as a result. In a battle situation, aether-breathing could mean a significant disadvantage.

Machkiel found himself gulping and gasping, the primary indication that his body would soon be forced to opt for an alternative energy source. Still, the angel continued his upward climb, hoping to lure his enemy into a wrong move.

Ezequeel responded to the thinning atmosphere by turning away. He scoffed at Machkiel. "If all you're going to do is run, Outcast, then you don't need me to help you do it."

Ezequeel turned in a graceful half-circle and began his descent, this time at a far more leisurely pace, gliding downward in wide spirals.

Machkiel paused for a moment and then reversed his own direction. He plunged downward but, unlike Ezequeel, actually increased his speed. Wings beating even more strongly, Machkiel aimed for a quick interception of the demon. He drew his sword in anticipation.

Ezequeel, gliding lazily, glanced upward, expecting to see the Outcast Angel retreating into the distance. Instead, he saw an outstretched sword pointing directly at him and coming closer with every passing second.

Ezequeel reacted instinctively, twisting and turning and diving to get out of the way of the unexpected threat. He was only partially successful—Machkiel's sword slashed through the lower part of one wing, restricting Ezequeel's maneuvering abilities. The demon veered away to the right and drew his own sword in response.

Machkiel didn't attempt to deviate from his current path but instead continued to accelerate downwards, then used his accumulated speed to loop up and around to the left. As Machkiel began climbing again, Ezequeel, tracking his opponent's moves, adjusted his own flying to follow.

Then, unexpectedly, Machkiel curved downwards towards the ascending demon. The two were accelerating towards a seemingly inevitable head-on collision.

Neither seemed likely to turn away. They each raised their swords, anticipating a fight to the death.

FIFTY
The Margus River, Moesia,
Night, pridie Idus Iulias (July 14) 285 AD

Perhaps it was the white-hot glow that began emanating from Machkiel's sword that unsettled Ezequeel—or it might have been the undiminished speed at which the Outcast Angel bore down on his adversary. In any event, Ezequeel turned aside a moment before the expected collision. Just out of reach, the Darke Warrior waved his sword ineffectually as Machkiel flashed past.

Machkiel couldn't resist a taunt as he channeled his downward momentum into yet another upward loop. "Losing your appetite for battle, demon? I didn't think Darke Warriors ever turned away from a fight."

"Come back down and fight face to face and we'll see who's afraid," retorted Ezequeel, once again altering his flight to head upwards, directly towards his opponent.

Machkiel reached the top of his loop and re-oriented himself downward, once more aiming at Ezequeel. The angel's wings were beating at maximum speed, driving Machkiel closer and closer to his opponent.

Ezequeel raised his sword. "Ready," he snarled, expecting Machkiel to slow and engage—or, if not, to be skewered as the angel attempted to pass.

Instead, at the very last moment, Machkiel tossed his sword aside and smashed into Ezequeel at full speed, body to body. Although Ezequeel was better protected because of his armor, the demon was not expecting the impact and was momentarily stunned. Machkiel had been braced for the collision and recovered more readily. He stretched his arms around Ezequeel, enveloping him in an unwanted embrace and pinning Ezequeel's upper arms to his sides.

The demon's upper arms might be held in place, but Ezequeel could still move his lower arms—in particular, his right arm, which wielded the still very-deadly sword. Ezequeel struggled against Machkiel's stifling hold, attempting to manoeuver the sword into a position where he could slash out at the Outcast. He swung the blade once, twice, but he could only reach Machkiel's back, still well-protected by the shield of Evalach.

Before the demon could find a more damaging target, Machkiel reached down with his left hand and managed to grab a portion of Ezequeel's sword blade.

Ezequeel attempted to twist and turn his sword to cut Machkiel's hand to ribbons, but the Outcast ignored the cuts and concentrated, sending intense heat through the demon's blade and hilt until Ezequeel was simply unable to maintain his hold on the weapon.

As soon as Machkiel felt the sword go limp, he released his own hold on the blade. The deadly weapon instantly dropped away and was soon lost from sight.

What remained was a spitting, snarling, kicking bundle of demon, struggling to get free from Machkiel's clutches. The Outcast Angel could feel his own strength ebbing, the combined effects of the slashed shoulder and the still bleeding wounds on his hand taking their toll. *I can't hold Ezequeel much longer.*

Concentrating as best he could against the pain, Machkiel sent heat energy surging into Ezequeel's armor. As the metal grew hotter and hotter, Ezequeel knew exactly what was happening and struggled violently, trying to escape. He reached out, managed to grab hold of Machkiel's left wing and began tearing at its feathers. Then, leveraging his hold, Ezequeel reared back and slammed his helmeted head into Machkiel's unprotected skull.

Close to blacking out, Machkiel took the only action he could, the final step that he had thus far avoided. He sent a white-hot burst of energy surging through his hands and into Ezequeel's armor, scalding the demon horribly and knocking him out.

Ezequeel's wings vanished as he lost consciousness and Machkiel found himself bearing the full weight of both angel and demon on his own set of wings.

Desperately, Machkiel wrestled the wristband containing the pathgem off the arm of the unresisting demon and slid it onto his own wrist. *If I can get to Nowhen, then our wounds can be healed.*

Machkiel mimicked the action he had seen Ezequeel taking, touching the blue gem with a finger.

Nothing happened. Machkiel had no idea how to make the pathgem work. He tried again, increasingly agitated—one finger, two fingers, the whole palm of his hand. Still no effect. He sent a prayer skyward to the God he had rejected long ago, but it went unanswered.

Head groggy, pain still flooding through from hand and shoulder and with one wing damaged, Machkiel desperately struggled to stay awake and make a safe return to the ground far below.

It was an impossible task. Before Machkiel could descend even a hundred feet, he could feel himself blacking out.

He tried desperately to hold on, but his efforts failed. Machkiel lapsed into unconsciousness and his wings also vanished. The two bodies, angel and demon, plummeted to the earth below.

FIFTY-ONE
Outskirts of Pisa, Duchy of Tuscany,
3 p.m. Tuesday April 20 1610

Chrymos and Carracci arrived back at the clearing where the Academy's carriage waited for them. What Carracci did next came as a surprise to Chrymos, who had expected the silent treatment again throughout the journey back to Naples. The priest indicated that she should walk with him over to a fallen tree several feet away from the carriage. He sat down on the trunk of the tree and beckoned her to join him.

Once she was seated, Carracci began to speak. "You know, Chrymos, originally I had such high hopes for you."

Naturally, Chrymos looked surprised, given the disdainful manner in which he had treated her, almost from the very first day that she had met him. Carracci was quick to explain further. "Oh, I don't mean when you arrived at the Academy in January. I meant five years before that, when you first came to our attention."

"What do you mean?" asked Chrymos.

"In 1605, the Contessa arranged for you to be brought to the Academy. You were in chains, kicking and screaming threatening to kill us in a thousand different ways. I was most impressed."

Chrymos could only stare at Carracci in disbelief. "I don't remember any of that," she said.

"Of course you don't," said Carracci. "Nor should you."

Chrymos grew increasingly puzzled, but Carracci wasn't finished with his revelations. "The Contessa told us that you are the daughter of the murderous Hungarian Count Ferencz Nadasdy, known as the 'Black Knight of Hungary', and his wife Countess Erzsebet Bathory, the 'Blood Countess'. You would have grown up in Čachtice Castle in Transylvania, surrounded by the bodies of the very many peasants and servants that your parents slaughtered over the years. Such a shame that you can't remember it now."

"No, it's not true, it can't be true," denied Chrymos, horrified.

Carracci gave her a broad smile. "Oh yes, it certainly is. And you know who they are, don't you? It's public knowledge now, but it was mere rumor and speculation back then, that between them the Black Knight and the Blood Countess killed hundreds of their workers over the last twenty years. By all accounts, your mother was worse than your father—after he died, she killed more of her people than ever."

Carracci sighed. "On the day we first met you, you were so vicious and violent we were definitely glad you were in chains. We were so sure you would be a great soldier—perhaps our greatest ever. Like mother, like daughter."

Chrymos shook her head. "No, no, no."

"We thought we were onto a winner," said Carracci. "The problem we had was that you didn't believe in our cause. Your family was heathen—Protestant. And your parents were high up in the nobility of Royal Hungary. Naturally, you had no interest in fighting for us. Not for the Spanish Empire—and certainly not for the Catholic Church. So we had to do something about that."

Chrymos gave up protesting—she was wasting her breath. And, for all she knew, Carracci could be telling the truth. She remembered nothing of her life before she woke up in Florence in early 1605. She listened to Carracci with morbid fascination as he continued his tale.

"We concocted a special mixture that took away your memory. Don't blame Doctor Odaldi, he did the mixing but to this day he still doesn't know whom it was intended to treat. You wouldn't go quietly—it took a dozen men to hold you down so that we could force you to swallow the drink." Carracci smiled at the memory.

"Once we'd wiped your memory clean, we dropped you off in a nunnery in Florence, so you could get exposed to the true faith. We also wanted to see if the 'new you' still had the necessary attitude to survive on your own on the streets. For some time, we had people watching you to see what you would do."

Chrymos felt momentary vindication of her decision to leave Florence and re-settle in Naples. *So I was being watched! I was right.*

Carracci brushed some dust off his breeches as he continued. "To be honest, if you had failed we wouldn't have saved you. We want warriors, not weaklings. You surprised us—not only because you were able to survive but also because of the manner in which you did so."

He smiled. "Based on your lineage, we fully expected you to lie and steal and kill your way through Florence. We even had a plan to rescue you if you were arrested for any crimes you committed."

Carracci shook his head sadly. "As far as we could tell, you didn't do any of that—no stealing, certainly no killing—which frankly was a great disappointment to us. All that time and effort wasted—we really drew the lemon with you."

Carracci's obvious displeasure brought the first smile that Chrymos was able to summon all day. *Great—whatever annoys you makes me happy.*

Carracci continued. "We were about to move in and pick you up, to wipe your memory and start again, when you vanished. Our people scoured Florence but there was no sign of you."

Chrymos then realized how narrowly she must have escaped. She gave a quick prayer of thanks for her deliverance.

"We didn't find you again until earlier this year," said Carracci, "when the Contessa predicted that you would be picked up in Naples by one of our recruitment raids. You led Henricus and his team on such a merry dance that I was sure you must have changed. Perhaps the streets of Naples had stiffened your spine."

Carracci went on. "Sadly, that wasn't true. You're still the same mollycoddling girl we saw in Florence, nursing every little stray that comes along. Argumentative, yes, self-opinionated, indeed, even bloody-minded. But you are certainly not a killer."

Chrymos nodded.

"And that," said Carracci, raising his voice at last, "is what the Academy needs right now. A hardened killer, someone willing to do whatever it takes, now that we're on the brink of the Lost War."

Carracci stood up. "I wouldn't even bother sending you back to the Academy, but the Contessa still believes that you have a part to play in the war." He spat on the ground. "Sure, if we have some babies to nursemaid."

At that moment, another horse and cart arrived and drew up near the Academy carriage. Carracci had apparently been expecting it. He looked over and nodded to the driver, a nun from Father Carracci's order. Then he turned back to Chrymos.

"I don't have time for you now, I have business in Paris. Sister Maria Benedetta will take you back to Naples."

"Okay," said Chrymos, "I get it. You're not going to let me take the Exousía potion. You might as well leave me behind here in Pisa, then."

"I'm afraid that's no longer an option," said Carracci. "You know too much. Now, *sāmek lāmedhēhē pēnūn ayinyōd tāwyōdlāmed yōd sām ek ālepyōd.*"

This latest spell caught Chrymos off-guard. She immediately lost interest in everything around her.

Carracci summoned the newly-arrived driver and issued appropriate instructions. Then he turned once again to Chrymos.

"I'll deal with you when I get back, once I've had a chance to talk to the Master and the Contessa. A word of warning, though. You should prepare yourself, Chrymos. Whatever your fate, you won't like it."

Chrymos simply sat on the tree trunk, unmoving, until Sister Maria Benedetta escorted her to the cart. She watched incuriously as Carracci climbed into the other carriage and left the clearing, heading to an unknown destination. If at that moment the Lost War had broken out around her, she would not have noticed.

Nor did Chrymos give any thought to Carracci's revelations about her parents. Her mind was completely blank.

Chrymos remained in this nearly-comatose state for what was a fourteen-day journey back to Naples. When instructed by Sister Maria Benedetta she would mechanically eat, sleep, or perform necessary ablutions. Otherwise, Chrymos had absolutely no awareness of the days passing by.

FIFTY-TWO
Fourteen Days Later
**Academy of Secrets, Naples, Kingdom of Naples,
Early Evening, Tuesday, May 4 1610**

"bēthēgīml ayinnūnhē." With that single incantation, Master Della Porta removed the spell from Chrymos and she found herself back at the Academy, in the Master's office. It was as if the journey from Pisa back to Naples had never happened.

Della Porta turned to Sister Maria Benedetta, who had nursed Chrymos throughout the journey. He issued brief instructions. "Take her to her room. After she has climbed down remove the ladder. She can help in the kitchen each day but she must stay locked up in her room every night until Father Carracci returns."

# # #

Within a few minutes, Chrymos was indeed restored to her room. She barely noticed when the ladder was withdrawn and the entry hatch closed. She didn't even feel the usual panic attack at her claustrophobic surroundings.

Her mind, quiescent for a fortnight, was now racing.

Chrymos tried and failed to summon up any memory of the Black Knight and the Blood Countess who were supposedly her parents. *If Doctor Odaldi truly did manage to wipe memories of people like that from my mind, then I must congratulate him—he did a fantastic job.*

Eventually, Chrymos abandoned any attempt to remember the past. Instead, she tried to consider her options for a new future.

They all seemed desperately grim.

FIFTY-THREE
The Margus River, Moesia,
Early morning, Idus Iulias (July 15) 285 AD

Marcus Augustus, Diocletian's deputy commander, was the first on the scene. He had attempted to watch the battle between angel and demon—although in the darkness he could only see the occasional flashes of fiery red and blue-white—and had heard the final impact as the bodies hit the ground. He had gathered a hand-picked squad of soldiers, along with a wagon carrying burial cloths and spades, just in case. Together Marcus Augustus and his men had ridden through the pre-dawn hours, carefully making their way along the riverbank, their journey guided by flaming torches.

Not long after dawn, the squad arrived close to where Marcus Augustus thought the bodies must have fallen. They dismounted and climbed the hillside. After some time spent searching, one of the soldiers shouted, "Over here."

Two bodies lay smashed and broken on the uneven ground. The demon was largely unrecognizable, smeared across the rocks, but at least some of his body still held together thanks to his armor. The angel, on the other hand, looked surprisingly undamaged, given the height from which he had fallen. Marcus Augustus spotted one of his soldiers waving his hand, sketching out a crude cross shape over the body.

"What was that all about?" demanded the deputy commander.

The soldier, horrified to be observed, stammered out an explanation. "Sir, the Bishop—Bishop Januarius—told us that the shield would preserve our champion. Look—he's still in one piece, not like the other one. You would think he was only sleeping."

Marcus Augustus had to admit that the soldier had a point. "Still dead, though," he added. "Tell you what, you, you, and you—" The deputy commander indicated three of his men, including the soldier who had administered the blessing. "—take some of the burial cloths we brought, wrap up this one and take him quietly to Januarius. Tell the bishop that we don't want it known that Machkiel is dead. Such news would weaken our soldiers' morale. Ask the bishop to bury the body somewhere in total secrecy."

Marcus Augustus looked around at all of his troops. "And if any of you so much as breathes a word about this to anyone, then may you be accursed in your blood and eyes and every limb and have all your intestines eaten away. As far as any of you know, the angel triumphed over the demon and then flew away. Is that clear?"

A chorus of "yes, sirs" followed, the others carefully looking away as the designated soldiers completed their task and carried their cloth-wrapped burden down to where the horses were tethered. Marcus Augustus waited until he could hear the three men riding away. Machkiel's body—the pathgem still firmly attached to his wrist—would be taken away for a decent burial. *More importantly*, mused the commander, *what our men don't know and don't see won't diminish their fighting spirit.*

Next, the commander turned his attention to what remained of the demon. "This one," he said with a great deal of satisfaction, "this one goes on display so that our brave men can see what happens to those who oppose the true emperor!"

The cheering was instant and prolonged. Marcus Augustus waited until the noise had subsided and then added: "And we'll parade the creature in front of that pretender Carinus and his lily-livered troops as well. That should teach them not to trifle with the true Roman Empire!"

Shouts and cheers continued to ring out through the morning, as the soldiers happily lashed the remains of the demon—now more armor than flesh—to a cross roughly assembled from nearby tree branches.

Diocletian's men had their new standard, and it would lead them to victory against their soon-to-be-thoroughly-demoralized human foes.

PART THREE

FIFTY-FOUR
23 Rue de la Ferronnerie, Paris, France,
Early Morning, Friday May 14 1610

Ravid arrived in Paris early in the morning after a relatively uneventful night flight. He skimmed the note that awaited him. "Impressive," he remarked to his Outcast Angels colleague Archimedes, "Bishop de Richelieu hasn't had much luck encouraging the palace guard to increase King Henri's protectors, so he's dreamed up another little ruse. He's put the fear of eternal damnation into the king's carriage driver and convinced him to stay away from the Les Halles area of Paris in general—and, of course, from this street, the Rue de la Ferronneri, in particular."

"If that doesn't keep the king safe, at least today—" said Archimedes.

"—then nothing will," finished Ravid. "I agree—and yet Jesse has not advised me of any change to the king's fate. He is, as far as we know, still destined to be assassinated on this street this afternoon. Our presence here is still essential, even if—" Ravid glanced around the overcrowded room. "—it's a bit of a squeeze in here."

Ravid, Archimedes and the five new recruits brought over from the Stonehenge training facility were currently crammed into the small upstairs bedroom of a two-level Paris appartement at 23 Rue de la Ferronnerie, the only accommodation they could find that had a clear view of the Rue de la Ferronnerie itself. The appartement itself was not officially available for rent, but earlier in the week its owners had felt a sudden urge to visit a sick aunt in Toulouse, many days' travel from Paris. This humanitarian gesture came as a result of an overwhelming compulsion planted by team member Elias. *Hopefully,* thought Ravid, *our business here will be concluded before Monsieur and Madame Gombaud realize that neither of them actually has a sick aunt, in Toulouse or anywhere else.*

Ravid looked at Archimedes. Time was running out. "Okay, Archimedes, introduce me to your team."

Archimedes called the recruits to order. "We've talked about him on many occasions, now you finally get to meet him. Gentlemen, it's my pleasure to introduce you to Ravid. Like me, of course, he is an Outcast Angel. Before the Rebellion, he was the leader of the Kingdom Guards, responsible for protecting the Kingdom of Heaven. In that role, he was blessed with superlative fighting skills and with enhanced hearing and vision, abilities he retains to this day."

Ravid bowed his head slightly, embarrassed by the introduction. Archimedes continued.

"Ravid, let me introduce you to the team. I picked them all personally for this mission, selecting them from the volunteers who have been taking part in our enhanced powers program. Over here—" Archimedes nodded towards a young man in his mid-twenties, of average height, with a generous beard and frizzy light brown hair. "—we have Martin Wintour. Martin has been with us at Stonehenge since early 1606, ever since the unfortunate events of the Gunpowder Treason which led to the execution of Martin's father and his uncle."

Ravid couldn't help himself—he looked startled.

Martin sighed. He'd obviously been through this often. "I swear to you, I was not part of the gunpowder conspiracy. I was cleared of any involvement five years ago, by the king's interrogators." He winced in remembered pain. "And Archimedes will tell you that your own people have examined me thoroughly and declared me innocent."

"Your pardon, Martin," said Ravid, "I was not at all concerned that you might have been involved in the Treason. I reacted the way I did because I was reminded of—another situation. If Archimedes trusts you, why should I do otherwise?"

Martin visibly relaxed. Archimedes continued with the introduction. "Martin's unique ability is to control light and darkness." At a nod from Archimedes, Martin waved a hand, plunging Ravid's half of the bedroom into total darkness. Ravid could still see the others, thanks to his enhanced powers, but they couldn't see him. "Thanks, Martin. That will be sufficient demonstration for now," said Archimedes, and the light returned.

"If you find yourself needing to hide in broad daylight, Ravid," said Archimedes, "Martin's your man."

Ravid nodded in acknowledgement. "A useful skill, Martin, thank you for volunteering."

Martin managed a brief smile. "I am grateful for the opportunity. I cannot atone for the sins of my father and my uncle but at least I can make myself of some use for the greater good."

Archimedes next beckoned to a stocky middle-aged man with flaming red hair. "Our next volunteer is Lochloinn, who comes to us from Scotland. There is—" Archimedes attempted to find a diplomatic phrase to describe the situation. "—a little bit of 'history' between Martin and Lochloinn."

"Aye, and ye canna blame me fer that," argued Lochloinn. "This man's da tried to kill ma king." The Scotsman all but snarled at Martin.

<*Well, he has a point,*> Ravid thought at Archimedes. <*James was king of Scotland long before he became king of England. And James was the primary target of the Gunpowder Treason.*>

Archimedes responded aloud to Ravid's mind-call whilst at the same time attempting to address Lochloinn's spoken comments. "Fortunately, since we have proven Martin to be innocent of any involvement in the Treason, the two should be able to work together against our common enemies." <*I hope,*> he added by mind-call.

"Lochloinn has the ability," Archimedes continued aloud, "to mimic any muscle movement he can observe. His training at Stonehenge has included careful observation of many of the warriors in our ranks, and we have sent him undercover into a number of European battles to learn even more. He makes a formidable opponent, instantly learning the moves of those he fights against and as a result can quickly blunt their attacks."

Ravid smiled at the Scotsman. "Thank you, Lochloinn, I look forward to working with you."

Lochloinn inclined his head and then moved to the back wall of the tiny appartement, scowling at Martin as he did so. Archimedes turned his attention to the next recruit. "This is Sean FitzGerald," announced Archimedes, indicating a clean-shaven blond-haired man with flashing green eyes. "Sean comes to us from Munster in Ireland. He and his brother Niall over here—" Archimedes indicated Sean's brown-haired companion, eyes also an emerald green. "—are grandsons of the Earl of

Desmond, who—met an unfortunate end whilst leading an unsuccessful Irish rebellion against Her Majesty Queen Elizabeth. Sean and Niall are—you might style them 'political refugees'. They are under our protection and have been enhanced to help us with our crusades."

"And what power do you have, Sean?" asked Ravid.

"Oi kin stop people from movin' jest by touchin' 'em," offered Sean. "Archimedes here calls it 'pah—'." He struggled to find the correct English word.

"Paralysis," ventured Archimedes. "The effect is temporary but in the right circumstances the skill can be life-saving."

"And you, Niall?" Ravid turned to Sean's brother.

Niall didn't believe in wasting words. He crossed to the appartement door, bent down and slithered through the tiny gap between the door and the floor. He was obliged to leave his shoes behind but all the rest of him somehow oozed through the gap. Ravid, stunned, looked to Archimedes. "Yes, he can squeeze and stretch and bend and twist into or out of almost anything," Archimedes confirmed. "I have no idea how that's even physically possible—but Niall has acquired that power through our enhancement program."

Niall squeezed back into the room, this time through the gap at the top of the door, and then flowed down to the floor. He then restored his body to normal human dimensions, retrieved his shoes and, with a cheeky grin, bowed low to Ravid and then rejoined his brother.

Archimedes cleared his throat to regain Ravid's attention. "There is one more of us for you to meet, Ravid. This is the last but not least of the volunteers, Elias. I chose him especially for this assignment, not simply for his powers but because he was raised in Calais—his mother is French, his father English. As a result, he can speak both languages fluently."

Elias, black-haired and strikingly handsome, beamed a mighty smile at Ravid as he bowed low in greeting. He spoke English with a slight French accent. "It is a true pleasure to meet you, Ravid. And I believe you feel the same about me." Despite himself, Ravid responded to Elias's words with a fulsome smile and bow of his own.

"Be careful, Ravid," said Archimedes, "I suspect you may be falling under Elias's spell. His powers are not physical but mental. Through his words, he can convince anyone to do his bidding. In fact, this room is only available to us because of Elias."

Ravid was instantly on his guard, but his resistance was futile. Words of coercion emanating from Elias convinced Ravid that the recruit was harmless, despite the evidence to the contrary. "Well met, Elias," said Ravid, "I look forward to seeing your powers at work."

Archimedes smiled, but let the comment stand. "Thank you, Elias," he said. "We may need your services shortly." He turned to Ravid. "What now?"

"Now," said Ravid, "we wait for an update from Jesse. He has remained in London and has been reviewing the futures of the guards who will be accompanying King Henri on today's journey, in case one of them sees and can identify the assassin for us."

Jesse's mind-call was not long in coming—and the message was triumphant in tone. *<One of the king's personal bodyguards will recognize the assassin after the murder today. The killer is a Catholic fanatic, François Ravaillac, who has already attempted three times to have a meeting with the king. The bodyguard recognized Ravaillac from his most recent visit, earlier this week. Ravaillac had claimed to have a vision that the king, himself a former Protestant, must convince the Protestant Huguenots to convert to Catholicism.>*

<I assume you have now scanned Ravaillac,> replied Ravid, *<and can tell us where to find him.>*

<Yes, and his future actions reveal that he is indeed the assassin,> responded Jesse. *<He is currently staying at the house of Charlotte du Tillet, mistress of the Duke of Épernon. If you hurry, you can catch Ravaillac at the du Tillet estate and detain him before he can make his move.>*

<Oh, I think we can do a bit better than that,> mind-called Ravid, glancing over at Elias. *<We'll send one of our team who should be able to—convince Monsieur Ravaillac to chart a different course.>*

Ravid took notes as Jesse described Ravaillac as he would appear at the assassination. *<Narrow, beady, brown eyes. Dark, shoulder-length hair. Closely-trimmed beard. Plumed hat. White doublet, grey over-tunic. Brown breeches, black hose and brown boots.>*

Jesse had nearly finished the mind-call, but he had one last request, for Archimedes. *<I need you back in Stonehenge as soon as you can,*

Archimedes. We're now moving into a very critical period, with more and more leaders about to face deadly challenges. We desperately need more recruits for our teams.>

<Absolutely,> replied Archimedes, *<I'll leave Paris right away. I can't fly out of the city in daylight without attracting unwanted attention, but I'll catch a coach ride into the countryside and then fly home from there.>*

Ravid said his goodbyes to Jesse and shortly later farewelled Archimedes as well. Next, Ravid gave Elias the description of Ravaillac that Jesse had just provided.

"Lochloinn." Ravid turned to the Scotsman. "I need you to accompany Elias, in case Ravaillac needs to be persuaded physically." Lochloinn nodded eagerly.

Ravid then dispatched the pair in search of their prey.

FIFTY-FIVE
Later That Day
Paris, France, Early Afternoon, Friday May 14 1610

"I'm bored."

"Well, there's a change, Pascol. That must be only the twelfth time you've told us that today. Much better than yesterday's record. What was that—twenty-five times? Twenty-six?" Johannes was understandably sarcastic. As the most senior member of this group of Alchemae, he was in charge of—or, as he put it, babysitting—three of the current crop of Academy graduates, Flaminio, Pascol, and Bitino. So far, they had all been sitting around in their inn in the Les Halles region of Paris, just waiting.

Johannes had been assigned the leadership role because he had the ability to detect intense emotions from a distance. If anyone who came within range radiated an intense desire of any sort, Johannes could interpret that emotion and, if appropriate, dispatch the Alchemae team to deal with the problem.

At this moment, Johannes was hard at work, mentally scanning for unusual emotions amongst a busy lunch crowd at the Les Halles food market. The rest of his team had nothing to do—and had been busily doing exactly that for most of the week. It was not helpful that only Pascol spoke French, so there was little that the rest of the team could do in the French capital. Inevitably, they were bored and fractious.

Earlier in the day Johannes had been obliged to break up a scuffle between Flaminio and Bitino—a disagreement reinforced by the virtual boulders and minor blizzards that they tossed at each other—and he was at the end of his patience.

Johannes was on the verge of lashing out verbally at his team members, which would almost certainly have triggered another unpleasant confrontation, when he began to detect a very strong emotion somewhere in the streets outside. He desperately sought to interpret the emotion he was receiving.

It's—intense satisfaction. With overtones of—murder! And it affects the king—

With a gasp, Johannes alerted the others. "This is it—the reason why we're here. We'll need everyone for this. Let's go!"

FIFTY-SIX
A Few Minutes Later
**Rue de la Ferronnerie, Paris, France,
Early Afternoon, Friday May 14 1610**

Elias and Lochloinn strode jauntily along the Rue de la Ferronnerie, returning to the appartement where their colleagues awaited news of the mission's outcome. Elias in particular was in a very satisfied mood. "Lord Ravid should be delighted with us," he said to Lochloinn, "now that François Ravaillac is no longer a problem."

"Aye, ye already said as much, laddie," said Lochloinn, "but I will nay be convinced until this day is but a memory." Still, the unexcitable Scotsman had a spring in his step that had not been evident earlier.

Lochloinn had watched Elias weave his magic with Ravaillac, convincing the French Catholic that on this occasion he had in fact managed to have his desired meeting with the king. Elias had also made Ravaillac believe that Henri had given secret undertakings regarding the Huguenots.

Certain of this new truth, Ravaillac had undertaken to leave Paris immediately. Elias and Lochloinn had accompanied Ravaillac to the coach depot and then watched him depart on the midday coach.

Elias's compulsive persuasions were not permanent, but they would easily last for some weeks, which should be long enough for the LOA to make alternative arrangements to protect the king from Ravaillac in the future.

Elias began humming to himself, very satisfied with his day's work. He and Lochloinn headed to the front door of their appartement, rapped on the door twice as a coded courtesy, and then let themselves inside.

They had no idea that they were being watched.

FIFTY-SEVEN
Palais du Louvre, Paris, France,
Afternoon, Friday May 14 1610

The King of France was in a very, very bad mood, and the subject of his displeasure was his carriage driver.

Henri IV made his intentions plain. "No bishop is going to tell me when and where I can ride in my own city. Today, I have urgent matters to discuss with my trusted advisor Maximilien, the Duke of Sully. The duke lies on his sickbed. He cannot come to me, so I will go to him—and that means we will travel through the Les Halles area and along the Rue de la Ferronnerie. Several of my *Quarante Cinq*, my royal guardsmen, will accompany me—they can protect me from any dangers that might arise. If you, driver, are not willing to take me on that journey, then my new carriage driver will be happy to oblige—while you enjoy your own trip to the Bastille. Do I make myself clear?"

The unfortunate driver, terrified out of his wits, could only nod in obedience.

"Good," said the king. "Then let's go. I have a war to plan."

King Henri, dressed in what his queen assured him was the latest Parisian fashion style, climbed into the royal carriage and took his accustomed place on the elevated throne at the rear, from which he liked to wave at his subjects. Two guardsmen joined him inside the carriage while a third sat outside, next to the driver.

The driver reluctantly took the reins and encouraged the horses to begin their journey towards the area that Bishop de Richelieu had described to the driver as "the accursed maggot pie of Paris."

FIFTY-EIGHT
23 Rue de la Ferronnerie, Paris, France,
Early Afternoon, Friday May 14 1610

"This one?" asked Pascol, gesturing to the door of an appartement. He stood outside the building that the two suspects had entered a few minutes earlier.

"Correct," agreed Johannes. He reached out and turned the doorknob, which opened easily. Warning the other Alchemae to silence, Johannes led the way into the appartement. They found themselves in a small room furnished with couches and chairs.

On the right, through an open doorway, they could see a fireplace, flanked by pots and pans and the usual cooking utensils.

On the left, a flight of stairs led upwards. They could hear voices above, speaking a language with which Johannes was not familiar. He looked across quizzically at Pascol, who had the greatest language expertise of the group.

"English, I think," whispered Pascol.

Johannes nodded. *The great enemy.* That made his next decision easier.

He turned back to Pascol, pointed up to the two huge wooden beams that crisscrossed the ceiling of the lounge, providing support for the upstairs rooms, then held up one hand and began lowering each finger—a five second countdown.

With his other hand, Johannes gestured for the remaining members of the team to move into the kitchen area, an instruction to which they quickly responded.

Johannes joined them by the fireplace as his countdown reached its conclusion. Two—one—zero.

Pascol stretched out both hands, one touching each support beam. In an instant, both beams liquefied, pouring their essence onto the room below.

A moment later, as Pascol hastily joined the other Alchemae in the kitchen, the ceiling planks, deprived of their underlying support, sagged, splintered, and broke into a thousand pieces. The contents of the upper rooms—beds, furniture, people—cascaded into the room below.

FIFTY-NINE
At The Same Moment
23 Rue de la Ferronnerie, Paris, France,
Early Afternoon, Friday May 14 1610

Ravid and the other members of his team were upstairs, listening as Elias and Lochloinn reported on their success with François Ravaillac. Ravid was about to mind-call Jesse for an update on the king's changed future when the floor collapsed.

None of the team had any chance to react—they simply fell, collecting deep cuts and scratches from the splintering floorboards and then finding themselves buffeted by the beds, cabinets and desks as the furniture tumbled as well. Martin was the first to hit the ground below, breaking his left leg on impact. He screamed in pain before losing consciousness.

Even as the rest of the team fell, Ravid heard a voice from the kitchen, shouting in the Napoletano language, "Now—hit them!" Ravid urgently summoned his wings and managed to slow his own fall but was unable to reach any of the others to help with their descent.

Sean, clinging desperately to some bedding to attempt to break his fall, now found himself bombarded by snow and ice, driven by a vicious windblast.

The sneak attack caught him off-guard and he lost his grip on the bedding, landing with a sickening crunch on the wooden frame that formed the edge of one of the couches. Ravid saw Sean hit the frame and then slump to the floor. *Has he broken his back?*

Ravid had little time to consider the consequences if that was truly the case—the Outcast Angel was too busy throwing himself over to the left hand corner of the room, where the team's weapons had fallen.

Elias and Lochloinn, who had been standing alongside each other when the floor collapsed, were mostly unharmed, thanks largely to Lochloinn's physical prowess. As a key part of his training, Lochloinn had spent more than a year visiting various circuses across Europe and parts of Asia, learning the muscle movements of acrobats and tightrope-walkers. As a result, he was able to contort his body in mid-air, directing his path so that he landed in a clear space—and then immediately positioned himself to catch Elias.

In the moments that followed, both teammates were on the receiving end of invisible blasts of energy, fired at them by one of their attackers. They unbalanced and fell to the floor, bowled over rather than injured. The energy blasts continued, effectively pinning Elias and Lochloinn to the spot.

Niall, though caught unawares by the collapsing floor like everyone else, had managed to stretch his arms and upper body over to the upstairs window and seize a handhold on the windowsill as the rest of the room fell around him.

He next lowered himself to the ground, taking advantage of his amazing elasticity to ensure a painless landing. Unfortunately, the blizzard conditions stirred up by his opponents hampered his further movements—the raging wind pounded Niall's elongated body against the wall, and although he wasn't hurt, he couldn't escape the unrelenting pressure of the wind.

That left Ravid, who had finally managed to reach the team's stockpile of weapons. In his case, the wind torrents had actually helped, blowing him in the direction he needed to go.

Ravid selected two of the weapons, a heavy broadsword and a narrow-bladed stiletto dagger, and then turned.

In front of him lay chaos. Beds, bedding, furniture, planking—all lay strewn through the room, incessantly stirred up and tossed around by the relentless blizzard. The air in the room was filled with snow and ice in constant motion, blending with splintered wood and pieces of furniture driven by a nearly unstoppable tornado. Sean and Martin, both seemingly unconscious, lay on the ground—not motionless, because the blizzard winds kept pushing their bodies around, but certainly not moving of their own volition.

Niall, over against the right hand wall, attempted to slither and slide under the wind, towards the attackers, but bursts of energy tossed in his direction impeded his progress. Thankfully, the raging wind blew most of those bursts harmlessly away.

Over to the left, out of the direct path of the wind, Lochloinn climbed to his feet, intending to rush towards the kitchen where the attackers still lurked. Elias, sheltering behind one of the couches, tried shouting at the kitchen, "We're friends, you know us, you don't want to hurt us."

Unfortunately, Elias, thought Ravid, *your persuasive powers are probably wasted here. You're shouting out in English, and, even if they can hear you over the wind, I don't think that these people understand English. It's a pity you don't speak Napoletano, the language of the Kingdom of Naples.*

Lochloinn was making good progress in his attempt to reach the kitchen, until his movements caught the attention of the person controlling the blizzard.

That individual redirected the blizzard at Lochloinn, instantly driving him backwards—but at the same time providing a clear opportunity for Ravid. For the moment, there was no wind between the Outcast Angel and the blizzard-maker.

Ravid lifted his stiletto dagger, balanced it carefully—and then threw it directly at his foe. The stiletto flew straight and true—and its hilt impacted against the skull of his target, knocking him out and instantly stilling the blizzard.

Ravid preferred to incapacitate rather than kill his human opponents, if he had the choice, because he knew exactly what lay in store for them if they died in sin and went to Hades. However, sometimes the choice was taken out of his hands—given the supernatural powers arrayed against him in this sneak attack, Ravid feared that his broadsword would need to drink deep of their blood if that was the only means of stopping these people and saving the French king.

Ravid looked around. Now that the wind had stopped, Niall had rushed over to the weapons cache, grabbed two swords and thrown them over to Elias and Lochloinn, before selecting a sword of his own. In the kitchen, several of the attackers also drew their weapons. *This,* thought Ravid, *is not going to be easy.*

Lifting his broadsword high above his head, Ravid shouted out a challenge. "We fight in the name of Henri IV, to protect him and to save his life from these treacherous assassins!" As his three colleagues roared their assent, Ravid repeated the challenge in the Napoletano language. *Might as well let these killers know that they have to get through us first.*

What happened next caught Ravid by surprise. The leader of the attackers replied in the same language. "Wait! Stop! What are you saying? Our purpose also is to protect the French king."

SIXTY
Seconds Later
23 Rue de la Ferronnerie, Paris, France,
Early Afternoon, Friday May 14 1610

That proclamation must be a trap, thought Ravid, *a diversion to distract our team before we can strike back. If it is a trick, he's wasting his time—I'm the only one of our team who can even understand their language.* Meanwhile, Ravid's team members continued to approach the kitchen, very much ready and eager to fight after being on the receiving end of most of the punishment so far.

The attackers paused, looking to their leader for guidance. Now that the two teams were so close, Ravid could see just how very young their opponents were. *Perhaps this attack really was in error,* he thought.

Ravid spoke quickly to his team. "Wait, we may be able to resolve this before anyone else gets hurt." His three team members, eager to retaliate, were slow to respond at first, so Ravid had to reinforce his instructions. "There may have been a misunderstanding. We may actually share the same goal, to protect the King. Wait a moment while I talk with their leader."

More resistance and then, finally, Ravid was obeyed. Niall—keeping one eye carefully fixed on the attackers—went to look after his brother, Sean. Elias crossed over to Martin. Lochloinn stood where he was, glaring at his opponents and ready to strike at a moment's notice.

Ravid spoke at some length with the leader of the attackers, who identified himself simply as Johannes. "How can I trust what you say," said Ravid. "You attacked us with no explanation, destroying this place and injuring our people. Then, when the tide turns against you, you claim that we are on the same side. How am I supposed to believe that?"

"I'm sure that it's difficult for you to believe me," said Johannes, "yet for the sake of the king, I beg you to try. We have been sent here because of the treaty between France and Savoy. Our Master believes that the King of France and the Duke of Savoy are both in mortal danger as a result, and he has sent us here to guard the king while another team is tasked with protection of the duke."

"If you expect me to believe that," said Ravid, "then you must tell me the name of your master."

"I'm afraid," said Johannes, "that I cannot tell you that."

The two leaders stood staring at each other for a long moment—until they were interrupted by sudden shouts and screams coming from outside.

SIXTY-ONE
Rue de la Ferronnerie, Paris, France,
Afternoon, Friday May 14 1610

The king's carriage turned briskly out of St Honoré and onto the Rue de la Ferronnerie, the king waving not quite so enthusiastically at the crowds along this part of the route. The royal arm, in fact, had grown quite weary through prolonged waving because, until the king had finally noticed and spoken very vehemently indeed, the driver had guided the carriage on an extended, circuitous route through the city, trying to avoid the Les Halles region.

Now that the royal carriage had finally arrived in the Rue de la Ferronnerie, the driver was attempting to rush through the damned street at a gallop—but he was suddenly forced to rein in and then bring the horses to a complete halt because the path ahead was blocked. A cart filled with wine casks had broken down on one side of the road and a haycart blocked the other side of the narrow thoroughfare.

Neither cart showed any signs of moving, so two of the king's guardsmen climbed out of the royal carriage and strode over to the carts, determined to clear the road quickly so that the king's journey could proceed.

The third guardsman remained beside the king. However, when it became apparent that another pair of hands would in fact be needed, The king sent his sole remaining protector over to help, leaving just himself and the driver in the carriage. That proved to be a fatal misjudgment.

Before the driver could react, before he could cry out a warning to the guardsmen, a figure rushed out from the crowd, clambered up a carriage wheel and jumped into the carriage beside Henri. Pulling out a wickedly sharp knife, the intruder then stabbed the king through the ribs.

His mission completed, the assassin threw himself down from the royal carriage, stumbled and then recovered and dashed away into the crowd. A moment later, there were shouts and screams from onlookers as the king could be seen lurching forward from his seat, blood pouring out from his side. Before anyone could reach him, the king collapsed onto the floor of his carriage.

Witnesses would later describe the assailant as wearing a plumed hat, white doublet and grey over-tunic and having dark, shoulder-length hair and a closely-trimmed beard. One of the king's guardsmen, Medoro, who had seen the killer leap from the carriage after striking the fatal blow, rushed back from the cart he had been attempting to move and frantically chased after the assassin. Medoro was certain that he recognized the man as one François Ravaillac, a Catholic loyalist who had attempted to meet with the king without success on several occasions.

Too late to prevent the tragedy but determined to bring the killer to swift and brutal justice, Medoro plunged into the crowd in desperate pursuit of the assassin. He was not close enough behind to observe that the object of his pursuit had lingered in an alleyway, nor did he see the man's appearance somehow flicker and change. The wanted man no longer sported a beard, his hair had shortened and lightened in color and his face had become cherubic rather than haunted. He had also grown three inches taller than the man the bodyguard thought he was seeking.

To complete his escape, Ruben tossed aside the conspicuous plumed hat and the grey over-tunic and straightened the plain doublet underneath. He then exited the alleyway and walked easily to safety, moving slowly past the devastated guardsman who was searching in vain for the now-discarded François Ravaillac.

SIXTY-TWO
Moments Later
23 Rue de la Ferronnerie, Paris, France,
Afternoon, Friday May 14 1610

Niall opened the window so that the two teams could hear the shouts from outside. The loudest and most heart-wrenching cry, taken up and echoed by many voices, was the last thing that either team wanted to hear: "Le Roi est mort!"

"We've failed," said Ravid, speaking to his team. "Henri IV has been killed." He repeated the announcement in Napoletano, but that wasn't truly necessary—the realization that the king was dead was already evident on the faces of the opposing team's members.

Ravid moved closer to the kitchen, broadsword at the ready. He called out to Johannes. "Keep your team where I can see them. It appears that you have succeeded in your evil scheme."

Johannes was quick to respond. "I told you, our mission was to protect the French king. If he is truly dead, then we have failed as well."

Ravid ignored that comment. He called out to Elias. "Please go and find out exactly what has happened and report back as soon as you can."

Elias slipped out into the street, leaving the two teams facing each other warily. While they waited, each team tended to their wounded. Niall cleared one of the couches and lifted a gradually awakening Sean—whose back was badly bruised but thankfully not broken—into a more comfortable position. Martin was still unconscious but Lochloinn straightened and then bound his colleague's leg, using a broken piece of planking and some fabric from one of the curtains that now lay shredded on the appartement floor.

While this was happening, Johannes and his team members worked on the young man who was responsible for the blizzards. They applied some of the scattered snow to his head in an ultimately successful effort to revive him. Ravid watched carefully, ready to deliver a more permanent blow if the slowly-recovering attacker attempted to launch any more blizzards.

A short time later, both groups turned expectantly as the door handle began to turn. Elias was back and ready to report—but he wasn't happy.

"We can't blame this group," said Elias, indicating the other team. "It was François Ravaillac after all—he stabbed the king, exactly as Jesse foretold."

"But we watched Ravaillac leave Paris!" shouted Lochloinn.

"I know," said Elias, "he must have slipped back into the city once he was out of our sight."

Elias was naturally devastated. "I don't know what happened. I don't understand how Ravaillac was able to resist my compulsions."

Ravid quickly explained the situation to Johannes. "The king was killed by a French Catholic assassin. From what we know so far, it seems that your team was not involved. I suggest that you leave here now, while you still can."

Johannes and his team quietly left the appartement, taking their still-groggy colleague with them. Ravid locked the door behind them, hoping to avoid any more unexpected guests.

The volunteers were not happy. Lochloinn in particular was incensed. "Are ye jest lettin' 'em skip away, laddie?" he asked Ravid. "After all th' damage they've caused ter this wee hoose—and what they done ter Sean 'n Martin?"

Ravid responded by addressing the whole team. "These were simply foot-soldiers. We want their leaders—which means we need to find out who sent them. For now, though, our primary concern is to get out of this appartement—and we need to leave at once. The king's guardsmen, the Quarante Cinq, must already be racing towards the Rue de la Ferronnerie, determined to interrogate witnesses and capture the king's assassin. It won't take long before they hear from some of our neighbors about the chaos emanating from this building—the Quarante Cinq will soon be crawling all over this place demanding answers."

He looked at each team member in turn, noted their tattered clothing, their cuts, and bruises and—in Martin's case—broken bones. "We've all obviously been in a fight, one that we don't want to answer any difficult questions about. Get changed into fresh clothing, gather your belongings and let's get out of here. We'll split up. Leave the Les Halles area as soon as you can and then get out of Paris. We'll rendezvous at Dijon in a week."

Ravid paused a moment, looking around the shattered appartement. "And I'll send a message to Jesse, asking him to arrange for this appartement to be repaired. It's the least we can do for Monsieur and Madame Gombaud."

They had barely begun when there was a mighty pounding on the front door.

SIXTY-THREE
A month earlier
**Academy of Secrets, Naples, Kingdom of Naples,
Morning, Wednesday April 7 1610**

Luca stood behind the hidden peephole, ready to eavesdrop on the meeting about to take place in the room below. Thanks to whoever had designed this secret chamber, Luca expected to be able to see and hear the conversation clearly.

Luca and his classmates had been released from their three-week isolation training in the Tower that very morning. Luca had been heading down to a morning meal when he overheard two servants gossiping about an imminent meeting. *Thankfully,* he thought, *I had time to get into place here before the meeting started.*

As Luca settled in to watch, the Master arrived in the room below. *That's odd,* thought Luca, *Della Porta hasn't given his visitor much of a greeting, simply a brief nod of his head.*

The visitor was seated with his back to the wall on which the peephole was mounted, beside one of the several desks in the room. Della Porta chose a seat alongside rather than opposite the visitor, another apparent sign of disrespect, and then took out parchment and pen from the desk and began writing.

Luca was puzzled. *What kind of meeting is this?*

The mystery was finally resolved when the visitor moved his chair slightly and Luca finally had a good view of his face. It was one of the Janus twins. *Ah,* realized Luca, *it's a long-distance conference between the members of the Consiglio.*

The Janus twins—not really twins, there were eight of them, and in fact they were not even related—had all gained the power of telepathy thanks to the Exousía potion. The twins could share thoughts with each other over vast distances and the Council of Four made use of their talent to maintain instant communications between the four groups. The Academy itself also used several of the twins to enable remote communications when it sent groups of Alchemae on long-distance missions.

Luca had seen the twins in action only once before, from this very vantage point—as a just-graduated student, he was certainly not authorized to know about such secrets.

"Ready—Ready—Ready." *That's so weird.*

The Janus twin spoke in three different voices—one gruff, one cheerful and the third somewhat deep—channeling messages from three different twins. Della Porta nodded and Luca knew that the three twins at the other ends of the conversation would be translating that nod into a "Ready" of their own.

Della Porta began the discussion, reporting on progress with the Plague project. Judging by the pointed questions forwarded by the Janus twin, this project had been proceeding far more slowly than other members of the Council expected. Della Porta fielded the queries with mostly non-committal answers. *I don't know what this 'Plague project' is about, I should do some digging.*

"What about the tomb?" asked the deep-voiced Janus. "Any luck?"

"None so far," said Della Porta. "We're still convinced it's down in the catacombs somewhere but so far no-one we've sent has managed to find it."

"Keep trying," said the deep-sounding voice. "The Darke Warriors have always been extremely keen to find that body. I think we can assume that it carries something worthwhile—we must find it before they do."

The discussion turned to the package captured two days earlier. "It's on its way to you," said the cheerful-voiced Janus. "Let us know when you receive it."

Finally, the meeting became interesting—at least, from Luca's perspective. The Janus twin began to speak again, this time channeling the gruff voice. "This is Killigrew speaking for New Phoenicia. We have organized a treaty between France and Savoy to drive Spain out of the Italian peninsula. Master Della Porta, we need your Alchemae troops to protect the French king and the Duke of Savoy. We fear that Spain will try to have them killed before the treaty can be fully implemented."

Luca nearly jumped with excitement. *This is my chance! The Spanish Empire will reward me handsomely—restore our family to our proper place in the Kingdom of Naples—if I can stop this treaty. Now I have to figure out the best method of doing that—and who can be trusted to help me.*

The meeting continued. The discussion had now turned to a problem in the Tsardom of Russia, a more contentious topic. Luca would normally have found it fascinating to watch the different voices of the twin arguing with each other. This time, he no longer paid much attention as he began to make his own plans.

SIXTY-FOUR
A clearing on the outskirts of Paris, France,
Early Evening, Friday May 14 1610

Father Carracci sat alone in his carriage reading. He looked up as Luca and Ruben entered and sat down opposite him. "The word's been spreading all over Paris this afternoon," Carracci said, "that the king is dead. I gather that you succeeded."

Luca nodded triumphantly. "We certainly did! Ruben turned himself into a duplicate of that fanatic who was at the palace demanding to see the king. I bribed one of the palace guards with my transmuted gold, so that we could find out exactly where the king was going this afternoon. Then we got ourselves into position. As soon as we saw the king's carriage heading towards the Rue de la Ferronnerie, I bribed two cart drivers with more instant gold, so that they blocked the street. Ruben did the rest."

Carracci turned his attention to Ruben, who stared back blankly. "Oh, right," said Carracci, "You're still in that trance." Carracci turned to Luca. "Ruben won't remember anything that's happened while he's been enchanted. I thought that was best, for all our sakes. I'm not sure that Ruben shares our desire to protect Spain's interests in Naples. I'm so glad that you came to me with your plan, Luca."

Luca nodded. "I don't understand why the French people have been so willing to believe in Henri IV's supposed conversion. It's always been obvious to me that he was still Protestant at heart, and simply pretended to be Catholic in order to claim the throne."

Carracci smiled. "That's exactly how I saw him as well. And I was prepared to take any action, pay any price, to ensure that Protestant pretender did not gain any more footholds on Catholic soil."

Carracci looked at Luca thoughtfully. "You do realize, Luca, that you won't be able to speak of this to anybody at the Academy? Master Della Porta will not be happy if he should learn that we killed Henri IV. He was more than willing to carry out New Phoenicia's instructions—it suited his insane dream, to see the Roman Empire reinstated. His goal was to have France, Savoy, and Spain battling amongst themselves, creating a power vacuum which he somehow thought he could exploit."

"My lips are sealed, of course," said Luca, "as long as you live up to your part of the bargain, to use your connections in the Church and in Spain to see my family reinstated to its rightful place in the Kingdom of Naples." He smiled at the thought.

Carracci nodded and then spoke swiftly. *"hēthē yōdzayin ʾālepnūndālet nūn ʾālep mēm ʾālep rēšyōd."*

Luca froze. His face went completely blank. Father Carracci bent over and peered into the young man's eyes which were now, like Ruben's, uncomprehending. Carracci shook his head softly. "I'm sorry, Luca," he said, although Luca could no longer understand him. "I can't take that chance. You're too much like me—you would try to exploit any weakness to achieve your aims. You would use your knowledge of my part in this regicide to destroy me."

Carracci stepped down from the carriage and walked around to the back, where his luggage was stored. A few moments later, he had retrieved the rapier that had been part of his civilian costume in Pisa. Thus armed, Carracci strode to the front of the carriage and untied the horses from the hitching post to which they had been secured. He climbed up to the driver's seat at the front of the carriage and, after carefully stowing the rapier beside him, gathered up the reins, preparing to begin the long return journey to Naples.

That ravine I passed a week ago, on the Mont Cenis pass, Carracci thought as he tugged on the reins. *That would make a nice burial spot. Very deep and deserted and no unwanted witnesses.*

The horses slowly began to pull the carriage in response to Carracci's urging.

SIXTY-FIVE
23 Rue de la Ferronnerie, Paris, France,
Afternoon, Friday May 14 1610

The pounding on the appartement door intensified. "Open up, in the name of the king!"

Sounds of splintering wood followed, as whoever was on the other side mounted a savage attack on the door.

That wood won't last for long. Ravid quickly looked around for an alternative exit. Niall, gesturing frantically, pointed to the skylight far above. The distance might not have been very great when there was an upper floor, but the skylight was now a long way from where the team currently stood on the ground floor.

Ravid wasn't convinced. *How is the team going to reach that?*

As if Niall had read his mind, the Irishman stretched his arms up, up, up, his fingers reaching and then unlatching the skylight. Meanwhile a jagged hole appeared in one of the wooden door panels as the attack intensified. Niall waved frantically to Lochloinn. Once he had the Scotsman's attention, Niall pointed to Martin.

A hand snaked in through the newly created hole in the door, reaching around for the door key. Lochloinn rushed over to Martin, carefully hoisted the Englishman's body over his shoulder and then, using Niall's stretched body as an impromptu ladder, began climbing towards the skylight.

At that moment, the door was driven open by the combined pressure of what turned out to be at least six soldiers, their red and blue livery proclaiming that they belonged to France's elite Quarante Cinq, the royal guardsmen. The soldiers rushed into the room, pikes lowered and ready to attack—and then came to a crashing halt. Most of the room was plunged into darkness as Martin, despite his precarious position on Lochloinn's shoulder, had recovered enough to use his powers.

The leading guardsman, unsighted, nevertheless stabbed out with his pike—until a hand reached out from the darkness and touched the soldier's outstretched arm. Instantly, the guardsman froze in place. *Good—Sean has recovered enough to use his powers of paralysis,* realized Ravid.

Before any of the other guardsmen could move, Elias announced to them, in French: "The assassins have escaped through the back door. If you hurry outside now you should be able to capture them."

The Quarante Cinq guardsmen—except for the temporarily paralyzed soldier—responded to Elias' powers of persuasion by turning and feeling their way towards the door. Once outside, they shared the news with their comrades. "They've gone—they escaped out through the back door. Quickly, follow them."

Martin was still being carried upward by Lochloinn. The Scotsman continued to climb, using Niall's body as a ladder, until he finally reached the skylight and was able to bundle Martin through and onto the roof. Niall, relieved of the dual weight of Lochloinn and Martin, gamely called down. "Who's next?"

"Don't worry about us, Niall," whispered Ravid. "Just get yourself to safety."

Once Niall had done exactly that, Ravid summoned his wings and made two flights up to the skylight, first carrying Elias, and then a second time for Sean.

Ravid's team then made their way across a series of rooftops, leaping, stretching, or flying across any gaps too wide to navigate on foot, only pausing once they were well away from the Les Halles region. Meanwhile the Quarante Cinq guardsmen searched fruitlessly at ground level.

While the team took a few moments to rest, Ravid considered their next move. The super-powered team was obviously from somewhere in Naples—but which part? He mind-called Jesse. *<If there's any more information you can provide about the origin of these super-powered teams, please let me know immediately. In the meantime, I'm sending the team to Dijon. Please ask Zophiel and a healer to meet them there in seven days.>*

Once he had completed his mind-talk with Jesse, Ravid turned to his team. "We need to leave Paris. It will easier to avoid the guardsmen if you each make your way out of the city separately. Meet at Dijon in a week—

another Outcast Angel, Zophiel, will join you there."

"I'll be takin' Martin wit' me," volunteered Lochloinn, "odderwise he won't be goin' far wit' that leg."

"I've asked Jesse to send a healer to Dijon as well," said Ravid. "Hopefully he'll be able to fix up your injuries." Martin nodded thankfully.

The team shook hands with each other and prepared to split up. Elias came over for a quiet word with Ravid. "What about you, Ravid? What are you planning to do?"

"Before I leave Paris, I'm going to have a little talk with Bishop de Richelieu."

SIXTY-SIX
A Few Days Later
Smolensk, Tsardom of Russia,
5.30 a.m. Wednesday May 19 1610

Shamar landed lightly on the hill overlooking the Russian walled city of Smolensk as dawn broke over the besieged city. He dismissed his wings with a thought and stood for a few moments taking stock of his surroundings.

From this elevated perspective, it was clear why Smolensk had not yet fallen despite nine months under siege by the forces of the Kingdom of Poland. The entire central core of the city was encircled first by a moat and then by massive outer stone walls that shrugged off any blasts from the heavy guns fired by the Polish attackers. Inner walls provided a further layer of protection for the determined defenders. *If any cannon do manage to blow a hole in one of those outer walls, it's unlikely that the attackers will be able to reach it anyway—the parapets behind the walls are bristling with Russian soldiers armed with arquebuses and muskets, thirsty for blood. They'll eagerly pick off anyone attempting to reach the city, especially when they try to cross the moat.*

Shamar turned his attention to the forces besieging the city. Normally at this hour of the morning, most would have been asleep—a siege is a long-term action, so early morning attacks are not common—but the previous day's arrival of King Sigismund III of Poland had clearly spurred his local commanders into a pointless display of action intended to impress the royal entourage.

The attackers' camp hummed with activity. Infantrymen could be seen moving into position near the front line, firing largely ineffective shots at the Smolensk defenders. Every few minutes one of the Polish cannon would roar into life, belching fire and smoke and a single cannonball which would hurtle itself inadequately at one of the city's walls, serving merely to dislodge a few stone splinters from the grimly unmoved fortification.

In response, Smolensk defenders took occasional potshots at Polish positions. The Polish camp was only slightly out of range, and some of the Smolensk attempts were too close for comfort—fragments of musket shot bounced off the ground, forcing the attackers to take cover.

Dozens of Polish and Ukrainian Cossacks on horseback, armed with long pikes, rode purposefully around the camp. *I'm not sure what they're expecting to skewer with those pikes, they certainly don't have any hope of using them anywhere within musket range of the walled city.*

Shamar mind-called Jesse. *<What exactly should I expect to find here?>*

Jesse was quick to reply. *<Get to King Sigismund and then see if you can identify anyone nearby who looks out of place. The king doesn't see anything before he is afflicted but maybe you can.>*

<Why, what's going to happen to the king?> Shamar asked. *<And why did you insist that I had to be here so fast? There wasn't time for anyone but angels to get here.>*

<I needed you here immediately,> said Jesse, *<because everything happens this morning. In the next hour or so, the king is going to start hearing voices in his head, in a language that he doesn't understand but that I've tentatively identified as a Napoletano dialect—so you are probably after someone from the Kingdom of Naples.>*

<Another one? I think we're finally starting to identify where our enemies are located.>

<Indeed,> agreed Jesse. *<The king will complain of hearing loud voices in his head - voices that no-one else can hear. The voices will go on day after day, shouting at him in nonsense languages he does not know. The royal doctors cannot cure him, and will eventually conclude that it is better for the country and for the king if they simply lock him up for life. They think he is crazy—but I know he is not, for I too can hear those voices, through him. Those who oppose us will attack him through his mind, but he will simply not be believed.*

<Once the king tells his generals that he's hearing voices, they lock him up—there are always plenty of military leaders who crave more power—and Sigismund remains imprisoned for the rest of his life. I didn't call for your help earlier because I didn't think it was part of the same

problem—Sigismund isn't killed, as so many of his peers are. But yesterday I looked into what happens as a result of the king's incarceration—and I found that Poland doesn't survive the experience, it descends into civil war and anarchy. Clearly, this is all part of the same attack we're seeing elsewhere.>

<Okay,> said Shamar, heading towards the Polish army's camp, *<leave it with me and I'll see what I can find out.>*

SIXTY-SEVEN
Smolensk, Tsardom of Russia,
5.45 a.m. Wednesday May 19 1610

A short time later, Polish sentries hailed Shamar as he approached the main camp.

"Halt! Who goes there?"

Security was tight with the king in the camp. Shamar smiled—in such circumstances, his own supernatural abilities came into their own.

"You know who I am," he said, "I'm with the king's entourage. I arrived here yesterday."

The two Polish soldiers manning the forward guard post looked at each other and nodded. Shamar's heavenly gift was that when people looked at him, they saw a close friend who they unconsciously recognized as being on their side, whose word they would take at face value.

The guards readily allowed Shamar to have unfettered access to the camp—and everyone who saw him treated him as one of their own, despite his inappropriate clothing and lack of documentation.

Shamar walked through the camp, nodding and smiling. He was warned not to get too close to the city below, lest the Russian snipers use him for target practice.

A group of otherwise-vigilant guards recognized Shamar—or believed that they did—and he was soon directed to the command tent close to the front line, where the king was talking with his generals. Once he entered the tent, Shamar inspected the Polish and Ukrainian troops inside, searching for anyone who didn't belong.

Shamar had barely begun his inspection when, out of the blue, King Sigismund spoke to those around him.

"What was that? I didn't understand you?"

His generals looked at each other. One, braver than the rest, spoke up. "Majesty, we didn't say a word."

"Of course you did," said Sigismund irritably. "I'm not deaf—I heard you, plain as day. I didn't understand the language, that's all."

The king paused, listened. "There you go again. What is it you're saying? Speak in Polish or be damned!"

The generals looked at each other, embarrassed and perplexed. Whatever was happening here, they didn't want the common soldiers to see it. They ordered everybody out of the command tent except senior officers and the king's staff. Shamar, of course, was left alone—those who saw him were convinced that he had a perfect right to be there.

That makes my task much easier, thought Shamar. He took a close look at those who remained in the tent, as the king shouted out again. "What do you want? Leave me alone!"

One of the king's aides attempted to calm him down, but the king was having none of it. "Don't waste your time with me. Find whoever's shouting at me. Make them stop!"

Everyone in the tent was now openly staring at King Sigismund. Everyone, that is, except one Ukrainian Cossack officer, who was actively attempting to avoid looking at the king. *Is he trying to be polite or does he have another agenda,* wondered Shamar.

Shamar took a closer look. He saw a very young man, overweight, greasy black hair, wearing an ill-fitting Ukrainian Cossack uniform and sweating nervously. *Surely he's too young to be an officer. He must be the one.*

Shamar walked up to the purported Ukrainian officer and spoke to him in Napoletano. "Hi. I'm Shamar. Don't I know you?"

The soldier smiled, in recognition and relief. "Of course—Shamar. Nice to see you again. I'm Niccolo."

"Right, Niccolo, of course," said Shamar. "Stop what you're doing for a moment. We need to talk."

Niccolo was instantly wary, but Shamar's apparent status as a friend gave sufficient reassurance that Niccolo paused his mental bombardment of the Polish king.

Shamar made a further suggestion. "Let's take this conversation outside the tent, shall we, so we don't—talk about matters that others here don't need to know about."

"I don't think anyone else here speaks Napoletano," objected Niccolo, before agreeing to Shamar's request. "Still, we should take appropriate precautions." He bent down, picked up his pack, and followed Shamar outside the command tent. There was a deserted area in front, a few feet down the hill from the tent.

Shamar stopped there, confident that they were out of earshot of any Polish or Ukrainian troops, and resumed his careful questioning.

"So, why exactly are you doing this, Niccolo?" As he asked the question, Shamar waved vaguely in the direction of the command tent that they had now exited.

Convinced that he was talking to a friend and co-conspirator, Niccolo answered quickly. "King Sigismund is responsible for the siege of Smolensk and the invasion of Russia. New Phoenicia has demanded that he been removed, he is interfering with their plans for the Tsardom—but because he is Catholic, Father Carracci insists that the king must not be killed." Niccolo smiled proudly. "The Academy chose me because I have the ideal talent to provide a solution that will keep both New Phoenicia and Father Carracci happy. Once I'm done, King Sigismund will be forced to abdicate but he won't be killed."

Ah hah, thought Shamar, *conflicting agendas. And New Phoenicia is involved as well. That explains many things.*

Shamar considered his options and then spoke again to Niccolo. "The situation has changed, Niccolo. I've just come from Naples."

"From the Academy?" asked Niccolo.

"Yes," said Shamar, grateful for the confirmation. "Father—?" Shamar couldn't quite remember the name Niccolo had mentioned. Niccolo helpfully supplied the missing ingredient.

"Carracci."

"Right. Father Carracci has sent a message, which I've been asked to deliver. The priest wants you to stop what you're doing, for now. He wants you to come back to Naples with me. He has an even more important task for you."

"Really?" Niccolo fairly glowed with self-importance. "Certainly, I'd be glad to get back home. It's been so difficult here. They only speak Polish or Ukrainian and no-one speaks any languages that I know. But I'm nearly finished with the king. All I have to do is lock my words into a mind loop and—"

"No!" said Shamar, too quickly. "That—that—" He stuttered, trying to find a credible excuse. "That won't be necessary. New Phoenicia has come up with a new plan."

"Oh?" said another ill-dressed Ukrainian Cossack, suddenly enlarging into view and growing and growing until he was a veritable giant, eight feet tall. He had been hidden in miniature size within Niccolo's pack, watching for any problems. "And exactly what is this new plan?"

The sudden appearance of this midget turned giant caught Shamar by surprise, but he struggled on gamely, attempting to explain himself. "It's—well, honestly, I'm not at liberty to share that with you. If Father Carracci wants to tell you, that's up to him. I'm afraid I'm not authorized to do so."

"Is that right?" The giant sounded suspicious. "And you are—who, exactly?"

"I'm Shamar, of course," said the Outcast Angel. "You do remember me, don't you?"

"Well, you are familiar," agreed the giant, "but I can't quite place you. Where do I know you from?"

"From Naples," insisted Shamar, desperately hoping that this super-powered newcomer came from the same place as Niccolo.

"Well yes of course from Naples," said the giant, "but exactly where and when? Did you meet us at the Academy—?"

"Yes, yes, it must have been at the Academy," said Shamar, desperate for more information about this mysterious Academy.

"When?" demanded the giant.

"Umm—last month?" suggested Shamar.

"We were long gone by then, weren't we, Simon?" said Niccolo, rejoining the conversation. "It's taken us nearly two months to get here from Naples."

"If you were in Naples last month, then how did you get here so fast, Shamar? Fly?" The giant, now identified as Simon, had adopted a scornful tone. Shamar could feel that he was losing this discussion, a sinking feeling that was reinforced when two knives appeared in Simon's hands.

"Whoa," said Shamar, backing out of reach of the giant's long arms. "There's no need for those. We're friends."

"Well," said Simon, stepping in front of Niccolo and staring at

Shamar, "my heart tells me that, as well. But we have a task to complete here, and nothing that you've said so far has convinced me that we should abandon our duty. If you're going to get in the way—" Simon waved the knives threateningly. "—then I'll have to stop you."

SIXTY-EIGHT
A Moment Later
Smolensk, Tsardom of Russia,
6.00 a.m. Wednesday May 19 1610

Shamar tried to defuse the situation. "Come on fellows. You know me. We're on the same side."

"Are we?" Simon was now on heightened alert, and Shamar's persuasiveness was no longer exerting its usual influence. "Then why are you so eager to prevent us doing what we have been specifically instructed to do, yet you can provide no proof that the instruction comes from either the Academy or the Council of Four?"

Despite the increasingly hostile reception, Shamar was delighted. *Council of Four? Whoever they are, Jesse will be delighted to learn about them.*

Simon was still waiting for a response so Shamar attempted to concoct a convincing explanation. "As you said, it's a long journey between here and Naples. The proof is on its way but it isn't here yet."

Simon scoffed. "Why not simply send a message by Janus twin? They can talk to Niccolo. Why send you in person?"

Shamar had absolutely no idea what Simon was talking about. The Outcast Angel tried to bluff. "The—Janus?—couldn't get through, for some reason. I was not far from here so they asked me to come and tell you myself."

If Simon looked doubtful, Niccolo was immediately certain. "I've just been talking to a twin. This man is lying. Deal with him, Simon, while I get back to the tent and finish off the king."

Niccolo turned and began heading back to the command tent. Shamar tried to stop Niccolo, attempting to circle around Simon, but the giant stepped across and blocked Shamar's path. "I don't think so, Shamar. Niccolo, get inside."

Shamar made an instant decision, one that he desperately hoped he would not have cause to regret. "Sorry, Niccolo, I can't let you do that."

Before either Alchemae could react to his words, Shamar summoned his wings with a thought and launched himself into the air, lifting himself well above Simon and then swooping down to seize Niccolo.

Though Niccolo struggled in his grasp, Shamar was able to lift the young man a dozen feet in the air. He was about to leave the area with his reluctant passenger when Shamar felt his ankle grabbed. He looked down in shock, to discover that Simon had pushed himself to grow even further. The giant now towered alongside the Outcast, had a firm hand around one leg and attempted to pull him out of the sky. In his other hand, Simon clutched one of his knives, waving it menacingly towards Shamar.

SIXTY-NINE
Instants Later
Smolensk, Tsardom of Russia,
6.05 a.m. Wednesday May 19 1610

Shamar tried to shake his leg free, to no avail—the giant would not be so easily dislodged. Worse, Niccolo, stunned at first by the appearance of the angel's wings, had recovered and began a mental assault on Shamar. *<Let me go! Let me go! LET ME GO!!!>*

Then the situation turned ugly—and Shamar finally understood why the ground in front of the command tent was so deserted. That area was within firing range of the walled city and a fusillade of shots rang out as Smolensk's defenders finally saw targets that they could reach.

A flurry of musket balls screamed towards the trio. Shamar, pinned to the spot thanks to Simon, attempted to dodge and was mostly successful, apart from a couple of shots that inflicted minor damage to his right wing. Niccolo, largely protected within Shamar's grasp, escaped unscathed.

Simon, an almost unmissable target at full stretch, was not so lucky—four musket balls slammed into his back. The giant shuddered and then fell heavily to the ground, releasing his grip as he did so.

Shamar, who had continued to strain mightily against Simon's restraining grasp, shot up into the air at great speed once the giant's hold was released. Niccolo was shocked into silence, firstly by what had happened to Simon and secondly by the fact that someone who must be an angel was lifting him high into the air.

The pair, angel and Alchemae, were nearly a hundred feet above ground when Niccolo finally regained his composure enough to resume his mental attack. Shamar gave the young man a powerful whack on the side of the head. "Listen, you little addle-pate, before you get us both killed," hissed Shamar. "My mind powers my wings. Knock me out, or distract me enough with your black-mouthing and we will both plummet to the ground—which, in case you haven't noticed, is getting further and further away."

One downward glance by Niccolo was enough to confirm his plight. He wisely halted his mental barrage and without further protest let Shamar carry him away.

# # #

Whilst it might have seemed that Niccolo had given up the fight, the reality was otherwise. Instead, he was furiously transmitting to the nearest Janus twin. *<The Outcast Angels now know about the Academy, thanks to Simon.>* Inevitably, Niccolo neglected to mention the fact that he himself was actually the one who had first revealed the Academy's existence. *<Warn the Master.>*

PART FOUR

SEVENTY
The Tower, Academy of Secrets, Naples, Kingdom of Naples, Midnight Friday June 18 1610

Once again, the Contessa found herself at the top of the Academy's Tower, waiting for Nekhbet.

The Darke Warrior soon arrived and wasted no time getting to the point of her visit. "It's been a hundred and fifty days since we entrusted Chrymos to your care. The critical moment is approaching. How is she doing?"

"Festering nicely," replied the Contessa. "She thinks she's been rejected. We have her helping with the food and cleaning out the stables. She's on a knife edge—nearly ready to run."

"Then you should move to the next phase."

The Contessa ventured a deadly smile. "Another couple of days and we'll set the trap. I'm waiting for one more piece of the puzzle to fall into place."

"You know what you have to do?" asked Nekhbet.

The Contessa nodded. "Someone she trusts will help her to escape. But before she can get away, she will come face to face with her past."

"And that—"

"—will trigger the Lost War," said the Contessa, "just as you intended."

SEVENTY-ONE
Two Days Later
**Academy of Secrets, Naples, Kingdom of Naples,
Early morning Monday, June 21 1610**

The kitchen simply buzzed that morning. Apparently, the Contessa had been in a very pleasant mood the previous night and had even praised the cook for her *panettone*. The reason for the Contessa's unexpectedly good humor was quickly evident—the Academy's mistress had just received an invitation to Naples' opening night of the opera *Euridice*, to be performed by a touring French cast. "The opera starts this weekend," burbled the cook, "and they say it has plenty of handsome young French monsieurs on display."

Chrymos didn't share the cook's enthusiasm for the opera, but still was happy because as a beneficial side effect, Cook was willing to give Chrymos extra work in return for an early and peaceful breakfast. The Master's food had already been prepared and sent upstairs, so instead Chrymos was tasked with delivering a cart of leftover food to the Academy's mortality room, where charitable medical care was provided to a few of the lazzaroni of Naples.

Like the kitchen, the mortality room was on the lowest level of the Della Porta mansion, which ensured that the Academy's students and teaching staff would not be exposed to any of the diseases that might be raging outside the Academy's privileged walls.

Although it was known as the mortality "room," the medical facility was in fact a whole series of chambers. The main treatment area included a half-dozen beds and was the place where new patients were assessed. The floor also boasted a large number of ancillary rooms that could each house as many as a dozen patients.

Chrymos was supposed to simply knock on the main door to the mortality room and then leave the food cart for the medical staff. But Chrymos knew how frantic the mortality room could become, so she preferred to bring the cart inside and on occasion would even feed some of the patients herself.

This time, however, as Chrymos pushed the cart inside the mortality room, she caught the slightest hint of a smell that she knew only too well from her days on the streets—putrefying flesh, an odor that Chrymos instantly associated with the deadly plagues that regularly killed their way through Europe.

Is the Black Death sweeping through Naples again? Is the city at risk? And what about my children? Chrymos still thought of Olivia, Madalena, and Sirus as 'hers,' despite not having seen them for months. *How can they avoid the plague?*

Chrymos was cautious, but she wasn't afraid. She quickly looked around for fresh flowers. The floral fragrances, according to common wisdom, should protect her from the miasma, the cloud of poisonous gas by which the plague was spread. Such safeguards had protected her in Florence while she tended to several of the other street urchins who had fallen sick during one of the plague's regular incursions. *Surely, they will do the same here?*

There were no fresh flowers in sight, although there was the usual collection of herbs to minister to the sick and wounded, including cayenne, comfrey, horsetail, and juniper. Before Chrymos could go looking elsewhere for suitable floral protection, one of the Academy's doctors entered the room. Chrymos' instincts were confirmed—the doctor wore a plague mask and full protective clothing. Chrymos couldn't help staring—she had never seen a plague doctor up close.

The doctor wore the mask strapped to his head, covered by a sturdy cloth hood. The plague mask had a long curved beak shaped like that of a bird, with glass eyes so that the doctor could examine his patients without being exposed directly to the disease. The beak itself was stuffed with many herbs and blossoms, all designed to filter out the deadly miasma.

A heavy overcoat, which swaddled the doctor from his shoulders to his feet, afforded further protection from the plague. Gauntleted gloves hid the doctor's hands and he carried a wooden cane with which, Chrymos realized, he could probably examine patients without touching them.

Chrymos called out. "What I can do to help, doctor?"

Caught by surprise as he was about to enter one of the inner rooms, the doctor stopped, looked over at Chrymos, shook his head. His voice, when it came, was muffled through the mask. "No, no, we're fine. Besides, you're not exactly dressed for dealing with these patients."

Instantly becoming aware of her own slight attire, which offered scant protection from the deadly disease, Chrymos backed away through the mortality room door, leaving the doctor to look after his patients. *I'll come back for the cart later.*

Chrymos scurried back to the kitchen and sought comfort in the millet bread and gruel that was her reward for her morning's labors. Her mind, though, was still in the mortality room, wondering what she could do to help—and desperately wishing that she could somehow warn the three children.

SEVENTY-TWO
Later that evening
Academy of Secrets, Naples, Kingdom of Naples,
Night, Monday, June 21 1610

As usual, Chrymos was locked in her basement pit for the evening. For once, though, she had a different concern to occupy her mind and minimize any panic attacks. If the plague had returned then now, more than ever, she wanted to escape so that she could find her three former wards.

Her thoughts were interrupted by the sliding sound of the ceiling hatch that guarded her basement prison. *Is Luca finally back? I wouldn't even mind his puerile attempts to scare me, after all these weeks of silence night after night.*

Instead of her enemy, Chrymos was delighted to see a friend's face, illuminated by a lantern he carried. Her visitor was Henricus. He lay prone on the floor above, peering down through the hatchway and he had a big smile on his face.

"Hi, Chrymos! I just arrived back, heard you were under house arrest, and wanted to say hello."

"Hi to you too, Henricus. Good to see you as well—though I expect I'll probably see you at breakfast tomorrow."

Henricus shook his head. "No, you probably won't. And, if you do, you almost certainly won't like me."

"What do you mean?"

"At dawn, I'm scheduled to receive a fresh dose of Exousía potion. I came to say goodbye tonight because, frankly, I won't be the same tomorrow. We're now being given an altered potion—and it changes our personalities.

"There is a new ingredient, a crimson liquid. I don't quite know how to describe the effects except to say it toughens people up, makes them more aggressive, more willing to act violently. I suppose it's necessary if we are to have any hope of winning the Lost War. But it makes the recipients very unpleasant and nasty. I've already lost several of my friends to this new mixture and I expect to lose all of them once I take the new potion—including you."

"That explains at least some of the changes I've seen around here," said Chrymos, nodding thoughtfully. "Do you think they tried it out on Simon when he was given his potion? He was so different afterwards."

"Yes, he was one of the first," said Henricus, "and the change was extremely noticeable. Of course, with some Alchemae, it wouldn't have been necessary—they were mean enough as it was."

"Yeah," said Chrymos, thinking of Luca in particular. "Thanks for the warning, Henricus, you've been a good friend. Even if I seem to lose you, I'll understand—it's not actually you, it's the potion speaking."

Henricus looked very unhappy.

Poor Henricus, you're dreading tomorrow, aren't you? Chrymos tried to help by changing the subject. "Anyway, where have you been? I haven't seen you around for ages."

Henricus brightened. "Mostly I've been on sentinel duty, on the lookout for people with powers, but every so often I get to go out on a mission. This last week, that's exactly what I've been doing and Doctor Odaldi even allowed me to use the Járngreipr. I'm heading to the Tower to return them."

He showed Chrymos the enchanted gauntlets. "I can't tell you about the mission, of course, you know how it is."

Chrymos nodded.

"And how about you?" Henricus continued. "What have you been doing with yourself since last I saw you?"

"Not much," admitted Chrymos. "Helping out with meals and cleaning and so on. But it's been very quiet—Cook hardly prepares any meals for the Alchemae these days. I gather that they're all out on 'mysterious missions'."

It was Henricus' turn to nod. "Yes, there's a lot of that happening. I guess that's normal, in the lead-up to a war."

"How long have you been back?" Chrymos had a few more questions she wanted to ask Henricus, but there was no point if he had only just arrived.

"I arrived back just after lunch today."

"So—have you seen Adric? Is he around? Does he know what his power is yet?"

Henricus shook his head. "He was one of your classmates, right? He's still here, I'm told, though I haven't seen him myself. I don't think his powers have shown up yet."

"And what about Ruben?"

"That's right, he was in your class too. I'm not sure where he is. This afternoon I heard one of the teachers searching for him but no one seemed to know where he'd gone. That's the trouble with secret missions—those who know about them can't say anything."

They both smiled.

Then Chrymos asked her most important question—although it wasn't one to which she really wanted an answer. "Is Father Carracci back yet?"

Henricus sobered. "Yes, I believe he has just returned—I overheard the servants talking as I made my way here." He looked down, saw the sparkle fade from Chrymos' eyes and carefully considered his next words. He beckoned to Chrymos to stand up and move directly under the hatchway so that he could speak more softly.

"I understand that his first words were about you," Henricus half-whispered. Chrymos had to strain to hear as he continued. "The servants were gossiping about it. Apparently, he said 'by the time I'm finished with her, she'll wish that the Blood Countess had strangled her at birth'."

"Sorry," he added, seeing the impact that the priest's words had on Chrymos. "But I thought you'd better know—before you find out the hard way tomorrow."

SEVENTY-THREE
A few moments later
**Academy of Secrets, Naples, Kingdom of Naples,
Night, Monday, June 21 1610**

After hearing that news, Chrymos couldn't stand still—she paced around and around her small prison cell, thinking, desperately seeking a solution. Henricus looked down helplessly.

Finally, after a few minutes' pacing, Chrymos stopped almost directly under the hatchway and stared into Henricus' eyes. He stared back unhappily.

"Henricus," she finally said, "I hate to ask you this—I don't want to get you into trouble—but are you willing to get the ladder and lower it down so that I can escape from here?"

For a moment, Chrymos thought that she must have presumed too much. There was no reply from Henricus. She looked up and his face was gone.

Fortunately, before she could start to despair, Henricus reappeared.

"Sorry, Chrymos, I've inspected the ladder," he replied. "It's been locked down with heavy chains—and I suspect it's protected with enchantments as well. That's usually what happens around here."

Chrymos slumped down on the straw of her basement floor and let out a heartfelt cry. She looked so miserable. Henricus looked down, pondered her plight, and then made a decision.

"Chrymos." He called softly.

She looked up. Henricus held out the Járngreipr, indicating that she should catch them. As he released the gauntlets, he added, "You can use them to climb out of this place, they can grip through solid rock."

Chrymos caught the two gauntlets, which were surprisingly heavy. She looked quizzically at Henricus, who shrugged.

"I'm supposed to return the gauntlets tonight," he said, "but I'll say that I forgot."

"Won't you get into trouble?"

"Probably. But once you escape from here," Henricus added, "if you can leave the Járngreipr outside my room, I'll return them in the morning instead."

Chrymos was profusely grateful but Henricus waved her thanks away.

"No need, I know you would do the same for me. Oh, one more thing," he added. "The guards patrol the main entrances. You'll need to slip out through the mortality room."

"There's a way out through the back?"

"Yes, there's a separate entrance. That's how they bring in the poor to be treated. The guards are too afraid of catching any disease so they don't go near that part of the Academy."

Chrymos wasn't surprised. *Most of the guards are very superstitious. And with what goes on here in the Academy, they have every reason to be.*

"We found the door several years ago," Henricus continued, "and of course you know what some of the students here are like. When we were supposed to be studying at night, we would often slip out through that room and head to the city. We usually returned through the same back entrance, without anyone noticing."

"Simpler times," he added with a sigh. "I'll just go and make sure there's nobody still around in the kitchen or on this floor. Give me five minutes and then, unless you hear me whistle, you'll know it's safe to climb out and get away."

Henricus looked down at Chrymos and blew her a kiss. "Safe travels, my dear. It has been a true pleasure."

With that final endearment, Henricus walked out of sight.

SEVENTY-FOUR
Academy of Secrets, Naples, Kingdom of Naples, Night, Monday, June 21 1610

Chrymos gathered her few possessions into her precious swete bagge, slipped an arm through its handle so that she could carry the bag over one shoulder and prepared for the climb ahead.

Even with the Járngreipr, it was not easy for her to escape from the basement prison. By trial and error, Chrymos discovered that by pushing hard with one of the gauntlets she could poke holes in the stone wall, creating footholds and handholds that enabled her to climb up to the wooden ceiling of her basement home. It was slow going, and the pace slowed even further once she reached the ceiling.

Yes, it was much easier to poke holes in wood than stone, but once she had left the wall behind, Chrymos had to hang on grimly with one hand whilst using the other to carve out her next handhold.

Twice, she simply could not maintain her grip long enough and dropped to the floor below. No broken bones, but more than enough scrapes and bruises. Thankfully, there was nothing breakable in the bag, which ended up under Chrymos' body after her second plunge, winding her briefly.

On the third attempt, Chrymos was finally able to make enough progress to drag herself all the way across the ceiling to the hatch. With her right hand, she grabbed at the nearest edge of the hatchway then tried to swing her left hand across to reach the other edge.

For one eternally long moment, Chrymos feared that she would fail. Her heavy-gauntlet-clad hand, already weakened from supporting her weight through much of the ceiling-wide traverse, simply would not swing far enough across to make contact with the far edge.

Twice, three times, four times she tried to swing her left hand into position while her right hand trembled from the extended effort of holding her body in place. Then, finally, on the fifth attempt, she succeeded. Her left hand found the edge and she was finally able to use two hands to cling to the hatchway.

A few more moments to steady herself and then Chrymos was able to lift herself enough to slip her elbows above the hatchway edges. Then it was a relatively easy task to leverage herself out of the hatchway, first crawling then kneeling and finally standing on the floor above.

A minute to catch her breath, a few seconds to remove the gauntlets and stow them in her beloved bag and then Chrymos began to walk towards the mortality room and freedom.

SEVENTY-FIVE
Academy of Secrets, Naples, Kingdom of Naples,
Night, Monday, June 21 1610

Henricus, who had been observing from a nearby alcove as Chrymos made her escape, smiled. He went to make his report to the waiting Contessa.

# # #

"—and then Chrymos headed towards the mortality room."

"Good work, Henricus. I'm glad that we gave you the new potion this afternoon. You've been most helpful," said the Contessa. "Now I have one more task for you tonight. Please take this to Doctor Odaldi." She scribbled a quick note, folded the paper over, and handed it to Henricus. "Tomorrow, you'll be free to resume your sentinel duties."

"Thank you, mistress," acknowledged Henricus, "I will take this to the doctor at once."

He bowed and left the Contessa's offices.

# # #

Henricus couldn't resist. He waited until he was in a servant corridor where he would be unobserved and then peeked at the message he carried. It was a single sentence. "Doctor, please leave the potion cupboard key on the bench." The Contessa had signed it with her usual flamboyant 'S'.

That's hardly worth disturbing the doctor about at this time of night, especially if he gives me a bollocking about the Járngreipr. Henricus was sorely tempted to leave the delivery until morning.

SEVENTY-SIX
Academy of Secrets, Naples, Kingdom of Naples, Night, Monday, June 21 1610

Chrymos quietly pushed open the door to the mortality room. *Great, nobody here.*

She tiptoed through the room, barefoot, her sandals safely stowed within her bag. A number of doors led off from the main chamber to unknown destinations. *Henricus said that the entrance door is right at the back.*

Chrymos walked quietly to the far end of the chamber, found the back entrance and slipped outside. *At last!*

She wasn't quite free yet. Although it was a moonless night, a flaming torch lit the entranceway and Chrymos could still be seen if anyone happened to gaze down from the windows above. So she quickly began to walk down the stone stairs that led away from the door and into the gardens.

She had managed about a dozen steps when she heard a loud whisper behind her.

"Chrymos?"

Chrymos spun round. There, staring back at her from one of the windows, was Olivia. Chrymos rushed over.

The window was locked, and crisscrossed with iron rods, but there was a small gap for ventilation and the two were able to talk through that gap.

"Olivia," said Chrymos, "what are you doing here? Where have you been? Have you seen the others?"

Olivia stared at her accusingly. "Are you telling me you didn't know?"

"Know what?"

"They came for the three of us, a few hours after you abandoned us. They said that you had sent them."

Chrymos was dumbfounded. "No! Olivia, I swear to you, I knew nothing of this. I searched for you everywhere, for months."

"You didn't need to look very far. We've been down here the whole time, all three of us, locked in these rooms with just the poor and wretched for company."

Chrymos felt sick to her stomach. "Oh Olivia, if only I'd known. I'm so sorry." She gazed miserably at the young girl.

Chrymos' grief was clearly visible to Olivia, who grudgingly admitted, "I suppose it hasn't been too bad. They've treated us well and fed us every day. Better than the stale bread you used to give us, anyway."

Chrymos managed a bleak smile and then ventured a question. "Did anyone explain why you were here?"

"No," said Olivia. "All they would tell us was that you would come and see us after you'd finished your studies. That wasn't very comforting, especially when you had told us the training would take years. So far, it's been, what, five or six months?"

"Well, it's all over now," said Chrymos, "I'm finished. I—failed. I wouldn't do what they wanted."

Olivia looked quizzical, but Chrymos waved aside any questions. "I'll tell you the whole story later, but right now that's not important. What matters is getting the three of you out of here."

Chrymos tugged at the window trying to open it but it wouldn't move—the lock was too strong.

Before Chrymos could try a different approach, Olivia interrupted. "Chrymos, I'm worried. Over the last few weeks, some of the other patients here have gone missing—usually those with broken bones or other minor illnesses. Then, a day or so later, they return—and they are all, without exception, suffering from the plague. Of course, they all soon die.

"Tonight, Sirus vanished as well."

SEVENTY-SEVEN
Academy of Secrets, Naples, Kingdom of Naples,
Night, Monday, June 21 1610

The news shocked Chrymos, but she quickly rallied. "Don't worry," she told Olivia, "I'll find him. Can you get to Madalena and warn her to get ready to leave?"

Olivia nodded. "Yes, there's a crack in our wall through which we can talk to each other."

"Good. I'll go back inside and try to track down Sirus." Chrymos returned to the door through which she had just exited. To her dismay, it had latched behind her, preventing her re-entry. She tried turning the door handle up and down, but to no avail.

Chrymos looked back at the window. Olivia had already gone to speak to Madalena. And even if she hadn't, the young girl was locked in her room and there wasn't anything she could do to help Chrymos.

With Sirus in danger, getting back inside was suddenly urgent. *But how? This entrance door is locked and all the other doors are closely guarded. Think, Chrymos, think—there must be another way.*

Very briefly, Chrymos considered going into the city to get help. A moment's thinking ruled out that possibility. *Master Della Porta is a respected citizen while I'm a nobody, a lazzarone. Who would listen to me?*

At that moment, Chrymos remembered. *The Járngreipr!*

She reached into her swete bagge and dug out the gauntlets, which in her haste to escape she had brought with her. *Sorry Henricus, looks like I need these more than you do.*

Donning the gauntlets, Chrymos set to work.

Like most of the Academy's exterior entrances, this door was a sturdy wooden arch construction that opened inwards, housed within a solid stone frame. The edges of the door were covered by the overlapping stone casing, a security precaution to prevent enemies slipping a lever between door and frame.

However, something more than simple structural design protected this door. Even with the Járngreipr, Chrymos found it nearly impossible to gain any sort of purchase on the wooden surface. And something— *probably one of those enchantments that the Academy loves so much—* prevented the gauntlets from digging into either the stonework or the wood.

No matter how much she prodded and pushed, the door wouldn't budge.

SEVENTY-EIGHT
Academy of Secrets, Naples, Kingdom of Naples, Night, Monday, June 21 1610

I can't fail the children again! That guilt-laden thought kept pounding away at Chrymos as she stood staring at the door, which had become an impenetrable barrier. *There has to be another way to get inside.*

She crossed back to the window and attempted to use the ventilation gap to gain a handhold. Yet again, the powerful spells protecting the Academy were more than enough to resist the efforts of the Járngreipr.

Chrymos tried picking away at the mullions, the metal strips that crisscrossed the window, to no avail.

Finally, she hammered away at the window itself with the heavy gauntlets, trying to break the glass. Again, her efforts ended in failure.

In the end, she simply stood there, waiting for Olivia to return. *I gave her fresh hope. Now I'm about to rip it away again.*

It was a devastating thought—too much for Chrymos to bear. She began to sob.

As her eyes filled with tears, Chrymos' vision blurred. And that small, insignificant moment triggered a months-old memory.

The sunlight that I couldn't see. In the Tower. Odaldi's laboratory. There may still be one unguarded entry into the building after all—if that hole in the Tower still hasn't been fixed, perhaps I can get in through there.

Chrymos didn't waste another moment. She seized the flaming torch from the entranceway and then dashed along the path that led through the Academy's extensive gardens.

SEVENTY-NINE
The Gardens, Academy of Secrets, Naples, Kingdom of Naples, Night, Monday, June 21 1610

The Della Porta estate was situated at the very top of the Capodimonte hill, with the main building's upper floors offering spectacular views of the city of Naples that stretched out far below. The Academy's gardens, which provided a luxuriant perimeter of at least half a mile around almost all of the estate's buildings, were as richly indulgent as the mansion's interiors. Exotic plants and trees acquired from all over the known world shared their space with elegant statuary featuring the luminaries of the once-mighty Roman Empire.

The path that Chrymos was following was specifically designed to take visitors past the finest features of this garden showplace, which included such attractive novelties as vibrant red tomatoes and bright yellow papaya imported from the Americas. The Academy's students were ushered through the gardens only once—and even then begrudgingly—at the beginning of their time at the Academy, but were otherwise not allowed into that part of the grounds lest they damage the prized decorations.

Because of those restrictions, Chrymos was unfamiliar with the general layout of the gardens and, with no moon, needed the fiery torch to find her way through. In particular, Chrymos was keen to ensure that she did not stumble into the large man-made lake that formed the centerpiece of the gardens on this side of the property.

The lake, fed by the same viaduct system that struggled to meet the daily needs of Naples' expanding population, was presided over by a gigantic sculpture carved out of the bare rock of the cliff that formed one side of the lake. The sculpture—*at least one hundred varas tall*, decided Chrymos when she first saw the magnificent creation—represented, she was told, the mythical Neptune. The Roman god of the sea, heavily bearded with unruly hair, was depicted astride a mighty throne, gazing down at his aquatic kingdom. In one hand, he grasped an outstretched trident, as he commanded his waterborne subjects. *That looks like the sort of god I would respect,* thought Chrymos, *supremely powerful yet caring. Hardly,* she reflected as she walked along the pathway, *the type of deity the Academy prefers. I don't imagine the Master was very impressed when the sculptor unveiled the finished work.*

Once she was safely past the water, Chrymos quickened her pace. Another hundred yards and the gardens began to look distinctly less manicured. *Visitors aren't usually allowed to come this far.*

Another dozen yards and Chrymos was reminded why few ventured this way. In the flickering flame of the torch, she could see the outline of the Tower. More importantly, she felt its threatening influence beginning to pound away at her mind.

EIGHTY
The Tower, Academy of Secrets, Naples, Kingdom of Naples, Night, Monday, June 21 1610

As she neared the base of the Tower, Chrymos slowed—not because she was any less desperate to get inside but rather because of the enchantments protecting this cruel edifice.

The entrance serum Odaldi gave us—he said it would last for about two months. It's been longer than that now since I received it—the effect will have worn off.

Under any other circumstances, Chrymos would have followed the instructions that screamed at her—"Turn and run, you are not welcome here." But her mind kept replaying the conversation with Olivia, kept picturing the accusatory glare with which Olivia had viewed her former caregiver. She kept thinking of Sirus and the very real possibility that he was already doomed to the most painful and horrific death. Those images, playing through her mind, were enough to drive her forward despite the Tower's relentless curses.

Chrymos placed the flaming torch on the tiled floor surrounding the Tower and retrieved the gauntlets. Hitching the swete bagge over her shoulder again, Chrymos pulled on the gauntlets and began to climb.

It was almost impossible to resist the fear cascading from the grim Tower—and Chrymos didn't even try. Instead, she soaked it up and channeled that raw emotion to power her climb up the outside of the building. The gauntlets couldn't dig into the incantation-protected stone slabs but they could help her cling to the small mortared crevices between slabs.

No, I am not worthy, she told herself, as she stretched up from one slab to the next. *I will fail Olivia as I have failed myself, I will fall from here and the ravens will peck out my eyes and devour my living flesh.*

Her thoughts turned to a gravely ill Sirus. *By now, his face will be covered in weeping sores and he will have swellings as big as eggs under his arms. His skin will have turned the most odious black. He will be tossing and turning in his bed, coughing and spitting out blood.*

Perversely, Chrymos' focused imaginings on the very worst that could happen helped shield her from the exhortations streaming from the Tower. *You cannot possibly condemn me more than I condemn myself. My fears drive me forward because I cannot go back.*

Minute by minute, Chrymos clawed her way up the side of the Tower. Were it not for the Járngreipr, she would have fallen a hundred times, whether by accident or as a deliberate result of throwing herself off the Tower to distance herself from the hate spewing into her mind. Yet those empowered gauntlets refused to relax their grip as she clambered in search of the illusion-cloaked cavity that would readmit her to the Academy.

Each time that Chrymos stretched upward, she hoped desperately that she would be within reach of the hidden entranceway. On each occasion, she encountered yet more unyielding stone. Success, when it finally came, was anticlimactic. Chrymos had actually climbed past the camouflaged hole. It was only when her right foot was questing for a foothold that it plunged into nothingness, almost causing Chrymos to lose her balance and fall.

Chrymos carefully crabbed across, gingerly reaching out sideways to determine the edges of this entranceway. At last, she eased her way inside. As she crossed the threshold, the Tower's enchanted curses eased, though they did not dissipate entirely.

Remembering how crowded and chaotic Odaldi's laboratory had been, Chrymos lowered herself down very carefully to the floor. She removed the Járngreipr and stuffed them into her swete bagge.

Chrymos stood motionless for a long moment, attempting to take stock. Earlier, she had been grateful that there was no moon, which had enabled her to climb the Tower without being seen. Now, however, she wished otherwise. *It's pitch black in here, some moonlight would have been a great help.*

Before she could succumb to her rapidly-rising feelings of panic, another distant memory stirred and Chrymos glanced over to her left. *I can use that red powder to find my way out of here and down into the Academy.* She carefully walked over to the bench that housed a number of small glass jars containing the glowing red powder.

She picked up one jar, loosened its lid, and then gave the jar a slight shake. To her delight and relief, the powder within, exposed to the air, began glowing more brightly.

Next, Chrymos began searching for the two glass vials that had so caught Adric's attention when their class toured through the laboratory. *Doctor Odaldi said that when those two liquids are mixed together they could melt through solid iron. I'll need that for the locks and chains at the Tower entrance.*

Chrymos quickly found the two vials and placed them in her bag, being extremely careful to place them well apart. Then she used her makeshift lamp to guide her passage to the door of the laboratory. She reached forward to turn the door handle.

It wouldn't move.

EIGHTY-ONE
The Tower, Academy of Secrets, Naples, Kingdom of Naples, night, Monday, June 21 1610

Puzzled at first, Chrymos shook the door handle firmly. It still wouldn't turn.

She took a closer look. There was no sign of a lock anywhere on the door. *Another enchantment? I hate this place.*

Chrymos once again donned one of the gauntlets and applied its pressure to the door handle. Again, nothing happened. *I didn't actually think that would work.*

She slowly peeled off the gauntlet and replaced it in her bag.

Then, conscious that precious minutes were slipping away, Chrymos lifted up her red powder lamp and began exploring her surroundings. *Something in this place must work on this door, surely.*

The first, obvious answer was to use the two vials that she had already placed in her bag. *Those two liquids when combined are supposed to melt through metal.*

A quick glance at the vials unfortunately confirmed what Chrymos had already feared. *There isn't enough in those vials to melt through both the laboratory door and the main lock at the Tower entrance. I'd better save them for now and try to find some other alternative.*

Chrymos began to search the laboratory, revisiting some of the exhibits she had noticed the last time she was here.

She heard scurrying sounds and looked over with distaste at the glass jars filled with the creatures responsible for the noise. *Scorpions? No, I don't think so.*

Next, Chrymos walked cautiously past the snake enclosure, mildly surprised to find it empty. *I'm glad they're not here, I hate those creatures.*

She crossed over to the benches that contained a wide array of glass jars containing assorted mysterious liquids. She moved her red-light lamp close to the jars and discovered that they were labeled, but not in any language Chrymos knew. *I could try mixing some of these together, but*—she looked over at the part of the wall which had been blown up—*who knows what would happen if I did that?*

Then Chrymos found herself in front of the cabinet containing the Exousía potion that she had been so desperate to receive. The cabinet was locked—but a small key on a chain lay on the bench in front of the cabinet.

Chrymos tried the key in the cabinet lock. *Something's gone right, for once. The key works.*

Inside the cabinet were three small jars of liquid, exactly as Chrymos had expected. *Two parts blue, one part yellow,* she reminded herself, *and avoid the crimson, it will make me nasty.*

Chrymos wasn't expecting, however, that the three liquids would be the wrong colors. One liquid was black and the other two were red.

EIGHTY-TWO
The Tower, Academy of Secrets, Naples, Kingdom of Naples, night, Monday, June 21 1610

Chrymos nearly smashed the jars in rage. *Of course those aren't the Exousía ingredients,* she thought bitterly. *Little else has gone right tonight, why would that?*

She left the jars beside the cabinet and resumed her search of the laboratory. Most of what Chrymos saw, she couldn't use—the mysterious labels continued to defeat her. But then she came across a sealed container carrying a small strip of metal and another memory returned. *Odaldi said this would burst into flames if we took it out of the container. Perhaps I can use it to burn down the door.*

Chrymos picked up the container, intending to try out her theory. As she moved towards the door, however, she tripped on yet another of Odaldi's hoarded treasures and the container flew out of her hands, landing heavily on one of the benches.

The glass container cracked, letting in air. The metal strip burst into flame, momentarily blinding her with its brightness in comparison to the dim red light that she had been using.

As the bright white light flared, Chrymos instinctively looked away—and in doing so, she caught a fresh glimpse of the liquids in the potion jars. *I don't believe it. The liquid have changed color.*

In the light from the new white flame, the black had become blue and one of the red liquids had apparently turned yellow. The other red—stayed red.

Before the fire could die down, and before she lost her nerve, Chrymos grabbed an empty goblet and poured in 'two parts blue, one part yellow'. The combined mixture sparkled and snarled. *That's exactly what the Exousía potion is supposed to do. Now let's see if Adric was right about the foul taste.*

She quickly swallowed the potion. *He was.*

EIGHTY-THREE
The Tower, Academy of Secrets, Naples, Kingdom of Naples, night, Monday, June 21 1610

Chrymos stood for a moment, watching and waiting. She could feel her stomach fighting valiantly against the foreign invader. Other than that, she felt no different.

Please, please, Lord, let me receive my powers immediately so that I can save the children, she prayed.

Nothing seemed to be happening, except that the white light grew dimmer and then went out completely as the thin metal strip finally consumed itself. All that remained was the red glow from the powder.

Chrymos again shook the glass jar containing the red powder, and was once more rewarded with an increase in the light's intensity. *Might as well keep looking through the laboratory for some useful tool or weapon, there's not much else I can do.*

She started afresh in a separate section of the laboratory and was thrilled to discover that she could actually read the labels on the jars in this area. *That's more like it!*

Even though Chrymos could read these labels, that didn't mean she could understand how to use the ingredients that the jars contained.

Weremilk. Phoenix feather. Dragon tooth. Owl eye. What am I supposed to do with these? Maybe they covered this stuff in the two and a half years of the training that I missed.

Chrymos worked her along the bench, growing more and more frustrated as she read and discarded jar after jar.

After completing her review of all the ingredients in one section of the laboratory, Chrymos moved on to the next bench.

She read label after label, quickly dismissing each jar. None provided anything that she could use.

She stopped in shock when she recognized a particularly distinctive jar containing desiccated vulture beaks. *I've already been through this section before—but I couldn't read the labels then.*

Chrymos sank to her knees in despair. *This is my power? To understand languages? What use is that? Is this the 'world-changing power' for which I gave up the children?*

EIGHTY-FOUR
The Tower, Academy of Secrets, Naples, Kingdom of Naples, night, Monday, June 21 1610

Come on woman. Feeling sorry for yourself isn't getting you anywhere. Get off those knees and keep looking for something that will get you out of this place in time to save Sirus and the girls.

Chrymos' self-talk may not have been inspirational but at least it pushed her to start moving again. She stood, lifted up the red powder-lamp, and continued inspecting the ingredients on display, searching for anything at all that she could use.

After another fifteen minutes or so, she had narrowed her selection down to a couple of options. One, labeled 'Greek Fire', seemed to promise explosive possibilities. A second, the 'poison-fog magic smoke eruptor,' was intended, according to the notes on the label, to 'choke enemies with a formidable spray of poisonous smoke.' *If I have to call the guards to get me out of here, maybe I could use this to escape,* she thought, not entirely convinced.

What else? Chrymos circled around the laboratory—and then paused when she spied the emerald tablet that Odaldi had called his most precious possession. *I wonder?*

She picked up the tablet and began reading, pleased to discover that she could understand this ancient writing.

She skipped past the opening honorifics and the subsequent warnings that the tablet's contents were intended only for alchemic adepts.

The next few section headings alone made for horrifying reading: 'how to destroy an enemy and his entire family, how to control the unliving, how to conjure a sand-demon, how to mummify your enemy alive, how to convert a believer—'

Chrymos had read enough. *Right now, I may be the one person who can read this tablet—but I doubt that will always be the case. The secrets it contains must never be revealed.*

She lifted the tablet high in the air with both hands and then threw it with all her might against the stone floor beneath her.

The tablet shattered noisily into a thousand pieces.

A few minutes later, she heard shouting and the clatter of footsteps.

EIGHTY-FIVE
The Tower, Academy of Secrets, Naples, Kingdom of Naples, night, Monday, June 21 1610

Chrymos hastily gathered the only real weapon she had found, the 'poison-fog magic smoke eruptor', and took up a position near the door, waiting her chance.

The footsteps slowed and then stopped in the corridor outside. She heard a chant. <Remove your bindings from this door, mighty lord of light>. This time she understood what was being said, even though it was spoken in Mystikó, the language used by the Academy's senior staff and adepts.

She waited.

The door opened, slightly. Before Chrymos could unleash her smoke weapon, a snake slithered inside, hissing angrily. She tried to stand up and move out of its way but Cleopatra, Odaldi's favorite snake, was too quick to unleash its fury.

Even as she stood up, Chrymos could feel the deadly venom hitting her lower leg. She backed away desperately as the creature reared up for another attack. Already Chrymos could feel a burning sensation as the venom began its work.

At first Chrymos was able to dodge as the snake spat another load of poison. She scrambled onto a bench and might even have managed to lift herself out of reach of the murderous creature.

Unfortunately, while she was otherwise occupied, one of the guards had slipped into the laboratory. Armed with a blowpipe, he fired a dart into Chrymos at pointblank range. She crumpled over within seconds.

EIGHTY-SIX
Academy of Secrets, Naples, Kingdom of Naples,
Night, Monday, June 21 1610

Chrymos awoke to find herself seated in the office of Giambattista Della Porta. She felt terrible—her head was splitting and the whole left side of her body throbbed in intense pain. She looked up to find the Master of the Academy sitting at his desk watching her, shaking his head.

"You amaze me, Chrymos," he said.

"Oh?"

"I'm surprised that you can even move, let alone talk. That snake spat venom at you a half-dozen times before my men dragged you out of there. Still," said Della Porta, pausing to make a note on a piece of parchment, "it's only a matter of time. Doctor Odaldi tells me that the venom should kill you within forty-eight hours."

"Then why am I here?" asked Chrymos. "What's the point if I'm dead already?"

"Father Carracci arrived back this evening," said Della Porta.

"So I heard," said Chrymos. "What does that have to do with me?"

"He asked for this meeting so we could discuss what happened with Galileo."

Chrymos winced in pain as the poison continued to burn through her body. "I'm dying, remember. Why should I care?"

"We do have a medicine that will relieve your pain," said Della Porta, noting her reaction to the news. "Cooperate with us and your final hours will be much less agonizing."

"Not a cure, though," observed Chrymos.

"I'm afraid not." Della Porta didn't even bother to look sympathetic. He turned his attention back to his papers while the pair waited on the priest to arrive.

Carracci bustled into the room a few minutes later. He ignored Chrymos and greeted the Master in their shared language, which had previously been such a mystery to Chrymos.

"<Thank you for seeing me at this hour, Master. I wanted to tell you about Galileo and the angel that saved his life. If you have any questions that I cannot answer, we may be able to get them out of this one before she dies.>"

"Charming," muttered Chrymos.

Carracci looked over at her for the first time. "What did you say?"

"I said 'charming,' the way that you're talking about me. I'm not dead yet, you know."

"<How did you know we were talking about you?>," asked Della Porta.

"I may be dying but I'm not deaf." Chrymos broke off, noticing how shocked the pair looked. "Oh—you were speaking in your secret Mystikó language, weren't you?"

"We were," said Carracci, "but somehow you understood us. How is that possible?"

"Oh, didn't I mention it before?" Chrymos tried not to grimace as a fresh burst of pain shot through her. "I swallowed a little dose of Exousía potion while I was up in the Tower. Turns out I can now understand languages." She coughed and shuddered simultaneously. "Not for long, I guess."

Carracci and Della Porta exchanged glances that were simultaneously incredulous and hopeful. "The manuscript?" said Carracci.

"Perhaps," said Della Porta cautiously. He turned to Chrymos. "I need to evaluate your supposed ability. If it proves valuable to us, then you just might survive after all."

"I thought you said that there isn't a cure," said Chrymos.

"That was before I realized that you might still be of some slight use to us," replied Della Porta.

EIGHTY-SEVEN
Academy of Secrets, Naples, Kingdom of Naples, Night, Monday, June 21 1610

Della Porta reached over to a nearby shelf, selected a book, and opened it on his desk. Then he took out a fresh piece of parchment and carefully wrote a note, referring to the book as he did so.

Then he closed the book and turned to Carracci. "Bring her to the desk."

The priest walked over to Chrymos and reached out to help. She shrugged off his assistance. "I can do this myself," she said and slowly, painfully, stood up and shuffled over to the desk.

"Read this back to me," said Della Porta, pointing to the newly-written parchment.

He moved aside and watched intently as Chrymos began reading from the parchment. "Natural Magick by Giambattista Della Porta". She looked up at the Master. "You've translated your own book into Mystikó. I never did get around to reading the book in class, so let's see if it's any good."

Chrymos lifted up the piece of parchment, supposedly to see it better—but in reality so that she could see what other documents Della Porta had on his desk.

She resumed reading aloud, pausing occasionally as if stumbling over words, in reality snatching brief moments to look down at another piece of parchment on the desk that carried tantalizing notes.

"What is the Nature of Magic? There are two sorts of Magick; the one is—" *The parchment on the desk is headed 'Possibilities in the tomb'.*

"—infamous, and unhappy, because it has to do with foul Spirits, and consists of incantations and wicked curiosity; and this is called—" *There's a list. 'The Thirteenth Chronicle.'*

—Sorcery; an art which all learned and good men detest; neither is it able to yield an truth of reason or nature, but stands merely upon fancies and imaginations, such as vanish presently away, and leave nothing behind them; as—" *'The pathgem.'*

"—Jamblicus writes in his book concerning the mysteries of the Egyptians. The other Magick is natural; which all excellent wise men do admit and embrace, and worship with great applause; neither is there anything more highly esteemed, or better thought of, by men of learning—" *'The Key to the Abyss.'*

Before Chrymos could read any further, Della Porta walked over, took the parchment out of her hand, and placed it back on the desk, obscuring her view of the list below.

"Enough. You've demonstrated your ability sufficiently. Go and sit down."

Disappointed that she wasn't able to read more of the mysterious list, Chrymos slowly returned to her chair. By the time that she was seated again, Della Porta held a loosely-bound pile of papers in his hand.

"We call this the *Medici manuscript*, because of where it was found. We want you to translate the document for us. If you agree to the task, we will give you a medication to dull the pain. If you complete your work successfully we will provide you with another medicine that will cure you completely."

Chrymos was finally in a position to do something for Olivia, Sirus, and Madalena. "Your offer is an acceptable starting point. But I will only translate the document if you free the children."

"What children?" asked Della Porta, genuinely puzzled.

"The ones in the mortality room—those three on whom you are about to experiment."

"Oh, those—the brats that you were living with. Very well, then, if that's what it takes to get you to carry out the translation, certainly we will spare them."

"I need you to release them," demanded Chrymos. "Tonight. Right now. I haven't much time, you know."

"I said 'Yes,'" snapped Della Porta. "My word is enough."

"No it's not," said Chrymos. "I want Adric to take them into the city and set them free. He's the only person here that I trust."

"Alas," said Carracci, "Adric—isn't available." Before Chrymos could protest, the priest held up one hand. "He's on a mission. But I do have an alternative. Sister Maria Benedetta—the nun who brought you back from Paris—could take the children into the city. Do you agree?"

Chrymos had fond, if foggy, memories of the nun who had cared for her while she was entranced, including a few hazy and extremely one-sided conversations. "Yes, she is acceptable."

"Very well," said Della Porta. He turned to Carracci. "Make it so." The priest nodded and left the Master's office.

Della Porta crossed to a side table and poured some purple liquid into a goblet. He handed the goblet to Chrymos. "Drink this. It will give you some relief from the pain. Then get started on the manuscript. As you said, you don't have much time."

EIGHTY-EIGHT
Nearly one hundred and fifty years earlier
Verrocchio's workshop, Florence [Italy], September 1 1469

Andrea del Verrocchio was behaving strangely that day, all his apprentices remarked upon it—but not until he was well out of earshot. Verrocchio was supposed to be crafting the golden *palla* for the Duomo, but instead he wandered around aimlessly, standing behind each apprentice in turn and peering silently over their shoulders at their latest painting or sculpture. The whole experience was most unsettling.

Verrocchio came over and stood behind eighteen-year-old Leonardo da Vinci on four separate occasions, scrutinizing his work intently. Then, finally, a fifth time, Verrocchio bent low and whispered in Leonardo's ear. "Come with me."

Bemused, Leonardo followed Verrocchio outside the workshop. "Leonardo," said Verrocchio quietly once they were alone, "I have a very, very important job for you—but it must be completed in total secrecy and you must promise never, ever to speak of it to anyone. Are you willing to do this?"

Da Vinci may have only been a teenager, but even so, he recognized the enormity of the vow he would be required to swear. "Is this a right and just task in the sight of God?"

Verrocchio nodded briskly. "This is easily the most important task you will ever undertake—and in doing so you will totally serve the will of the Father."

"Then of course I am prepared to take on this assignment, and to swear total and utter secrecy, in the name of Almighty God."

Satisfied with his apprentice's response, Verrocchio beckoned for da Vinci to accompany him and they set off through the streets of Florence, arriving shortly at a stately home. Leonardo recognized the property at once. "This is the home of your patron—"

Verrocchio finished the sentence: "—Piero di Cosimo de' Medici, the deeply revered Gonfaloniere of Justice. Indeed it is. And he has a vital commission that I have chosen you to fulfil."

A smartly-clad servant admitted the pair to the house, disappeared briefly to confer with his master. He returned a few minutes later to indicate that the visitors should wait in a lavishly decorated antechamber until de' Medici was ready to receive them. Da Vinci looked about in wonder.

Shortly, the two men were led into the bedchamber of the Florentine leader. The old man was clearly ill but his intelligent gaze was undiminished as he inspected his visitors.

Verrocchio introduced his apprentice and then announced that he would leave the pair alone to discuss their business.

De' Medici waited until Verrocchio had departed before he started to explain exactly what was required. He beckoned to Leonardo to come closer and half-croaked, half-whispered into the young artist's ear.

EIGHTY-NINE
The mansion of Piero di Cosimo de' Medici, Florence, September 1 1469

"I am dying," de' Medici whispered to his visitor, "and there is one secret that must not die with me—but which is too dangerous to remain in its current form."

De' Medici started coughing, and Leonardo fetched a goblet of water, which the old man gratefully accepted. De' Medici sipped some water and then resumed his tale.

"This secret concerns a very special 'book of the dead' which has been in the possession of my family for nearly three centuries. The document itself is a thousand years old and the pages are crumbling away. I fear the document will soon turn to dust. Its contents must be preserved."

More coughing. Leonardo waited patiently until the coughing fit had passed and de' Medici continued.

"The document reveals the location of a tomb that is vitally important to the future of Christendom. No," the old man said, holding up his hand to stop Leonardo from interrupting, "not the tomb of the Savior, but one nearly as important. This tomb holds secrets that could either destroy or save us all."

The old man paused for another drink of water. Leonardo had the impression that the elder statesman had not spoken so much since contracting his illness.

"I asked Verrocchio to choose an apprentice he trusted, one who could copy the contents while concealing them behind an unbreakable code. Are you that man, Leonardo da Vinci? Do you have the skills necessary to protect these secrets from those who worship death and destruction?"

NINETY
The mansion of Piero di Cosimo de' Medici, Florence, September 1 1469

"Yes, of course," Leonardo told the dying Gonfaloniere. "I will hide those secrets so deeply that only those with the key to the code will be able to decipher what is written. And even they may struggle, unless they are actually near the tomb itself."

# # #

The young Leonardo worked for nearly three months on that sacred task, firstly developing and refining an unbreakable code and then using that code to translate the text of the Book of the Dead into impossible letters and symbols. He rendered the instructions that explained how to find the tomb within simplistic illustrations of plants and people and stars. The resulting manuscript, provided to a grateful Piero di Cosimo de' Medici shortly before he died, bore no resemblance to the original book of the dead. Leonardo had personally fed that perilous document page by page into a raging fire.

# # #

Half a century later, as the sixty-eight-year-old Leonardo lay on his deathbed, he instructed his assistant Francesco to send a sealed package to the Vatican Secret Archive. The package bore a simple note. "This contains the solitary key to the de' Medici manuscript. Keep it safe."

Unfortunately, the code that Leonardo had worked so diligently to create would not remain unbroken forever.

NINETY-ONE
Academy of Secrets, Naples, Kingdom of Naples, Night, Monday June 21 1610

Chrymos was not willing to begin work on the manuscript until she was satisfied that the children were safe. Father Carracci returned with the news that they were in Sister Maria Benedetta's care, soon to be taken into the city. Even then, Chrymos demanded to be taken to the balcony overlooking the main gate, from where she could watch the carriage that was taking the children to safety. Thanks to the lanterns mounted on the carriage, she could see all three children, sitting alongside the nun. *Sirus looks okay, I guess they didn't actually give him the plague.*

Chrymos waited until the carriage was safely out of sight before she returned to Della Porta's office.

"Thank you," she said to the Master. "At least now the children are safe. But why would you give people the plague intentionally?"

Della Porta frowned. "Foolish girl! We're not giving anyone the plague. Doctor Odaldi is attempting to develop cures to help plague victims. How could you possibly believe otherwise?"

Chrymos wasn't convinced, but there was no point in arguing. She began to examine the document.

"Can you tell me any more about this—what did you call it—Medici manuscript?" asked Chrymos. "Where did you get it?"

"I can tell you," said Della Porta, "that before it came into our possession, the manuscript belonged to the Holy Roman emperor Rudolf II. A short time ago, the emperor loaned it to some of our—enemies. As it happens, we were able to retrieve it from their care."

"How old is it, do you know?"

Della Porta looked at Carracci. The priest answered reluctantly. "According to Vatican records, the best guess is that it is between one hundred and two hundred years old."

Chrymos thumbed through the document, surprised to find that there were already translation notes attached to most pages. She looked across at Della Porta. "You've already translated parts of this document?"

"We've been working on this for more than a month," admitted the Academy's leader. "Father Carracci was able to call on some assistance from colleagues in the Vatican, who had access to certain documents in the secret archives. There are still a number of gaps in our knowledge with which we hope you will be able to help. In particular, there are very few directions to help us find—" Della Porta broke off, unwilling to share the secret with someone he knew was not committed to their cause.

"I'll find out soon enough, you know," Chrymos pointed out, "once I translate the document. So you might as well tell me now, to speed up the process."

Della Porta and Carracci looked at each other. "True enough," Carracci reluctantly conceded, leaving Della Porta to tell the story.

"Thirteen hundred years ago, in the third century after the birth of Our Lord, there was a mighty battle between a demon and what we now understand to have been an Outcast Angel," explained the Master.

Chrymos listened intently as Della Porta continued. "According to contemporary reports, the demon was defeated and its corpse paraded in front of the enemies of the eventual victor, emperor Diocletian. The angel is assumed to have flown away."

Carracci chimed in. "However, we have learned otherwise. According to Church records, the angel perished as well."

"How is that possible?" asked Chrymos. "Aren't angels immortal?"

"Kingdom Angels are, according to Holy Scripture," agreed Carracci, "but this was an Outcast Angel, one who had been exiled from Heaven after the Great Rebellion. Who knows what the rules are for those banished by Almighty God?"

Della Porta continued. "Until very recently, all we knew about what might have happened to the angel were rumors and legends, most of them based on comments supposedly made by one of the Roman soldiers who took away the body. Father Carracci's Vatican contacts have now discovered that the body was entrusted for burial to Bishop Januarius— better known to us all as the patron saint of Naples, San Gennaro."

"Normally, that would be the end of the matter," added Carracci, "but one of the bishop's assistants was secretly a member of the Brotherhood of Judas."

"They're part of the Council of Four, aren't they?" Chrymos struggled to remember an old lecture that Carracci had given a few months earlier.

"Ah, you were listening," said Carracci. "Yes, they are—although they were much more powerful thirteen hundred years ago than they are now. Anyway, their spy followed an old Egyptian tradition and wrote a 'book of the dead,' supposedly to help the spirit find its way out of the tomb—but in fact to help the Brotherhood find the body and defeat any safeguards that the Church might have put in place to protect it."

"Ironically," added Della Porta, "the Brotherhood's spy was executed by the Romans before the 'book of the dead' could be handed over to the Brotherhood. Supposedly, Diocletian began persecuting Christians because Januarius wouldn't tell him where the angel's body was buried—yet one of the first few to be executed would have readily shared that information if anyone had listened."

"So what happened to the book?" asked Chrymos.

"We don't know," said Della Porta. "It was lost from sight until the fifteenth century, when it was listed as part of the estate of Cosimo de' Medici of Florence. When his heir Piero died in 1469, the book was gone and this manuscript was listed in its place.

"We now believe that this is an encrypted copy of the original book. If we can decode it properly, it should reveal where the body is buried."

Chrymos was stunned. *An actual angel, just like the one I saw in Pisa?* She tried to think through the implications.

Della Porta wasn't finished. "From what we've translated of the manuscript so far, we've been able to confirm that the body was indeed buried here in Naples, in what's now called the Catacombs of San Gennaro—our nearest neighbors." He smiled. "We've been looking for the angel's body for a great many years—my grandfather started the quest nearly a hundred years ago.

"Long before we acquired the Medici manuscript, we were convinced that the body must be buried in the catacombs, which is why we set up the Academy nearby, here on the Capodimonte hill. What we've been able to establish from our translation efforts so far is that we are indeed correct. The Outcast Angel is buried somewhere in the oldest levels of the catacombs. What we don't know is exactly where. And that's what we need you to find out from the manuscript."

"Why?" asked Chrymos. "What could you possibly expect to learn from the body of a long-dead angel? It'll only be bones anyway."

"That, Chrymos, is none of your concern," said Carracci. "I suggest that you focus on the fact you now have less than forty-eight hours in which to help us locate the angel's tomb. Otherwise, say your final prayers."

NINETY-TWO
Academy of Secrets, Naples, Kingdom of Naples, Early morning, Tuesday June 22 1610

Chrymos had slaved tirelessly through the night, scribbling furiously, correcting the most glaring errors in the translations as she worked on the manuscript.

One particular passage gave her pause. The translator had interpreted a key phrase as 'which Almighty God finds amusing'. The description didn't make sense, but Chrymos couldn't fault the literal translation. *But it just feels wrong.*

Chrymos stood up, stretched, and walked over to the balcony to admire the approaching dawn. *Each day promises a new beginning, an opportunity to see Divine providence in action,* she thought.

And then she realized. *Not 'things that Almighty God finds amusing'. Rather, 'Divine Comedy'.* The unknown author of the manuscript was directing her to a particular passage in Dante Alighieri's fourteenth-century masterpiece.

Chrymos rushed out of Della Porta's office, startling the two guards who had been stationed outside. She explained what she needed and one of the guards went to the Academy's library to fetch a copy of the classic book by Florence's most celebrated creator.

Once Chrymos was alone again, she flicked impatiently through the pages of the Divine Comedy until she found the particular section referred to in the manuscript:

"Languages diverse, horrible dialects, accents of anger, words of agony, and voices high and hoarse, with sound of hands, made up a tumult that goes whirling on forever in that air forever black, even as the sand doth, when the whirlwind breathes.

"And I, who had my head with horror bound, said: 'Master, what is this which now I hear? What folk is this, which seems by pain so vanquished?'

"And he to me: 'This miserable mode maintains the melancholy souls of those who lived without infamy or praise. Commingled are they with that caitiff choir of Angels, who have not rebellious been, nor faithful were to God, but were for self. The heavens expelled them, not to be less fair; nor them the nethermore abyss receives, for glory none the damned would have from them.'"

Unfaithful Angels, who were not rebellious but yet were expelled from Heaven. Is Dante describing the Outcast Angels?

Chrymos noted down her thoughts and continued translating the document.

Several hours later, Della Porta strode back into this office. He skipped past any pleasantries and simply asked "What have you found?"

Chrymos considered her words carefully. "Some of this you will already know, from what has been translated so far. But I will give you the complete overview, to put everything into perspective."

"Yes, yes," said Della Porta impatiently, "Go on."

"The initial goal of Bishop Januarius, according to the original author of the 'book of the dead', was simply to give the angel's body a good Christian burial," began Chrymos. "Januarius was from Naples so it was perfectly understandable that he would bring the body back here to be buried appropriately."

"But?" prompted Della Porta.

"But," she continued, "when the emperor Diocletian demanded to know where the body was buried, Januarius grew suspicious. He knew that the emperor had been raised with traditional Roman beliefs, and decided that it was too dangerous to allow Diocletian to get his hands on the corpse. The manuscript doesn't explain what the danger might be, but I expect you already know. Otherwise you wouldn't be so obsessed with finding the body."

Della Porta ignored the jibe and simply motioned for Chrymos to continue.

"Januarius issued orders for the angel's burial chamber to be moved to a hidden part of the catacombs."

"You're sure of that? Moved within the catacombs?" Della Porta asked anxiously.

"Yes, according to the manuscript," replied Chrymos. "By then, Diocletian had begun to persecute Christians. Januarius wanted to keep the body where he could still arrange to protect it."

"Go on."

"Clearly your Brotherhood spy realized that this was his opportunity to find out the safeguards put in place to protect the angel's body, so he managed to convince Januarius to let him oversee the transfer," said Chrymos.

"The Brotherhood spy was a woman," said Della Porta, "but otherwise your report rings true. So what did she discover?"

"That there are seven ways in which the angel's body is protected," said Chrymos. "Firstly, there's the entry portal itself. According to the manuscript, it's on a lower level that was never documented anywhere, a secret section of the catacombs where many of the early church's martyrs are buried."

"My father and grandfather spent months exploring the catacombs until they stumbled upon the level by accident, when the upper levels flooded and afterwards the water drained away somehow," said Della Porta. "They dug great holes in various *arcosolia*—the larger family tombs—until they finally found a way down to the next level. Of course, that was before we had secured the manuscript."

"Secondly," added Chrymos "there's the main chamber, which is essentially a labyrinth filled with poisonous gases."

"Yes, we found that out the hard way," said Della Porta. "We lost a few—volunteers—until we discovered an elixir that works. What else?"

"The third protection appears to be a series of passageways, most of which are booby-trapped. Your people have managed to translate most of that portion of the manuscript correctly. Where they've run into problems is in deciding which passageway leads to the tomb."

"Yes, yes, don't you think we know that?" said Della Porta impatiently. "So which one is it?"

"Whoever goes searching for the tomb needs to stop and listen first," said Chrymos. "If they hear voices, strange noises that seem to come from nowhere, in one specific passageway, then that's the path they should choose."

Della Porta looked at her, initially in disbelief, then took out a fresh piece of parchment and made some notes. "Noises to choose the correct passage. Right. What next?"

"This is one section of the manuscript that I don't yet fully understand. It talks about the Acheron River, gateway to Hades, but its meaning in terms of the fourth safeguard is unclear. Again, the manuscript quotes Dante. 'By other ways, by other ports thou to the shore shalt come, not here, for passage; a lighter vessel needs must carry thee.'"

"That will have to do for now, Chrymos. Tell me about the fifth protection."

Chrymos turned a few pages in the manuscript. "The fifth protection is finding the correct tomb. There are more than three hundred bodies buried in this section of the catacombs, some in simple graves, the *loculi*, others in more extravagant arcosolia. The arcosolium you seek belongs to 'the bishop himself', according to the manuscript, and is again referred to by a quote from Dante."

"And what exactly are the words?" asked Della Porta.

"They're surprisingly straightforward. 'Through me the way is to the city dolent; through me the way is to eternal dole; through me the way among the people lost.' *Dolent* means 'sorrowful'—"

"I know what the word means, Chrymos. What's the sixth protection?"

"The bishop's arcosolium, according to this section that your people don't seem to have translated, is only the starting point. The tomb itself is even further within—and it's protected, I gather, by what the manuscript describes as a prophecy rather than something that actually existed when the original Book of the Dead was written. According to the manuscript, that prophetic protection is known simply as the *militum mortuorum*, 'soldiers of the dead', whatever that may mean."

"Soldiers of the dead, very well," noted Della Porta. "And the seventh and final protection?"

"I don't know," said Chrymos, "or, rather, your spy didn't know. Januarius wouldn't let him—sorry, her—accompany the body into the burial chamber. In fact, Januarius himself moved the angel's body from its original tomb to its new home. The spy never saw the actual body."

Della Porta made another note and then prepared to leave. "That will have to do. I hope for your friend Adric's sake that your translation is accurate."

"What do you mean?"

"Oh, didn't we tell you? We're sending Adric down into the catacombs shortly. His powers still haven't manifested themselves, so we can't make much use of him up here. Adric will be following your instructions to try to find the tomb. If you've translated the text incorrectly, I'm afraid that he will be the one to pay the price for your mistakes."

NINETY-THREE
Near the City of Naples, Kingdom of Naples, Midday, Tuesday June 22 1610

The carriage containing Sean, Niall, Lochloinn, Elias, Martin and Zophiel rattled over the hill near the imposing Castel Sant'Elmo fortress which stood guard over Naples.

Sean, who was driving, pulled the horses to a stop so that the team could have their first look at the port city stretching out below.

"Impressive view from here," said Elias, "shame it's wasted on a military fortress."

"Where's the Academy?" asked Martin, keen to know their enemy. They looked over at Zophiel, who had been accompanying them since Dijon.

Zophiel, in turn, mind-called Shamar and then reported to the others.

"According to the information that the student Niccolo gave Shamar, the Academy is over in that direction." Zophiel pointed off to the left. "It's on the Capodimonte hill, not far from the Catacombs of San Gennaro."

"So what are we waitin' for?" asked Lochloinn, always impatient to get started.

Zophiel could see that, despite their long journey, the LOA team members were eager to engage their enemy. He reminded them that they were not yet at full strength. "As you well know, we're waiting for Shamar and three new enhanced he's bringing here from Wallachia. And, of course, we're still waiting on Ravid. They should all be here soon. Ravid has asked us to find a hiding place near the catacombs and to do some preliminary scouting so that we know exactly what we're dealing with."

Lochloinn grumbled but couldn't argue. Sean encouraged the horses to change direction and head towards the catacombs.

# # #

None of them noticed Henricus, who had hidden himself in the shadows on a ledge near the top of the Castel Sant'Elmo fortress. He nodded to his companion, a Janus twin, who sent a quick mind-message to the Academy. <*They're here.*>

NINETY-FOUR
Academy of Secrets, Naples, Kingdom of Naples,
9.30 p.m. Tuesday June 22 1610

Chrymos' head was spinning, after hour upon hour of trying to understand not just the words of the manuscript but also the cryptic pictures—and the hidden meanings behind both. *Whoever put this together was a genius,* she decided yet again.

The debilitating pain from the venom had returned, but no-one would bring her more medication—the current shift of guards wouldn't listen and would only say "get back in there and keep working".

Resigned to her discomfort, Chrymos returned to the desk and began to decipher the next section, which talked about angels and demons 'falling from the sky'.

Two hours later, by which time her whole body was convulsing at regular intervals, Chrymos heard rapid footsteps approaching. Della Porta and Carracci walked briskly into the office.

Della Porta was blunt. "You've failed. Your translation must be faulty."

"What do you mean?" asked Chrymos.

"We sent off Adric eight hours ago, armed with your instructions. He hasn't come back."

Chrymos didn't understand. "Perhaps the search is just taking longer than you expected, even with the instructions in the manuscript."

"It doesn't matter why Adric is late," said Della Porta impatiently. "What matters is that he hasn't come back. We want you to go in there and find the tomb and bring back what it contains. You can bring back Adric as well, if you can find him."

"You're joking. After everything that you've done to me, you expect me to help you?"

"If you return successfully with what's in the tomb," said Della Porta, "we will give you the antidote for the snake venom and save your life."

"You already promised that to me if I translated the manuscript successfully," Chrymos pointed out.

"Adric had your translations but he hasn't come back," said Della Porta. "Therefore, you haven't completed your task. I'm giving you another chance."

That would almost sound virtuous, if someone else had said it. "Why not send another one of your lackeys?"

"None of the other students trust your translation," said Carracci. "You can't blame them, after seeing what you've let happen to a person that you say is your friend."

Chrymos protested angrily. "What? You didn't even tell me that Adric was the one going inside until after I had completed the translation."

"Would it have mattered? Would you have changed anything?" asked Della Porta.

"Well, no," admitted Chrymos. "I've done the very best I can."

"Then you should have no problems following your own instructions," said Carracci. Chrymos glared at him.

"Enough, we're wasting time," said Della Porta. "Get your translations and let's go."

"Why are you in such a hurry?" asked Chrymos, making no attempt to get up. She crossed her arms behind her head and leaned back in her chair.

"Our enemies are almost upon us, so we need to prepare for their attack," said Della Porta. Chrymos gave a silent cheer.

"Not that you would care about our problems," said Carracci, "but there is the missing Adric. As you know, the main chamber is filled with poisonous air, one of the safeguards mentioned in the manuscript. We gave Adric a special elixir, to enable him to breathe as he passed through that section."

"So?"

"The elixir we gave Adric lasts for about twelve hours. He's been down in the catacombs for eight, so his protection will wear off in another four hours. If he does not come back, or receive a fresh draught of elixir, he won't be able to escape. If you hurry, there's a possibility that you may be able to save him."

That hit home. "Can't you send someone else in to rescue him?"

"We could, but as I said, no-one trusts your translation," Carracci pointed out. "And also we need to get ready for this impending attack. We still have plenty to do. Get moving."

"What, when I'm like this?" Chrymos had been struggling to contain her convulsions but instead allowed them to show. Her body twisted and turned in agony as the poison took its grim toll. "And I haven't slept for more than thirty-six hours."

"We'll get you some more pain relief," said Della Porta, "along with medicine to keep you awake and some elixir to help you breathe down in the catacombs." He seized Chrymos' shoulder roughly and began to urge her to get moving.

Chrymos started to gather up the translations, along with the manuscript itself, and stuffed the documents into her belt so that they lay flat against her body. At first, Della Porta tried to stop her.

"Just take the translations, you won't need the original."

"How do you know? You said it yourself, my translation might be faulty," replied Chrymos. "If I have the original with me, I may be able to solve any outstanding problems on the spot."

Della Porta was reluctant but eventually agreed. "Very well. But be sure you bring back what you find in the tomb, with or without Adric, and we will spare those children that you profess to care so much about."

"What? But they left the Academy last night. I watched them being taken to safety by Sister Maria Benedetta," said Chrymos.

"Alas," smirked Carracci, "you cannot always believe your eyes, especially when Apollinaris the illusionist is around."

Chrymos was horrified. Before she could respond, Della Porta spoke again.

"We said we would spare the children, and so we have—thus far. But their final fate—and yours—is in your own hands."

NINETY-FIVE
The Academy of Secrets, Naples, Kingdom of Naples, Midnight, Tuesday June 22 1610

Della Porta, Father Carracci, and Chrymos stood outside the entrance to the Tower. "Please go and get Doctor Odaldi," Della Porta instructed the priest. "Tell him what we need. Oh, and make sure he brings something so that she can see in the catacombs. She won't be able to use a torch once she gets into the poisonous gas."

The pair waited while Father Carracci went to fetch Odaldi. Chrymos could once again feel the oppressive Tower enchantments, but they barely registered compared with the crippling effects of the snake venom.

After a few minutes, Carracci returned with Odaldi. The teacher regarded Chrymos with hatred in his eyes. "You? The destroyer of my most precious possession? You'll receive nothing from me!"

Odaldi would have turned and gone back to his laboratory, but Carracci held the teacher firmly.

"Time enough for revenge later, Doctor," said Della Porta. "For now, we still need Chrymos. Give her the necessary protections. Make her functional—don't try for 'comfortable.'"

Odaldi had brought along a large bag carrying various alchemic preparations. He proceeded to administer several different liquids to Chrymos.

"This one," said Odaldi, mixing up the same purple medication that Chrymos had already been receiving, "is for relieving the pain of the snake venom." She hurriedly drank it down although she knew from previous doses that its effect would not be immediate.

"And this," noted Odaldi as he mixed together a nasty-looking brown liquid, "will keep you awake for another 24 hours. It won't be pleasant, however." Odaldi smiled coldly. "Every minute will feel like an hour, your skin will crawl and your senses will cry out for sleep." Chrymos had no choice but to gulp down the foul-tasting drink.

Odaldi took several more ingredients out of the bag but then stopped, concerned. "These jars were full this morning, but now—" He examined each jar in turn. "Now there's only about a quarter of each ingredient left. I don't understand."

Della Porta frowned. "Can you, or can't you, still an elixir to get her through the gas?"

"Well yes, I can," Odaldi said, "but with the quantities remaining I can't guarantee that the effects will last any more than seven or eight hours at most."

"Give her enough now to keep her going for six hours," said Della Porta, "and put the rest into an additional, emergency dose that she can take with her just in case."

Odaldi proceeded to create a potent black cocktail, which he handed to Chrymos. "Six hours, no more," he told her.

While Chrymos swallowed the elixir, Odaldi created a separate mixture, and poured it into a vial for her to carry with her. He added in one additional ingredient. "To preserve its potency until you need it," he explained as he handed over the vial to Chrymos. She stowed the emergency vial in one of the pockets of her tunic dress.

"Thank you, Doctor," said Della Porta. "Did you bring what she needs so that she can see down there?"

Odaldi nodded, retrieved two containers from his bag, and handed them over to the Master. "Either of these should provide the necessary light."

"Many thanks, Doctor, you can go now," said Della Porta. Odaldi gathered up his bag and left, though not without another glare at the tablet-destroyer.

"Now let's get started," said Della Porta. He took a flaming torch from the foyer and then led the way down past the kitchen and into the very basement of the Academy.

In the flickering flame, Chrymos could see that the sides of the basement were just tightly-packed earth—and what appeared to be the entrance to a tunnel had been roughly dug into one corner. A shiver of fear ran through her as she realized that the Master expected her to enter the tunnel.

"It leads to the catacombs," said Della Porta. "Public access to the catacombs is limited because the tombs have been looted so often over recent centuries. We realized ten years ago that we needed to have our own entrance so that we could come and go when no-one else is around. Don't worry," he said, seeing Chrymos' reaction, "the tunnel is perfectly safe, we've sent many people through here over the years. You need to go about four hundred varas and then you'll find yourself at the second level of the catacombs. It's lucky that you're small, though," he added, "I'm told the tunnel is very narrow in a few places. A few landslips over the years, nothing much to worry about."

Clearly, you haven't been through there, not when there are plenty of flunkies you can send to their doom instead. Chrymos tried to gulp down her panic and focus on the instructions she was being given by Carracci.

"When you emerge from the tunnel," said the priest, "you'll find yourself in one of the family tombs on the second level. Try not to disturb any bones as you make your way out to the main corridor." Carracci gave a half-grimace to suggest he was joking. "Then turn left, straight down the main passageway until you come to the steps leading downwards. After that, follow the instructions in the manuscript."

Della Porta handed the flaming torch to Chrymos. He also gave her a small vial filled with the same glowing red powder that Chrymos had used to good effect in Doctor Odaldi's laboratory. "You won't be able to use the torch once you get to the section with the poison gases," said the Master, "so that's when you will need the powder." Chrymos stuffed the vial into a pocket of her tunic.

"And you're already familiar with this, I believe," noted the Master, handing over another small container, this one housing a familiar strip of metal. "The red powder may not be sufficient once you get inside the angel's tomb. You may need the very bright light that this can create, so that you can see—" The Master finished his sentence weakly, not wanting to say too much. "—whatever treasures the angel's tomb may have for us."

Chrymos nodded and slipped the container into her tunic pocket as well

Finally, Della Porta held up a small mechanical device.

"This is called a timepiece. We liberated it from the craftsman who made its cousin for Cosimo de' Medici", said Della Porta. "Observe—it has a strip of metal, a 'hand' that moves. It takes precisely one hour for the hand to travel from one number to the next. If you're not back here with what's in the tomb—or at least the manuscript—before that hand touches the VI, then your elixir will run out and you'll choke to death down there." The single hand on the miraculous timepiece had just left the XII.

Chrymos placed the curious device into her pocket beside the other items. Then with great trepidation, she bent over double and eased into the tunnel. In one hand she clutched the spluttering torch that threatened alternately to burn her or to choke her with its foul-smelling smoke whilst her other hand kept a tight grip on her belt and the manuscript that might spell the difference between death and survival.

NINETY-SIX
The Academy of Secrets, Naples, Kingdom of Naples, Midnight, Tuesday June 22 1610

Della Porta and Carracci watched her go.

"You don't really expect her to come out of there alive, do you?" said Carracci. "Hardly anyone else has, in all the years we've been sending students into that death-trap. And no-one has ever found the tomb."

Della Porta shrugged. "Stefani believes that Chrymos has the best chance of anyone we've ever sent. Perhaps she does, after all she did manage to translate the manuscript and identify many traps that we simply didn't know about."

He crossed to the basement exit. "If she succeeds, if she brings back whatever treasure that the tomb is protecting—"

"—then, according to the prophecy, that will trigger the Lost War." Carracci completed the sentence. "And if not, we're well rid of one troublesome student." Carracci followed Della Porta out the door and they proceeded up the steps. "What do you want me to do about her precious children?"

"Oh, put them back into the Plague project, at least then they can be of some use," said Della Porta. "Don't waste any more time on lazzaroni. We need to get the next phase of our plans underway. Has Odaldi developed an immunity pill yet?"

"He tells me he's very close," said Carracci. "It could be days, it could be hours."

"Good," said Della Porta. "In the meantime, let's get ready for the Outcast Angels."

NINETY-SEVEN
The Tunnel from the Academy of Secrets, Naples, Kingdom of Naples, 12.05 a.m. Wednesday June 23 1610

The tunnel between the Academy and the catacombs was poorly constructed, largely unsupported except in a few places where planks of wood and columns of bricks had been employed to bolster particularly unstable ground.

The tunnel was barely wide enough for one person to squeeze through and for much of its length required Chrymos to crawl and wriggle rather than walk. It was the perfect punishment for a claustrophobe and only the knowledge that others had successfully passed through the tunnel kept Chrymos from a total panic meltdown as she agonized through the tight passage. That did not stop her from imagining the worst. *What if the tunnel has collapsed since Adric went through? What if the Master lied to me again and no-one has been through the tunnel in years? What a way to go—buried alive, with no chance to save the children!*

Despite her fears, Chrymos pushed forward. Her right hand was stretched out in front of her, clutching the flaming, smoking torch, whilst her left hand held the manuscript close to her body. She propelled herself forward mostly using her knees and her right elbow. It made for slow going.

After Chrymos had been crawling through her living nightmare for what felt like an eternity—but must have been no more than an hour at most—she came to a complete standstill. It wasn't because the passage was blocked—it was still tight-going, though no more so than it had been for most of the journey—but rather because she had become totally overwhelmed by her fears.

No more. I can't do this. Surely, the children would understand? Adric, he will. He knows how I feel about being trapped underground.

For a long moment, Chrymos lay there, paralyzed by fear and doubt. Eventually, brutal realization set in. *I will die here. I can't turn around, I can't go back. If I don't go forward—but I can't, I just can't.*

She bent her head. *Father God, you know what I am facing. It's too much for me. I cannot cope. Help me, Almighty Lord. Send me a sign so that I know what I should do.*

Silence at first. But then Chrymos coughed. She coughed because some of the smoke from the torch blew into her face.

Wonderful. Now I'm going to choke to death.

It took a few moments for Chrymos to realize what had happened. For most of her journey through the tunnel the smoke from the torch had blown away from her, fanned by the air coming from behind, from the Academy. *If the smoke is now being blown towards me, then I must be getting close to the catacombs. Halleluiah!*

Chrymos offered grateful thanks to the Father as she scrabbled forward. Now that it seemed that her destination might be within reach, she was able to dampen down her fears and get moving again. More and more smoke blew towards her as the fresh air coming from the catacombs grew stronger—but now she happily coughed and spluttered, regarding every puff of smoke as a milestone bringing her closer to her goal.

Finally, she reached the end of the tunnel and emerged into the Catacombs of San Gennaro.

NINETY-EIGHT
In the skies above Naples, Kingdom of Naples,
12.30 a.m. Wednesday June 23 1610

The grossly overweight blob that was the Darke Warrior Chosek was on surveillance duty above the city of Naples, and none too happy about that task, even though his ability to see in the dark made Chosek the obvious choice. His black leathery wings struggled to propel his oversized body over the city as Chosek watched for any stealthy nighttime attacks on the Academy.

Even when Chosek was just another angel in Heaven, he tended to over-indulge—and since he became a Darke Warrior, Chosek had really let himself go. He had always been short, five foot two inches when barefoot, but since the Rebellion, he was best known for his extreme gluttony. Like angels, demons have no need for physical food—they draw their power and their sustenance from the radiation emanating from the sun. Chosek alas had double-dipped, drawing energy not only from solar radiation but also from the souls of those trapped in Hades—and then doing very little with that energy. The inevitable result: an overweight, unattractive little demon, out of condition and prone to sweat and complain whenever his duties required him to exert himself in the slightest.

Chosek bombarded Nekhbet with yet another question. *<Why are we even bothering to do this? Once we have the pathgem—>*

Nekhbet interrupted him. *<There are no guarantees, you know that. Yes, there is a strong probability that Chrymos will find the pathgem—but there are other possibilities too. Until the pathgem is found and returned to us, we will continue to assist the Council of Four with their plans. Is that clear?>*

<Yes,> agreed Chosek grudgingly.

<Good. Then devote your attention to watching for Outcast Angels and stop bothering me.>

NINETY-NINE
The Catacombs of San Gennaro, Naples, Kingdom of Naples, 1.00 a.m. Wednesday June 23 1610

The tunnel opened into an arcosolium, a family tomb within one of the upper levels of the catacombs. From there, Chrymos found herself in one of the main corridors. She was delighted to discover that the corridors in these catacombs were far wider than she had expected—a blessed relief after the constrictions of the tunnel. This level of the catacombs, she belatedly recalled from the manuscript, had been constructed from an old stone quarry, dug out by highly skilled workers known as *fossores*. They used picks to carve corridors and chambers out of the soft Naples rock.

Chrymos stood for a moment, stretching out her body and breathing in the fresh night air. The Catacomb's upper levels were punctured at regular intervals by *luminaria*, shafts that extended from the surface down to the catacombs to provide light and fresh air.

She reached into her pocket for the timepiece. Its hand had moved and now pointed to the I. *One hour gone—no time to waste.* She stuffed the device back into her pocket, brushed the worst of the dirt off her tunic, and began her search in earnest.

As Father Carracci had instructed, Chrymos turned left and proceeded down the main corridor until she came to a set of steps leading downwards. According to the manuscript, she needed to go down two levels—but the steps would only take her down one. To descend any further, she needed to look for Shadrach, Meshach, and Abednego.

The manuscript had been typically cryptic at this point, simply containing a reference to Chapter Three of the Book of Daniel. Because of her memory loss, Chrymos was unsure what the chapter contained. Fortunately, Della Porta did have a bible in his office—*doesn't look like he's ever used it*, she noted to herself—and Chrymos soon found the scriptural reference, to three young men who had been thrown into a fiery furnace but emerged unharmed. *Now all I have to do is find an inscription or some other item on this level that links to the bible story.*

Flaming torch held high, Chrymos walked through the lower level of the catacombs as she dared. She ignored the loculi, the basic graves which were little more than slots in the wall, and focused her attention on the more elaborate arcosolia. These larger burial chambers, usually housing Naples' wealthier citizens, often bore friezes illustrating Christian images—although the oldest, dating back to the years of persecution in the third and fourth centuries after Christ, were less transparently Christian and instead used traditional Roman icons such as grapevines or peacocks.

When Chrymos finally walked past the burial chamber for which she had been searching, she didn't recognize it at first.

She had been expecting some sort of illustration of three men surrounded by flames. Instead, the chamber carried a wall painting depicting three birds perched on a nest of fire, while a fourth bird flew above, wings outstretched.

Oh, that's clever, gasped Chrymos once she had interpreted what she saw. *Three phoenixes—a classic Roman icon signaling death and rebirth—representing the three men untouched by the fire, while the fourth represents the angel. To Roman eyes, it's a typical grave emblem—but to Christians it's a celebration. And for me it's a pointer.*

Chrymos climbed over the small wall that bordered the burial chamber and headed to the marble slab on top of the sarcophagus in the center. She carefully laid the manuscript down on the floor and then propped up the torch against one wall of the burial chamber.

Wish I still had the gauntlets, Chrymos grumbled, as she struggled to push the slab across, to uncover whatever was inside the sarcophagus.

Once she had started the slab moving, however, it slid smoothly across, pivoting around on one corner. *It's obviously been designed as an entry point that many people can use, probably so that Christians could secretly visit the martyrs' graves during the persecution years.*

Chrymos peered down into the sarcophagus. The tomb simply contained a set of stone steps leading downwards.

And then she noticed the gas billowing up through the sarcophagus towards her.

ONE HUNDRED
The Catacombs of San Gennaro, Naples, Kingdom of Naples, 1.30 a.m. Wednesday June 23 1610

Chrymos reacted quickly, sliding the slab back into place. That stopped most of the gas from pouring out and contaminating the air around her, giving Chrymos valuable time to think.

First, she took the timepiece out of her tunic pocket and held it near the torch. *The hand is halfway between the I and the II. That's good enough.*

Next, Chrymos retrieved the manuscript and placed it flat on top of the sarcophagus slab. Then she retrieved the torch and held it close while she flipped through the relevant pages of the manuscript. *This is the last chance I'm going to get to use the torch so I'd better re-read this while I can.*

Chrymos spent about ten minutes refreshing her knowledge from the manuscript and then, reluctantly, left the torch propped up against the wall. *Here we go.*

She picked up the manuscript, flattened it out, and slipped it between her belt and her body. Then, breathing what might be her last gasp of fresh air, Chrymos again pushed hard until the slab slid open.

Again, the gas began to pour out. Chrymos was ready. She swung herself over the side of the sarcophagus and reached down with her right foot until she touched the top step. *Let's see how good this elixir is.*

Chrymos slipped down onto the steps and began climbing down, holding her breath as she did so.

The moment that her leading foot touched the fifth step, Chrymos heard a grinding sound above her. The slab was sliding shut—and the last faint light from the torch was quickly disappearing.

ONE HUNDRED AND ONE
The Catacombs of San Gennaro, Naples, Kingdom of Naples, 1.45 a.m. Wednesday June 23 1610

Before she could start to panic, Chrymos hurried thrust her right hand into her tunic pocket and—when her questing fingers found the glass vial they sought—she breathed a deep sigh of relief.

Well, a deep breath was what she intended to take. That breath turned into a nasty hacking cough as Chrymos inhaled her first lungful of the poisonous gas. After the inevitable coughing fit that followed, Chrymos switched to taking very shallow breaths. *It seems that the elixir does work, but the experience certainly isn't pleasant.*

Chrymos now found herself in complete darkness. While she was coughing, the slab had closed completely. However, despite the coughs racking her frame, Chrymos hadn't moved and she certainly hadn't let go of the vial.

Moving her right hand very, very carefully, Chrymos slowly withdrew the vial from her pocket. She brought her hand in front of her face and with great patience gently shook the vial. She was rewarded with a faint red glow as the powder reacted with the small amount of air within the vial. Chrymos was just about to open the vial to make the powder glow more brightly when she realized that there might be a problem.

What if the gas makes the powder stop glowing? What will I do then?

Chrymos decided not to take any chances. She gave the vial a slightly more vigorous shake but kept the cork lid firmly closed. The powder glowed a little more brightly, but not much.

Chrymos began to head down the steps towards her next destination, the labyrinth. She tried desperately to dispel the thought that had stabbed through her. *If the red powder doesn't work in this gas, I may have already doomed both Adric and myself.*

ONE HUNDRED AND TWO
Certosa di San Martino, City of Naples, Kingdom of Naples,
1.45 a.m. Wednesday June 23 1610

The monks of the Certosa di San Martino monastery, gathered for a midnight service to commemorate the *Sollemnitas Sacratissimi Cordis Iesu*, looked at each other in horror. Their monastery, perched high on the Vomero hill overlooking Naples, began shaking uncontrollably, accompanied by what appeared to be rumbling thunder.

Several monks rushed out of the service to the nearest balcony. They looked towards Mount Vesuvius, expecting another eruption.

The monks quickly realized that the disturbance was not coming from that direction. Instead, it seemed to be centered on—no, below—the water fountain that sat in the middle of the monastery's gardens.

The noise and the shaking grew and grew in intensity and then—the water fountain split into two sections, each piece sliding aside to reveal a deep chasm below.

Transfixed, the monks stared in shock as first one carriage and then many more emerged from the very bowels of the earth. As one of the watching monks would later describe the scene to his superior, "these were carriages crawling with demons, pulled by unearthly creatures from Hades—their heads glowing balls of fire, their bodies unnaturally wide and covered with armor, their legs stripped of their flesh and gleaming like metal."

That monk was one of the braver ones. Most fled as soon as the first carriage began to emerge, without stopping to observe the arrival of the rest of the carriages through a tunnel entrance that had never previously been used for such a purpose.

New Phoenicia had sent five carriages, each carrying six warriors, to aid the Academy in the impending clash with the Outcast Angels and their enhanced colleagues.

Most of New Phoenicia's fighters were pirates, drawn largely from the most bloodthirsty and battle-hardened of Peter Easton's pirate crews.

Nekhbet had specifically requested their presence when she met with New Phoenicia's leader Sir Robert Killigrew two months earlier.

The carriages clattered out through the main gates of the Certosa di San Martino and headed towards the city.

ONE HUNDRED AND THREE
The Catacombs of San Gennaro, Naples, Kingdom of Naples, 1.50 a.m. Wednesday June 23 1610

Chrymos emerged from the stairwell, greatly relieved to find that, for once, her worst fears had not been realized. *I can see red powder numbers marked on the walls. My plan does still work.*

The manuscript had described a bewildering number of crisscrossing passages and doorways in this part of the catacombs but had offered up a simple solution—"keep right." The accompanying illustration, of a man with the head of a bull, had given Chrymos her inspiration.

In her translation notes, she had repeated the injunction to "keep right." But, borrowing an idea from the story of Theseus and the Minotaur that the illustration had referenced, Chrymos had suggested that whenever the searcher—*who has turned out to be Adric*, thought Chrymos regretfully—had to make a choice about which way to go, he should use the red powder to mark his chosen route with the number 1. Then if had to retrace his steps at any point, or if the labyrinth took him around in circles and he found himself in the same area again, Adric could simply make a different choice, this time marked with the number 2.

It seemed like a good idea, but did it actually work?

Chrymos began tackling the maze, taking her own advice—she kept right wherever possible and she followed the numbers. There were a gratifyingly large number of 1s, with only a few 2s indicating where Adric had been obliged to retrace his steps—and just a single 3. *It must have taken Adric a lot longer to get through here than it's taking me, but the plan seems to have worked.*

Soon enough, Chrymos found herself in what appeared to be a large, open area filled with row after row of stone sarcophagi, blatantly decorated with Christian symbols. *The final resting place of the Christian martyrs*, decided Chrymos, and a glance inside several sarcophagi confirmed her suspicions—each housed at least one set of skeletal remains, some two or even three skeletons. It was a sobering sight, even more than a thousand years later, and Chrymos paused for a few moments to offer up prayers for their souls.

She was, however, conscious that the hours were passing too quickly. She retrieved the timepiece from her pocket and squinted at it in the dim red light. The hand now pointed to the II. *I need to get moving.*

The next destination, the next hurdle, was the passage. The manuscript provided a less-than-helpful guide in the form of a complex illustration of a plant with three overlapping roots. *My best guess is that I'll find the three passageways at the far end of this chamber.*

Chrymos began to move forward and then stopped. She fancied she'd heard a noise.

Is that Adric? Is this as far as he got?

She tried calling out. "Adric? It's Chrymos! Are you here?"

Chrymos listened for a response. Nothing—at least, not at first. Then she heard another slight noise, coming from behind her.

She turned around. At first, she could only see the faint glowing red of the powder vial in her hand. Then, as Chrymos concentrated, she thought she could see a pair of eyes over to one side, staring at her. The whites of those eyes seemed to reflect the red powder.

Adric? Chrymos almost called out again, until she saw another pair of eyes, and then another and still another. All four sets of eyes were watching her, unblinking. *How is this possible? How can anything survive in these poisonous fumes? And, if any of these creatures do live down here, why weren't they mentioned in the manuscript?*

Slowly, those eyes—and whatever creatures lay behind them—began moving directly towards Chrymos.

ONE HUNDRED AND FOUR
The Catacombs of San Gennaro, Naples, Kingdom of Naples, 2.00 a.m. Wednesday June 23 1610

The creature gazed hungrily at its next meal.

It—he—had, twenty years earlier, answered to the name of Vittorio. He had been a promising student at the Academy of Secrets, still a year away from graduating. Then one day the Master of the Academy, the great and powerful Giambattista Della Porta, had sought out Vittorio and proposed a fine adventure—a hunt for buried treasure in the nearby Catacombs of San Gennaro.

"What you will be searching for," Della Porta had told the young student, "is a weapon that we can use against the English and their vastardo queen."

Della Porta had found an eager participant. In 1590, many young men of Naples were still burning with rage over the treacherous defeat of the Spanish Armada two years earlier. Any quest that promised to avenge that defeat would be vigorously championed.

And so it was that, a few weeks later, Vittorio and four other classmates broke into the catacombs—the connecting tunnel from the Academy had not yet been dug—and began their search for a mysterious tomb. All they knew, all that Della Porta knew in those long ago days, was that a white shield marked with blood had been buried with the body. It was a slim clue but Vittorio and his friends were confident that they would be able to find the body and recover any weapons that had been buried in the same tomb.

"One more point," Della Porta had told the five students before they left the Academy. "We understand that there is bad air that lingers in some parts of the catacombs. This—" Della Porta handed several vials of elixir to each student. "—will enable you to breathe freely if you do encounter such air."

The adventurers had set off with several weeks' supply of food and water—they did not intend to return to the Academy until they had secured their prize. Days went by as they explored the upper levels, opening each and every tomb and searching in vain for the white shield. Their enthusiasm dimmed as tomb after tomb yielded nothing but bones, but still they persevered.

Eventually, the students came across the sarcophagus which led to the labyrinth. They, like Chrymos two decades later, were greeted by foul gas flooding towards them. They too hastily resealed the sarcophagus until they were ready to descend. They swallowed their first vials of elixir and then gingerly began to make their way down the steps. They too inadvertently triggered the switch that resealed the sarcophagus behind them.

What Vittorio and his friends lacked was any means of illumination. They had brought along flaming torches, but these spluttered and went out, extinguished by the deadly gas. The students found themselves in total darkness, uncertain dangers below, escape blocked above.

What happened next was predictable. One of the students panicked, slipped, and tumbled down the stairs. The others, navigating by feeling their way slowly, carefully downwards, arrived at the bottom of the stairwell in due course and almost tripped over the dead body of their former colleague. He had broken his neck in the fall.

For the next six weeks, the students divided their energies between cursing the Master and exploring the stairwell by touch, trying to find something that would release the slab that stood between them and freedom.

As food and water supplies ran low, they began to fight amongst themselves for the last remaining rations. Their elixirs ran low but by then their bodies had adapted somewhat to the poisonous fumes. They became more beast than human, the gases warping both body and mind.

Finally, all supplies were exhausted and the four became three and then two and finally one. The lone survivor, Vittorio, was forced to choose between death and cannibalism.

# # #

Vittorio's living death evolved into a regular routine. Every few months, the Academy would send a fresh batch of students to search the catacombs. Some made their way downward through the holes in the arcosolium floor that had been dug by Della Porta's father and grandfather. Several discovered the secret passageway and entered through the sarcophagus. Whichever route they took, most ended up suffering the same fate as Vittorio's colleagues, becoming a food source for the creature within. A mere handful proved sufficiently hardy to transform themselves into near-dead creatures like Vittorio. Their eyes adapted—a side-effect of the elixir, perhaps—so that they could see in the near-total darkness but their bodies withered away through lack of proper sustenance.

And they had all become more animal than human. Their body hair had largely fallen out, their muscles had wasted away and their skin was deathly pale and clammy to the touch.

By the time that Chrymos entered the tomb Vittorio had three bestial companions. Each relied on consuming human flesh and blood to survive.

ONE HUNDRED AND FIVE
The Catacombs of San Gennaro, Naples, Kingdom of Naples, 2.00 a.m. Wednesday June 23 1610

Chrymos attempted to back out of reach but was only partly successful. *Whatever these creatures are, they aren't stupid,* she noted, as the four moved to surround her, blocking off her exits. Then, at a signal from the one she gathered must be the leader, they began to close in.

Surprisingly, Chrymos brightened as the four creatures attempted to catch her. *This is a game I very much know how to play.* She had been chased many times when she lived on the streets of Florence and Naples, usually because a local shopkeeper had been robbed and any nearby lazzaroni were automatically suspects. Chrymos usually escaped without being captured. *This should be no different.*

Chrymos' first move was to gain a height advantage on her attackers, which she achieved by climbing onto one of the sarcophagi nearby. While the sarcophagus she scaled did have a cover slab on which she could stand, she couldn't stay there. *This area is too vulnerable.*

Instead, she stretched across to the next sarcophagus, this one without a cover, and stood with one foot on each stone side as she considered her options. Meanwhile the four creatures reoriented themselves and began moving towards her again. *First thing I need to do is to get beyond their immediate reach.*

Chrymos leapt from sarcophagus edge to sarcophagus edge, dodging outstretched hands, until at last she found herself on the far side of the creatures' perimeter. She looked back as best she could, relying on the dim light generated by her vial of red powder. The four had not given up their pursuit, even though they shuffled along at a far slower pace than she did.

Two more leaps and Chrymos decided it was finally safe enough to get back to ground level. With a final surge, she jumped down from the sarcophagus—and landed heavily, twisting her right ankle as she did so. Chrymos had protected the vial of powder by sheltering it within her right hand, so that at least was undamaged.

A few choice words escaped her lips but she dared not linger—the four creatures were still close behind her. Chrymos limped in search of her next goal, a passageway filled with voices.

Here's where I find out if the clue about voices makes sense, she realized. *If it doesn't, I could be in big trouble.*

Actually, she reflected, risking another glance behind her, *I'm in big trouble already. I still need to find my way past these creatures to get out of the catacombs—and now I'm moving at about the same pace as they are.*

ONE HUNDRED AND SIX
Catacombs of San Gennaro, Naples, Kingdom of Naples, 2.15 a.m. Wednesday June 23 1610

Chrymos had subconsciously hoped that the third protection would be relatively straightforward. *I was wrong.*

In the dim light generated by her makeshift torch, Chrymos could see that she faced a wide range of options. Instead of perhaps three or four entrances from which to choose, the back wall of the chamber was riddled with passageways—at least a dozen, if not more. Some were at ground level, enticingly easy to enter, but most were at least six feet above ground level, with no obvious access. *This could take hours.*

Chrymos didn't have hours. She glanced back, confirming that the creatures were still shuffling towards her. She had a minute or two, at most, to escape them.

Moving as fast as her injured leg would permit, Chrymos went to the closest ground floor passageway and poked her head inside the entrance, listening. *Not a sound.*

Chrymos' next choice was nearly her last. She limped over to the second passageway and, stooped over because of her injury, leant inside to listen. Her forehead pushed against a rope that had been strung chest-high across the entrance, triggering the release of an arrow that whooshed past, mere inches over her head.

Chrymos could not spare the time to admire her narrow escape. She limped on to the next passageway and, far more tentatively, listened just inside the archway. *Still nothing.*

Despairingly, she looked over at the two remaining ground floor entrances. *Those are highly likely to be booby-trapped as well.* She glanced back at the creatures, still moving inexorably towards her. *There's probably only enough time to try one of the higher passages. But which one, Lord, which one?*

Chrymos stepped back a pace, so that she would be better positioned to select the most promising possibility from the many passages on the second level. *But how do I judge from down here?*

As Chrymos swept her gaze along the wall, her eye registered a faint red glow. *Is that what I think it is?*

One of the entrances had been marked in red powder with the number 1. *Adric, you made it this far!*

Chrymos scanned the other passageways, in case any of them bore a higher number. As best she could tell from where she stood, the others were unmarked.

Well, Adric, if you've made the wrong choice, then I guess we'll both share the same fate.

The creatures were now less than ten feet away. There were no easy paths for Chrymos to climb to reach the chosen passageway directly, but a few cracks and indentations showed promise. And there was a narrow ledge, which should enable her to cross over to the entrance that Adric had marked.

Tucking her precious vial back into her pocket, Chrymos began climbing for her life. She had almost reached a safe height when she felt a bony hand grab at her left ankle.

ONE HUNDRED AND SEVEN
The Academy of Secrets, Naples, Kingdom of Naples, 2.20 a.m. Wednesday June 23 1610

"You're out of time. You need to get those plague-hosts out of the Academy now, before the Outcast Angels attack." Killeen, speaking via Janus-twin, was typically blunt.

"But we're almost there," argued Della Porta. "Odaldi is promising a protective pill in a matter of hours."

"Too late," said Killeen. "If we lose those hosts, then the Lost War may be over before it's even begun. Get them out of there, that's an order!" The Janus twin shouted that last sentence, no doubt mirroring the manner in which his counterpart in New Phoenicia had been addressed.

Della Porta wearily waved away the twin. Once the telepath had left his office, the Master of the Academy turned to his wife. "Any more news on the Outcasts?"

The Contessa shook her head. "Nekhbet has one of her demons watching above us, but he hasn't reported any movements yet. We're probably safe enough until dawn, but then we can expect an attack for sure."

"Then we'd better start getting those plague-hosts ready for travel. My dear, please advise Doctor Odaldi that he has—" Odaldi looked up at the clock on his wall. "—no more than three hours remaining with the hosts. If he can't complete his pill by then, we'll have to launch the Plague project without it."

ONE HUNDRED AND EIGHT
Catacombs of San Gennaro, Naples, Kingdom of Naples, 2.25 a.m. Wednesday June 23 1610

Chrymos might have fallen then, with one of the creatures grasping her ankle. She kicked backwards. Perhaps her desperation put enough power into her kick. More likely, it was the creature's greatly weakened condition after being entombed for so long with minimal food and water. Whatever the cause, Chrymos managed to successfully dislodge its grip and pull her foot away.

Free at least for the moment, Chrymos scrambled up the rock, to the ledge that was her interim destination. She took a deep breath in relief, and then had to fight off a coughing fit as once again the poison gas forcefully reminded her of its presence.

Once she was settled, standing on the ledge, Chrymos pulled the powder vial out of her pocket. She shook the vial briskly and then used the ensuing light to gain a better view of the creatures below.

Two of them were pawing away ineffectually at the wall, as if attempting to climb, and Chrymos almost felt sorry for them—until she noticed what appeared to be red blood stains around each creature's mouth.

For a heartbeat, she panicked, thinking that the blood must be Adric's—then she remembered that he had left his mark on the passage she was about to enter. *If what I'm seeing on their faces is Adric's blood, hopefully he isn't badly hurt*, she told herself, though with little conviction.

Leaving the creatures milling around below, Chrymos returned the vial to her pocket and then—as slowly and carefully as she dared—inched along the narrow ledge towards the marked entrance. Her head was half turned, her cheek pressed hard against the rock. Both her arms were fully extended, with each hand doing its best to cling to the surface of the wall.

Behind her back, she could almost feel the creatures watching her pitiful progress, willing her to fall, salivating at every stumble. Once or twice, as she rested her weight on her injured right leg, she nearly did tumble.

Finally, her outstretched left arm found the edge of the target passageway and she was able to pull herself across to relative safety in front of the entrance that Adric had marked.

Chrymos paused, listening. *I assume that Adric has marked this as the correct entrance, but I still should listen for the noises that the manuscript suggested.*

At first, she couldn't hear anything. Then, as she focused, she thought that she could hear a low buzz, as if of people talking. *Am I truly hearing that,* she wondered, *or am I simply imagining it?*

Once again, Chrymos removed the vial from her pocket and shook it, awakening a fresh glow. She held the vial out at arms' length in front of her, but saw only a plain passageway, receding into the distance. *There are no obvious signs of booby-traps, but then there wouldn't be, would there?*

She took one limping step inside the entrance, fearing the worst but praying for the best.

ONE HUNDRED AND NINE
Catacombs of San Gennaro, Naples, Kingdom of Naples, 2.33 a.m. Wednesday June 23 1610

The noise seemed slightly louder. Chrymos chanced another step and was rewarded with a further increase in volume. More importantly, her actions triggered no traps.

Chrymos patted the manuscript, still held firmly in place by her belt. *Thank you, unknown genius, your story continues to serve me well, I seem to have survived the third protection. And thank you Adric, wherever you are, you just saved my life.*

She took several more limping steps into the passage, and the noise grew in intensity. *Definitely angry voices,* she decided. The noise seemed to be coming from somewhere up ahead.

Finally satisfied that the passage she had chosen was the correct one, Chrymos stepped up her pace as best she could, trying to avoid putting too much weight onto her right leg. Half-limping, half-dragging her injured foot, she forced herself along the corridor, which seemed to have a slight downward incline. As she progressed, she found that the passageway was becoming very damp, with little pools of water dotted along the ground.

With every step that Chrymos took, the noise grew louder around her. Soon it was almost a roar, yet there was no obvious cause.

Chrymos grew more anxious as the path began to wind around itself as if in a spiral. *Where is this taking me?* Still, with known perils behind her and with time running short, she had little choice but to proceed. The noise continued to increase in intensity.

The passage continued to curve around and then abruptly opened into a large circular chamber. Chrymos followed into the central part of the chamber, where the path stopped abruptly, forcing her to do likewise.

She held up the glowing red vial as high above her head as she could and inspected her surroundings, turning in place as she looked for possible exits.

Apart from the passageway that had brought Chrymos here, she could see no other exits. The chamber was like the inside of a bowl, with smooth sides all around. *Did I miss a side-passage that I should have taken?*

Chrymos fished the timepiece out of her pocket and groaned aloud when she saw its face. *Three-quarters of the way to the third hour.*

Her options were dwindling as well. *This chamber appears to be a dead end.*

Chrymos resolved to retrace her steps, searching for an alternative exit. She put away the timepiece and then, with the aid of her glowing vial, began to climb out of the chamber, limping back to the passageway. She had gone a few tentative steps when she stood on something that moved under her left foot.

There was a click, and then a mighty rumble. A series of stone blocks began to slide out from one side of the chamber, creating a stepped effect from floor to ceiling. Then huge volumes of water began cascading down from a newly revealed hole in the ceiling, bouncing angrily off the stone blocks. The torrent of water thundered towards Chrymos.

ONE HUNDRED AND TEN
Catacombs of San Gennaro, Naples, Kingdom of Naples, 2.45 a.m. Wednesday June 23 1610

With her damaged right foot, Chrymos had few options. She braced herself for the impact as best she could. The first wave smashed into her, knocking her off her feet, and then pushing her along as the seemingly endless torrents of water rushed to fill the bowl that the chamber had become.

She instantly became a mere passenger, tossed around in this maelstrom like a twig and her mind conjured up the horrific drowning memories from her nightmares. *Were those dreams prophetic warnings?*

Chrymos had little time for such thoughts. Around and around the water swirled and Chrymos felt herself starting to be pulled under by the powerful current. She struggled mightily to keep her head above the furiously-boiling surface. *If I go under, I'm dead.*

Chrymos still clutched the glowing vial in her right hand but as often as not that hand was being sucked underwater, muting the effectiveness of the light. Even so, she caught occasional glimpses of the series of four-foot-square stone blocks that protruded from one side of the otherwise smooth chamber, the water pouring down from somewhere in the ceiling and then ricocheting from one block down to another. Already the lowest block was completely submerged and the water level continued to rise very rapidly. *If I can grab hold of one of those blocks*, she told herself, *perhaps I can climb out of this.*

It was the only idea that seemed to hold any promise, so Chrymos attempted to make it happen. With great difficulty, she managed to stow the vial within her tunic. Then with both hands free, she began to fight through the currents towards the walls. Chrymos was still being tossed around and around in the turbulent waters but hoped that as she was driven past the blocks, she could somehow cling on to an edge.

That idea was nearly her downfall. With the vial stowed away inside her clothing, Chrymos could see very little. Consequently, even though she managed to reach the periphery of the water, she was still borne along by its circular motion. She found herself thrown against the side of the lowest block of stone before the relentless current scraped her off again.

Chrymos wasn't badly hurt but the impact drove the air from her lungs. For a moment, she thought she would surely drown as she struggled to get above the raging torrent.

From deep within herself, Chrymos found a reserve of extra strength and managed to push herself enough to get her head out of water and gulp down a couple of mouthfuls of that foul air.

She prayed for divine guidance as she struck out once more for the walls of her aquatic prison, extending her left hand in an effort to snag an edge of the block she had targeted.

As soon as her fingers touched the stone edge, Chrymos wrapped her body around the block and hung on desperately. Inch by inch she pulled herself along the block until she had reached the next, higher block. She found a firm handhold on one of the eroded edges of this block and finally was able to pull herself mostly out of the fast-flowing current. She still had to avoid the water cascading down from above but at least Chrymos was now able to regain her footing.

ONE HUNDRED AND ELEVEN
Catacombs of San Gennaro, Naples, Kingdom of Naples, 2.55 a.m. Wednesday June 23 1610

At last, Chrymos had a moment to think. Again, she fished the glowing vial out of her tunic and used it to inspect her surroundings. From this vantage point, she could see that the whole chamber below had clearly been designed to create a dangerous water trap. *No obvious exits at ground level.*

Chrymos looked upward. The water still poured steadily through a large hole in the ceiling high above. *An underground river,* she decided, *that gets diverted to become the fourth protection.*

She checked her timepiece again, grimacing when she saw that it was nearly at the third hour. *Not much time left. I doubt that it will be enough to complete my mission and return to the Academy.*

With no other options evident, Chrymos began climbing from block to block, moving ever higher. There were a half-dozen blocks still to climb, each about four feet in height, so the task was achievable but taxing, especially whilst she was nursing her right foot and actively trying to avoid the dancing, splashing water.

Eventually, Chrymos was able to reach the highest of the blocks, which took her to a few feet below the ceiling. To her great relief, Chrymos saw that stretching out from the top of the block was a dark passageway. *There is a way out of here! Praise the Lord!*

Chrymos took a few limping steps into the passageway and then stopped in horror. Again, she had stepped on some secret trigger. Again, there was a mighty rumble.

This time, the noise came from behind. Chrymos turned, and watched in wonder as hidden mechanisms began to close off the flow of water and the stone blocks began to recede into the chamber walls. Far below, she could hear the water begin to drain away, as the trap re-set itself to await its next victim.

Chrymos' clothing was soaked, so she took a moment to squeeze out as much water as she could, although in truth she achieved very little—her tunic dress still clung to her body, chilling her.

Then, with a gasp, Chrymos touched the manuscript and realized that it too was sodden. She lifted it away from her body and placed it carefully on the ground, then sat down in the passageway next to the precious document.

Propping the glowing vial against the passage wall, Chrymos began to inspect the manuscript. The outside covers were soaked but the inner pages, though often stuck together at the edges, seemed to have escaped relatively unscathed. She turned the pages one by one, where necessary gently separating them from their companions. *I don't have time for this,* she acknowledged to herself, *but I may need to refer to the book urgently later.*

Nearly at the end of the manuscript, she found two pages that seemed even more sealed together than the rest—not merely at one edge but at three edges. She spent several minutes painstakingly working a fingernail between the pages. Eventually, she was able to separate those pages—to discover a hidden section that no-one must have seen since the manuscript was first created.

With mounting excitement, she began to read.

ONE HUNDRED AND TWELVE
Catacombs of San Gennaro, Naples, Kingdom of Naples, 3.15 a.m. Wednesday June 23 1610

"There is a portion of the Book of the Dead," declared the author of the manuscript, "that I have been unable to read. It is in a language completely unknown to me. From the information provided elsewhere, I believe that this section reveals what great or terrible thing is to be found buried with the angel.

"I have carefully copied the unknown symbols here, so that those who come after me, if they have the knowledge, may be able to decipher the passage and discover the secret.

"However, because I cannot trust that this manuscript will remain in safe hands, it is my intention to seal these pages so that none will see their contents except those to whom God chooses to reveal His mysteries."

Below that introduction, Chrymos could see the copied characters. Thanks to her Exousía-gifted powers, Chrymos could translate the words easily.

"To my Brothers in Judas, glorious greetings," wrote the long-dead author of the original Book of the Dead. "I write these words in the hope that this report will get safely into your hands. This portion I have written in our own secret tongue so that our Brotherhood alone will learn what treasure lies within the angel's tomb.

"I have assembled these facts at great personal cost, after seducing two of the Roman soldiers who removed the body of the angel from the battlefield and after plying Bishop Januarius himself with enough wine that he answered my questions. My efforts lead me to believe that the tomb contains a glowing blue gem that enables the wearer to travel instantly from one place to another."

Chrymos sat up, stunned. *Was that the 'pathgem' that was on Della Porta's list? No wonder he wants to find the tomb. Such a weapon would grant power beyond belief.*

The spy's report continued. "I understand that one of the Darke

Warriors was using the gem until he was stopped and killed by the angel. I beg you, do not tell the Darke Warriors where the gem is, they will want it for themselves. There are so many ways that we can use the gem for our own cause, before eventually we may be forced to hand it back to them."

With that, the report ended. Chrymos turned the page, but there was nothing more.

I have to get the pathgem to Della Porta before he will release the children. But I just can't let him have the pathgem, it's too powerful. What am I going to do?

It was all too much for Chrymos, especially with time running out. She wedged the manuscript back inside her belt and stood up. *Right now, I have to keep going and try to find the tomb. If I do find the pathgem, that's when I'll decide what to do with it.*

The journey through the rest of the passageway was uneventful, for which Chrymos was undeniably grateful. By now, she was feeling the effect of so many hours without sleep, despite the medication that Odaldi had so grudgingly given her—and the snake venom began to reassert itself as well. Chrymos' head was starting to pound and she could feel her leg muscles protesting as the poison attacked anew.

I am so weary, Lord. What other challenges do you have for me before I can rescue Adric and free the children?

Chrymos' question was abruptly answered, not necessarily in a manner she would like, when she limped around a corner and found a large waterfall blocking her path. Water gushed down from above and into a large crevasse that spanned the entire passageway.

ONE HUNDRED AND THIRTEEN
Catacombs of San Gennaro, Naples, Kingdom of Naples, 3.30 a.m. Wednesday June 23 1610

Is this where the river normally empties out, wondered Chrymos, *when it isn't diverted into that chamber?*

Then she realized that she was asking the wrong question. *What I need to know,* she decided, *is how wide that crevasse is and whether the passageway continues on the other side.*

There was no easy way to find out. The manuscript hadn't even mentioned the waterfall. *Unless there are other secret pages, I'll find no help there.*

Chrymos tried to reason out her options. *Surely, this whole elaborate scheme is designed to allow the chosen people to enter the tomb? So there must be some means of passing through. All I have to do is find it.*

Then she had another thought. *What was that quote from the Divine Comedy?*

She retrieved the manuscript once again and thumbed through her notes until she found the right reference. 'By other ways, by other ports thou to the shore shalt come, not here, for passage; a lighter vessel needs must carry thee.' *What does that even mean? And is the quotation talking about this waterfall, or about the earlier trap?*

She referred to the timepiece once more. *Three and a half hours gone.*

Chrymos was sorely tempted simply to take a running jump through the falling water, hoping to connect with a passageway on the other side. *That's what I would usually do. But with this limp, I can't exactly run. Perhaps I can try to jump from the edge of the precipice.*

With so much depending on her choice, Chrymos hesitated. And thought, long and hard. *If the Divine Comedy is actually referring to this waterfall, then I guess the message is straightforward—this isn't the right path. So where do I find 'other ways' and 'a lighter vessel'? There weren't any forks in the passage I've just been through.*

More out of frustration than expectation, Chrymos lifted up the glowing vial and looked around to see if there were any other exits. *No.*

She did notice that one wall was more pockmarked than the others. Lifting the vial as high as she could, Chrymos inspected the top part of the wall, seeing even more indentations further up. *I think I could climb up there—perhaps I'll see something I can use.*

Chrymos set to work climbing the wall. It wasn't easy with her injured leg, especially as her various medications were starting to wear off, but after a few minutes she had managed to climb up to what turned out to be a 'shore,' a ledge alongside the raging river.

From her new elevated position, Chrymos could see that at this junction the underground river split in two. Most of the water poured down into the depths below but a small portion continued flowing forward beside her, diverted along another channel carved into the rock. A few feet away from Chrymos, several small coracles stood empty alongside the waterway, paddles nearby.

Chrymos grinned for the first time in what seemed like forever. *The lighter vessel!*

She inspected the nearest boat, in search of any leaks. The wickerwork construction seemed sound enough, and the hull itself was covered in the skin of what must once have been a very large bear.

Without further ado, Chrymos lifted the coracle into the water and clambered aboard. Before she had even settled herself properly, the current began hurrying the boat forward to its next destination.

ONE HUNDRED AND FOURTEEN
Catacombs of San Gennaro, Naples, Kingdom of Naples, 3.40 a.m. Wednesday June 23 1610

Chrymos had little idea how to steer the small boat, so was content to use the paddle primarily to ensure that she faced forward as she was carried along. She used one hand to hold tightly to the side of the craft whilst with the other she wielded the paddle. As a result, Chrymos had no hand free to hold the glowing vial so her journey was in darkness. In any other circumstance, she might have been terrified. Not this time. *I'm really too exhausted to worry.*

Fortunately, most of the energy of the river had been leeched off to feed the waterfall, so Chrymos' journey proceeded at a much more sedate pace than she might have expected. She didn't have any idea where she was going, but was grateful for a few minutes' rest.

The boat floated quietly along through the darkness. Then, about ten minutes into her journey, Chrymos sat bolt upright. Up ahead, she could hear what sounded like a waterfall—and she was powerless to do anything about it. *Are we about to sail off the end of a cliff?* Chrymos gripped the edge of the coracle even more tightly.

She didn't have to worry for long. The waterfall she could hear was actually a gentle flow of water pouring down from above and into the river channel itself. The boat and Chrymos sailed serenely through the curtain of water, which turned out to be simply a few inches thick. The boat rocked a little as it briefly absorbed the force of the water and Chrymos found herself a little damper, but otherwise her journey continued unimpeded.

Chrymos wasn't able to rest quite so easily after that close call. *Here I am, in an out of control boat, in pitch darkness, heading to some place I know will have more booby-traps.* To her credit, she didn't panic but her heart did race a little faster.

A short time later, Chrymos noticed a change in her surroundings. *It's getting lighter ahead.*

Almost abruptly, as her boat entered what turned out to be a large cavern, Chrymos found herself bathed in soft white light. She looked around for the source of this light, only to find that the walls and ceilings of this cavern seemed to be glowing by themselves. *It's amazing—but what's causing it?*

Before she could worry too much about this puzzle, Chrymos was faced with another, more immediate concern. She could see that the watercourse was narrowing ahead.

Soon, Chrymos found that she had arrived at some sort of dock. A strip of wood stretched across the waterway, forming a barrier against which the coracle gently bumped and came to a halt.

Chrymos disembarked and then pulled the small boat out of the water. She left the coracle near several other similar craft on the dock. *Hopefully, I'll be able to use it for the return journey—if I'm lucky.*

Chrymos checked her timepiece again. The hand pointed straight at the IV. *It seems hopeless now—two hours left to find Adric, and somehow make a return journey in half the time it took me to get here. And Adric's elixir has now officially run out.*

Chrymos gave a deep sigh—and then realized that somewhere during the journey, the air had changed. She was no longer breathing poisonous gases. She took several long, deep breaths. *There must be luminaria around here letting in fresh air,* she decided. *At least when my elixir runs out I won't be instantly poisoned—and, if he's in this part of the catacombs, neither will Adric. But we still have to get back through the gas to return to the surface.*

She shook her head. *There's no point agonizing over matters that are out of my control. I need to find the fifth protection—the tomb with the 'dolent' inscription.*

Chrymos limped away from the dock and began to explore what was clearly the entrance to a series of large burial chambers. The giant cross that dominated the back wall of the entranceway declared that this was an unapologetically Christian part of the catacombs.

Perhaps a dozen passages led off from the entrance chamber. Chrymos cautiously chose the nearest passage—like the others, handily lit by glowing walls and ceilings—and began inspecting the plaques mounted in front of the arcosolia, the burial rooms.

The inscriptions mounted near the first couple of arcosolia confirmed her suspicions. *These were martyrs killed in Diocletian's Great Persecution at the beginning of the fourth century. No wonder their graves were hidden behind so many protective layers—their families would have wanted the bodies buried in peace, in a place where believers could safely visit without being persecuted themselves.*

Chrymos limped from arcosolium to arcosolium, scanning each inscription and then moving on. Many of the arcosolia had obviously belonged to some of the most powerful Christians of the era—the tombs were elaborate and bore carefully carved plaques. Whilst many of the inscriptions told heartbreaking tales of lives snatched short in their prime by their Roman persecutors, they weren't what Chrymos sought. She limped on, wincing occasionally from the pain.

The first passage, housing perhaps twenty arcosolia, proved unfruitful. Chrymos had no more joy in the second passage. The third passage was different. Only three arcosolia led off from this passageway— but each bore inscriptions claiming that theirs was the final resting place of Bishop Januarius.

One of these must be the arcosolium that Chrymos sought—but which one?

ONE HUNDRED AND FIFTEEN
Catacombs of San Gennaro, Naples, Kingdom of Naples, 4.15 a.m. Wednesday June 23 1610

Two of these arcosolia will be booby-trapped, Chrymos realized. *So how do I choose?*

She also knew that in reality Januarius's body was nowhere near any of these tombs. *San Gennaro's body is buried in the Succorpo under Naples Cathedral. And his blood liquefies once or twice a year in response to the prayers of the faithful.*

But was Januarius ever laid to rest here? I think the bishop's body was moved to its current resting place. Did it come from here? That, Chrymos didn't know.

She loosened her belt, removed the manuscript, and re-read the relevant passage. 'Through me the way is to the city dolent; through me the way is to eternal dole; through me the way among the people lost.'

None of the plaques actually bore that inscription. *That would be too easy.*

The first arcosolium, on the left side of the passage, was marked with an inscription highlighting the saint's role in hiding many Christians who were in danger of execution. It concluded by noting that Januarius was captured and sentenced to death as a result.

The second plaque, on the right, talked about the miracle of the wild bears at the Flavian Amphitheater at Pozzuoli.

The third arcosolium, at the far end of the passageway, simply bore the name Januarius and the inscription 'Gethsemane'.

Without hesitation, Chrymos slipped the manuscript back into her belt and limped inside the third burial chamber. *There is nothing more 'dolent' than the Garden at Gethsemane, where Jesus Himself was overwhelmed by sorrow.*

ONE HUNDRED AND SIXTEEN
Catacombs of San Gennaro, Naples, Kingdom of Naples, 4.17 a.m. Wednesday June 23 1610

As soon as Chrymos entered the burial chamber, she saw Adric's body lying on the ground. She limped over, knelt beside him, and shook him gently. "Adric. Adric."

He didn't respond. She laid her hand on his forehead. *Still warm.*

Just to be certain, Chrymos lifted Adric's wrist and felt for a pulse. *It's beating, he's alive, praise God!*

She sat back and looked over Adric's body. *No sign of any injuries.*

Adric was dressed in his typical manner—dark, knee-length cloak, loose white shirt, black breeches, leather boots with rolled-down cuffs. His sword-belt dangled around his waist, its usual occupant the schiavona lying on the ground a few feet out of reach of its owner's hand. *Adric, what have you been doing that required your sword?*

Belatedly, Chrymos remembered the sixth protection. *The soldiers of the dead? Did you meet them, Adric? Did they attack you?*

She stood up and gazed down at the unconscious body of her friend. *Sorry, I can't do much for you right now, Adric, but I'll be back.*

The chamber in which Chrymos now found herself was very different in comparison to those that she had already visited. First, it was far larger. *About forty varas high and fifty varas along each side*, reckoned Chrymos.

Secondly, each wall had been intricately carved so that it resembled a series of temples, one on top of each other, stretching around the chamber. Each 'temple' included at least three doorways and perhaps a half-dozen windows, each leading to a possible angelic resting place. Chrymos did a quick calculation in her head. *Fifteen temples, that means maybe fifty doorways and ninety windows. I'll be long dead before I finish exploring all these.*

Chrymos had been brutally reminded of her short life expectancy a few moments before, when she once again felt a stab of pain through her body. *The snake venom. Of course. Because things couldn't get much worse.*

Then they did get worse. Chrymos heard clattering sounds—only a few at first and then a virtual avalanche. The noises came from all around her.

She stood still, not daring to believe her eyes, when a walking skeleton, clad in a Roman military uniform and brandishing a *spatha*, the standard Roman longsword, strode jerkily into view in one of the temple doorways. Then a second skeleton, similarly attired, made its entrance at a second doorway. And then a third, a fourth, a fifth—more and more, until perhaps fifty skeletons stood staring down, one each in almost all of the doorways, their swords pointed menacingly at Chrymos.

ONE HUNDRED AND SEVENTEEN
Catacombs of San Gennaro, Naples, Kingdom of Naples, 4.25 a.m. Wednesday June 23 1610

The message was clear—'come no further'—but it was not a message that Chrymos could heed. "Sorry," she called out, "I need to find what remains of the angel." *Am I crazy talking to skeletons? But these must surely be the 'militum mortuorum' mentioned in the manuscript.*

One, just one, of the so-called soldiers of the dead left its post and advanced on Chrymos, its sword raised. Chrymos could hear a low chant beginning in the background, but the words were too soft to hear. *The other soldiers must be urging their champion to attack me.*

Chrymos slowly backed away from the approaching skeleton, glancing rapidly backwards and forwards between the apparition and the prone figure of Adric that lay behind her.

When she had managed to limp close enough to Adric, she bent down and scooped up his schiavona.

"Now", she said as she turned towards her skeletal opponent, "let's see if the art of sword-fighting has improved at all since the days when you were alive." *If you ever were*, she added to herself.

The skeleton was quickly upon her, lunging forward with its sword. Chrymos defended herself, content for the moment simply to parry the stroke, allowing herself room to remember at least some of the swordsmanship principles that she had learned at the Academy.

The skeleton drew back its longsword, preparing for another thrust. Chrymos seized the opportunity to aim a sweeping blow at the skeleton's legs but the creature jumped high into the air and her blade swept harmlessly under its bony feet. As the skeleton landed back on the ground, it raised its blade high, aiming to hack downward at Chrymos' head.

Chrymos quickly raised her own sword and managed to deflect the attack. If the basket-hilt of the schiavona had not protected her hand, the ferocity of the downward assault would most likely have cut it to ribbons.

Come on girl, lift your game, you've made it this far.

Chrymos limped out of the way as the skeletal soldier attacked again, sweeping its sword from side to side. Even with her limited experience, Chrymos could see that such a move was tactically ineffectual, leaving the soldier open to counterattack. *That's encouraging. I don't think this soldier knows what he's doing.*

She took a closer look at her opponent. The creature wore classical Roman armor from its shoulders to its waist, on top of a simple cloth tunic that stretched down to its knee bones. Its arms, legs, and skull were unprotected—but Chrymos was unsure which, if any, of its bones were most vulnerable.

The skeleton lunged at her once again, its sword aiming straight towards her ribcage. Chrymos instinctively parried, her broadsword sliding down her attacker's blade and bouncing over the small hilt of the longsword before slicing into the skeletal finger bones gripping the sword.

To Chrymos' great surprise, her heavy broadsword cut straight through her opponent's fingers. The bones fractured and the skeleton howled with pain. A moment later, its longsword fell to the ground— most of the fingers in the creature's right hand had broken off and it was no longer able to grasp the sword.

ONE HUNDRED AND EIGHTEEN
Catacombs of San Gennaro, Naples, Kingdom of Naples, 4.30 a.m. Wednesday June 23 1610

Chrymos stepped back, confused. She watched, trying to understand the situation, as the skeleton crouched down and scrabbled around with its other hand to pick up the fallen sword. *What's really happening here? How can I hurt a skeleton?*

The creature stood up again, now holding the sword rather clumsily in its left hand. A few forlorn finger bones dangled from its now useless right as the skeleton advanced towards Chrymos.

She twisted her body aside as the skeleton attempted to slash at her head. The creature made a few more wild sweeps in her direction, which Chrymos easily dodged even with her injured leg. She hastily formulated a plan. *Okay, let's see if this works.*

Chrymos positioned herself so that the skeletal soldier had its back to the nearest chamber wall. Then she went on the attack.

Her blade lunged at the skeleton's chest, an attack that the creature instinctively if clumsily attempted to parry. It failed and the point of Chrymos' blade pushed hard against the skeleton's armor, forcing it backwards. Chrymos repeated the maneuver several times until the skeleton's back almost touched the wall of the chamber. Then she struck in earnest.

Chrymos slammed her broadsword against her opponent's longsword, pushing it against the wall and then holding it there so that both swords were temporarily out of play. Then, ignoring the pain as she balanced on her right leg, Chrymos raised her left foot and kicked out at the skeleton's right knee.

Because of her carefully-chosen position, Chrymos succeeded in crushing her opponent's bones against the back wall of the chamber. The bones splintered immediately and the skeleton again cried out in anguish.

Chrymos limped back two paces. The skeleton simply slid down the wall, its ruined leg no longer able to bear its weight. The creature's sword fell noisily to the ground.

Behind Chrymos, the chanting that had been a low buzz throughout the fight now grew louder.

Finally, Chrymos could hear what the skeletons were saying. Each was repeatedly chanting "*meque his exsolvite, ignosce me.*" And, thanks to her new language skills, Chrymos knew exactly what the words meant. They were begging "release me, forgive me."

ONE HUNDRED AND NINETEEN
Thirteen hundred years earlier
Flavian Amphitheater, Pozzuoli [Italy],
Idus Augustus (13 August) 303AD

The lone figure stood quietly in the middle of the Flavian arena. The crowd, which had been cheering and baying for blood a few seconds before, fell deathly quiet when the wild bears began backing away instead of attacking.

Silence turned to urgent whispers when several in the crowd recognized the person in the arena as Januarius, the Christian bishop who had been defying the authorities in neighboring Naples. Most of the onlookers simply wanted their afternoon's entertainment to continue and began shouting at the guards. A few, however, whose Christian friends or family had previously been saved by the bishop, prayed quietly but fervently.

The stadium guards, fearing a revolt, tried to appease the crowd. The soldiers prodded the bears with long pikes, attempting to push the beasts forward to attack. But even though the bears continued to snarl and roar, and lunged out at the guards with their powerful claws, they simply would not move towards Januarius.

Finally, as the crowd continued to make its displeasure loudly known, the guards acted. They dragged Januarius out of the arena and tossed in several criminals instead. Only once the bishop was completely out of sight did the bears move menacingly towards their new quarry.

Januarius, back in the rooms that stretched under the arena, found himself hauled in front of a clearly-shaken captain of the stadium guard. "What dark magic is this?" demanded the captain. "How did you enchant those bears? And do you think you will escape your fate with those tricks?"

Januarius stood firm. One by one, he inspected each of the dozen assembled guardsmen before turning a withering gaze towards the captain. Despite the deafening noise from the arena above, the bishop's words, when they came, echoed through the very soul of every man present.

"Quintus Ostorius," Januarius began, drawing a sharp intake of breath from the captain.

"How do you know my name?" demanded the bewildered captain.

"I don't," replied Januarius, "but my God does. On His behalf, I speak to you all. To you, Rufinus Silvanus, and to you Vibius Hortensius—" The soldiers stared in shock as one by one the bishop named every single one of the guards present in the stadium that day.

"To each of you and to all of you, I tell you this, not as a curse but as a prophecy. For what you have done here, killing innocent people merely because their beliefs are different from those of your emperor, none of you will find comfort in death. Instead, you will guard my tomb, all of you, for year upon endless year, protecting its contents, until someone finds it in their heart to forgive you."

ONE HUNDRED AND TWENTY
Catacombs of San Gennaro, Naples, Kingdom of Naples, 4.40 a.m. Wednesday June 23 1610

For the first time, Chrymos took a close look at the skeletons standing in the doorways overlooking the chamber. *Why didn't I notice earlier? That skeleton has no arms. The one over there only has one leg.*

Many of the skeletons were maimed, with broken or missing bones. Just a few were wearing armor. Chrymos held up her hand for silence and the chanting ceased. *It's almost as if they're holding their breath,* she thought.

She turned to the skeleton with the missing leg. "Did you lose that leg when you died?" she asked.

"Yes," came the quiet response.

"The bones don't grow back?"

The skeleton shook its head.

"Does it hurt?"

"Yes!" came the shout from many of those around her. "All the time," added the soldier with whom she had been talking.

Chrymos shed a tear for the endless pain these men must have suffered. "And you want me to release you from this torment?"

"Yes!!" The shout was deafening.

"How?" Chrymos asked.

The response came from behind her, from the soldier that she had just defeated. "We are cursed to guard this tomb until we are forgiven."

Forgiven? I may be able to do that. But first things first. "I can help you. But first I need to know which entrance leads to the angel's tomb."

The fallen soldier told her what she needed to know. "Go through the fourth doorway from the left, here on ground level. But you should be aware that the doorway is protected. Even we cannot enter there."

"Thank you." Chrymos crossed over to the door and placed the schiavona near the entrance, to mark the doorway and make it easier to find again. Then she returned to the center of the chamber and spoke to the skeletons. "Now let's focus on the redemption that you've been waiting on for all of these years." She raised her voice so that everyone could hear her. "Do you believe in God the Father and His Son Jesus Christ?"

"We have believed in your God's power for many years," said the fallen soldier, "ever since His bishop put this eternal curse on us, and it came horribly true."

"Then, all of you, all those who believe," said Chrymos, addressing all of the skeletons assembled in that place, "repeat after me, 'Forgive me, Father, for I have sinned'." Each and every one of the soldiers echoed her words.

Chrymos didn't know if she had truly been raised a Catholic or not—*though if I really am the daughter of the Black Knight and the Blood Countess, I guess not*—but she had been to Confession on a great many Sundays over the past few years, in both Florence and Naples, and easily remembered the protocols and prayers that constituted the sacrament of penance. *I am no priest, Lord, but I believe that if You so choose, You can act through me.*

She led all of the men—she no longer thought of them as skeletons—through the confession process, inviting them to acknowledge their sins and then had them recite prayers of contrition.

Finally, Chrymos lifted her hands up to Heaven and pronounced the words of absolution that the Roman soldiers had waited so very long to hear. "Through the ministry of the Church may God give you pardon and peace. I absolve you from your sins in the name of the Father, and of the Son and of the Holy Spirit. Amen."

At the exact moment that Chrymos spoke the final "Amen", every skeleton collapsed into its constituent parts. The assorted body parts of the fifty departed souls tumbled from the doorways and rained down on the unprepared Chrymos, burying her beneath a pile of bones.

ONE HUNDRED AND TWENTY-ONE
Outside the Academy of Secrets, Naples, Kingdom of Naples, 4.55 a.m. Wednesday June 23 1610

It was nearly dawn. Soon Naples would begin to wake up and it would no longer be safe to fly above the city's streets and buildings.

For the moment though, Zophiel and Shamar could still fly through the city in the semi-darkness and not be seen. Or at least that's what they thought as they flew above the lane that led to the Della Porta estate, accompanying their eight colleagues who were briskly striding along below.

Viewed from the sky, the Della Porta estate was shaped much like a raw peanut—two roughly circular ends joined in the middle by a narrower section of land. Most of the buildings were on the right hand side or in the center of the property, with the man-made lake, trees, and gardens dominating the left.

An eight-foot-high wall, surrounded the entire estate, with just a single entranceway. The wall might not have proven much of an impediment to angelic visitors but it certainly served to deter more-earthbound intruders.

<*You're right, Zophiel,*> mind-whispered Shamar, <*we won't be getting past those guards in a hurry.*>

The entrance to the estate was blocked by two imposing iron gates, patrolled by what appeared to be at least a half-dozen armed and armored guards. The walls nearest the buildings were also well covered, lit by a number of strategically-placed metal baskets filled with brightly-burning logs. In stark contrast, the walls around the left-hand side of the property were dark.

<*Odd,*> said Shamar, <*it's almost as if they're inviting us to break in through the forest area.*> He circled down for a closer look. <*Or maybe I'm simply being too paranoid. The trees are growing very close to these walls. It wouldn't take much to set the whole area on fire if they had placed flaming baskets around here. And it's not as if this section is undefended,*

there are metal blades embedded all along the tops of the walls and—> He flew even lower. *<—and some very sharp stakes hidden in the undergrowth, all along the other side of the wall. Friendly fellows.>*

The two Outcast Angels flew quietly above the estate. Zophiel attempted to fly close to a tall dark tower, only to be warned away by voices inside his head. *<Better not go anywhere near that tower,>* he warned Shamar.

Despite the early hour, it was evident that plenty was happening at the Academy. The courtyard outside the main building streamed with light from many flaming torches and dozens of servants were hard at work loading supplies onto carriages. People were bustling in and out of buildings, clearly getting ready for something.

Shamar and Zophiel flew back up the road to meet up with their teams, who were still several hundred yards away from the estate itself. They both landed quietly and then proceeded to report what they had just seen.

Lochloinn was inevitably the most eager to get started, but Mircea—one of the three enhanced that Shamar had brought from Wallachia—counseled caution. "There are very few of us," he pointed out, "and we know that we are facing supernaturally-powered opponents. Perhaps we should wait until Ravid can join us."

"It's already nearly too late today," said Zophiel. "Dawn will be upon us in a few minutes. If we don't go now, we won't be able to sneak onto the property while it's still dark enough. We'd have to postpone our attack until tomorrow. And, based on what we saw, I don't think that any delay is a good idea."

Zophiel's sentiment carried the day. "Shamar and I can each carry two of you," he told the group. "We'll fly over the top of the wall near the forest, get past the sharpened stakes, and drop you amongst the trees. Then we'll come back for the others."

Zophiel linked arms with Lochloinn and Niall while Shamar did the same with Radu and Sean.

"Okay, hold tight," said Shamar, struggling to launch with such a heavy load, "this won't be easy."

Slowly but surely, both angels managed to lift off the ground and head towards the estate.

They had just cleared the walls and were starting to fly over the sharpened stakes when a voice rang out from far above.

"Now!"

A split second later, from somewhere within the estate's woodland area, a dozen musket shots fired as one.

ONE HUNDRED AND TWENTY-TWO
The Academy of Secrets, Naples, Kingdom of Naples, 5.10 a.m. Wednesday June 23 1610

Muskets are very unreliable weapons. That assertion, made by Archimedes during a training session that seemed so very long ago and far away, replayed itself again and again in Lochloinn's head as he fell out of the sky, his shoulder burning from the pain of a musket ball tearing through it a moment earlier. *Aye, unreli'bl—but if'n dey hit de arm you're usin' ter hold onter an angel, muskets kin still kill ya.*

Lochloinn twisted and contorted in mid-air, well aware that he was falling towards a bed of sharpened stakes. It's doubtful that he would have survived the plunge if Niall hadn't stretched out an arm and managed to pull Lochloinn over into the bushes. It wasn't a comfortable landing—the bushes were wiry and their leaves were prickly—but at least it wasn't fatal.

Niall's heroic stretching caused problems for himself and Zophiel as well, pulling the angel off-balance, and causing the pair to crash heavily into one of the trees on the estate. Neither suffered serious injuries but scratches and bruises weren't helpful.

Shamar, Radu, and Sean were more fortunate. All of them avoided the musket-fire, and if their landing amongst the estate's trees wasn't easy, at least it was controlled.

Shamar quickly mind-messaged Zophiel.*<Are you okay?>*

<Nothing that a warm bath wouldn't fix,> replied Zophiel.

<Okay, we have about twenty seconds until they reload,> said Shamar, *<let's go and get the others over the wall.>*

Whatever reply Zophiel might have made was lost when hundreds of crows suddenly filled the sky directly above the Outcast Angels, effectively grounding them both and leaving half of their team on the other side of the wall.

ONE HUNDRED AND TWENTY-THREE
Catacombs of San Gennaro, Naples, Kingdom of Naples, 5.00 a.m. Wednesday June 23 1610

Silence returned to the Catacombs of San Gennaro—in stark contrast to the thunderous clatter of a few moments earlier, when so many skeletal human remains had come cascading down, forming a large mountain of skulls and bones. Of Chrymos, there was no sign.

Then came a gentle rustling from deep beneath the pile of bones. That turned into a frantic flurry of activity as Chrymos fought her way to the surface, pushing aside skulls and limbs and emerging relatively unscathed. Painfully, her injured leg hurting more than ever, Chrymos pulled herself out of the mound that had threatened to bury her and slid down the side of the heap of broken bones to rest for a moment on clear ground.

She coughed, attempting to clear her throat of the centuries of dust that had accompanied the dislodged skulls and bones—and was immediately reminded of the snake venom ravaging her body. Chrymos doubled over with the pain, shuddering in agony.

A minute or more passed, and then Chrymos straightened up. Again, she took out the timepiece. *Five o'clock. One more hour until my elixir runs out. Time is running short for Sirus and Madalena, and Olivia as well. If I don't get back to the Academy before they're exposed to the Black Plague*—she couldn't bear to finish the thought.

Chrymos pulled herself upright and then limped over to check on Adric. *Still breathing, but no closer to waking up. I hope he's okay.*

Now to tackle the seventh and final protection. Chrymos steeled herself for the challenge. *Let's see exactly what else the good bishop has in store for me.*

Chrymos dragged herself over to the doorway where she had left Adric's sword as a marker. She prepared herself as best she could and then stepped inside.

ONE HUNDRED AND TWENTY-FOUR
Catacombs of San Gennaro, Naples, Kingdom of Naples, 5.05 a.m. Wednesday June 23 1610

The instant that Chrymos limped across the threshold to the burial chamber, an invisible force held her in its grasp. She could neither move nor speak.

She felt her very essence being scanned. *It feels like I'm being stabbed with pins and needles, from the top of my head to the soles of my feet.*

Then, a moment later, it was over. Chrymos found herself able to move again.

That can't be all there is, surely? Is this a test, a trap or perhaps the first part of a more complex protection scheme? Chrymos didn't know. For now, all that mattered was that she was finally inside the tomb. *I'm the first one to get inside for more than a thousand years, if this dust is any guide.*

Chrymos saw nothing at first. *There's no glow inside here—I guess whatever makes the glow can't get inside either.*

Chrymos reached into her right pocket for the vial of red glowing powder, only to find her hand touching fragments of glass. The vial had shattered. *Probably when the bones fell on me,* she decided. *I guess now's the time to use that brightly-glowing metal instead.*

Chrymos pulled her hand out, intending to reach into her other pocket for the jar that contained the metal strip. She quickly realized that her hand, coated in red powder, was actually casting its own glow, enough to check out her surroundings.

Chrymos held the powder-covered hand high and used it as a torch to explore the tomb. There wasn't much to see, just a single sarcophagus at the very back of the burial chamber. The stone slab covering the sarcophagus looked very heavy, yet Chrymos was able to push it aside with surprising ease.

In doing so, Chrymos disturbed the layers of dust covering the slab. As a result, she sneezed violently, triggering another round of venom-induced convulsions. *They're getting worse,* she admitted to herself as she grasped the side of the sarcophagus tightly, coughing and spluttering.

Only once she had recovered did Chrymos look inside the sarcophagus. Something gleamed in the darkness below—an unearthly blue-white light.

ONE HUNDRED AND TWENTY-FIVE
Catacombs of San Gennaro, Naples, Kingdom of Naples, 5.06 a.m. Wednesday June 23 1610

Outside the tomb, the arcosolium remained undisturbed.

Adric's body was all but motionless. He might have been dead, were it not for the occasional rising and falling of his chest.

A few moments passed. Then a figure appeared at the entrance to the arcosolium. Its head darted from left to right as it surveyed the scene before deciding on a course of action.

The new arrival moved quickly, lifting Adric's prone body and carrying it out of sight. Quiet rustling could be heard.

A short while later, the newcomer, now wearing Adric's cloak, returned to the place where Adric's body had rested—there was an outline in the dust where Adric had been lying. The interloper carefully lowered himself to the ground, positioning his body to match the outline almost exactly.

There was a flicker, contrasting oddly with the white glow that illuminated the arcosolium.

Then, to all intents and purposes, Adric's body once again appeared to occupy the same position.

The whole exchange had taken less than two minutes, while Chrymos was busy exploring the inner tomb.

ONE HUNDRED AND TWENTY-SIX
Catacombs of San Gennaro, Naples, Kingdom of Naples, 5.08 a.m. Wednesday June 23 1610

Because it was so dark in the inner chamber, Chrymos could clearly see the faint blue-white glow. *Surely, that must be the pathgem?*

When Chrymos reached down and touched the gemstone it flared brightly, illuminating a perfectly preserved body lying within the sarcophagus.

That's not possible! This body is more than a thousand years old. It can't still be flesh and blood.

And yet, that's what Chrymos saw—a body that appeared as fresh as if it might have just died in the past few hours. It bore a bloody wound on its shoulder that looked as if it could have been inflicted mere moments ago.

But the biggest surprise came when Chrymos looked into the face of the corpse. *I know him! I don't understand how, but I'm almost certain that I recognize this angel.*

In her shock, Chrymos lost her grip on the pathgem. Instantly the jewel dimmed, plunging nearly everything in the chamber into darkness. Only the red powder coating Chrymos' hand remained as a source of illumination.

Chrymos held her glowing hand over the body in the sarcophagus and looked more closely. It had a kindly face, unmarked by the passage of time. *How do I know you?* She had no answer.

Chrymos moved her hand further down above the sarcophagus so that she could inspect the rest of the body. There wasn't much to see. The corpse wore a light mail shirt, undamaged except for the brutal gash at the shoulder, over a long brown robe. A belt that ran from shoulder to waist carried an empty sheath that presumably had once housed a sword.

Under the body, Chrymos could see some type of shield strapped to the corpse's back. She reached out to touch the shield, only to find it pulsing with an unknown energy. *That feels very much the same as the mystery force that stopped me when I tried to enter this chamber. Is this shield the protection that's been preserving you in here, angel?*

Chrymos decided to leave well enough alone. She let go of the shield and returned her attention to the pathgem, which still glowed faintly. She avoided touching the gem directly but instead brought her arm near so that she could use the red glow to inspect the sought-after treasure more closely.

It's attached to a wristband of some sort that the angel is wearing. I can probably unfasten that band and remove it from the body without actually touching the gem.

That's exactly what Chrymos did. She was squeamish at first, trying to avoid touching the body at all as she reached around and loosened the band from around the angel's wrist. As soon as she had worked the wristband free, Chrymos lifted the band out and away from the sarcophagus, gratefully turning her back on the corpse.

She held the wristband in her hand, careful not to touch the gemstone. *So this is the treasure that Della Porta has been searching for all these years—the deadly pathgem that so many people have been sacrificed for. Now what do I do with it?*

Her train of thought was interrupted by a noise that came from outside the tomb. She stuffed the wristband and gem into one of her pockets.

ONE HUNDRED AND TWENTY-SEVEN
Catacombs of San Gennaro, Naples, Kingdom of Naples, 5.12 a.m. Wednesday June 23 1610

Chrymos went to the tomb entrance and peered cautiously out into the main chamber.

Adric was stirring—the noise that she had heard was him coughing. *All the dust from the bones,* Chrymos thought as she limped over to her friend as quickly as she could.

Adric was understandably groggy, but brightened when he saw Chrymos. "C, what are you doing here? Don't you know how dangerous this place is?"

Chrymos helped Adric to sit up. "I have so much to tell you," she said, "I don't know where to start."

"You can start by telling me why you're here," said Adric, "although I think I can guess."

"The Master sent me—" began Chrymos.

"—because I hadn't returned," said Adric. "Why? What did he think you could do that I couldn't? No offence," he added hastily.

Chrymos was unimpressed. "I was sent because I had the best chance of rescuing you. Who do you think translated the instructions that helped you make it this far?"

"You did? Zooterkins—that's amazing, C. I never knew you could do that," said Adric.

"Well," admitted Chrymos, "previously I couldn't, not until I had some Exousía potion." She tried not to show Adric how much pain she was feeling as she helped him to stand up. "Now I can understand any language. What about you," she added, "have your powers come through yet?"

"Alas, no," said Adric, as he brushed the dust of his clothing and satisfied himself that he was still in one piece. "But you know what they say, 'the mills of God grind slowly.'"

Chrymos nodded. She watched as Adric glanced around at his

surroundings, seemingly unfazed by the large mound of bones that for him must have appeared out of nowhere.

Adric seemed to be staring at everything with some bemusement, not saying a word. Finally, Chrymos simply had to ask. "So what happened to you?"

"I don't know," said Adric. "Obviously I made it into this room, and then—that's all I remember until I woke up right now."

"Did you see any of the skeletons?"

"Skeletons? No. At least, I don't think so," amended Adric. "Did you? What happened?"

"It doesn't matter," said Chrymos. "What matters is that I found the angel's tomb."

"You have?" Adric shouted. "Curse me for a cumberground, I've been no use here at all." He jabbered excitedly, dancing around Chrymos. "Tell me—what was in it, what did you find?"

"This," said Chrymos, removing the wristband from her pocket while taking great care not to touch the glowing gem. "I believe it's called a pathgem. They say it can be used to travel anywhere, instantly."

Adric stared at the gemstone. "How does it work?" he asked. He couldn't take his eyes off the precious stone.

"I don't know," said Chrymos. "All I know is what it's supposed to do, not how to do it."

Adric reached out and, before Chrymos could warn him, touched the stone with his finger. The gem flared up brightly.

Adric dropped his hand and jumped back in surprise. "Gadsbud! How does it do that?" The gem had dimmed again once Adric had lost contact.

"I have no idea," said Chrymos, lifting up the wristband and staring at the pathgem. "The manuscript writer didn't know much about it or how it worked, so there are no instructions. We'll simply have to try to work it out for ourselves."

Adric came back in for a closer look. "Can I hold it?"

Chrymos wasn't comfortable with that idea but she didn't know quite how to refuse her old friend.

ONE HUNDRED AND TWENTY-EIGHT
Catacombs of San Gennaro, Naples, Kingdom of Naples, 5.15 a.m. Wednesday June 23 1610

The four members of the LOA team stranded outside the Academy walls didn't know what they should do. The musket-fire of a few minutes earlier had been followed by the sounds of crashing bodies and then by the relentless cackling of hundreds of crows as they circled around and around the Academy. And the first rays of sunshine were beginning to touch the top of the Capodimonte hill.

"Clearly there won't be any flying in or out of that wall, not with all those crows around," said Martin. "Anybody have any suggestions?"

"They were obviously expecting us," said Mircea, "I will say it, if no-one else does—it must be a trap."

"So do we go in there and try to rescue any of our team who survived," asked Elias, "or do we hang back and wait for Ravid?"

"We know these people, their leaders," said the other Wallachian newcomer, Doamna, in his rudimentary English. "They make no prisoners. We have small choice—we must rescue, now, before too late."

"Even if we agree with you, Doamna, how do we get inside now that the wall is off-limits?" asked Elias.

"How about a direct, front-on approach," said Martin unexpectedly, "through the main gate?"

"You are joking," said Mircea.

"No, really," said Martin. "I can spread darkness so that they don't see us coming until too late. Elias, you can talk us inside."

"And I make stone. Might work," said Doamna. "Of course, if fails, we—" He lacked the vocabulary but everyone understood the risk.

"Then let's do it," said Martin.

ONE HUNDRED AND TWENTY-NINE
Catacombs of San Gennaro, Naples, Kingdom of Naples, 5.20 a.m. Wednesday June 23 1610

Before Chrymos could respond to Adric's request to hold the pathgem, they both heard what sounded like singing coming from the main chamber outside. They looked at each other in disbelief.

Adric was first to respond. "I'll go, C, you don't look like you're in too good a shape." *Ah, so he has noticed,* thought Chrymos, *that's nice.* She felt unexpectedly flattered.

Adric crept quietly to the entrance of the tomb and then slipped out into the main chamber beyond. Chrymos waited nervously. *It can't be those gas-creatures again, can it? They couldn't even talk, let alone sing. And I'm sure all the skeletons are gone.*

Adric was only gone a couple of minutes. He returned, ashen-faced. "It's a creature out of a nightmare. Two and a half vara tall, at least, black armor everywhere, carrying a sword and an axe. It must be some sort of demon, like the ones that the Academy warned us about."

Chrymos nodded in horror, her own dream-fueled memory even more vivid.

"He's here," whispered Adric. He gulped. "Coming straight for us. He was singing out 'I can see you!' I'll bet he's after that." Adric pointed at the pathgem.

Chrymos froze. "He mustn't get it, he mustn't. We need to hide." She looked around frantically.

"Where do you hide from a creature like that?" Adric was also looking around but he seemed almost resigned to his fate.

Chrymos glanced around the chamber, and suddenly smiled. "I don't think he can enter the angel's tomb," she said, beckoning to Adric to come with her, "that's why the pathgem is still here."

She dragged Adric over to the tomb. "This is what we've been searching for. I think it's protected from creatures like him."

Adric seemed oddly reluctant to enter. "Are you sure? If the protection you're talking about doesn't work, we'll be trapped in there—easy prey."

"Sure," said Chrymos, professing a certainty that she didn't actually feel. "Come with me, you'll see."

Chrymos pulled Adric into the entrance to the tomb. Again, she felt that she was being scrutinized from head to toe. Again, she passed the test.

But Adric—he remained frozen in place. Then, suddenly, the tomb appeared to spit him out. Adric was sent flying, arms frantically waving in an attempt to stop his flight. He came to a sudden stop crumpled against the wall of the burial chamber.

ONE HUNDRED AND THIRTY
Catacombs of San Gennaro, Naples, Kingdom of Naples, 5.24 a.m. Wednesday June 23 1610

As fast as she could, Chrymos limped over to Adric. By the time she reached him, Adric had picked himself up and was checking for injuries. "I guess the angel doesn't like Napoletanos," he said ruefully, satisfied that merely his pride was battered.

"I don't understand," said Chrymos, still shocked at the turn of events. "Why could I get inside but not you?"

"Never mind," said Adric. "We have a real live demon to worry about—and he'll be coming through that entrance in a couple of minutes. We don't have many options left."

He turned to Chrymos again, gesturing at the pathgem. "What about that gem? You said it could be used to take us anywhere. Can we try to make it work to get us out of here?"

Adric held up his hand to forestall Chrymos' objections. "I know what you said—you don't know how it works. But perhaps I can get it going. Why don't you hand it over—"

Chrymos was instantly on alert. *That's the second time you've asked for the gem. What's going on, Adric?* Even so, despite her concerns she replied mildly. "How about we both hold it?"

Adric nodded in agreement—but Chrymos seemed to sense some reluctance on his part. *I must be imagining it.*

She slipped the band onto her wrist and then held it up so that Adric could touch the gemstone. Then everything seemed to happen at once.

A dark, demonic figure, exactly like the creature in Chrymos' nightmares, appeared at the entranceway. It was clad in black armor and armed with a deadly curved sword. The demon's first words, as soon as it saw Chrymos, made no sense to her at all. "Oh, it's you. Nekhbet's pet."

Chrymos shuddered despite herself. *I don't know that name and yet it sends shivers through my whole body.*

The demon wasn't finished speaking. "Did you really think that I

341

wouldn't be aware that people were searching for the pathgem? That I wouldn't notice that the pathgem was activated? My name is Ezequeel and the pathgem is mine!"

The demon—Ezequeel—started towards her. At exactly that same moment, Adric reached over and touched the pathgem. As the gem burst into light, Adric spoke a charm that he should not have known, in a language that he should not have been able to speak. Chrymos instantly translated his words in her mind. "<Take me to Nowhen.>"

Chrymos and Adric vanished.

ONE HUNDRED AND THIRTY-ONE
Catacombs of San Gennaro, Naples, Kingdom of Naples, 5.25 a.m. Wednesday June 23 1610

The idea of a frontal attack had seemed like a good idea a few minutes ago, but as the LOA team started to put the plan into practice, Martin began to have second thoughts. *Those are armed soldiers at the gate,* he told himself, *heavily armed soldiers, with swords and knives and guns and who knows what else. What am I doing?*

Martin led the way because he was the only one able to darken the rapidly-lightening sky around the Academy entrance. He was still limping a little after the battle in Paris, but his leg was mostly healed.

He risked a glance back towards his LOA teammates. The new fellow, the man from Wallachia with his horrible grasp of English, gave him an inane grin. *Thanks, Doamna, that's just the encouragement I needed to get me through this next patch.*

Once he was within about fifty feet of the main gate, Martin began to concentrate, picturing the wall, gate, and roadway getting gradually darker. As usual, reality obliged, reversing the recent effects of dawn on a highly-localized basis. Martin imagined the designated area getting blacker and blacker, and indeed that's what happened. As the darkness began to take hold, Martin could hear a few shouts and instructions called out by those affected.

Martin waved the others forward to join him as he came close to the center of the darkness, where the main gate was located.

"Okay, Elias," he whispered as the younger man came forward, "time to do your work."

Elias launched into a typical warm, caring speech, in English, French and hastily-learnt Napoletano, intended to convince the guards to come out of the darkness with their weapons left behind.

Unfortunately, that part of the plan didn't quite work. All that emerged from the darkness was a volley of musket balls.

ONE HUNDRED AND THIRTY-TWO
Outside The Academy of Secrets, Naples, Kingdom of Naples, 5.26 a.m. Wednesday June 23 1610

The musket balls weren't aimed anywhere in particular and no-one in the LOA team was hit. They were encouraged to move out of range, however.

The reason for the plan's failure suddenly became apparent, at least to Martin, who still stood close to the main gate. From there, he could hear the soldiers talking amongst themselves—and he realized that whatever was being said was in a language he couldn't understand. *It's not English, French or Napoletano. No wonder they weren't affected by Elias, they didn't understand what he was saying.*

Martin felt highly exposed. He needed to be near the gate to maintain the cover of darkness, but if any of the soldiers thought to open the gate and take a handful of paces out from their current position, they would easily spot him. *Now what do I do?*

He was seriously considering making a run for safety—which would have meant allowing the darkness to dissipate—when he heard an excited buzz of voices coming from the gate area. Gales of laughter and much chatter followed. Then, one by one, the voices fell silent.

Before Martin could consider his next move, a head popped out through the darkness.

"You can get rid of the blackness now Martin, thanks," said Zophiel, "it's done the job quite nicely."

Delighted to see Zophiel, Martin gratefully released the darkness. As daylight returned, he could see the main gates open, the guards roped together and tied to the gate pillars. Martin's missing teammates were standing around smiling.

"What happened here?" Martin asked Zophiel.

"A combination of you and Shamar and Sean," said Zophiel. As Ravid may have told you, Shamar has the ability to make people think that he's a good friend of theirs. Under the cover of your darkness, he was able to get close to the guards by convincing them that he was their best mate. Then Sean paralyzed them one by one, until we could tie them up. Simple."

Sure, thought Martin as he and the rest of the LOA team followed Zophiel through the gate and onto the Della Porta estate. *What could possibly have gone wrong?*

Then the thought passed when Martin was forced to throw himself to the ground trying to avoid a furiously-whirling tornado.

ONE HUNDRED AND THIRTY-THREE
Nowhen

Chrymos found herself in a glorious clearing surrounded by giant trees. She immediately felt blessed relief from all her aches and pains. The limp was gone. Her exhaustion disappeared and her head cleared. The healing powers of Nowhen instantly nullified even the deadly effects of the snake venom.

But Nowhen's healing powers reached beyond the merely physical. Chrymos' mind was healed as well. The heavenly environment instantly restored the memories that had been grafted over by demonic enchantments, false imaginings and the lies told by Carracci and others in the Academy. Chrymos finally knew who and what she was. *I'm an Earth-born Outcast Angel.*

With that realization came an overwhelming flood of memories, both wonderful and horrific.

# # #

Chrymos was but seven Earth years old and her mother—her glorious, beautiful, Outcast Angel mother, Ayil—was singing her to sleep. Chrymos felt so loved, so happy, so secure.

# # #

Chrymos was nine and the mighty Outcast Angel Shamar—her strong, handsome father—was teaching her to fly, swooping in and out of the clouds far above their home, the island they called Sanctuary but which humans called Atlantis. Chrymos felt that she could achieve whatever she wanted.

# # #

Chrymos was thirteen when she finally realized that, even though she was an angel, she would never receive any powers because her parents had rebelled from Heaven. She raged, shouted, and abused her parents dreadfully. She cried herself to sleep for weeks.

# # #

Chrymos was fifteen when her father explained why the Outcast Angels had opposed the Darke Warriors so bitterly and for so long. "If Lucifer ever takes control of Heaven, our mortal bodies will be destroyed and our spirits will be tormented for eternity," Shamar explained. "Banishment may seem like a terrible punishment but Lucifer's alternative is far, far worse."

# # #

Chrymos was eighteen when she was presented to the Elders. "Now that you are old enough," said the Outcast Angels' leader, Eyphah, "you can be trusted with the knowledge of the location of our next Sanctuary. Jesse tells us that Atlantis will not last forever," he added, when Chrymos reacted with surprise at the news, "and it is essential that a few of us know where to go next after Atlantis falls. Yours is one of just five families entrusted with this vital secret. It is a great privilege and a powerful obligation. You are finally old enough to be entrusted with this information and we Elders have judged you worthy of our trust." Chrymos glowed with pride for days afterwards.

# # #

Chrymos was nineteen when the citywide alarums sounded. The Darke Warriors had finally discovered Atlantis, despite the protective enchantments put in place by the Elders and despite the prophetic powers of the angel Jesse. Now the island city was under attack, as the Darke Warriors, led by the thunder demon Hurakan, pounded its coast with tidal wave after gigantic tidal wave. Chrymos should have been safely housed in one of the city's shelters but her young brother was missing and she went searching for him.

The tidal waves swept her far out to the unforgiving ocean. She might have made it back to shore safely—but her seven-year-old brother, also swept away, cried out for her help. But before she could reach him, she was snatched out of the sea by the Darke Warrior Ezequeel.

Chrymos was still conscious when Ezequeel took her to the cavern at Alepotrypa, the single earthly entrance to the otherworld of Hades. She experienced every agonizing moment as her body was ripped into its microscopic components and translated across the abyss to Hades.

# # #

Chrymos was nineteen when her name was stripped from her and she was given the designation Prisoner Number Eleven, the seven-hundred-and-eleventh Outcast Angel to be imprisoned in the heinous underworld that was Hades.

# # #

Eleven was nineteen—and then a hundred and nineteen—and then one thousand, three thousand, five thousand and nineteen—as the most sadistic of Lucifer's lieutenants, Nekhbet, tortured her and conducted countless experiments on her, trying to force her to reveal the location of the new Outcast Angels Sanctuary.

# # #

Eleven was seven thousand and nineteen and had been imprisoned in solitude in a tiny cavern for decades. At first she called out, she begged, she screamed, she whimpered but no-one came. Her only sustenance was moisture and moss from the wall of the cave, which lay in the deepest underground region of Hades.

As far as Eleven knew, she was the only living being in the netherworld. All others there had died at least once and had been sent to Hades if they had not accepted Jesus as their Lord and Savior or if they were angels or demons who had rebelled.

Consequently, Eleven was the only prisoner in Hades who required any energy to keep her still-mortal body alive. Normally, she consumed solar radiation, but in Hades she was already so very, very far from the sun. In her new prison, in a deep underground cavern and screened from even those feeble rays by demonic protections, that energy source was denied her.

Eleven resisted and resisted and resisted, until finally her mortal body was minutes from death. Only then, with her life ebbing away, did Eleven allow herself to reach out and draw energy from the tormented human spirits that were also trapped in Hades. Eleven took just the bare minimum, enough to restore her body for a few days—but as she absorbed even that small amount of energy, she could feel the vampiric thirst building in her and knew that next time she would be more easily driven to feed on the helpless slaves around her.

The following day, Eleven was freed from her isolation and separation from solar energy. Nothing was said, then or ever, but Eleven knew that she had failed, had shown herself to be no better than her demon captors. She had also developed a deep and lasting fear of confinement that she would continue to feel even when her conscious memory was lost.

# # #

Eleven was eight thousand, six hundred and eighty-one when the angel Machkiel was paraded through Hades. As an outcast, Machkiel was resurrected in the netherworld rather than in Heaven when his body died.

He was the first angel to be consigned to Hades in a very long time and the demons celebrated loud and long.

That was the exact moment when Eleven first resolved to escape. *If I don't get out of here while my body is still alive, she realized, one day they will kill me and then I will be completely in their power.*

From that day forward, Eleven exercised in her small cell whenever she could, training her muscles and her reflexes. The demons guarding her would peer in to her cell, laugh, and make fun of her. "Go ahead and fatten yourself up for the kill, Eleven, you're never going to get out of here."

It took more than thirteen hundred years, but when her opportunity came, Eleven was ready.

# # #

Eleven was ten thousand and nineteen or thereabouts when the day came that the demons were distracted, rejoicing over their successful assassination of Pope Leo XI.

After millennia of imprisonment, Eleven made a daring escape from Hades and slipped through the portal to Alepotrypa.

She did not escape unnoticed. She found herself pursued by hundreds of demons and was eventually struck by fireballs that incinerated her wings and sent her plummeting into the sea far below.

Eleven was still conscious, though barely, when several demons dragged her out of the water and tossed her battered body onto the ground in front of her tormentor, Nekhbet.

Eleven could once again recall the amused look on Nekhbet's face as the Darke Warrior looked down at her where she lay. And in a daze, before the pain from her injuries drove her unconscious, she heard Nekhbet's final words to her. "Since your escape from Hades, your possibilities have been transformed. Now, you might become the one who actually triggers the Lost War. Wouldn't that be spectacular?"

Eleven lay on the ground while Nekhbet examined her closely. "Yes," said the Darke Warrior at last, "I believe it's worth taking the risk. Eleven my dear, you're finally going to be working for us. But first, we need to rid you of your memories. Let's go and visit the Academy."

# # #

Eleven had struggled, fought, and kicked as the men from the Academy tried to force her to drink some sort of liquid. Her very last recovered memory was of a man she now recognized as Father Carracci, hitting her over the head with a stout piece of wood.

# # #

And then she had woken up in Florence, with all knowledge of her past and her identity stripped from her.

# # #

Chrymos turned to Adric, not sure what to say to him now that she knew what she really was, only to find him whispering a few words to her in the secret Mystikó spell-language—which, thanks to the Exousía potion, she now understood.

He said, "<Freeze her where she stands. Bind her tongue, in the name of the light-bearer.>"

Then Adric reached out and removed the pathgem band from her wrist.

ONE HUNDRED AND THIRTY-FOUR
Nowhen

Chrymos couldn't move, couldn't talk—but her heart could still break. Even though she knew Adric couldn't possibly hear her thoughts, she still tried to mind-call him. *<Oh Adric, I'm not your enemy. The Academy was wrong—the Outcast Angels are a force for good, not evil. Remove the curse so that I can explain.>*

To her surprise, Adric reacted as if he could actually hear her—and he smiled, but it was a twisted, evil caricature of his normal smile.

And then, without warning, Adric flickered. His whole body transformed, his features stretching and melting, his hair shrinking into itself and changing color.

If Chrymos could have gasped, she would have done so, for the person emerging in front of her was not Adric—it was Ruben.

"Hello, sis," said Ruben. "How nice that you finally know who you are. Remember me yet?"

ONE HUNDRED AND THIRTY-FIVE
Villa belonging to Phaon, 4 miles outside Rome,
Ante diem quintum Idus Iunias (June 9) 68 AD

It had been a bad day for the man whose birth name was Lucius Domitius Ahenobarbus. His fourteen-year reign as Emperor Nero had just come to an inglorious end.

A messenger had arrived at Phaon's villa two hours earlier, bearing the news that the Roman Council had declared Nero to be a public enemy and that armed men were being dispatched to seize the emperor and take him to the Forum for execution. The report was premature—the directors were still debating the action—but not by much.

Nero, hiding out in a villa outside Rome that belonged to his freedman servant Phaon, quickly moved from denial to despair. He paced from room to room, muttering, "What an artist dies in me" and threatening to take his own life.

"Self-obsessed to the last," whispered Phaon to Nero's private secretary, Epaphroditos. "It never occurs to him to wonder why so many want him gone."

Epaphroditos never had a chance to reply, because at that moment the demon Ezequeel appeared out of nowhere, the deadly stench of brimstone leeching out of his every pore. Nero—the most powerful man in the Roman Empire, the man whose merest whim could mean death for any of his millions of citizens—threw himself to the floor and begged for his life.

"Has Orcus himself sent you to take me to the netherworld? Mercy, oh mercy, I beg you."

Ezequeel looked down unimpressed at the blond, blue-eyed wretch quaking at his feet. *This is the human that Hurakan wants to install as leader of a new Roman Empire? What a worm.* Still, Ezequeel had his orders. *Better act nice.*

"Hail Caesar!" *Hurakan said not to say any more until the human responds.*

Nero was momentarily perplexed, and then his imperial instinct reasserted itself. He stood up again and tried to stare at the apparition without shaking. Swallowing hard, he spoke in a quavering voice. "What do you want? Why are you here? Speak or be gone."

Ezequeel managed to sound momentarily obsequious. "I come to rescue you, mighty emperor—to save you from those who would mean you harm this very day."

Nero, never one to miss an opportunity, brightened at the thought. "You offer allegiance to your emperor?"

"Oh yes," said Ezequeel, struggling not to laugh. "But we must be gone from here at once, your enemies are nearly upon you."

With that pronouncement, the Darke Warrior seized the emperor by the shoulder and then stretched out a finger to the blue jewel that Ezequeel wore on a band around his wrist. Ezequeel muttered an incantation and the pair, nervous emperor and triumphant demon, began to fade from sight.

Moments before he vanished, Nero managed to cry out one last word to Epaphroditos: "Reddam."

Before nightfall, news of Nero's disappearance and that last word, Nero's final promise, "I will return", had echoed across half of Rome. By the next full moon, it was established legend through the length and breadth of the Roman Empire that Nero would be back. A few cheered— but most shivered in fear.

ONE HUNDRED AND THIRTY-SIX
Nowhen

For Chrymos, it was the final shock. Ruben was her brother. Like her, he was also an Outcast Angel born in exile. Like her, he had been washed out to sea when Atlantis fell. The last time she remembered seeing him, in the surging waters, he had been just seven. Now, many thousands of years later, he looked like a young man in his twenties—but Chrymos could still recognize the features of the young child she had adored as they grew up together. <*Ruben? Is it really you? Did you recognize me at the Academy? Why didn't you say something?*>

"Yes, Chrymos, it's me," said Ruben, "and I've known who you were all along. The Academy didn't need to wipe my memories like they did yours—I was happy to join them."

<*But why? Why would you want to become part of them? You know the evil they represent.*>

"Hello?" said Ruben, "I know you're in the middle of recovering your memory and all that, but have you taken a look at yourself lately? We're angels, but we have no powers because we were born outside heaven. All we can do is fly—but if we're discovered, the humans will do their best to try to kill us. Our parents rebelled, we didn't, but we're still stuck, banished to a single miserable planetary system, powerless, hiding from virtually everyone. As the humans say, 'the sins of the fathers will be visited on the children and the children's children, to the third and the fourth generation'. Lucky us. Thankfully, the pathgem can change all that."

<*How?*>

"You'll see, in a few—seconds? Minutes? How does anyone tell time in a place like Nowhen anyway?"

<*What do you mean, I'll 'see'?*>

"What you don't know—because most angels never knew—is how to use the pathgem. Only Ezequeel knew, because when he was in Heaven the pathgem was his responsibility. Of course, after the Rebellion he told

Nekhbet how it actually worked—and she told me, so that I could use it if you managed to find it." As he explained, Ruben was gazing around at the thickly-forested area in which they found themselves. He chose a towering tree with a good view of the clearing and guided Chrymos behind its mighty trunk, whispering the words that let him control her movements.

Then he leaned back on a neighboring tree-trunk and looked at Chrymos. "I'm sure you have plenty of questions, dear sister. We have a little time, so ask away."

<Where have you been?>

"Recently? Oh, off assassinating the French king," replied Ruben, giving an unpleasant grin. "Carracci thought he forced me to do it, using one of his spells. The spell didn't actually work on me—the Darke Warriors gave me what I needed to protect myself from those sorts of spells—but I went along with his plan, simply to see what would happen. I didn't speak when Carracci killed Luca, either—although I thought it was a bit foolish, he should have forced Luca to transmute large quantities of gold before he threw him into the ravine."

<How did you even find me in the catacombs?> asked Chrymos.

"I followed you, of course. My camouflage capabilities allowed me to blend into the background. You had a couple of close calls, didn't you, sis? I must admit, my heart was in my mouth for a while there—all the trouble I went to, only for you to stuff it up." He smiled unpleasantly. "Thankfully, you came through—persistence runs in the family, I suppose."

<But how did you survive the poison gases?>

"I stole some of Odaldi's elixir. I bet he was furious, right?"

<He was. And you obviously managed to get through the catacombs' passageways and avoid the traps.>

"That was easy—I waited until you were out of sight and then I flew through the empty passages. I'm an angel, remember?"

With an enabling thought, Ruben summoned his wings. Chrymos gasped—Ruben's wings were still feathered but they had turned a dark grey, reflecting the changes in his heart. Ruben flew up into the Nowhen sky, gawping like a tourist, before reluctantly flying down to land near Chrymos.

"I never ever thought I'd get to see this place. Nowhen—it's awesome. You should see it from up there—oh, yes, you can't move, I forgot, sorry about that." Another unpleasant smirk.

<How can the Academy's spells even work in Nowhen?>

"Because they're not Academy spells—they're Darke Warrior spells. How could any mere human spells work, whether here or back on Earth, without angelic or demonic powers behind them?"

<And getting past the creatures?>

"Also easy. They were in fact former students who were, let's say, 'surplus to the Academy's needs'. I used an appropriate spell to freeze them in place."

Ruben decided he'd given enough explanations. "Honestly, Chrymos, you need to concentrate on getting your mind back together, not chatting with me. Here, this'll help."

Ruben cast another spell. "<Still your mind-calling, in the name of the light-bearer.>" Now Chrymos couldn't even mind-call. Her eyes stared helplessly at Ruben.

He shrugged. "Sorry. We're about to have visitors—in particular, Ezequeel. We just escaped from him of course but I imagine you also remember him from the fall of Atlantis and from Hades, right? I can't have you spraying your thoughts around like a water-fountain—that would interfere with my plans."

He looked over at Chrymos and saw the obvious question in her eyes.

"How do I know that Ezequeel is coming soon? Before he was killed in his battle with Machkiel, he came here with a very special guest, the true Roman emperor, Nero. Ezequeel embedded this—Time? Place? Sorry, I don't have an adequate description for Nowhen. Anyway, Ezequeel mentally embedded this destination into the pathgem because he planned to come back to the very same moment. When I chose our own destination, I set it for just before Ezequeel's next arrival here, which was his previous visit—whatever 'just before' and 'previous' mean in this crazy place."

Time passed and then out of the corner of her eye Chrymos noticed a disturbance in the air in the clearing, a shimmering where two shapes seemed to fade into existence. The shapes gradually became two people.

One was the horrific Darke Warrior Ezequeel, and he was indeed wearing the pathgem. His companion appeared to be a human in his thirties, short curly blond hair, dressed in a simple Roman tunic.

Ezequeel released his grip on the human, took a couple of paces back, and bowed low. "Mighty Emperor, I must go now to prepare for your glorious homecoming. I will be gone but a moment. When I come back, it will be to escort you to your triumphant return to lead the Roman Empire. The citizens of Rome will shout for joy: 'Nero is back to lead us, as he promised! Hail Nero! Hail Caesar!' By your leave, sire."

With those farewell words, Ezequeel vanished, heading to the year 285 AD and his battle with Machkiel.

Ruben moved quickly, transforming himself into a duplicate of Ezequeel. He removed Adric's cloak, revealing dark clothing that might easily be mistaken for Ezequeel's armor. Mouthing the words "Bye sis" to Chrymos, he walked over to Nero and announced himself. "Here I am, Caesar. We need to go."

Nero started to speak. "But we—" Before Nero could even finish the sentence, the Rubenesque Ezequeel reached out to seize the arm of the deposed emperor and the pair vanished.

Chrymos found herself alone, trapped in Nowhen, unable to move.

She had two conflicting thoughts on her mind. *How can I go after Ruben and convince him to change his mind? But how can I also get back to the Academy, to save the children?*

ONE HUNDRED AND THIRTY-SEVEN
Nowhen

Time (or its equivalent in Nowhen) passed. Chrymos, still frozen by her brother's spell, could neither move nor speak. She could only think—but there was so much to think about, much of it agonizing.

Her first thoughts were of Ruben. *My poor, darling brother. You were seven when you were taken. Did the Darke Warriors convert you while you were still so very young? Or did you have to suffer through endless torments like me, before you finally agreed to do their bidding? At least you were too young to know any Outcast Angel secrets that they might have tried to get out of you. How can I hope to save you from the evil that surrounds you?*

Next, Chrymos tried to picture her parents, last seen so very long ago. *Would I even know you if I saw you? Are you even still alive? I've missed you so much, Mom, Dad. God willing, let me see you both again soon.*

Chrymos felt even more pain when she thought about the three children. *What must you be thinking right now, Olivia? Two days ago, I said I was going to get you all out—and, as far as you know, I simply ran out on you again. Will the Master keep his word and protect the three of you until I return—if I can? I certainly don't trust him to do so.*

And You, Father God? So many times, I've prayed to You, when I thought I was human, and You seemed to answer, to provide me with help and guidance. But my parents and all the Outcast Angels have told me that since the rebellion You have been deaf to our prayers. I don't understand.

And what of the new Sanctuary, the one that Nekhbet tried for so long to find out about? Does it even still exist? Was all my suffering for nothing? How can I even know?

In due course, another shimmering transformed into a phenomenon that Chrymos had heard about but never before witnessed—the blinding light of an arriving Kingdom Angel. Chrymos could see little, dazzled by the brilliance of the light pouring from this guardian of Heaven.

The angel, a veritable giant, looked down at Chrymos. He paused, communicating with the Lord, and then waved away the curse that had rendered Chrymos both dumb and motionless. She staggered, able to move for the first time in what seemed like forever.

Chrymos was torn. *Should I ask to be sent in pursuit of Ruben and the pathgem or should I ask to be sent back to the catacombs so that I can help the children?*

Before Chrymos could even find any words, her decision was made for her. The Kingdom Angel spoke in her mind, his voice both thunderous and yet soothing. *<You should not be here, Outcast. Return from whence you came.>*

The Kingdom Angel waved his hand again and Chrymos was gone from Nowhen.

ONE HUNDRED AND THIRTY-EIGHT
Catacombs of San Gennaro, Naples, Kingdom of Naples, 5.25 a.m. Wednesday June 23 1610

Chrymos instantly found herself back in the burial chamber within the Catacombs of San Gennaro. The stench of brimstone was still in the air and for a moment, Chrymos feared that she would find herself facing Ezequeel once more. Thankfully, the chamber was empty but Chrymos could hear heavy footsteps stomping away down the passageway—the demon must have only just left.

Chrymos took the timepiece from her pocket. The hand was pointed nearly halfway between the V and the VI, which meant that almost no time had passed between her departure from this place and her return. *The elixir that protects me from the poison gas is nearly exhausted—and Adric's has definitely run out.*

At first, Chrymos didn't know what to do next. It was such a relief to find that all her aches and pains—including those inflicted by the deadly snake venom—were gone, thanks to the healing environment of Nowhen. However, any excitement that she might have felt now that she remembered who and what she was—*I'm an angel*—was tempered by the bitter reality that her brother had seized the pathgem and intended to use it for evil. Anything that Chrymos might do now seemed pointless in the face of such betrayal and failure.

And then, after an absence of ten thousand years, Chrymos heard the mindvoice of her father, Shamar. He was not far away, and he was mind-talking another nearby angel.

Chrymos waited until Shamar had finished talking and then tentatively reached out to him. <*Father?*>

<*Who? Chrymos? My precious one? Can that really be you? After all these years? Where are you, honey?*> Shamar's response was a cascade of emotions, a mixture of hope, disbelief, caution, excitement, and above all love for his long-missing daughter.

The two of them soon established each other's current situation.

<We're under attack,> said Shamar, <from a group called the Alchemae. Nothing we can't handle, though.>

<As soon as I get out of here,> Chrymos promised, <I'll come and help you.>

<Don't worry yourself, child,> said Shamar, <I'll be fine. In fact, don't overexert yourself, I'll come and help you myself once we deal with this group.>

It was almost time to cease the conversation, but Chrymos had one very unpleasant task to complete. <Father,> she said, very reluctantly, <I have to warn you about Ruben. He's gone over to the Darke Warriors— and he has the pathgem. Don't let him get close enough to hurt you, I beg of you.>

It was the second major shock of the day for Shamar, and for a moment, Chrymos was afraid that she had gone too far. At first, Shamar was silent. However, just before Chrymos felt that she simply must speak again, her father responded. <Thank you, Chrymos. I know how hard it must have been for you to tell me that. I won't judge Ruben—we don't know what he's been through since the Darke Warriors took him—but I won't let him get close to me, either.>

And that, for the moment, was that. Tearful reunions would have to wait.

ONE HUNDRED AND THIRTY-NINE
Outside The Academy of Secrets, Naples, Kingdom of Naples, 5.30 a.m. Wednesday June 23 1610

It was a stalemate. The LOA team was pinned down beside one of the estate walls, unable to get past the tornado that whirled backwards and forwards in front of them, blocking their access to the Academy buildings.

On the other hand, the tornado couldn't move any closer to the team, despite the obvious desires of whoever had conjured up the mini-storm. Zophiel, frozen in concentration, was able to manipulate the air in front of the team, creating a barrier that the tornado couldn't pass.

Shamar sent a mind-message to Ravid. *<Are you here yet?>*

<Still about two to three hours away,> replied Ravid. *<We're nearly there—we only need some more wind.>*

Shamar smiled at the irony. *<We have plenty of wind here but we can't quite get it to you.>*

<Great, well, I'll see you as soon as I can. Do try to leave a few pieces for me to pick up.>

With that, Ravid terminated the mind-call, leaving Shamar alone with his thoughts. Inevitably, they now focused on his long-lost son and daughter.

ONE HUNDRED AND FORTY
Catacombs of San Gennaro, Naples, Kingdom of Naples, 5.35 a.m. Wednesday June 23 1610

Chrymos rapidly searched the burial chamber area close to where Adric's body had lain. *I was only in Machkiel's tomb for a few minutes. Ruben wouldn't have had much time to move Adric.*

Thankfully, Chrymos was correct. She found Adric's body a short distance inside a doorway to one of the many false tombs within the burial chamber. Adric was still unconscious, but was finally beginning to stir. She waited for a few minutes, staring down at him, until he opened his eyes.

Adric peered around at his unfamiliar surroundings, before focusing on Chrymos. His first words were faint but typically cheerful. "Hi, C, what are you doing here—wherever 'here' is? Did I sleep in again?"

"Adric, I'm very glad to see you," said Chrymos. "Take it easy, though," she added as Adric tried to get up. "Allow yourself to recover."

"Recover from what?" asked Adric, still dazed but determined to get to his feet. He did manage to stand up, but was still very wobbly. "Woah. Did anyone get the name of that donkey that kicked me in the head?"

Chrymos held Adric's arm to steady him, only releasing her grip when it was clear that he could walk by himself. "What happened to you?" she asked. "What actually knocked you out?"

"I'm not sure," said Adric. "All I remember is trying to get into one of those tombs. Something sent me flying and I hit my head. I have no idea how I ended up in this tomb, though, it isn't the one I was trying to enter."

Chrymos helped Adric make his way out of the tomb and into the main burial chamber. "Hey," he said, doing a double take, "where did that pile of bones come from? It wasn't here when I arrived."

Chrymos smiled. *That's more like it.* "It's a long story. Let's just say that it was one of the protections surrounding the tomb—but it won't bother us anymore."

"Wait, the tomb?" said Adric. "Of course, the mission—find the tomb, save the world. Let's get back onto it."

Chrymos looked at him sadly. "Mission's over, Adric. That's the tomb, over there." She pointed at the real tomb. "But the pathgem—that's the treasure in the tomb that the Master was after—that's gone. Ruben has it—he took it from me."

"Ruben? Our Ruben?" Chrymos nodded. *Oh yes—or, rather, 'my' Ruben.*

"I didn't even know he was back from whatever secret task Carracci had him performing," said Adric. "How long ago did he take it?"

"That's complicated," said Chrymos. "From one perspective, though, about fifteen minutes."

"Fifteen minutes? Then what are we waiting for? Let's go. We can beat him back to the Academy," said Adric, bustling Chrymos towards the main exit of the burial chamber. "If he's going to attempt to take credit for what you did, then we can tell your side of the story first."

"Wait a moment," said Chrymos. She rushed over to Machkiel's tomb and stepped over the threshold, pausing until she had been scanned and cleared to enter. She looked down at her fellow Outcast's body. Now she could finally remember when and where she last saw Machkiel, being dragged through Hades by crazed demons after dying to protect the pathgem thirteen hundred years earlier. She bowed her head, a moment's silence. *Machkiel, I pray that I have not undone your heroic sacrifice.*

Then, reaching down into the sarcophagus, Chrymos freed the shield and strapped it to her back. As she did so, she heard rather than saw Machkiel's bones crumble into dust. *<Farewell, Machkiel, you will be avenged.>*

Chrymos emerged from the tomb just as Adric bent down and reclaimed his cloak, which lay on the ground. When she'd last seen the cloak, Ruben had been discarding it in Nowhen. *I didn't realize that the Kingdom Angel sent back everything that we brought with us. Didn't want any trace of us still left there, I guess.*

"Now where's my sword?" grumped Adric.

"It's over here," said Chrymos, fetching the schiavona which still lay where she had left it an eternity ago, beside the entrance to the angel's tomb.

Adric slipped the sword into his belt and looked over to Chrymos. "Let's get out of here."

Chrymos was happy to let Adric lead the way back to the underground river port—a simple task, at least for this part of the return journey, thanks to the illumination cast by the glowing walls and ceilings.

All the while, she wrestled with how best to explain to Adric everything that had been happening. There didn't seem to be any easy explanations. *Actually, Adric, we're Outcast Angels, Ruben and I. He's my brother but he's gone bad. And if you're planning to fight for the Academy, you're on the wrong side. Oh, and my dad's out there as well, and at this very moment, he's battling against the Academy and if we get out of here I'm going to help him.* Chrymos couldn't think of any approach she could safely use with Adric. *Oh, this is a nightmare!*

ONE HUNDRED AND FORTY-ONE
Catacombs of San Gennaro, Naples, Kingdom of Naples, 5.45 a.m. Wednesday June 23 1610

Adric chattered away to Chrymos as they headed back to the underground river, not noticing that she was uncharacteristically silent. "The biggest challenge for me," he said, "was the labyrinth. I followed the instructions—your instructions, I guess, C—to number the paths that I took, but it was so dark and confusing in there that I almost chose the wrong way several times." He waited for Chrymos to respond.

"What about the creatures?" she asked.

"Creatures? There was no mention of anything like that in my notes. I thought I heard noises, some distance away from where I was, but I didn't see any creatures. Mind you, it was so horrible down there that I simply rushed through that section as fast as I could. I could hardly breathe in that poisonous air."

Chrymos started, uncomfortably reminded of the dangers that still lay ahead. "Wait a minute," she said to Adric, and reached into her pockets. She brought out the small jar of elixir that Doctor Odaldi had given her. "This will get us through the gases," she said. "If we move quickly there should be enough for the two of us to share."

"That's great, C," said Adric enthusiastically, "I knew there was a reason I invited you along to this little picnic."

The pair resumed their journey, arriving shortly alongside the river. "And here we are," announced Adric unnecessarily. "Did you sail here in one of these little boats too?"

"Yes I did," said Chrymos. "Though the river did most of the work."

They stood on the riverbank for a couple of minutes, preparing for their next move. "When I first arrived," said Adric, "I checked out where the river goes after it leaves here. It appears to curl round in a circle and head back to the waterfall."

"That makes sense," said Chrymos. "It was designed to bring pilgrims to see their loved ones. You'd expect there would be a return path. It's all very tricky, though, if you don't know how to escape the waterfall."

"Indeed," agreed Adric. "I stood watching for a while after I managed to escape from the whirlpool. Even if you don't trigger the trap by standing in the wrong place, it goes in cycles all by itself, forming a waterfall, creating a deadly water trap and then draining away." He looked around for a suitable boat. "Here, this should carry both of us."

Between them, Adric and Chrymos carried the chosen coracle into the river. Adric held the little boat steady while Chrymos climbed in. Then it was her turn to hold the coracle in place while Adric clambered aboard, bringing an oar with him.

"Ready?" he asked.

"Sure," said Chrymos. "Let's go."

Chrymos released her grip on the side of the wharf and the coracle responded, leaping forward into the flowing current. Adric, a more experienced sailor, confidently guided the boat into the center of the river.

Chrymos was still uncertain exactly how to explain herself so she settled for a safer topic. "Any sign of those powers yet, Adric?"

Adric shook his head. "Nope. Still, you know what they say— 'nothing should be done in haste but gripping a flea.'" He laughed. "I guess I'm expecting some rather major powers, since they still haven't shown up."

"So what have you been doing, these last few weeks?"

"Apart from this, you mean?" replied Adric. "Mostly I've been a carriage driver, taking Janus twins all over the place so that they can give us advance warning if the Outcast Angels show up."

That was Chrymos' cue, and she was about to start talking about Outcast Angels, and perhaps sound out Adric's opinions before revealing the changes in her circumstances. Before she could do so, Adric spoke up.

"Hold on tight now C, the river's turning rough ahead."

Sure enough, the coracle started rocking as the water became more turbulent. Chrymos clung to the side of the boat while Adric rowed energetically to keep the vessel upright and centered.

A few moments later, they could see the cause of the turbulence—

another waterfall pouring down from above and blanketing the river.

Thankfully, the waterfall was again mere inches thick, and they were soon safely on the other side.

Within seconds, however, Chrymos could feel a burning sensation in her throat. Once again, she was in the midst of the poisonous gases.

She looked across at Adric. He was bent double, coughing and choking.

ONE HUNDRED AND FORTY-TWO
Catacombs of San Gennaro, Naples, Kingdom of Naples, 5.55 a.m. Wednesday June 23 1610

Chrymos fumbled in her pocket for the jar of elixir. She opened it and handed it across to Adric. Then she took over the rowing so that he could hold the jar with both hands and drink deeply.

That's exactly what Adric did, between coughs.

Then he handed the still-half-full jar back to Chrymos. "Thanks, C," he said, still coughing. "That's exactly what I needed. Pity they can't make it taste any good. It still seems like swallowing the cow and then choking on its tail." Adric sat back in the boat, waiting for the elixir to do its work.

The section of the catacombs within which the river now flowed was once again pitch black. *We left the glowing walls behind when we lost the fresh air*, thought Chrymos. So once again, she put her hand into her pocket to coat it with more red powder.

When she drew her hand out again, Chrymos could once again dimly view her surroundings. The boat was being carried along through a narrow tunnel that might lead anywhere.

Chrymos glanced across at Adric to see how he fared. *He looks relaxed and comfortable. The elixir is starting to have an effect. I'll need to take my share soon—my last batch must be nearly worn off.*

Chrymos was too busy rowing. She didn't have a hand spare to check her timepiece but she knew what it was likely to indicate. *About five minutes left until my elixir runs out, I think.*

A strange rasping sound intruded into her thoughts. She turned towards the noise, only to find that it was Adric, snoring. *How can he sleep in all this? He must have been extremely tired.*

Pausing in her rowing for a moment, she reached over and shook Adric, but he didn't even stir. Then, and only then, did Chrymos think back to the moment when Odaldi had given her the additional vial of elixir. *He added an additional ingredient. What if that contained something to make me sleep?*

The more that Chrymos thought about it, the more that seemed the most likely explanation for Adric's current state—and for Odaldi's odd behavior. *He was very, very angry with me, he would see this as the ideal means of getting back at me without Della Porta blaming him.*

The realization sent chills down Chrymos' spine. *I'm about to run out of elixir—but I dare not take what's left in that jar or I might never wake up.*

At that moment, Chrymos was as close to panicking as she had been since her memory had returned. *Here I am, deep underground, a river carrying me towards who knows what—and I soon won't be able to breathe.* All the pain and anguish of her isolation in Hades came flooding back.

ONE HUNDRED AND FORTY-THREE
Catacombs of San Gennaro, Naples, Kingdom of Naples, 5.57am Wednesday June 23 1610

Perhaps it was the shield strapped to her back, which still seemed to vibrate with hidden energies. Or maybe it was her long-suppressed emotions finally coming to the fore. In any event, Chrymos felt a powerful reminder of her duties yet undone. *Adric is depending on you. Your father needs you. The children will die without you.*

Chrymos dug deep within herself—her new/old self. *I can do this.* She now remembered only too well how fiercely she had resisted the Darke Warrior Nekhbet as the demonic creature sought to break Chrymos' spirit during her thousands of years in captivity. *You didn't destroy me then, I won't let you win now.*

Little had changed in terms of her circumstances—Chrymos was still heading into the unknown in a barely-controlled boat, her friend Adric unconscious beside her, poisonous gases burning her throat and perhaps mere minutes away from causing her to die in agony—but Chrymos had her attitude back.

Not a moment too soon, as the river widened, joined by other tributaries. The coracle, which had been floating gently along, was now bouncing around from side to side. Chrymos could barely control the vessel in quiet waters, to do so in the midst of a full-blown torrent was next to impossible.

Chrymos knew what was coming next. She could hear the familiar rumble of the waterfall up ahead. *Unless I can somehow steer into that very narrow side river, this boat is about to go sailing over the edge of the waterfall. It's a long way down, and not a soft landing.*

ONE HUNDRED AND FORTY-FOUR
Catacombs of San Gennaro, Naples, Kingdom of Naples, 5.59am Wednesday June 23 1610

Chrymos abandoned any further attempt at controlling the coracle. Instead, she moved over behind Adric and managed to get his sleeping body into a sitting position, enough that she could slip her arms through under his armpits and clasp his arms with her hands. *I guess this is as close to an embrace as we're going to get, Adric.*

Chrymos braced, and then straightened herself up, lifting Adric as she did so. His head lolled forward, but the position seemed one that could work.

Now we wait for the hard part.

"You know, Adric," Chrymos told her comatose friend, "I always thought we could have made a half-decent couple, you and I, in other circumstances. Turns out, it wouldn't have worked, anyway—the age gap can get a little noticeable after a while. Especially when you're coming up to, say, fifty and getting a bit grey and saggy, and I'm ten thousand and fifty but still look like I'm twenty."

Chrymos offered a bitter-sweet smile. "Humans have such short lifespans. You barely have a chance to make an impact and then you're gone. But every life is precious, no matter how short."

Chrymos fell quiet for a moment, listening as best she could for the fast-approaching waterfall. "My mother, my real mother, Ayil, told me—" She struggled to remember the exact words. "—that 'humans are capable of great things within their far-too-limited lifespans. Amazing achievements, yes, but also matchless loyalty, unbreakable relationships, even love that prevails when all else is lost.'" Chrymos sighed. "You and I, we'll have to settle for friendship."

At that moment, the coracle was flung over the edge of the waterfall.

ONE HUNDRED AND FORTY-FIVE
Catacombs of San Gennaro, Naples, Kingdom of Naples, 6.05 a.m. Wednesday June 23 1610

Chrymos was ready. As soon as she felt the boat begin to tip over the edge, she launched herself and Adric into the air, summoning her ectoplasmic wings with a thought. It had been several years since Chrymos had last used her wings—and then only briefly, during the escape from Hades—but her mind connected with them immediately and she was easily able to hover in the air, holding the unconscious Adric tightly as she did so. *So far, so good. But you are heavier than I expected, Adric.*

Chrymos' immediate challenge was to avoid the cascades of water—*in the darkness, with only a few patches of glowing red powder on my hand to guide me*—and then find her way into the passage down below through which she had previously entered the water chamber. To make matters worse, the poisonous gases niggled at her throat as her own elixir began to wear off—and she was starting to loosen her grip on Adric.

In that moment, seeing the giant blocks of stone that had previously served as a stairway, inspired Chrymos' next move. She flew upward rather than down, and landed easily at the entrance to the upper passage that had served as her escape route a short time earlier.

Chrymos gently deposited Adric at the passage entrance, thought away her wings, and then took a few steps along the passageway. Once again, she stood on a hidden trigger that diverted the underground river and drained the chamber below. On this occasion, however, Chrymos returned to the entranceway and stood next to the sleeping Adric, watching from above as the waterfall was diverted and the chamber drained away. She dipped her hand into her tunic pocket for more red powder, but when she withdrew it from her pocket, only a small portion of her hand was coated in the glowing substance. *I'll have to conserve the powder more carefully from now on.*

Once the chamber below was almost completely emptied, Chrymos reached down, hoisted Adric onto her right shoulder, and plunged over the edge, summoning her wings as she did so. Her destination was the lower passageway, the curved path that she had originally followed to enter this chamber. *Seems like a lifetime ago.* She glided smoothly in to land near the beginning of the passageway, but well past the secret switch that had triggered the waterfall.

"Okay, Adric. That's enough flying for now." This passage was too narrow for Chrymos to fly through, at least not whilst carrying a body, so she resorted to half-carrying, mostly-dragging Adric backwards through the tunnel.

The journey through this passageway had taken perhaps ten minutes when Chrymos had been limping along on her own. The return, dragging Adric, took at least twice as long—and, with every step, Chrymos found it more and more difficult to breathe. The poisonous gas was starting to take its toll.

ONE HUNDRED AND FORTY-SIX
**Catacombs of San Gennaro, Naples, Kingdom of Naples,
6.30 a.m. Wednesday June 23 1610**

Finally, after what seemed like a never-ending marathon, Chrymos arrived at the far entry to the passageway and gratefully relaxed her grasp on Adric, at least for the moment. *The labyrinth is coming up, I need to see what those creatures are doing.*

Chrymos crept to the edge of the passage, six feet above ground, and looked down at the sarcophagi below. She tried to breathe quietly and shallowly, but it was a losing battle—now every breath turned into a coughing fit as the poison burned through her system. She tried breathing through her tunic, holding the fabric over her mouth, but that didn't help very much. *I need to get back to the higher levels of the catacombs. If I don't escape these gases soon—*She left the thought unfinished.

Chrymos fought to get her breathing under control as she surveyed the landscape below. There was no movement and at first, she thought she had a clear run. But then something—some shapes—caught the corner of her eye. *What are they?*

She couldn't see very well in the semi-darkness, so she reached into her pocket for a little more of the red powder—nearly her last. The extra powder helped, a little—now Chrymos could see that several of the shapes down below were actually those of the creatures—*former students, according to Ruben*—that had been chasing her.

Then Chrymos remembered what else Ruben had said. "I used an appropriate spell to freeze them in place." And she also remembered, only too well, how helpless she had felt when first Carracci and then Ruben had used such spells on her.

What do I do? They're horrible, horrible cannibalistic creatures. But they'll die if that spell is not removed.

For the first time since she had remembered that she was an Outcast Angel, Chrymos felt the urge to pray, to help guide her decision. So she did. "Father God, now that I know how unworthy I am, I don't know if You will answer me. But still I pray to You for guidance. What should I do? Help these creatures or leave them to starve?"

She waited for some response. Whether it came from God or not Chrymos couldn't say, but words from a half-remembered sermon popped into her mind. "Whatever you did for one of the least of these my brethren, you did for me."

Put like that, the answer is obvious.

Chrymos launched herself into the air, wings forming around her, and flew down to the nearest creature. Through a medley of coughing and choking, she whispered the enabling spell. *"ālepwāw ālepkāp hēnūnbēt hēwāw rēšhēhē."*

Chrymos recited the same spell to each of the other three creatures and saw them all start to move again. Satisfied that she had done everything that she should, she flew back to the ledge.

As Chrymos prepared to land, she saw that Adric was awake. He was watching her, wide-eyed.

ONE HUNDRED AND FORTY-SEVEN
Catacombs of San Gennaro, Naples, Kingdom of Naples, 6.40 a.m. Wednesday June 23 1610

"Hi."

That, thought Chrymos, *is about the lamest thing I could have said to Adric. But what else can I say? He's caught me with my wings out.*

She landed lightly in front of Adric, waiting desperately for his reaction.

Finally, Adric replied. "That's a new look for you, C."

"Uh, yes," said Chrymos. "Turns out that I'm an Outcast Angel."

"I figured. Nice wings." Adric offered up a half-smile.

"Thanks." Chrymos might have said more, but another coughing fit cut her short. When she had recovered sufficiently, she explained. "Sorry, my elixir has run out."

"But you do have more," said Adric. "I only drank half of the jar you gave me."

"Unfortunately," said Chrymos, "I'm certain that Odaldi has added a sleeping mixture in there as well. That's why you fell asleep." She coughed again, her throat in agony.

"Then go ahead and take it," said Adric. "We're safe enough here, I can watch over you while you sleep."

"I can't do that," croaked Chrymos, "I'm not sure how long I'd be asleep. What happens if your gas elixir runs out again while I'm still sleeping? It's too dangerous. The real answer is to get to the upper levels of the catacombs as quickly as we can."

Adric attempted to persuade Chrymos, but her mind was made up.

Finally, he nodded in agreement. "Okay, then let's get going." He looked at her wings. "So, can you carry me with those wings?"

"I've already done so once this morning," said Chrymos, whispering to minimize further coughing.

"Then let's fly," said Adric. "We need to get to the top corner, over that way, to the right."

"That's not where I came in," said Chrymos.

"No, but it's how I got here," said Adric. "I don't know if the Master told you, but that's where they dug their way inside, long before they discovered the false tomb and the steps. It's a far easier exit out of this part of the catacombs, but it's quite a climb from this level. Unless you have wings," he added admiringly.

"Then that's where we'll go," said Chrymos. "Now stand up and face away from me so that I can carry you properly."

Adric quickly did as he was told. Chrymos stretched out her hands and grabbed him around his waist. Then she launched off the ledge, her wings flapping powerfully as she gained altitude. Adric, after reacting very nervously as they left the ledge, snuggled into Chrymos.

"Well, this is a nice way to travel," he said. "I guess this flying is one of the memories you lost, C?"

"Gone completely until a short time ago," whispered Chrymos. "Not a memory you'd expect to forget, is it?"

"So any idea how you lost your memory?" asked Adric. Chrymos started to bring Adric up to speed with what had happened to her, though glossing over the sheer number of years that had passed while she had been imprisoned. *I don't want him to think I'm an old hag.*

By the time that Chrymos had reported on the role that the Academy had played in her memory loss, they had flown halfway to their destination.

"So the Academy stole your memory and then just dumped you on the streets of Florence?" asked Adric. Chrymos was about to answer but then her body began convulsing wildly as the poison gas mounted a fresh attack. Her back arched and she could feel herself beginning to let go of Adric as her muscles went into spasm.

ONE HUNDRED AND FORTY-EIGHT
Catacombs of San Gennaro, Naples, Kingdom of Naples, 6.50 a.m. Wednesday June 23 1610

Adric started to slip out of Chrymos' grasp as she shook and twisted in mid-air. He grabbed at her arms and held on as best he could, but he could see that Chrymos couldn't stay aloft much longer.

He looked down. *We're still in the middle of the labyrinth.* "You need to land, C. I'll try to guide you down."

He wasn't sure if Chrymos heard him, but she definitely began to descend, so he decided to proceed as if she was listening. "Okay, down here, down, down, left, left, left—no, left!"

It wasn't exactly a controlled descent. They narrowly missed two labyrinth walls as they descended, too quickly. Chrymos lurched from side to side, her wings flapping unsteadily, her body jerking, as the foul gas took its toll. The pair fell the last few feet, as Chrymos' wings simply vanished. But they were down, more or less in one piece. Chrymos collapsed onto the ground, her body still convulsing.

Adric took command. "Chrymos, where's the elixir?"

Coughing and spluttering, Chrymos weakly pointed to the left-hand pocket of her tunic. Adric knelt down, reached inside her pocket, and took out the glass vial. He uncorked it and, lifting Chrymos into a sitting position, held the drink to her lips. "Here, Chrymos. Drink."

Between coughing fits, Chrymos managed to swallow the elixir down. The coughing didn't stop instantly but it gradually eased and her body, after much shaking and shivering, calmed.

Adric gently lowered Chrymos to the ground. He took off his cloak and wadded it into a ball, which he placed under her head as a makeshift pillow. She didn't seem that comfortable, lying on a shield, but it was easier to leave the shield strapped to her back than to try to remove it.

Adric watched and waited, until Chrymos began breathing more easily. *Looks like you were right, C, that elixir does seem to be making you sleep.*

Once he had ensured that Chrymos was as comfortable as possible, Adric stood up and looked around to see exactly where they had ended up.

I guess we're in the middle of the labyrinth. I can't see any of the red marks I made so I obviously haven't been through this part before. I hope it's not a dead end.

It was difficult to see much in the gloom—the patches of red powder on Chrymos' hand did very little to illuminate the area—so Adric fished his own vial of powder out from his pocket and held it above his head.

There still wasn't much to see. They were in a small room, about eight feet square, with twelve-foot-high walls. Two doorways at one end of the room seemed to lead off into other passageways. *There's no way of telling where those passages lead.*

At first, Adric simply propped himself against the wall near Chrymos, determined to wait until she woke up.

After about ten minutes, however, when Chrymos was still breathing steadily but little else was happening, Adric stood up, stretched, jumped up and down on the spot a few times, paced the room from one end to the other, and then went from side to side. That passed a few more minutes. Chrymos was still sleeping soundly, though, with no sign of awakening.

Eventually, Adric crouched down beside her. "Sorry, C, I'll go stir-crazy if I don't do something. I'm going to explore this labyrinth, to see if we can get out from here. I won't be long."

The sleeping angel gave no response.

Adric stood up once more, lifted his red powder lantern in front of him, and then headed out through the left-hand doorway.

ONE HUNDRED AND FORTY-NINE
Catacombs of San Gennaro, Naples, Kingdom of Naples, 7.30 a.m. Wednesday June 23 1610

One of the creatures shuffled into the room where the young woman lay on the ground.

Its name had been Mauricio and it was the newest of the four creatures to be transformed, having been banished to the catacombs a mere four months earlier after a student prank went horribly wrong. In the months that it had been trapped in the poisonous gases, the creature had shed much of its hair. It still retained a predominantly human appearance, but was merely a caricature of its former self.

The creature dragged itself over towards the woman.

First, it sniffed her, up and down, like a dog. What it could smell in the midst of the poison gases was a mystery. At any rate, the creature seemed satisfied with what its nose told it about its prey.

Then the creature reached out and touched a finger to one of the glowing spots of red powder on the woman's hand. Some of the powder transferred to the creature's finger.

The creature lifted its powder-stained finger close to its eyes and stared at it, frowning intently. Then it touched the powder to its tongue and quickly spat it out again.

Next, the creature turned its attention to the woman's face. It reached out and held her chin, moving her face around so that it could be examined from various different angles.

It hesitated at one point. Perhaps it recognized her from the classes they had taken together at the Academy a few months earlier. More likely, it remembered seeing her a short time earlier, when she had released the curse that would otherwise have resulted in its death.

For whatever reason, the creature paused before attacking—just long enough for a figure to rush into the room, sword raised, hollering a bloodcurdling war cry.

ONE HUNDRED AND FIFTY
Catacombs of San Gennaro, Naples, Kingdom of Naples, 7.40 a.m. Wednesday June 23 1610

The creature jumped backwards, away from Chrymos, which was exactly what Adric had intended.

Wielding his sword expertly in his right hand, Adric prodded and poked at the creature, forcing it further backwards, towards the right-hand doorway.

"Get out of here," he shouted. "Leave her alone!" The words probably went unheeded but the constant pricking of the sword had the desired effect. The creature kept backing into the passageway, and then turned and made its escape.

Adric offered up one final piece of advice from the safety of the doorway. "Don't come back or—I'll slice you up," he finished weakly.

Once he was satisfied that the creature was indeed gone, Adric crossed back to Chrymos and squatted down beside her. "Sorry, C. I thought you'd be quite safe here."

Chrymos gave no sign that she had noticed either the activity or the apology. She continued to sleep serenely.

Adric breathed a deep sigh of relief. *No harm done, after all.*

He settled himself down not far from Chrymos, this time determined to wait until she woke up.

ONE HUNDRED AND FIFTY-ONE
Outside The Academy of Secrets, Naples, Kingdom of Naples, 7.45 a.m. Wednesday June 23 1610

It had been a frustrating couple of hours for the LOA team. Every attempt to breach the Academy buildings had so far proven fruitless.

The tornado had finally dwindled away about thirty minutes earlier, which Shamar guessed was because its creator had run out of energy. "It seems that the Alchemae potions only last for a limited period," Shamar told the others. "I gather that the Academy bosses don't want their underlings to have too much power."

Even so, the LOA team was still pinned down. Occasional musket volleys, though not coming close to their position, kept the two angels earthbound. And a series of bitter blizzards—despite the crystal clear summer sky above—drove back any land-based attempts to storm the nearest building.

The team hadn't been idle. Doamna, who could transform soil into stone, had been hard at work building up a defensive wall. And Mircea— his Wallachian colleagues had affectionately nicknamed him the Mole— was equally industrious, with his bare hands digging out a trench behind the wall to serve as a shelter for the team. *I suppose it beats doing nothing, but I doubt he'll get very far with that trench before the Academy finishes whatever it is they're doing.*

At some point during this lull in the fighting, Martin had asked how the first team had escaped the trap in the woods. "It was quite easy," admitted Shamar. "As soon as the Academy men fired their muskets, we knew where they were—and we also knew that their vision would be restricted because of all the smoke from the musket fire. So Zophiel used his power over the air currents to gently push the crows out of the way directly above us, creating just enough room for me to fly Sean over near the attackers. Then we used the same tactics we used later at the main gate—I struck up a friendship with them all and then Sean paralyzed them."

"The only annoying part," added Zophiel, "was that one of the Academy men could make the trees grow by touching them. Sean couldn't get close enough through all the branches to paralyze him. That took ages, which is why we weren't able to help you at the main entrance."

Once that particular mystery had been solved, there wasn't much more to be said. The team members all retreated into their own thoughts while they considered what else they might do. In the end, that decision was taken out of their hands.

It was inevitable that the Academy tactics would eventually switch from defense to attack. That transition was marked by a series of explosions that impacted against Doamna's newly-built stone wall.

ONE HUNDRED AND FIFTY-TWO
Outside The Academy of Secrets, Naples, Kingdom of Naples, 8.10 a.m. Wednesday June 23 1610

The explosions shook the stone wall but had little direct effect. Behind the wall, however, the attack was more damaging. Some of the piles of soil and rocks—created by Mircea as a side-effect of his digging— were dislodged by the force of the blasts, and began raining down on the team members in the trench. They scrambled to avoid the falling debris, and in doing so nearly fell victim to the next phase of the Academy's attack.

Musket balls ricocheted off the impromptu stone wall as the guards fired yet another volley at the would-be infiltrators. Because of their unpredictable nature, the deflected missiles were even more dangerous than deliberately-aimed shots. Most careened safely away from their intended targets but a small number bounced off the wall at just the right angles to pose a threat to the LOA team. Both Martin and Elias suffered minor wounds as musket ball shrapnel tore at their flesh.

The third phase was far more concerning. Behind the wall, the LOA team members could hear a number of shouted commands, followed by the sounds of people moving about. Shamar and Zophiel exchanged mind-messages.

<*What now?*> wondered Shamar.

<*Whatever it is, they're moving their own people out of the way first,*> said Zophiel. Aloud, he warned his colleagues. "Brace for impact—this next one could be big."

The attack began slowly, a mild vibration that gently shook the ground around the LOA team. It was disconcerting, but not much more than that.

Then the vibrations intensified, the whole area beneath the Outcast Angels and their team starting to shake. They found it difficult to remain standing as the shuddering rolled on, growing stronger and stronger.

"Earthquake?" asked Martin, directing his query at the angels.

"A very tightly focused one," replied Zophiel, pointing at the Academy buildings, which remained unaffected. He clutched tightly to one side of the trench to avoid being knocked down as the shaking around them grew worse. "The work of a very powerful Alchemae, I think. He—look out!" That last shout was a desperate warning as the stone wall, overstressed by the sharply-intensifying tremors, cracked down the middle and began to topple into the trench below.

ONE HUNDRED AND FIFTY-THREE
Outside The Academy of Secrets, Naples, Kingdom of Naples, 8.15 a.m. Wednesday June 23 1610

The LOA team members scrambled to get out of harm's way as the two halves of the stone wall fell towards them. Niall had no problems stretching out of the trench and avoiding the wall. Lochloinn, his movements already restricted because of the shoulder wound he suffered earlier, wasn't so lucky. He found himself pinned against one side of the trench by a large left-hand piece of the wall.

Acting together, Shamar and Zophiel stood firm and were able to halt the collapse of the right-hand wall segment long enough for Sean, Radu, and Martin to scuttle out of the trench. That left Doamna, Mircea, and Elias trapped on the left-hand side, their exit blocked by the collapsed wall and by Lochloinn.

The tremors gradually subsided, leaving the LOA team dangerously exposed. Six of them were on the open ground, all cover gone now that the wall had fallen, while four were still imprisoned within the trench.

In the stillness that followed, the Outcast Angels could hear more orders being shouted out. Then came the ominous sound of triggers being cocked.

Shamar looked at Zophiel. <*Do we surrender? We can't run while our men are trapped.*>

<*Will they even give us the option?*> replied Zophiel wearily.

A split second later, a deafening volley of musket fire shattered the silence.

ONE HUNDRED AND FIFTY-FOUR
Catacombs of San Gennaro, Naples, Kingdom of Naples, 8.15 a.m. Wednesday June 23 1610

Chrymos finally stirred. She opened her eyes slowly. Mostly, she was surrounded by darkness. Then, on one side, she spied a red glow, accompanied by the anxious face of her friend Adric.

"C, are you okay?" he asked.

"I am, as it turns out, still alive despite my best efforts. And I feel much better thanks. Now please help me up."

With Adric's aid, Chrymos managed to stand up. She stretched, flexing her back. "Ow. That shield's not as soft as the straw back at the Academy, I can tell you that. Still, at least I can breathe again, though it's still not very pleasant in this stuff."

She looked around, getting her bearings. "Where did we end up?"

"In the middle of the labyrinth," said Adric. "We're about halfway to the exit point."

"Good," said Chrymos. "Before we go any further though, Adric, you and I need to talk."

"Sure," said Adric, "go for it." He stood back, ready to listen.

Chrymos came up to him and stared straight into his eyes. "You now know that I'm an Outcast Angel. And ever since we arrived at the Academy, Father Carracci and the other tutors have made it clear that the Outcast Angels are the enemy. I need to know, Adric, and I need to know now—do you believe that I am your enemy?"

Adric returned Chrymos' stare unflinchingly. "I've known you for three years, C, ever since you first arrived in Naples. I've watched you parent those children who weren't even yours. I've seen you look after the poor. I've seen you minister to the sick and help anyone with a hard luck story. So I can't put it any more plainly than this."

He paused for a moment, and then spoke with great passion. "I. Trust. You. If you are indeed an Outcast Angel—and those wings really were a bit of a giveaway, C—then I am more than willing to accept that the Outcast Angels are good, and that means that the Academy is not. And, frankly, given how badly Della Porta, Carracci, and the Contessa behave, I'm not that surprised. And in terms of whose side I'm on—did you ever doubt that?"

There was a moment's silence and then Chrymos hugged Adric fiercely. "Thank you, Adric, that means so much to me."

Adric returned the hug enthusiastically. "You're welcome, C." He coughed. "I think I'm ready for that fresh air, now."

"Well, let's get going again then. The sooner we're out of this foul place the better. Ready?" With that, Chrymos summoned her wings, primed for flight.

Adric gazed at the wings in a mixture of amazement and puzzlement. "How do those wings stick to your back through your clothes and even through that shield?" he asked.

Chrymos struggled to explain. "They're somehow linked to my body through what we call the aether," she said. "They're not true physical wings—they only look like they are. They draw on heavenly energy to help me fly. Or anyway, that's how my father explained it to me when I was nine."

"That's as good an explanation as any," said Adric. He bent down and gathered up his cloak, then positioned himself in front of Chrymos, back towards her. "I'm ready."

That was all the go-ahead that Chrymos needed. She reached around Adric's waist, grabbed him tightly, and launched into mid-air.

A few minutes later, she glided in for a soft landing at her destination. She released Adric and then dismissed her wings with a thought.

"That's zooks," said Adric, admiring the way that Chrymos' wings simply vanished when she no longer needed them. "Now, follow me."

With Adric in the lead, the pair walked up the remaining distance to the entrance to the next level. "This section has been deliberately blocked off with fabrics and heavy planks," said Adric, "to stop the gases befouling the upper levels." *And to keep the creatures from escaping*, thought Chrymos.

With both Chrymos and Adric pushing with all their might, they were able to move the heavy planks far enough apart to create an opening. They slipped through the gap, quickly replacing the planks as soon as they had passed.

Finally, Chrymos and Adric had left the poison gases behind. They had emerged into one of the larger arcosolia in the upper catacombs. There must have been luminaria in the passage outside, because some light shone into the room through the doorway at the other end. In the shadows, they could see a half-dozen sarcophagi standing in a line down one side of the chamber whilst a single, massive sarcophagus dominated the other side.

"Be careful C," warned Adric. "The floor of this chamber is riddled with holes—Della Porta's men did plenty of digging in here before they found a way down to the level below. Those sarcophagi may look sturdy enough, but at least some of them are probably going to collapse through the floor if there's another flood."

The pair gingerly tiptoed through the room until they reached what appeared to be a relatively safe spot. They stood for a moment, taking in welcome breaths of the fresh air.

"Free at last," said Chrymos.

"I don't think so," said a voice from behind them.

ONE HUNDRED AND FIFTY-FIVE
Catacombs of San Gennaro, Naples, Kingdom of Naples, 8.20 a.m. Wednesday June 23 1610

Chrymos and Adric both spun round, to see Ezequeel entering the chamber and striding towards them, his armored feet clanging with every step on the stone floor.

The demon was an imposing sight, clad in black armor from his neck to his toes. For the moment, his sword was sheathed and his axe secured to his belt. He wore no helmet, which accentuated his cruel, scarred face and greasy black, shoulder-length hair.

Ezequeel did not look happy. His voice rang out, echoing through the room. "I have been coming to these catacombs year after year after endless year, attempting to break into that tomb to retrieve my pathgem."

Adric drew his schiavona, indicating to Chrymos that she should get behind him. Chrymos shook her head. Instead, she removed the shield from her back and brought it round to the front. She slipped her left arm into the straps, preparing to defend herself.

Ezequeel continued to move towards the pair. As he grew closer, Chrymos could smell the mixture of mixture of brimstone and putrefying flesh that was uniquely Ezequeel's. Maggots and cockroaches scurried across his armor. "You had the pathgem in your hands," he said, "but now I can sense that the pathgem is gone. After all these centuries, Eleven, you gained the prize only to let it slip through your fingers. Tell me what has happened to my precious pathgem and I may even be merciful."

Ezequeel came to a halt about an arm's length from Adric and Chrymos. He glanced dismissively at Adric and then turned to his attention to Chrymos, staring intently at her through his demonic red and yellow eyes. "Well? Where is the pathgem?"

"It's safe from you, Ezequeel," said Chrymos. *I hope.*

"Leave—" began Adric, raising his sword and stepping between Ezequeel and Chrymos. Without even looking, certainly without drawing his weapon, Ezequeel casually raised his arm and swatted Adric away like a bothersome insect.

Adric went flying halfway across the chamber, ending up crashing into one of the sarcophagi. His sword clattered noisily to the ground beside him.

Chrymos dashed over to Adric and knelt down beside him. He was dazed but otherwise seemed okay. She whispered, "Stay here," and then stretched over and grabbed Adric's fallen sword.

Ezequeel hadn't bothered to move. He waited for Chrymos to return and then offered up a disdainful comment. "Touching, Eleven, the way you look after these little humans. Anyone would almost think you cared."

Chrymos, a good six inches shorter than Ezequeel, looked up at his sneering face. "The pathgem is long gone from here. I suggest you do likewise, demon, and crawl back into your hole."

Ezequeel laughed. "The pathgem may be gone, but you're still here. And Nekhbet isn't finished with you yet, Eleven. She wants you back in Hades—and this time she would prefer you dead."

Now, Ezequeel did draw his sword. The vicious barbed blade still bore flecks of dried blood from a previous victim.

ONE HUNDRED AND FIFTY-SIX
Outside The Academy of Secrets, Naples, Kingdom of Naples, 8.22 a.m. Wednesday June 23 1610

Shouts and screams rang out across the Della Porta estate—but they came from the Academy's men, not from Shamar or Zophiel or any of the LOA team.

To the Outcast Angels' surprise and relief, they and their team were unhurt. Their enemies had not fired the muskets. Instead, the shots had come from the main gate, which was currently shrouded in gun smoke.

Even before the smoke began to clear, six armed soldiers, clad in the distinctive red and blue livery of France's Quarante Cinq royal guardsmen, rushed through the gate and took up defensive positions facing the Academy buildings. Their arrival went unchallenged—any potential opposition now retreated inside the buildings.

A few moments later, the long-absent Ravid strode into the Academy courtyard, accompanied by another twenty or so French guardsmen carrying weapons, ammunition, and other supplies. Ravid spotted Shamar and Zophiel and came over to join them. The three angels embraced each other warmly before helping to extract their colleagues from what remained of the trench.

The French soldiers quickly freed the trapped team members, who gratefully accepted the food and water provided.

They took a break for a few precious minutes. Martin had two burning questions for Ravid. "Where have you been? And how on earth did you persuade the French to send their royal guardsmen to help us?"

Ravid smiled. "It's a long story."

ONE HUNDRED AND FIFTY-SEVEN
Six Weeks Earlier
**Palais du Louvre, Paris, France,
morning, Saturday May 15 1610**

The *Palais du Louvre* was in total uproar when Ravid arrived for his prearranged meeting with Bishop de Richelieu. The palace, seat of the French government and residence of the late King Henri IV, swarmed with guardsmen, court officials and functionaries, though few seemed to know exactly what they should be doing.

Ravid waited patiently until the bishop's right hand man, the Capuchin friar Father Joseph, arrived. The priest guided Ravid to Bishop de Richelieu, who now occupied temporary rooms in the royal palace in the immediate aftermath of the king's assassination. The Bishop nodded politely at Ravid as he was settled in the sumptuous visitor's chair alongside de Richelieu's desk.

"Thank you, Joseph, that will be all," the bishop announced.

If the bishop's closest aide had been surprised by being dismissed from a meeting that he might normally have been expected to attend, that fact was not evident in the manner in which the friar responded. "Yes, of course, Your Eminence," Joseph replied, bowing low and then removing himself discreetly from the bishop's office.

Ravid waited until the friar had closed the door firmly behind himself. Then he stood, crossed to where de Richelieu stood and hugged the bishop warmly. "Armand," said Ravid, "I am so sorry that the prophecy came true and that we were unable to prevent it. My heart goes out to you and your country in these troubled times."

"Thank you, Ravid, I deeply appreciate all your efforts," said de Richelieu. "I too am deeply saddened—but at least we quickly caught the killer."

"And he is?" asked Ravid, surprised by the news.

"François Ravaillac, a known fanatic," replied de Richelieu, sitting down at his desk and indicating that Ravid should likewise sit. "One of the King's guardsmen, Medoro, recognized the vermin. We were able to catch him on a coach heading out of Paris."

The Bishop smiled grimly. "We're interrogating him now, so we should have a confession soon. There was one odd curiosity, though—the coach on which Ravaillac was travelling actually left Paris at midday, several hours before the king was assassinated. We don't yet know how Ravaillac managed to catch up and get onto that coach mid-journey, but rest assured, we'll find out."

Ravid was also puzzled, especially since both Elias and Lochloinn had also previously reported that they had watched Ravaillac leave Paris on that same midday coach, well before the assassination was carried out. *There are other powers at work here*, he reminded himself. Aloud, he asked, "Have you arrested anyone else?"

"Two others of significance," said de Richelieu. "We arrested the two drivers whose carriages blocked the road at the critical moment. When we searched their carriages, we found these." He indicated two solid gold goblets and a pair of solid gold water jugs, lying on his desk. "This gold is worth a fortune. They were obviously bribed. At any moment, I should receive a report from the interrogators on exactly who bribed them. It could not have been François Ravaillac—he was only a handyman and did not have that sort of money."

Ravid might have spoken up then, since he knew that Ravaillac had been staying at the home of Charlotte du Tillet, mistress of the Duke of Épernon. *But what could I say? That the killer could be in the pay of the Duke? Or perhaps that he might have stolen the gold items from his hostess?*

Before Ravid could voice any suspicions, there was a gentle knock on the door. "Come," said the Bishop, and Father Joseph entered apologetically. "Sorry to disturb you, Your Grace, but the report you have been waiting for has arrived."

"And what does it say, Joseph?" asked de Richelieu. The friar glanced across at Ravid, obviously concerned that an unknown visitor would hear the report, but the bishop waved away any concerns. "He needs to hear this as well, Joseph. Go ahead."

Unconvinced, but deeming it unwise to question the bishop's instructions, the friar began reading the report aloud. "One of the drivers is still denying everything but the other has confessed. He admits that a stranger gave him the gold. In return, he was required to block the roadway when signaled to do so. He swears on the life of his mother that he had no idea why he was being asked to block the road and with his dying breath he cursed the man who bribed him in order to kill the king."

De Richelieu leaned forward over his desk. "Did the driver describe the stranger?"

"Yes of course," said Father Joseph, "otherwise he would not have been allowed to die. The man we seek is of average height, with short blond hair and, probably, blue eyes. He had a curved scar that stretched from one of his ears to below his chin. He was dressed all in black, with fancy boots and, to quote the driver, 'didn't look as if he had done a day's honest work in his life.'"

"So," said de Richelieu heavily, "not the assassin Ravaillac, then?"

"No, Your Grace," agreed the friar. "It would appear that we have a conspiracy on our hands."

De Richelieu pondered for a moment and then stood up. "We need to find this man, fast, before he has a chance to escape. Put the word out, Joseph. Get this description to every church within a day's riding distance from Paris. Let each priest tomorrow describe this conspirator to their congregation and ask their help to find him."

The friar scrambled out the door to put the bishop's instruction into action. De Richelieu turned to Ravid. "We will see into which rat's nest this man has burrowed. And then you and your Outcast Angels will track him down for me and bring him back to Paris where he will answer for his crimes."

ONE HUNDRED AND FIFTY-EIGHT
Palais du Louvre, Paris, France,
Afternoon, Sunday May 16 1610

Reports started flooding into the Palais du Louvre almost immediately after the earliest Sunday morning services. Parisians were outraged over the death of their king and eager to do whatever they could to assist with the hunt for his killers.

Naturally, there were plenty of false reports—in such incendiary times, plenty of people were willing to imagine the worst about their neighbors and acquaintances—but gradually the true picture began to emerge.

"The scarred one was seen walking briskly away from the Les Halles region shortly after the assassination, in the company of another unidentified suspect," reported Father Joseph to the bishop.

"A number of people saw the pair as they walked across the city. They met with a third man in a clearing on the outskirts of Paris, joining him in a carriage marked with the seal of the Kingdom of Naples. Then the carriage was last seen heading off towards the road that leads from Paris to Lyon."

"And from Lyon," said Ravid, "they will easily be able to slip through the mountains to the Italian peninsula."

"Ravid?" asked de Richelieu expectantly.

"On it," responded Ravid, rushing out of the Bishop's office.

ONE HUNDRED AND FIFTY-NINE
Near Mont Cenis,
Late afternoon, Saturday May 22 1610

Ravid had spent several long days and nights flying over carriages traveling towards the Italian peninsula before he finally caught up with the carriage that might be the one he sought. This carriage was slowly climbing up towards Mont Cenis and the mountain traverse between France and Italy. The carriage was marked, as several Parisians had reported, with the seal of the Kingdom of Naples. *But is this the one? Does it carry the man with the scarred face?*

There was no easy way to tell, at least not from the height at which Ravid was obliged to fly during daylight hours. The spyglass he carried, a gift from a grateful Galileo, was helpful but not perfect.

Ravid had a difficult choice to make. *Do I keep pace with this carriage until after dark, until I can fly much lower and get a closer look? Or should I fly further along the road and keep searching?*

In the end, Ravid based his decision on time and distance calculations. *I doubt that a horse-drawn carriage could have traveled any further from Paris than this, in the week that's gone by since the king's assassination.*

In order to be certain, Ravid opted to investigate more closely. Despite the risk that he might be seen in the late afternoon sun, Ravid flew down as close as he dared to the carriage. He aimed to get near enough to catch at least some view of the passengers through the carriage windows, all the while trying to avoid being seen by the driver.

Ravid was in luck, for once. Through the left-hand window, he could see that the carriage contained two people, strangely unmoving despite the bumpy progress of the coach along the rugged mountain track. A second glimpse revealed that one of the passengers had a curved scar. *That's him. Now what?*

Ravid flew sharply upwards to resume his position far above. He kept pace with the carriage as it struggled through the mountainous terrain.

As the afternoon faded into dusk, Ravid pondered how best to stop the carriage. *The driver must surely be part of the conspiracy. How can I force him to stop if he's determined to carry on?*

Ravid needn't have worried. As the carriage reached a particularly steep section of track, it slowed and came to a halt of its own accord. The driver stepped down from the carriage and peered cautiously over one side of the track, a sheer cliff where the ground fell away steeply to a valley far below. *He's up to something*, Ravid decided. The Outcast Angel carefully spiraled down to observe more closely.

The driver seemed in no hurry. He fed and watered the horses, taking a break. It became apparent that he was waiting until the twilight lengthened into night. Only when the last rays of the setting sun began to disappear behind the mountain did the driver make his move.

First, he looked up and down the track to ensure that there were no other coaches in sight. Then, as Ravid watched in horror, the driver reached inside the carriage and led one of the passengers to the edge of the ravine.

Wings beating frantically, Ravid managed to get into position halfway down the mountain slopes, just in time to witness the driver pushing his unresisting victim over into the void.

ONE HUNDRED AND SIXTY
Near Mont Cenis,
Night, Saturday May 22 1610

It was a moonless night, which meant that what happened next would have been impossible for anyone but Ravid.

In total darkness and in eerie silence, the body plunged into the depths. Because of his enhanced senses however, Ravid was able to see as clearly as if it was broad daylight. He judged that he only had split seconds to act. He dove frantically, trying to intercept the body before it hit the rocks below.

Flying as if his life depended on it, Ravid managed to catch the falling body before it touched the ground. *This is so strange, he's still alive but he's not moving,* Ravid told himself as he lowered the victim onto a flat strip of land on one side of the ravine. He checked the man's face. *Scar, yes, it's the man I'm after.*

Once he had landed safely, Ravid tossed some rocks into the ravine. They made a satisfying clatter on the way down. *If that driver is still waiting by the roadside, that should satisfy him that his victim is dead.*

Ravid crouched down in the darkness, next to the man he had rescued, waiting. *At least I don't have to tell him to be quiet,* he told himself. He inspected the young man who was now in his care. *I don't think I would have wished to know you. Even without the scar, your face looks distinctly unfriendly.*

Ravid remained hidden until he heard the driver urge the horses to get moving again, followed by a clattering of hooves and creaking of wheels as the carriage drove off towards Naples.

"Now let's get you back to Paris," Ravid told his unresponsive companion. "Let's see if we can shake that spell and find out what we need to know about your part in the assassination."

Ravid gathered the young man in his arms and launched himself back into the night sky.

ONE HUNDRED AND SIXTY-ONE
Paris, France,
Morning, Tuesday May 25 1610

Ravid and his motionless guest were settled in a room at *Le Meunier Heureux*, an inn on the outskirts of Paris that regularly played host to the Outcast Angels. The inn featured an interior courtyard, blocked off from prying eyes, where angels could land and take off without being seen. The proprietor, needless to say, was a long-time supporter of the LOA.

<He just sits there, not talking, Jesse.> Jesse could feel Ravid's frustration, even through the mind-call.

<Let me look at him.> Jesse, still hundreds of miles away in England, was able to 'see' through Ravid's eyes, view Ravid's companion and then examine the possibilities that might lie in store.

Jesse kept up a running commentary with Ravid while examining the comatose prisoner. *<Obviously, he is entranced. In most of his alternative lives, he died back on Mont Cenis. But in one of his possible futures, he is released by this spell. Ravid, say these words to him: ālepwāw ālepkāp hēnūnbēt hēwāw rēšhēhē.>*

Luca awoke with a gasp as soon as Ravid completed the recitation. The young student had no idea what was happening.

"Where am I? What is this place? You!" Luca addressed Ravid haughtily. "What am I doing here?"

Ravid stifled a smile. *This could be fun.* "And whom do I have the pleasure of addressing?"

"My name is Luca Raimondo Del Balzo Orsini, son and heir to Duke Orsini of Naples. But you shall call me 'sir' and answer my questions and bring me food and water, right now. Then I may choose to spare you the punishment that your impertinence would otherwise deserve."

<Feisty little fellow, isn't he?> laughed Jesse from afar, while Ravid tried not to smile.

"Well, young sir," he said to Luca, "as to exactly where you are, you are in Paris." Luca jumped with fright at that news, but Ravid wasn't finished.

"As to what this place is, you might call it Purgatory." Again, Luca jumped fearfully.

"And the reason that you would call this place Purgatory," said Ravid, "is that it is a waystation, between what we may choose to call Heaven and what you would most assuredly consider to be Hell. Because over there—" Ravid pointed in the direction of the city center. "—sits the Palais du Louvre, where the authorities are extremely eager to 'talk' to you about the role you played in the foul murder of their king."

Luca was on his feet in a moment, frantically denying everything, but Ravid waved away his protestations and insisted that Luca sit down. Because the instruction was supported by Ravid resting one hand on the sword in his belt, the unarmed Luca reluctantly acquiesced.

"And as to your third question," continued Ravid, "regarding what you are doing here. You are choosing."

"Choosing? Choosing what?" demanded Luca.

"Choosing your future, of course," said Ravid. "You may choose Hell, in which case we will take you to the Palais du Louvre, where the king's interrogators will quickly establish your guilt and determine whether your death will be very slow and very painful, or very, very slow and extremely painful. Or—" Ravid paused dramatically.

"Or what?" Luca asked, terrified.

"Or you could answer my questions, right here, right now, and then be taken to a place where you can serve out your life in peace."

Even Jesse struggled to keep up with the flow of information that Luca poured out in his eagerness to escape Parisian justice.

After Luca had babbled on for several hours, Ravid and Jesse emerged with a basic if slanted understanding of the Academy, the Council of Four and the combined forces awaiting them in Naples.

They had also established that Father Carracci was the man behind the assassination plot. <Bishop de Richelieu will be less than impressed to learn that a man of the cloth is behind it all> observed Ravid to Jesse.

ONE HUNDRED AND SIXTY-TWO
Palais du Louvre, Paris, France,
Afternoon, Tuesday May 25 1610

De Richelieu was furious. "A Dominican priest?" The bishop spent the next few minutes denouncing the failings of the Dominican order in general, and the shortcomings of that priest in particular, before turning to the very practical matter of what to do about him.

"And what happened to your informant, the conspirator?"

"We sentenced him to death, Your Grace," said Ravid.

"Very good, very good. Will it be a public execution? We can put the word out through the congregations this Sunday."

"Ah, no, Your Grace," said Ravid. "We have chosen to make Luca die very slowly. It will take a while." *<About fifty or sixty years by my calculations>*, added Jesse, in a private mind-aside to Ravid which earned the elder angel a mental rebuke.

<We did promise to spare him if he gave us what we needed,> Ravid pointed out to Jesse, while simultaneously carrying on a spirited verbal discussion with de Richelieu about the educational merits of public executions.

<True,> agreed Jesse, *<though I am not sure that the young man will be quite so grateful, once he realizes that his new role is to help feed the poor, by turning base metals into gold for the Cistercian monks of Cîteaux Abbey, at least until his powers run out. After that, I'm sure the monks will make good use of an extra pair of hands, no matter how soft and unskilled.>*

The conversation between de Richelieu and Ravid now turned to the issues that had emerged from the interrogation of Luca. "It's not only the priest, of course, or even the Academy," said Ravid. "Now that we know who we're really up against—this so-called 'Council of Four,' including the Brotherhood of Judas and New Phoenicia, and possibly some Darke Warriors—our small team will be greatly outnumbered by the forces gathered against us in Naples."

"Are there any more Outcasts or Enhanced that can be sent to join the fight?" asked de Richelieu.

"Jesse and I talked about that this morning," said Ravid, "and his view was that none can be spared. We're already stretched thin attempting to guard Maurice of Orange and the Ottoman Sultan Ahmad—and Captain Smith is pushing hard for us to send a team over to Jamestown, before the colony ends up lost just like Roanoke."

"Then the Quarante Cinq will come with you to Naples," proclaimed de Richelieu. "The king's guardsmen are devastated that they were unable to prevent his murder. They will demand to be part of this mission of retribution."

As far as the bishop was concerned, the matter was settled. Ravid still had some concerns. "Won't sending an army into Naples provoke a war with Spain?"

"You forget," said de Richelieu, "that our grieving queen is Marie de' Medici, daughter of Florence's ruling dynasty. Her family will support our efforts to capture her husband's killer—they can speak to their Napoletano counterparts and ensure their cooperation.

"However," said the bishop, pondering the issue further, "we will still need some plan to sneak the guardsmen into Naples. They can't exactly go marching into the city. That would demand an official response from the authorities."

"Not to mention tipping off the Academy," agreed Ravid.

ONE HUNDRED AND SIXTY-THREE
Palais du Louvre, Paris, France,
Afternoon, Tuesday May 25 1610

De Richelieu and Ravid spent the next hour or so tossing around ever more fanciful ideas to solve the problem, without success. The answer, when it emerged, came from an unlikely source.

Father Joseph, as was his custom, had been in and out of the bishop's office all afternoon, bringing papers to be signed and decisions to be made. The friar's latest delivery provided the solution, though that fact was not immediately evident.

"What's this?" asked de Richelieu as Father Joseph handed over a bill of accounts.

"It is a charge for the hire of the *Seintespirit*, Your Grace. It is part of your patronage arrangement with the Paris Opera Company."

The bishop looked momentarily puzzled, so Father Joseph explained. "The *Seintespirit* is a merchant ship that is usually hired out to the French navy to patrol the Mediterranean. We have arranged for it to ferry the cast and crew of the opera *Euridice* to Naples next month, from where they will begin their tour of the Italian states."

And then, suddenly, the answer was obvious. De Richelieu, alive with inspiration, had to wait until the friar had left the room before he could explain to Ravid. "The guardsmen can be smuggled into Naples aboard this ship, as part of the touring opera company. They can pretend to be performers and stagehands. You should accompany them so that you can brief them during the journey."

The bishop reviewed the travel details from the papers that Father Joseph had provided. "The ship is scheduled to sail from Marseille in a week. That means we will need to organize a series of fast carriages, and several teams of horses, to get you and the guardsmen to Marseille before the *Seintespirit* departs."

ONE HUNDRED AND SIXTY-FOUR
Catacombs of San Gennaro, Naples, Kingdom of Naples, 8.24 a.m. Wednesday June 23 1610

Ezequeel raised his sword, preparing to strike. "I'm going to enjoy this."

Instinctively, Chrymos raised Adric's schiavona with her right hand while her left held the shield of Evalach protectively in front of her.

Ezequeel's eyes narrowed as he recognized the white shield with its blood-red cross. "I see you've picked up Machkiel's shield from the tomb. It didn't do him much good so I shouldn't expect too much, if I were you."

He slammed his barbed sword against the shield, sounding impressed when the shield absorbed most of the impact. "Not bad, Eleven. Of course, the shield's usefulness does rather depend on the skill of the person holding it." With that, Ezequeel pulled back his arm and smashed his sword against the shield once again.

The sheer force of the second strike sent Chrymos sprawling backwards across the chamber, like Adric before her. She collided with one of the sarcophagi and slumped to the floor. She still clutched the shield, but the schiavona had been knocked out of her hand.

Ezequeel strode over to where she lay and lifted up his sword, planning to deliver a killing blow.

ONE HUNDRED AND SIXTY-FIVE
Catacombs of San Gennaro, Naples, Kingdom of Naples,
8.25 a.m. Wednesday June 23 1610

Ezequeel towered over his fallen opponent, gloating for a moment. "Not great, Eleven. You should have put your time back on Earth to better use."

"Actually," said Chrymos, pushing her back hard up against the side of the sarcophagus, "it was my father, a very, very long time ago, who taught me how to do this."

With that, she summoned her wings. As they shimmered into existence, they reacted to the presence of the sarcophagus wall behind Chrymos. Unable to co-exist with the solid stone, the wings squeezed themselves into the almost non-existent space between Chrymos and the wall, and then expanded like an uncoiling spring. Chrymos was catapulted forward so that she shot towards Ezequeel like a cork out of a bottle.

Chrymos had been planning for precisely that outcome. She had clasped the shield in front of her body and now used it as a battering ram, crashing into Ezequeel and knocking him off his feet. Then she flew to the top of the nearest sarcophagus and hovered slightly above it.

Ezequeel had been caught off guard but was unhurt. He spat out an angry challenge as he picked himself up. "Is that the best you can do? Then you'd better run as far from here as you can, Eleven, because nothing else will save you, girl."

"I'm done with running," said Chrymos, still hovering above the sarcophagus. "If you want me, come and get me. I'm right here."

Ezequeel sent the mental command to summon his wings but stopped before they were fully formed, belatedly realizing that the chamber ceiling was too low because his wings were much larger than Chrymos'.

Grunting with annoyance, Ezequeel was forced to use his hands and feet instead. He clambered onto the sarcophagus, making heavy going of the task.

"Putting on a little weight, are we?" Chrymos taunted the demon—but made certain she hovered just out of reach of his vicious sword.

Ezequeel growled as he straightened up and stomped across the sarcophagus towards Chrymos. "Stay where you are, angel spawn, and face up to your fate."

Chrymos flew a short distance backwards, until she was hovering over the next sarcophagus in line. She was still tantalizingly close to the increasingly more enraged demon. "I'm only over here," she said, "or is that a little too far for you to jump?"

Ezequeel snarled. He eyed up the distance between sarcophagi, took a couple of steps backwards, and then made the jump, landing heavily on the next sarcophagus. The stone slab almost seemed to shudder from the impact.

"You're nearly out of room, Eleven," Ezequeel told Chrymos. She glanced behind her. *Two more sarcophagi and then a wall.*

"Then you'd better come and capture me before I trap myself," Chrymos retorted, timing her own backward flight to match his stomping progress along the sarcophagus.

Once again, she moved across, hovering above yet another sarcophagus. Once again, Ezequeel leapt from one sarcophagus to the next.

This time, however, as the giant demon thundered down onto the top of the new sarcophagus, it shook unsteadily.

It shook and then, as Chrymos had been hoping, the sarcophagus collapsed through the weakened floor beneath, taking the demon with it in an uncontrollable avalanche of stone and rock.

ONE HUNDRED AND SIXTY-SIX
Catacombs of San Gennaro, Naples, Kingdom of Naples, 8.27 a.m. Wednesday June 23 1610

Chrymos flew above the collapsed sarcophagus and stared down at Ezequeel. The demon lay in the midst of the rubble, covered by slabs of stone and rocks.

As Chrymos watched, he began to stir, pushing the debris aside in an effort to get free.

Chrymos hovered above him and spoke from her heart. "I've spent the last five months hoping that some magical power would turn me into someone who matters and who could make a difference.

"Now that I know who I really am, even though I don't have any special powers, I realize that I don't need them. I was searching in the wrong place—I only needed to look inside myself.

"You, Nekhbet and the rest of your Darke Warrior kind have tried and failed to break my spirit for more than ten thousand years.

"You couldn't do it then, you won't do it today."

That last challenge goaded Ezequeel back into action, which was exactly what Chrymos had intended. As the demon pulled himself free of the collapsed sarcophagus, Chrymos reached into her pocket and extracted the glass jar, which she had carried with her throughout her catacombs journey.

Chrymos dashed the jar against the stone floor, closing her eyes just before the moment of impact. The glass shattered, instantly allowing the metal strip within to react to the air and flare into radiant bright light.

Even through her closed eyelids, Chrymos was momentarily dazzled by the brightness, especially in comparison to the semi-darkened catacombs.

Protecting her eyes from the worst of the glare, Chrymos looked over at Ezequeel. He staggered, clutching at his eyes. *As I hoped, he's been temporarily blinded.*

Seizing her opportunity, Chrymos clutched the shield of Evalach with both hands and slammed it down with all her strength on Ezequeel's unprotected head—once, twice, and then a third time. "My name," she said as she pounded the Darke Warrior, "is not Eleven. It's Chrymos."

Ezequeel slowly crumpled to the floor.

ONE HUNDRED AND SIXTY-SEVEN
Catacombs of San Gennaro, Naples, Kingdom of Naples, 8.28 a.m. Wednesday June 23 1610

Chrymos flew down to the ground to reassure herself that Ezequeel was definitely unconscious. Then she called to Adric. "Are you okay?"

After a moment, the call came back. "Yes, I'm fine. What's happening?" Adric's head popped up beside the sarcophagus where he had landed. He looked over at Chrymos, who was still brightly illuminated by the burning metal, though the light was diminishing as the metal was consumed.

"I've knocked Ezequeel out," Chrymos reported. "We're safe for now, but we won't want to be here when he wakes up."

Adric came over and joined her where she stood, near the fallen Ezequeel. His nose wrinkled at the smell. "Not pleasant."

"No," agreed Chrymos. "All the demons smell bad, but Ezequeel is the worst of the lot."

Adric examined the body, carefully avoiding the cockroaches and other vermin swarming across the armor. "Can demons die?" he suddenly asked.

"Not as such," said Chrymos. "Their bodies can be destroyed, yes, but they simply get resurrected in Hades. It's more of an inconvenience for them than anything else. Of course," she added thoughtfully, "then they have to retrain their bodies before they can become active again, which does take them out of our hair for some time."

Chrymos and Adric had clearly both had the same idea. Adric reached for Ezequeel's axe, but Chrymos pushed him away. "Best that I do it," she said. "The demons already hate me."

A few minutes later, the job was done.

"Now let's get out of here," said Chrymos, tossing the axe aside. "We still have to get back to the Academy and save the children."

She summoned her wings with a cheerful declaration. "And this time, I'm not taking any tunnels."

ONE HUNDRED AND SIXTY-EIGHT
The Mortality Room, Academy of Secrets, Naples, Kingdom of Naples, 8.29 a.m. Wednesday June 23 1610

Giambattista Della Porta was not happy, and everyone in the mortality room knew it. He screamed at Doctor Odaldi. "I've waited for you as long as I can. There's no more time. We have to get these hosts onto the ship NOW!"

"One more minute, Master, please," Odaldi begged. He wore a plague doctor mask and gown as he bent over one of the beds, trying to extract fluids from the dying woman who lay there.

"NO—MORE—TIME!" shouted Della Porta, pushing Odaldi roughly aside. Father Carracci, who had been standing quietly to one side, beckoned for the nurses to remove the remaining patients—two women, two girls and one young boy.

The nurses led their five charges outside, through the backdoor exit, while Odaldi followed, furious. He was not accustomed to being treated in such a manner, especially not by the Academy's leader. "I nearly had it," he muttered to himself.

Della Porta wasn't paying attention to Odaldi. Instead, he was listening to the sporadic bursts of musket-fire coming from the front of the building. He smiled when he heard screaming. *Finally, we're getting somewhere.*

He was still smiling when the Darke Warrior Nekhbet entered the room. Even Della Porta shivered whenever he saw the demon, especially during daylight hours.

Nekhbet spoke briskly. "You shouldn't be smiling, Della Porta— those are the sounds of your men and the men from New Phoenicia dying. You're losing this fight."

"What do you mean?" asked Della Porta.

"The Outcast Angels have brought reinforcements from the French Royal Guard," said Nekhbet. "The guardsmen are highly trained—and they're thirsty for revenge for the murder of their beloved king."

"Murder? We were not involved with the king's assassination. In fact, we tried to prevent it," protested Della Porta.

"I wouldn't be too sure, Della Porta," said Nekhbet, turning her attention to Thomas Carracci. "What do you think, Father? What mischief have you and the Contessa been stirring up behind the Master's back?"

Carracci tried to bluster his way out of the accusation. "I have no idea what you're talking about."

"We'll see," said Nekhbet with a sly grin. "Jesse was not the only prophet exiled from Heaven on the day of the Great Rebellion."

Whatever else might have been said at that moment was lost when the air shimmered and two figures appeared out of nowhere.

One appeared to be a Darke Warrior, a glowing blue gem on his wrist. The other was a blond man of average height, wearing a simple tunic.

The Darke Warrior bowed low to Nekhbet. "Mistress, may I present to you the Emperor Nero."

ONE HUNDRED AND SIXTY-NINE
At that very same moment
Stonehenge, England, 7.30 a.m. Wednesday June 23 1610

Jesse stood talking to Archimedes at the moment that the pathgem returned to Earth. The instant that the possible became the new reality, millions upon millions of dramatically-altered futures battered Jesse's mind.

Life after life after life changed, and always for the worst. Now it was no longer only the world's rulers at risk—every living human being was affected.

No mind, human or angel, could withstand such trauma. Jesse collapsed.

# # #

Archimedes instantly summoned the healers.

They ministered to Jesse for several hours. Finally, their leader Aceso, grim-faced, reported to Archimedes. "Jesse is in a very deep sleep from which he might never recover. All we can do is watch and wait."

ONE HUNDRED AND SEVENTY
Academy of Secrets, Naples, Kingdom of Naples, 8.30 a.m. Wednesday June 23 1610

Nekhbet executed a dramatic sweeping curtsey, greeting the newly-arrived Roman emperor. "It is my very great pleasure to meet you, Your Imperial Majesty."

Nero, still stunned, managed a brief nod.

Nekhbet turned to the Darke Warrior. "And I see that you have the pathgem back. Well done, Ezequeel—better late than never."

The Darke Warrior smiled.

Meanwhile Della Porta, once he had overcome his shock at seeing the pair appear out of thin air, scurried over to Nero, threw himself down on the floor, and attempted to address the emperor in halting Latin. "*Salutem imperator—et honorem multum—accipietis—a me est—honor recipiam vos—in domum meam.*"

The emperor looked down at the man lying in front of him, muttered one word, "*Barbarus,*" and stepped over the prostrate figure, speaking quickly to his Darke Warrior companion. Della Porta slowly pushed himself up off the floor, muttering. "He called me a barbarian. Me? Fifteen hundred years his superior?"

Carracci hurried over and helped the devastated Master to his feet.

Nekhbet was about to make a comment, when she received an unexpected mind-message. She listened, and then addressed the Darke Warrior. "I've just been advised that a few minutes ago Ezequeel was resurrected in Hades. Of course, I should have already seen your probabilities. It's not him, it's you."

The Darke Warrior nodded. His figure flickered, revealing his true identity.

Carracci and Della Porta gasped, virtually in unison. "Ruben? Is that you?" asked Carracci.

Nekhbet had her own questions for the unmasked mimic. "So your sister found the pathgem, then?"

Ruben nodded again.

"Amazing," said Nekhbet. "She really did it? I never would have believed it if I hadn't foreseen it with my own eyes. Well, good for her. I hope she enjoyed her triumph, while it lasted."

Nekhbet turned to Della Porta. "Thank you for providing the conditions that enabled Eleven—the one you know as Chrymos—to find the pathgem. We'll take it from here."

She sent a mind-message skywards. *<We have what we wanted, Chosek. You go ahead, we'll make our own way back.>*

Nekhbet turned back to Ruben. "Ready?"

"By your command, mistress," said Ruben, taking hold of Nero's arm once more.

"No, wait!" Della Porta rushed over.

Nekhbet looked at him quizzically.

"You can't leave yet. The Outcast Angels, the Plague project—" Della Porta spluttered.

Nekhbet waved a dismissive hand. "None of that matters anymore," she told Della Porta. "Not now that we have the pathgem. It's not important who wins this little battle. The Lost War has now begun—and that will change everything."

Nekhbet reached over and touched an armored finger to the pathgem, speaking an enchantment as she did so.

The three figures faded from view, leaving Carracci and Della Porta behind.

Della Porta was the first to react. He turned to Carracci. "It may not matter to Nekhbet who wins and who loses today, but it certainly matters to us. Let's get the rest of those children onto the ship."

Della Porta scowled. "And while we're doing that, you can explain exactly what the demon meant by 'mischief going on behind my back'!"

ONE HUNDRED AND SEVENTY-ONE
The Academy of Secrets, Naples, Kingdom of Naples,
8.35 a.m. Wednesday June 23 1610

Chrymos landed lightly on the path just outside the back door to the Academy, dismissing her wings. She was pleasantly surprised to find the area deserted and sent a mind-message to her father bringing him up-to-date.

In return, Shamar reported on the current state of the battle out front. *<Most of the Academy men are barricaded inside one of the front rooms, hiding from the Quarante Cinq's musket fire, although we still haven't seen any sign of the leaders. Let me know if you come across any of them—but be careful, I don't want to lose you before I've even had a chance to hug you in person.>*

Chrymos attempted to open the back door, which had given her so much trouble the last time she tried to enter—*was that truly only two nights ago?*—and was in for yet another surprise. The door was unlocked.

I could have brought Adric with me after all. Chrymos had deliberately left Adric to make his own way back from the catacombs, despite his angry protestations. *I didn't think it would be safe here. Looks like I was wrong.*

Chrymos quietly let herself in through the back door. There was no sign of anyone around, so she began to explore the whole ground floor.

The main mortality room itself was deserted. *Clearly, they left in a real hurry.* Bed covers were roughly pulled aside, as if the occupants had been speedily evacuated, and furniture and furnishings were simply scattered around the room.

Chrymos was desperately anxious for the children. She hurriedly searched the room until she found a set of keys. Then she headed towards the rooms that led off the main chamber.

Most of the doors that she tried were unlocked and the rooms empty. In desperation, she crossed herself and offered a prayer to the Lord, even though as an Outcast Angel she now knew she should not expect a response. *Almighty God, please give me the power, the strength, and the wisdom to save the children. Protect them and keep them safe, I beg You, Lord.*

There were three doors left to try. Chrymos tried the first door. *Locked.* She fumbled with the keys until she found one that fit. She unlocked the door and peered hopefully inside the room. *Empty.*

The second door was unlocked and, as expected, was empty. *One more.*

Chrymos tried the third door. *Unlocked.* She almost didn't even bother looking inside, until she thought she heard some sort of noise from within.

She did go inside, cautiously—*there could be Alchemae in here*—and saw, to her delight, that she had finally found Madalena. The poor girl was tied to the bed, with a gag around her mouth, but otherwise seemed unharmed.

As soon as Madalena saw Chrymos, she went wild, thrashing and turning in the bed, making unintelligible sounds through the gag and flashing her eyes.

Chrymos began to cross the room towards Madalena—and then, for no apparent reason, Chrymos had an almost overwhelming urge to summon her wings.

ONE HUNDRED AND SEVENTY-TWO
The Academy of Secrets, Naples, Kingdom of Naples, 8.50 a.m. Wednesday June 23 1610

Chrymos immediately rejected the idea—*Madalena is already terrified enough. What will she think if she sees me sprout wings?*—but the urge was so strong that it could not be denied.

With extreme reluctance, Chrymos called her wings from the aether—and as they sprang into ectoplasmic reality, the edges of the wings collided with an unseen presence behind Chrymos.

She spun around, knocking whatever was behind her to the ground as she turned. The invisible presence, momentarily disoriented by the fall, flickered and revealed itself to be Father Carracci—and the priest was armed with a long knife.

"I should have known," Carracci snarled as he regained his footing and started to turn invisible again. "All that self-righteous behavior—that's so rich, coming from a cursed Outcast Angel. Let's see how an angel manages against cold steel, shall we?"

Before Carracci could completely vanish from sight, however, he was hit from behind by a glass vial.

The vial instantly shattered, outlining the nearly-invisible priest in a coating of red powder.

Chrymos looked up to see Adric, freshly arrived from the catacombs, launching himself across the room at the red spectral Carracci.

The priest began to utter an enchantment that would give him the upper hand. "*Pēhēt rēshēhē zayinhē. Dālet—*"

Before he could complete the spell, Chrymos whacked Carracci across the head with her right wing. *Not quite the treatment I gave Ezequeel, but very satisfying nevertheless.*

Without his enchantments, the priest was no match for Adric and although they fought briefly over the knife, the outcome was never in doubt.

Carracci was quickly gagged with bandages before he could enchant his way free.

While Adric restrained Carracci, Chrymos quickly untied Madalena. As soon as the gag was removed from her mouth, Madalena almost shouted. "There's no time to lose, they've taken Olivia and Sirus to the lake."

ONE HUNDRED AND SEVENTY-THREE
The Academy of Secrets, Naples, Kingdom of Naples,
8.57 a.m. Wednesday June 23 1610

Chrymos sent a hasty mind-message to her father as she raced out of the Academy's back door and along the path to the lake. <*The man behind the assassination, Thomas Carracci, is secured in the mortality room. You must keep him bound and gagged—he can turn invisible and can cast spells.*> She'd left Adric and Madalena back at the Academy as well, to guard Carracci until the LOA team could relieve them.

<*Thanks, Chrymos,*> said Shamar, <*I'll see that Carracci is handed over to the Quarante Cinq, to be taken back to Paris for trial.*> Then he warned Chrymos to watch out for pirates from New Phoenicia. <*There aren't many of them but they're ruthless killers. Be careful.*>

<*Thanks, Dad, I will. Now I need to go.*>

Chrymos ran frantically towards the lake, and then realized that it would be much quicker for her to fly. *Out of practice*, she thought as she summoned her wings and soared into the air.

She stayed low, conscious that there were still armed Academy thugs and New Phoenicia pirates roaming around the estate, but even so, she was able to cover the remaining distance to the lake in less than two minutes.

As she rounded the final corner, Chrymos was so shocked by what she saw that she almost lost the concentration necessary to maintain her wings.

Beneath the giant statue of Neptune, a large section of the cliff wall was gone and the lake water poured through the gap thus created.

Not only that, but an overloaded boat packed with children was about to disappear through the gap as well.

ONE HUNDRED AND SEVENTY-FOUR
The Academy of Secrets, Naples, Kingdom of Naples, 9.00 a.m. Wednesday June 23 1610

Chrymos didn't even stop to think. She drove her wings faster than ever, chasing after the boat as it plunged into the gap.

Just in time, too. The gap began closing as soon as the boat had passed, and there was only enough room for Chrymos to slip through at full wingspan.

The underground watercourse was dark, of course—a far too familiar situation for Chrymos by now—but the boat carried flaming lanterns at front and rear, so at least she had a clear target to follow. But she could see that the tunnel grew narrower as it went along. *At this rate, I won't be able to fly in here much longer—there won't be enough room for my wings.*

Chrymos accelerated towards the boat and reached out to grab hold of the stern section, the transom. *The boat can pull me along.*

The moment that Chrymos touched the transom, she felt herself bombarded by the same types of enchantments that protected the Tower. *"Let go, leave or die, beware, doom, death."*

Chrymos almost lost her grip. The enchantments were relentless, drilling into her head, warning of pain and torture and unbearable despair—but Chrymos had a far greater inducement to hang on tight. *I can see the heads of the children in the boat. I'm sure that's Olivia—and that must be Sirus.*

In the end, concern for the children was enough to sustain Chrymos.

She dismissed her wings and held on tightly as the boat followed the underground waterway down under the Capodimonte hill, all the way to a hidden exit that led into the Naples harbor.

The boat emerged into the harbor at speed, still maintaining much of the momentum from its downward plunge.

The boat's captain, previously crouched in the bow watching for obstacles ahead, turned around and started shouting instructions for his crew—two servants from the Academy—to start rowing. He stopped short when he saw the bedraggled Chrymos clinging to the transom.

Chrymos froze as well. The man at the helm was Giambattista Della Porta.

ONE HUNDRED AND SEVENTY-FIVE
The Harbor, Naples, Kingdom of Naples,
9.20 a.m. Wednesday June 23 1610

Della Porta reached down into a box by his side and pulled out a loaded pistol. As he cocked the trigger, ready to fire, Chrymos tensed. *I have to time this just right.*

Della Porta squeezed the trigger. At precisely that instant, Chrymos threw herself backwards. She simultaneously summoned her wings and used them to propel herself deep down into the water, another trick that her father had taught her when she was a child. A fragment of a long-ago-and-far-away conversation slipped through her mind as she swam. *Da-da, look at the gannets, what they doing? Dear child, they are plunge-diving into the sea and using their wings to swim around in the water catching fish.*

A few seconds later, Chrymos reversed direction, powering herself up, up and out of the water. She adjusted her flight so that she hovered near the bow of the boat.

As Chrymos had hoped, she had not given Della Porta sufficient time to reload his pistol. In fact, he hadn't even tried. Instead, he stood still, waiting for her. He held out both his hands as if he was about to clap.

"Well, this is a day of surprises, Chrymos. Who would have guessed that you were an angel? And would you have guessed that I can do this?"

Della Porta raised his eyebrows ever so slightly—and suddenly held a raging ball of white fire between his hands. Chrymos could feel the intense heat from several feet away.

Della Porta smiled tolerantly. "Yes, I have powers too. Now we all know, Chrymos, that you can probably dodge this fireball fairly easily—but the children here can't." His expression hardened. "And while as an angel you might not care too much about human children in general, you and I both know that there are some children on this boat that you do care about. I'm not sure which particular children they are—Father

Carracci concerned himself with all that—but I want you to know that I can incinerate them all with this fireball faster than you can stop me."

He switched the fireball to his left hand and then used his right to point behind her. "See that ship over there? That's where I'm going, with these children, and if you know what's good for them, you'll get out of my way. In three. Two. One—"

Della Porta didn't need to finish the count because Chrymos had flown up out of reach. She flew fifty feet up into the air and mind-called her father. *<Dad, Della Porta and two of his crew are taking the children towards a Spanish galleon that's moored in the harbor. From what I can see from up here, it appears that the galleon has been taken over by a small group of pirates. Is there anything you or your team can do to stop them?>*

Shamar's reply came back quickly. *<The ship that brought Ravid here has a French naval crew. He reckons they'll be delighted to take out a few pirates.>*

<Great. I'll leave that galleon to you, then. I'm going to deal with Della Porta.>

<Wait!> said Shamar urgently. *<What are you going to do?>*

Chrymos sent one word, and then cut the connection. *<Gannet.>*

She ignored Shamar's frantic attempts to reconnect. *If I let him through, he'll just tell me how dangerous this is, especially in a shallow harbor. I know that, Dad, but this is my best—and probably my only—shot.*

Chrymos flew higher and higher into the sky, well aware that Della Porta and his boat would be drawing ever nearer to the Spanish galleon.

Then, satisfied that she was as high as necessary, Chrymos turned and plunged down, down, down, heading towards the small target far below. She tried not to think about what had happened when she had last attempted this stunt, at Alepotrypa.

Down, down, and then she was nearly there and the small boat grew larger and larger until it occupied all her horizon. And then she moved, so slightly, and missed the boat but plunged into the nearby water at an impossible speed, her impact generating a massive splash that rocked and soaked the boat—and, more importantly, extinguished the fireball in Della Porta's hands.

And Chrymos desperately flapped her wings underwater to reverse her plunge but the bottom grew closer and closer—

And then there was just, only just, enough room and time for her to alter her trajectory and curve round, scraping the very bottom of the harbor and head back towards the small boat, snatching Della Porta out of the boat before he had a chance to resist.

One of the older boys seized his chance, grabbed Della Porta's fallen pistol, and pointed it menacingly at the two servants still manning the boat. The pair immediately leapt overboard and frantically began swimming towards the Spanish galleon.

While this was happening, Chrymos had lifted Della Porta straight up into the air, higher and higher. Fifty, one hundred, two hundred feet.

Della Porta struggled to get free. Again, he summoned a fireball, presumably intending to burn Chrymos. But after a quick glance downward, he realized that harming the woman with the wings would not be a good idea while they were so far from the ground.

Higher and higher Chrymos flew, until Della Porta gasped for air.

"Some Outcast Angel bodies are adjusted so that they don't need air to breathe," said Chrymos. "Mine," she gasped, "is not—but I can hold my breath longer than soft and pampered scum like you!"

That last line fell on deaf ears. Della Porta was unconscious. If she'd had any breath left, Chrymos would have given a sigh of relief. Instead, she managed a slight smile as she started to descend.

What should I do with him?

In the city below, the most visible building that she could see was the *Chiesa di Santa Maria del Carmine*. The church's bell-tower was the tallest in Naples. She deposited the unconscious Master at the top, near its highest spire.

"It's more important for me to get the children to safety than to deal with you right now," she told the oblivious Della Porta, "but don't go anywhere."

ONE HUNDRED AND SEVENTY-SIX
The Harbor, Naples, Kingdom of Naples,
9.40 a.m. Wednesday June 23 1610

By the time that Chrymos had flown out of the city and back over to the harbor, the Seintespirit had begun moving into position to challenge the Spanish galleon. It looked likely to be a very one-sided battle. Shamar gave Chrymos an update. <*The French merchant ship is well fitted out for naval duties, with a dozen cannon, and has a full complement of sailors. And twenty Quarante Cinq guardsmen have come along in case there's any hand-to-hand combat. There aren't enough pirates to man all the cannons, so this battle shouldn't last for very long.*>

Chrymos swiftly flew over the harbor, searching for the small boat packed with children. She found it making good progress towards the nearest wharf, four of the oldest children manning the oars. Sirus, she was delighted to see, was one of the rowers.

The boat was still screaming out its enchanted threats so Chrymos opted to leave the children to steer the boat to safety. She flew down to the dock that was the boat's intended destination, landed lightly, and dismissed her wings. As she watched and waited for the children, she belatedly noticed that once again her clothing was soaking wet.

At least it's a sunny day, she observed.

A short time later, the boat docked at the wharf. The children quickly scrambled off and gathered shyly near Chrymos—except for Sirus and Olivia, who threw themselves into her outstretched arms and hugged her tightly. Any harsh words previously spoken in anger were forgotten and forgiven.

ONE HUNDRED AND SEVENTY-SEVEN
The Harbor, Naples, Kingdom of Naples,
11 a.m. Wednesday June 23 1610

Chrymos and the children huddled together on the wharf until the LOA team arrived to take the young ones under their care. Even then, Sirus and Olivia flatly refused to leave Chrymos, so they remained with her until Shamar drove up in an Academy carriage with Adric and Madalena.

"Come over here with me for a few minutes," Adric said to Sirus and Olivia, "Chrymos needs some time alone with her father."

He took care of the wide-eyed children—who were astonished to learn about Chrymos' father—while Chrymos and Shamar embraced and laughed and cried and chattered and mind-talked, all at once. It was the sort of reunion usually only seen in Heaven.

Finally, Chrymos had the chance to ask her father the question that she had been avoiding all morning. "What about Mother? Is she okay?"

Shamar was blessedly quick to reassure her. "Your mother is fine, just fine. She is safe in Sanctuary—the new Sanctuary."

Chrymos was delighted. "Is that—"

Shamar stopped her with an urgent mind-message. *<We don't talk about Sanctuary, now or ever. You of all people know what happens if the Darke Warriors discover its location. When you're ready to move there permanently, you'll learn where it is. For now, be content. You protected the secret for ten thousand years. It's still safe.>*

Out in the harbor, the battle between the pirates and the French navy simply fizzled out. The New Phoenicians, vastly outnumbered, quickly abandoned ship, many throwing themselves into the water, and attempting to swim to shore. Ravid and Zophiel flew aboard to oversee the difficult task of transferring the ship's plague-ridden passengers back to a safe location, where the healers could attempt to help them.

Chrymos could see the anxiety on her father's face as he exchanged mind-messages with Ravid.

"What's the problem?" she asked when he had finished his mind-discussion.

Shamar paused a moment, and then answered her with a question. "What do you know about the Academy's Plague project?"

"Nothing," said Chrymos, "except that the children were somehow involved."

Shamar switched to mind-messaging. *<We're still interrogating the Academy's people and piecing together the details, but the plan seems to have been simple enough. Aboard that ship are a number of what the Academy calls 'plague-hosts'. They have the plague but—thanks to the Academy's experiments—aren't dying. Instead, they're highly contagious—anyone who comes near them is likely to catch the plague.>*

Chrymos looked over at the children, happily chatting away to Adric.

Shamar followed her gaze and nodded. *<The Academy's intention was to sail the ship into enemy harbors, infect a few children with the plague, and then let them 'escape' into the enemy city. Being children, they'd be able to go almost anywhere, spreading the plague far and wide, without realizing what they were doing. Meanwhile, the ship would sail on to the next enemy port.>*

Chrymos was horrified. *<And the 'enemy' is—?>*

<Anyone who doesn't share the same beliefs as the Academy, from what we can tell. It gets worse. The Academy was very, very close to perfecting what they called an 'immunity pill'. If they'd succeeded, they could protect themselves—and their chosen ones—from the plague, and infect everyone else. It would have destroyed the world.>

He looked at his daughter with enormous pride. *<You've truly made a difference to so many lives by your actions, my dearest child—not only those you've saved here today, but all those who might have been exposed to the plague if not for you.>*

ONE HUNDRED AND SEVENTY-EIGHT
The Road from Naples to Rome,
Late night Thursday June 24 1610

Chrymos flew high above the carriage ferrying Madalena, Sirus and Olivia—and Madalena's mother, Caterina—to an LOA safe haven in Rome. From time to time, the carriage's driver, Sister Maria Benedetta, would look up to reassure herself that Chrymos still accompanied them. *I can't believe that they all took it so calmly that I'm an Outcast Angel. The nun, yes, she's used to dealing with heavenly things, but the children? They should have been running away terrified. Instead, they treat me the same as they always have.* She sent a prayer skywards. *Whether You are listening to me or not, Lord, I simply want to say thanks.*

It had been a whirlwind couple of days. The plague-hosts had been successfully transferred from the galleon and were, for the moment, back at the Academy and being examined by the healers. Father Carracci was being taken to Paris under close LOA and Quarante Cinq guard, to answer for his part in the assassination of Henri IV. And the four wretched creatures in the labyrinth were being kept under close observation and given regular food and water until some more permanent solution could be found.

Perhaps the hardest part for Chrymos had been saying goodbye to Adric. He had agreed to join the LOA and would shortly leave Naples for Stonehenge and the LOA training facility.

"It's not goodbye, C, just 'til we meet again'," he had told her brightly.

"I'm sorry we couldn't—" Chrymos started, but couldn't finish.

"Yeah, yeah," Adric had replied. "Me too."

There didn't seem to be any more that could be said. They had shared a final hug and then went their separate ways.

There were still a few loose ends. The Tower had been cordoned off until the LOA's experts could attempt to defeat its protective enchantments. The Contessa and Doctor Odaldi had simply disappeared.

And Della Porta had managed to climb down from the bell-tower and slip away before Chrymos could return. "We'll find them again before they can cause any more trouble," Shamar had said hopefully, though Chrymos wasn't convinced.

And, of course, Ruben, dear Ruben, my little brother, you are out there somewhere, with that pathgem. I fear for your immortal soul. But I swear this. I will do everything that I can to save you, to break you free from the curse that has you in its grasp. I will find you and bring you home.

EPILOGUE
Four and a half years earlier:
Under the Houses of Parliament, England,
Late morning, November 5 1605

The man known as John Johnson smiled as he heard the steady buzz of conversation and debate in the rooms above. The English Parliament was now in session and the despised Protestant king himself, James I, was presiding.

Johnson had been standing outside amongst the cheering crowds when the king arrived to open this long-delayed session of Parliament. Only after the king had been escorted into the Chamber did Johnson slip back down to the cellar and its carefully-hidden dangers.

As he rolled some of the thirty-six gunpowder barrels into the position where they would do the most damage, Johnson reflected on the last couple of weeks. It had been a very close call on two occasions, and only the active intervention of—*pinch me, I'm dreaming*—an actual angel had kept the conspiracy on track.

Johnson smiled to himself again as he began to run the fuse cord from the barrels to the front door of the chamber. *If ever I had any doubt that I am doing God's work, that angel absolutely confirmed for me that this is the right thing to do.*

Just over a week earlier, the conspirators had been horrified when a late-night caller came hammering at Thomas Wintour's door. The caller, a manservant of Baron Monteagle, revealed that the baron had received an anonymous letter warning him about the gunpowder plot. Before Monteagle could alert the king, however, an angel had appeared—*An angel? We didn't believe that at the time.* The angel seized the letter and killed the baron with a single thrust of his sword.

Then the heavenly creature had turned to the manservant and spoke, calmly and clearly. "Tell Thomas Wintour about this—but tell him it is still safe to proceed, his secret has not been revealed."

Johnson dragged another barrel into position, panting from the effort. *Only one more.* He started to wrestle with the last barrel of gunpowder as he thought back on what he had told his co-conspirator Thomas Bates earlier that morning. *"I doubt that you will believe this. I'm sure I wouldn't if I hadn't been there. Last night, in this very room, an angel appeared to me. In person. I know he was an angel because he appeared from nowhere and had glorious dark grey wings. His clothing was simple but he worn a wristband with a glowing blue gem. The angel spoke directly to me, saying 'I have just stopped a demon from warning the king. You are safe to proceed with your plans tomorrow.'*

I said to the angel, 'Wait, who are you and why are you helping me?'

He smiled and said, 'My name is Ruben and I am helping you because it is my glorious destiny.' I don't know what he meant by that. I probably never will."

Johnson prepared to make a hasty exit. He bent down, lit the fuse, made certain that it had ignited properly and then closed and locked the door. As he walked briskly away from the Parliament Buildings, he thought about his place in history.

The time for false names is over. No more John Johnson. He turned the corner to safety, just as the explosions began. *I want people to remember my real name. I want them to be saying 'Guy Fawkes saved us all.'*

King James I, and almost all of England's leaders, lost their lives that day, when the Houses of Parliament were blown into oblivion. They were just the first casualties of the Lost War.

THE OUTCAST ANGELS WILL RETURN IN

THE LOST WAR
http://TheLostWar.com

ACKNOWLEDGEMENTS

To my darling wife Celia, obliged once again to become a writer's widow while I wrestled with this manuscript.

To my wonderful sons Matthew and Paul.

To my Lord and Savior Jesus, for everything.

Grateful thanks also to Google and to Wikipedia for enabling me to turn slight imaginings into useful historical realities upon which to build a tissue of possibilities.

More about the Academy of Secrets and its founder, Giambattista Della Porta, can be found here:

http://en.wikipedia.org/wiki/Academia_Secretorum_Naturae

The Battle of the Margus River, between rival Roman imperial claimants Diocletian and Carinus, is described (with a few notable omissions) here:

http://en.wikipedia.org/wiki/Battle_of_the_Margus

The 15th century *Medici manuscript* is better known today by its more recent title, the Voynich Manuscript, but remains an enigma:

http://en.wikipedia.org/wiki/Voynich_manuscript

The Catacombs of San Gennaro are amongst the oldest underground burial chambers in Naples, dating back to at least the third century of the Christian Era and perhaps even earlier.

http://en.wikipedia.org/wiki/Catacombs_of_San_Gennaro

CPSIA information can be obtained at www.ICGtesting.com
Printed in the USA
LVOW10s0701180916

505100LV00008B/45/P